FEAR NOT GREATNESS

BY PETER J. MURGIO

dragon *tree* books

Fear Not Greatness

Copyright © 2018 by Peter J. Murgio. All rights reserved.

Cover Design: Kevin Craig

Interior Design: Pamela Morrell

ISBN (hardcover): 978-0-9995488-7-5

ISBN (softcover): 978-0-9995488-4-4

ISBN (e-book): 978-0-9995488-6-8

Dragon Tree Books
1620 SW 5th Avenue
Pompano Beach, FL 33060

To my loving and beautiful wife, Kathy, who is the best person I've even known and probably ever will. I can only aspire to be the person she is.

"Be not afraid of greatness. Some are born great, some achieve greatness, and others have greatness thrust upon them."

—William Shakespeare, *Twelfth Night*

CONTENTS

PROLOGUE

Hilltop House, 1978

E LIZABETH LOOKED AROUND THE PROPERTY FOR A LAST-MINUTE check, to make sure everything was just perfect.

The Hilltop House was a quintessential baronial estate in every sense of the word. The house was nestled in the middle of sixty lush acres that her husband's late grandfather, Fillmore Blair Carnegie, had purchased in the 1920s. The centerpiece of the garden was a reflecting pool with a large sculpture of a dolphin rising from the still pond. A delicate stream of water shot from the dolphin's mouth. When the sun hit the pond in just the right way, the stream of water transformed into a rainbow. Beds of flowers and carefully laid gravel paths radiated out from the fountain, each bed more lush than the last, teeming with daffodils, tulips, peonies, and wildflowers of every color and hue.

Satisfied that everything was perfect, she sighed and pushed back on the gnawing sadness that her husband, William, would be late for his eldest son's sixth birthday party, thanks to the demands of his job. She pushed the sadness away—it was a big day for Tyler, and not just because of the party. His grandfather, Harrington Carnegie, former

U.S. Ambassador to the United Kingdom, was coming in for the week-end to help celebrate his eldest grandson's birthday. The Ambassador was an imposing figure: cultured, fiercely intelligent, worldly, connected to capitals all around the globe, equally at home in Buckingham Palace and the polo fields of Palm Beach. His empire included dozens of daily newspapers, plus radio and media outlets throughout the United States and properties throughout the world.

Although Hilltop House was technically owned by the Carnegie Trust and listed as Ambassador Carnegie's principal residence, he spent the majority of his time at his townhouses in New York City and Georgetown, a stone's throw from Washington DC. The Ambassador wielded great power and influence in the world's most important city.

As if her thoughts had come to life, Elizabeth heard a stir from the front of the stone manor house. The Ambassador had arrived and was just now emerging from French doors onto the stone patio. His weathered face broke into a broad grin as the two boys, Henry and Tyler, flew up the stairs from the ground level to greet him, shrieking in delight as they ran.

"Grandpapa! Grandpapa!" shrieked the boys, one louder than the other. "You're here! Mommy said the party can't start without you!"

Henry, the younger and wilder of the two, pressed ahead of his older brother and grabbed his grandfather's hand while the old man laughed delightedly.

"Are the ponies here?" he pressed. "Please, Grandpapa, did you bring the ponies?"

Elizabeth watched in contented amusement as her father-in-law patted the boys on their heads and a stout woman in a starched apron huffed up the steps to scold them.

"Now, children!" Nanny said in her unmissable Irish brogue. "Stop hanging on the man's arms, for goodness' sake, and give him a proper kiss. Some space, children! Some space!"

The boys instantly let go of their grandfather's hands and stood back to offer a more dignified greeting. Liz laughed out loud, the shadow of sadness passing from her heart, and walked toward the steps. "And a handshake, too," she chimed in as she climbed the steps to greet the Ambassador. "A proper handshake!"

Two tiny hands were dutifully thrust out and the Ambassador shook each with great dignity. When he was done, he leaned down toward their tow heads and, with a mischievous glint in his eye, said, "And yes, the ponies aren't far behind!"

The boys both squealed with delight as the Ambassador straightened up and turned to Liz, who offered him a dry kiss on both cheeks.

"Tell me," he said, "where's William?"

"Oh, he'll be right along," she answered. "He's at the office, but he promised to be home in time for the festivities. How is Mother Fiona?"

"Fine, fine," the Ambassador answered. "Devastated she couldn't be here today. Would have meant the world to her, but her ship was delayed in Le Havre. Some kind of mechanical issue, so they couldn't make the Atlantic crossing as scheduled. A mess, if you ask me! You know she hates flying, so she must endure the slowness of the seas."

Elizabeth smiled. She well knew that the Ambassador held stock in multiple airlines and was betting that flight would someday very soon make transatlantic crossing as rare as hen's teeth.

"Well, the children will miss her," she said. "While we wait for William, perhaps you'd like to see the grounds?"

The Ambassador nodded. "Yes. Let's. As long as one of these handsome boys agrees to give me the tour!"

Henry, always the bold one, grabbed his grandfather's hand. "I'll take you, Grandpapa!" he said, then frowned. "But I have a question." He tugged on his grandfather's arm so the old man bent his white head closer to the shining hair of his handsome grandson. Henry whispered his next sentence, but like everything else about Henry, even his whisper was energetic and loud, so Liz could plainly hear him say, "I know it's Tyler's birthday and Mommy told me not to ask, but you didn't just bring a present for him, did you? You brought something for me too? You did, didn't you?"

Liz was about to shush her younger son, but the Ambassador smiled broadly and looked thoroughly charmed. "Don't you worry," he stage-whispered back, winking at Liz and the horrified-looking Nanny. "Grandpapa brought something special for you too!"

"What is it?!" Henry shrieked, too excited to whisper. "Can I have it now?"

"Henry!" Nanny said, unable to contain herself. "You're being very rude!"

"No worries," the Ambassador said to her, and it occurred to Liz yet again how obvious it was that Henry was the favorite grandson, despite being the younger child. He and Harrington seemed to have been cut from the same cloth. "As for you," the Ambassador said to the boy who was literally hanging from his arm, "you'll just have to wait. It is your brother's birthday, after all."

With that, the Ambassador descended the steps into the garden, a grandson hanging on each arm, and Liz and Nanny trailing, exchanging smiles at how easily two small boys had disarmed one of the world's richest, most powerful men.

The group toured the garden together, the boys racing ahead to chase dragonflies and Liz and the Ambassador linking arms with easy affection.

"Aren't you curious what I brought the boys?" he said. When she nodded, he said, "I hired the cast from that show, the Dukes of Hazzard, to come and bring that...car, the General Grant, I think—"

He was interrupted by Liz's laughter. "The General Lee," she said.

"Ah, yes. Well whatever it's called, their car. I thought the boys would like a ride."

"The Dukes are one of the kids' favorite shows," Liz said. "They love the antics of those two guys—what's their names?"

"I haven't the foggiest. All I can tell you is that we had to fly them in, car included, from Hollywood for this gig. Cost a fortune, but I knew the kids would never forget it."

Liz, rolling her eyes at the thought of the commotion that would undoubtedly ensue, agreed. "No doubt there."

If anything, Liz had underestimated the commotion. A few hours later, the estate was overrun with dozens of children, some of whom had flown in with their parents for the party. After all, it wasn't every day a family received an invitation to a party hosted by a Carnegie and his father, a former Ambassador.

Besides the children, the grounds were swarming with ponies, clowns, jugglers, and wandering magicians. One of the clowns made balloon crowns, and Tyler's head was nearly invisible under a giant golden crown. Children's songs drifted across the scene, and staff members circulated with platters and trays of goodies and snacks. Near the stone steps up to the patio, an enormous fountain flowed with chocolate, while a three-tiered birthday cake waited inside a huge pavilion. The cake was decorated with the famous red and yellow Superman logo—Tyler hadn't stopped talking about the movie since it came out. Liz hadn't thought anything could be more exciting than *Star Wars*.

A jangling of metal rang out, and Liz saw a tall young man wearing cowboy boots, chaps, and a wide-brimmed cowboy hat appear around the corner of the house, leading a string of ponies.

"Mummy, look! Ponies!" an excited Tyler shrieked. "I want the white one. Can I? Can I?"

"No, I want the white one!" interrupted Henry.

Liz, holding up her hand, spoke firmly to the boys: "Children, let's not be concerned, each of you will have a turn and all the ponies are the same."

"No, they're not. This one is white and the others are all different colors," Henry corrected.

The handler came forward. "Howdy, ma'am," he drawled in a thick accent that Liz suspected was fake. "Name's Cooper. I got a pony here says he's aiming to give the birthday boy a ride. Where is the lucky young man?"

"That's me," pronounced Tyler. "And I want the white one."

"Alright, buckaroo, the white one it is."

Cooper lifted the excited Tyler and placed him on the handsome white pony, while grabbing the lead and handing it to the bubbling-over youth.

When Tyler was done, the other children lined up for their turns. When it was Henry's turn, he decided he didn't want the white pony anymore, but picked out the biggest and most colorful, a large calico that stood almost as tall as a horse and wore a silver bridle. "Wow!" he said. "What's his name?"

"That's Show-Off," Cooper said. "He's a spirited pony, my favorite."

Henry sauntered up to the big animal. "Can I pet him? Does he bite?"

Cooper laughed. "No, siree, he does not bite and he loves to be petted. Go ahead and pat his nose."

Henry immediately reached up to pet Show-Off's warm muzzle.

"You want to ride him?" Cooper said. "He's about the only one hasn't given any rides yet today."

"Yes!"

A minute later, Henry was perched on top of Show-Off, his face beaming with pride as he held the reins. Cooper smiled and stepped back, starting to walk around the animal to check the stirrups, when the air was suddenly split with a mechanical roar. Every head turned to see a low-slung orange muscle car with a Confederate flag painted on its roof and its engine revving round the corner of the house on a gravel path. A dark-haired man was hanging out the passenger window, waving and smiling, while a blond man drove.

Kids started yelling at once—"It's Bo Duke! Luke! Luke!"—and running toward the car. The smile was still forming on Liz's face when she was pushed aside violently, as something slammed into her. She turned to see Show-Off rearing back, then plunging away from the car. Cooper saw it too and dove for the reins, but he was too slow, and the powerful pony took off with little Henry clinging to his back and screaming.

"HENRY!" Liz yelled.

Cooper took off at a dead run after the pony.

The Ambassador noticed what was happening, raised his hand, and yelled something.

But they were all too far away and watched helplessly as Show-Off careened toward a stand of trees and a garden shed. At the last minute, the pony veered around the shed, sending Henry sailing from the saddle and into the air. Liz watched in slow motion horror, her heart and breath freezing, as her youngest boy tumbled through the air and landed hard on the ground. He shrieked in pain, and she was running without realizing it when she saw why. The boy had landed on a pitchfork that had been left on the ground next to the shed. Two of its tines were buried deep in his side.

Liz heard herself screaming and only dimly realized that her husband William had arrived and was also racing toward his son. Most of the party was still focused on the car, unaware of the tragedy in the background. William stopped only long enough to grab a servant by the shoulder. "You!" he barked. "Call an ambulance! Run, damn you! Run!"

Liz collapsed to her knees next to her wounded baby and whispered to him. "It'll be alright, honey. The doctors are coming. It'll be alright."

Minutes later, the high whine of ambulance sirens could be heard racing toward the mansion.

CHAPTER 1
GOD SAVE THE KING, PART I

London, 1986

T HE GUN CARRIAGE MADE ITS SLOW WAY THROUGH CENTRAL LONDON, navigating streets packed with throngs of people. It was escorted by the royal family—the widow in black and her two teenage sons— and an honor guard representing each branch of the British armed forces. The bronze coffin carrying King William VI's body glittered in the rare London sunlight as the procession wound toward the Great Hall at Westminster, where William would lay in state, as English monarchs and prime ministers had for centuries.

A funeral for a king is always a solemn affair, but the BBC crew covering this one noted that the outpouring of grief from the crowd was muted. The anchor, Leland Broadmoor, observed several times during the procession that William VI had not only enjoyed one of the shortest reigns in English history, but that as an outsider he was virtually unknown to his people. The country was still absorbing the incredible series of events that had elevated him to the throne before he was assassinated by a lone IRA gunman. In the press, William VI was often referred to as The American King, or sometimes The American Who Would Be King.

When the procession arrived at Westminster, a group of soldiers resplendent in red approached and lifted the coffin onto their shoulders. Even this group, Broadmoor noted, was somewhat unusual. In typical circumstances, the pallbearers would be carefully chosen from among the king's family and close friends, or perhaps men he had led into battle or relied upon. But because William's connections to the kingdom were so tenuous, the Royal Office of Protocol had instead selected decorated soldiers from each branch of the military.

They carried the casket into Westminster and the scene switched to inside. The constellation of enormous chandeliers in the Great Hall had been dimmed, and the crowd of mourners stood in flickering shadows under the high, ornate ceilings. Hundreds of candles surrounding the catafalque emitted an eerie glow that played over the casket's bright surface. A heavy silence descended over the crowd, broken only by the crisp footfalls of the soldiers bearing the casket.

"And now," Broadmoor said in a hushed, respectful voice from the press pen where he was broadcasting, "the Queen Mother enters."

The camera shifted to show a woman in a wheelchair coming in, being pushed by two more soldiers in red. She was trailed by two handsome boys, her face obscured behind a veil. They wheeled her close to the casket, and she reached out and touched the flag with William VI's standard. As she did, the whirr of a thousand cameras clicking echoed in the hall.

"One can only imagine what she's feeling today," Broadmoor said. "It wasn't a week ago that her husband was elevated to the throne under the most remarkable ascension in centuries, only to be killed by an IRA terrorist in a grenade attack that also killed Solicitor Owen Crowley and several bystanders. Then to watch her eldest son, a 17-year-old raised in America whose claim is indisputable but who has never lived in the country, named the King of England. There are no words."

A man in robes and jewel-encrusted vestments joined Elizabeth and the boys on the dais: the Archbishop of Canterbury, the Most Reverend Tibias. He raised his hands, and silence descended as he made the sign of the cross and prepared to bless the dead king.

"Let us pray. In the name of the Father, the Son and the Holy Spirit," he intoned, as the congregation bowed their heads. "God, our refuge and strength, close at hand in our distress, meet us in our sorrow and lift our eyes to the peace and light of your constant care. Help us so to hear your words of grace..."

As he prayed, the camera zoomed in on the black veil covering Liz's face, then panned to the boys behind her: handsome and rugged 16-year-old Henry and his brother, the newly elevated King Charles. They both looked shocked and pale. Without seeming to think, Henry leaned forward and patted his mother's shoulder, and she raised her hand to pat his in return.

"As I say," Broadmoor whispered, "the entirety of the kingdom is wondering what this small family will do next."

———•••———

Under her veil, Queen Mother Elizabeth was wondering the same thing. The whole day—dressing in somber black, the long procession through a silent crowd full of faces that seemed a bit too eager, the ceremony here in Westminster—all of it seemed like a bad dream from which she couldn't awaken. It seemed so unbelievable that her beloved William was lying in the gleaming casket just feet away but separated from her by the gulf between life and death. She would have given up everything, the throne and William's coronation, to have him back. A savage sorrow gripped her as she imagined the life that could have been.

She felt the weight of Henry's hand on her shoulder and absent-mindedly reached up to touch him. His flesh was real, skin and bone, full of the life and vitality that had seemed natural to Henry since he was born, but she was alarmed to realize that she felt nothing as she touched him. Perhaps she was still in shock, perhaps she had no more feelings left other than sorrow. Looking up at him, the thought crossed her mind that she might never walk again. The doctors hadn't been sure. But even this thought aroused nothing in her but a blank indifference.

Her sight drifted past Henry to settle on Tyler. Charles, she corrected herself.

King Charles VII.

Normally, the reigning king would preside over a ceremony like this one, but the decision had been made to let Charles process as a part of the family, owing to the remarkable circumstances. Looking at her oldest son, Liz thought that was the right choice. Tyler—Charles, she thought again—looked pale and drawn. He wore his shock and sadness openly, along with something else. Fear. There was naked fear on his face, and Liz wondered if his youthful shoulders could bear the full burden of monarchy that was about to descend upon him. This thought only increased her sorrow. Her boys, although of unquestionable British ancestry, had been raised in America and had no way of truly understanding what the monarchy meant to the United Kingdom. They had no way of anticipating the pressure and scrutiny that would follow young Charles every day of his life.

Liz sighed and pondered. Henry, now the Prince of York and second in line to the throne, although the younger, would have been the better equipped to handle it—he was bolder than his brother, made of stronger stuff internally, more like his grandfather than his father. But such were the whims of destiny that the burden had fallen to her oldest son, a boy who still worked every day to prove himself worthy, even though there was no real question of his intelligence, decency, and charm.

She closed her eyes, and a new image sprang to life: William lying in his hospital bed, weak and mortally injured. She had spent every minute by his side after the attack, ignoring her own pain and injuries and cajoling him, almost begging him, to fight for his life. Slowly, though, she'd had to admit he was dying, and something had broken inside her. When he asked her to witness his abdication from the throne, she could only mutely nod and let her tears fall onto his bedsheet.

The hospital room ceremony that followed was ghoulish, like a funeral for a living person. The Prime Minister, Sir Harold Linden, had entered with a retinue of officials. Sir Harold presented the Letters of Patent naming Tyler Carnegie Bolin-Stuart the next king. At that moment, she had hated the Prime Minister for his brisk and formal efficiency. It was all so very British, this dry ceremony in which her husband signed away his kingdom, his destiny, and his life.

"Once you've executed this document," the Prime Minister had said, laying several printed pages on the long, narrow table that crossed William's hospital bed, "it will be delivered to Parliament, where they will accept it and act accordingly. All that is required for you to execute it is your signature, with witnesses testifying that you are doing this willingly and of sound mind and body, and the Great Seal of the Realm. I will handle the rest." And then, as if reminding himself, he added, "Your Majesty."

William scratched his name on the prescribed line, "William VI Rex," and fell back into the pile of pillows supporting him.

A tall, thin man, the Lord Chancellor, next opened an ornate velvet box and removed the Great Seal of the Realm. It was a wooden tool with a handle much like a pestle. At the end of the handle was a metal disc, cast in silver and engraved with the Great Seal used to authorize the Sovereign's approval of important state documents. Several sticks of sealing wax in various colors were last to be removed, and a small spouted vessel was placed on the table.

The Lord Chancellor produced a golden lighter and used it to melt wax into the vessel. When there was enough wax, the Lord Chancellor and Prime Minister helped William raise his weakened hand to grasp the seal, place it in the pool of green wax, and firmly affix the seal to the documents.

And so it was done and the official wheels of bureaucracy turned, already forgetting William and now focused on a pale, frightened 17-year-old Tyler.

"My husband," Liz whispered when they were alone again, after the officials had left with the documents. "You would have been a great king."

CHAPTER 2
THE GOOSE HEARD
'ROUND THE WORLD

STANDING NEXT TO HIS FATHER'S CASKET, HENRY FELT BUFFETED BY powerful winds. His mother's face was drawn and she had a far-away look in her eyes. She was looking into the past, he knew, and he wondered if she would ever be the same again. Part of him knew she wouldn't, and he was prepared to do what he had to do to help her.

Behind him, Tyler was looking seriously freaked out, like he had seen a ghost.

And that's when Henry, always ready to break up an uncomfortable moment, decided to have some fun. He sidled back a few steps, so he could stand next to his brother.

"Hey, bro," Henry whispered out of the side of his mouth. "Or is it Your Majesty now? Your Lordship? King Bro?"

Tyler ignored him, but Henry saw with some satisfaction that his brother turned another shade paler.

"Can you believe this?" he whispered. "I mean, why does every official in this place look like a chess piece? Seriously. Except for you, the king, who looks like a page boy."

Tyler still ignored him, but now Henry was warming up to his game.

"I got a riddle for you," he whispered, the Archbishop of Canterbury still droning on. "When is the king foul?"

This time Tyler glanced over at his younger brother and hissed, "Shut up!"

"When he's a goose!"

Then, quick as a flash, Henry's hand shot out and goosed his older brother.

There were unmistakable gasps from the audience, and the Archbishop stumbled over his words and glanced back. Even their mother turned halfway around and glared at them.

Henry stood ramrod straight, his eyes fixed in the middle distance and his hands clasped formally in front of him. His face was the picture of innocence, like an altar boy silently praying. Liz frowned slightly, looking confused.

Finally, Tyler leaned over and, covering his mouth with his hand, whispered, "You idiot! Don't you know they have professional lip readers watching us?! Every word you just said was broadcast to the whole world!"

Henry had to fight to keep his face straight, swallowing back the huge, mischievous grin that wanted to break out. "Awesome!" he said. "That's so cool! Good thing they can't read our minds!"

"Oh god, you're such an ass," Tyler muttered, and they both went back to listening to the Archbishop drone, even as newspaper writers around the world began dreaming up headlines about the goose heard 'round the world.

CHAPTER 3
THE REGENT

B EFORE THE CEREMONY CONCLUDED, THE PRIME MINISTER GATH-
ered a group of high officials representing both Parliament and the
monarchy in a side room. A television had been wheeled into the room
on a cart and a frozen image was on the screen: Henry's hand shooting out to goose his brother. A stack of printouts on the table screamed
with TV headlines about the Royal Gooser. The Prime Minister had
to hand it to the headline writers. They'd had a field day with this one,
even if some had gone too far. The leading anti-royalist talk show had
come up with "Goose Stepping Onto the Throne!"

Camden Stafford, from the official succession committee, cleared
his throat to get the Prime Minister's attention. "This is a most unfortunate way to start the rule of King Charles," he said with classic
British understatement.

"Indeed," the Prime Minister agreed.

"You'd think the press would find something else to focus on!"
huffed a leading member of the House of Lords, the Baron de Ros
Andrew Maxwell. "There are four monarchs in that assemblage, plus

a President of the United States, Lionel Keith, and all they can focus on is the pranks of an American brat!"

"An American brat who, for the record, is British, and also happens to be the Prince of York and now second in line for succession," the Prime Minister observed mildly, watching the Baron's narrow, elegant face turn scarlet.

The Prime Minister spoke again, addressing himself to the Baron and the MPs present. "The question now is what we shall do to promote continuity and calm things down. Seeing as the king is truly a boy king, only seventeen years old, we've already put in motion the process to appoint a regent to the throne. As you likely know, the Act of Settlement requires that although a minor may hold the rank and title of Sovereign, he or she must reach the age of majority, namely 18 years old, before taking on the official and sacred duties of the kingdom. At least for the next year, the regent will hopefully be able to keep these boys from the public eye as much as possible and, if we're fortunate, brush them up on royal protocol."

"A regent? Who shall it be?" Baron Maxwell demanded.

"Well," the Prime Minister said, "as dictated by law and fortified by tradition, the Parliament is obliged to appoint either the wife of the deceased Monarch or the next in line to succeed. Given the reality that the late king's wife was seriously injured in the assassination attempt and her full recovery is questionable, and the fact that the king's brother is younger than himself, the succession committee must cast a wider net.

"Unfortunately, this is where it gets dicey," he said with a glance at Stafford. "The next would actually be Prince John, the late Queen Mary's second son. However, he is not eligible to be king, again according to the Act of Settlement. As you recall, John was disqualified from succession because his wife is a Roman Catholic, which strictly excludes him from the throne and technically removes him from next in line to succeed. Very messy indeed. It could turn into a fiasco and may be in conflict with the Church of England and the law of the land. In short, a political hot potato."

The Prime Minister took a deep breath and plunged on. "The next choice would logically be Duke Edward. Although he had the throne for a short period only, his breeding is impeccable and he's nothing if not careful with his privacy."

A series of glances around the room carried an unspoken senti- ment: *not him*. The Prime Minister understood it perfectly well. Edward had ascended to the throne briefly before William had taken the throne, then abdicated almost immediately. He cited personal rea- sons, of course, but the truth of his situation was suspected throughout the highest levels of the government and monarchy. As a legal matter, homosexuality technically was decriminalized by Parliament in 1967, but still was pretty much closeted. As a practical matter, legal or not, it would be a searing scandal if the Royal Regent was caught with another man on his knees in the back seat of a car or, worse, trolling in some seedy men's room.

"As a matter of protocol," the Prime Minister continued, "I extended the offer to Edward. He was flattered, of course, and he did give it serious consideration. He slept on it for a night, then came back and said he was afraid it would be impossible under the circumstances for him to serve in such a public capacity."

An audible sigh of relief sounded throughout the office. Baron de Maxwell, a blatant homophobe, quipped, "Thank God, we don't need a fairy prince representing a boy king. Lots of tongues would wag on that kind of proposition."

"Right then, Baron. So with his stepping aside, that left only one logical choice. Richard, Duke of Gloucester, also a former and short-lived monarch and cousin to the current king."

"Good God!" the Baron exclaimed. "You can't be serious! The choice is between a pervert and a marauder!"

"Well, yes," the Prime Minister said. "There's really no way around it. But before I place the call, I need to know that Parliament will agree to it. With all the upheaval, we can't afford a crisis like this."

The moment drew out until the Baron said, "Is there no one else?"

"Not legally speaking, no," the Prime Minister said. "If we offer the position to someone else, Richard would have legal standing to sue, and most probably win. I understand your reservations, considering... but a suit like this, given the tenuous grasp the new king has on the country, could literally destroy the monarchy in the United Kingdom. And it's worth noting the regency will only last a year. For the sake of the country, this is the best step."

The Baron sighed heavily. "You know I can't compel a vote to go our way," he said. "But it's true that Richard does have his allies in the House of Lords, and no doubt the Commons will follow our lead on this. But before I assent, I must say. He's a dangerous man, Mr. Prime Minister. And he's an ambitious man. You can scarcely imagine his rage over being forced to abdicate when the late King William emerged with a legitimate claim to the throne. I'm afraid you could be inviting the fox into the henhouse, putting him in any type of position of power over our youthful king, whose inexperience will surely be no match for man of Richard's...considerable talents."

The Prime Minister didn't respond.

"Very well," the Baron finally relented. "I will do what I can on the vote. As for you and the whole of the Office of Succession, I hope for the sake of the country you keep an eye on Richard as much as possible. As regent, you know he'll have the whole power of the monarchy at his disposal."

"Of course," the Prime Minister said. "And thank you, Baron. We live in interesting times, indeed. But as they say, God and king."

"God and king," the assembled men murmured as they filed out to rejoin the ceremony.

Richard watched from between slitted eyes as the Prime Minister approached him, signaling with a slight hand gesture to join him for a private conference. Under different circumstances, of course, it would be rude to interrupt a funeral—but these were not ordinary times, and this was no ordinary funeral. This was the funeral for the King of England, and the business at hand was as old as the monarchy itself: self-preservation and the exercise of power. These were things Richard understood instinctively, and his heart thrilled at the anguish in the Prime Minister's face.

Of course Richard knew all about the offer of the regency to Edward and the meeting the Prime Minister had just concluded in an off-room at Westminster. As the former head of M15, he had moles throughout the government, some paid and some blackmailed. A fly could hardly fart in official London and he would know about it. As for the regency, it hadn't been hard to guarantee that the pervert Edward would turn the job down. All it took was a phone call to remind Edward of a certain set of photographs that Richard kept locked in a safe. Photos that showed Edward doing things that were likely illegal at the time, and certainly not the type of things a proper English gentleman would do. It turned out Edward had hardly needed any convincing at all—the fairy was planning to turn the job down anyway, rather than risk exposing his revolting love nest with that Addison fellow. Sometimes, Richard thought, getting people to do what he wanted was almost too easy. A little challenge would be nice now and again.

But following the Prime Minister into a private chamber was not the time to gloat. Just as he had known that Edward would be offered the regency, and that he, Richard, would guarantee that Edward turned it down, Richard had also known his name would be next. It hadn't taken his source inside the Succession Committee to predict that. Fact is, as a former monarch himself, he was legally entitled to the job.

Once the door was closed and he was alone with Sir Harold, Richard let the moment draw out uncomfortably, until finally Sir Harold cleared his throat. "Well then, I suppose I'll get down to it," he said. "As you perhaps know by now, we have a situation on hand, namely that we must appoint a regent for King Charles, as he is a minor and unable to rule until he reaches his eighteenth birthday. And as you perhaps also know, we are bound to offer the regency in order of succession. As it so happens, you are in that order of succession, by virtue of your relation to the king. And..." the Prime Minister paused, and Richard took a private glee in watching the man seem to choke down bile, "and all of the other eligible regents are either disqualified for one reason or another or have turned the position down."

"I see," Richard said in a neutral voice, his face perfectly disguising the joy exploding in his chest.

"I'm speaking with you now to see if you are ready, willing, and able to serve as regent to King Charles," Sir Harold choked out. He wore an expression that looked as if he'd been assaulted with a particularly foul odor—which in fact he had: Sir Richard was known throughout London for his powerful and constant body odor.

Richard pursed his lips as if in thought. "I'm deeply honored, Mr. Prime Minister," he finally said in a grave tone. "Just so I understand, you're offering me the regency? If I'm not mistaken, Parliament has to confirm the appointment, yes? Where are the representatives?"

"That's been taken care of," Sir Harold said. "The vote will go your way."

"I say," Richard said, in a tone that grew more oily with every word. "In that case, I wouldn't dream of not doing my bit for the kingdom. I shall be honored to accept the offer. Humbled beyond all measure, I will dedicate myself to serving with dignity, always keeping the well-being of the young King Charles first and foremost, followed only by my unswerving loyalty to the Crown and the nation."

"Right then," Sir Harold said. "I'll have everything arranged. Call my office in the morning and we'll take care of the necessary documents, then introduce an emergency measure into Parliament so it will happen as quickly as possible. I'm assuming you'll be available to take the oath as soon as possible?"

"Indeed! I will happily bow before your schedule," Richard said.

Sir Harold stared at Richard for a long time, and his eyes crackled with hostility.

Richard particularly loved these moments. He was no fool. He knew what other people thought of him. He knew he was considered grotesque in his obesity, and that thanks to a genetic condition he'd had since his early teen years, his body odor was a foul miasma that followed him everywhere. He knew he was mocked behind his back, and only received such social invitations as were mandatory to his station. And he equally knew that the women he handsomely paid for their company had to hide their revulsion when he began to make his peculiar demands of them.

It was because he knew all of this that he lived for these moments, when he could make even the Prime Minister bend to his will. Yes, he had the body of an ogre, but Richard also knew his mind was cunning and sharp, and that when it came to winning, he had no limits—nothing was out of bounds. Few men went toe-to-toe with him and emerged with their reputations, businesses, and families intact.

Sir Harold started suddenly, as if he had been able to see Richard's gloating played out plainly on his face. He began to turn away, not bothering to hide his disdain, but then he turned back. "I will say this," he said in a controlled, steely voice. "We will be watching you, Sir Richard. Your reputation is well known to me. And you wear your ambitions like a coat of arms. You are being entrusted with the care and guidance of not only a fine young man but also the King of England, to whom your fealty and allegiance must be beyond question. I swear it, man, if word comes back to me that you have put one toe out of line, you will regret the day you accepted this position."

Richard couldn't help it: he was a little impressed. Perhaps the Prime Minister was a worthier adversary than he had first thought.

"Sir Harold," he said in a shocked tone, "I'm wounded you would feel it necessary to speak to me like this. I can assure you that not only will I conduct myself in a way that will make all of England proud, but that from the day of my installment, my office will operate with complete transparency. We are on the same side, Mr. Prime Minister. God and king."

Sir Harold stared at Richard for another minute, then whirled and left the room.

CHAPTER 4
"YUCKINGHAM" PALACE

T HE DAY AFTER THE OFFICIAL FUNERAL, THE NEW KING CHARLES and his brother were still trying to settle into their very strange new home. But home is hardly what you might call a palace, for that would be the understatement of all understatements. The boys were used to opulent surroundings, but nothing could compare to Buckingham Palace. With over 775 rooms, including 52 bedrooms and suites, the palace was a symbol of power, wealth, and history.

When they arrived, the young brothers decided to share rooms, since they were still a bit awestruck by the size and scale of the place. Even their palatial bedroom was fitted out in gold brocade wall coverings and massive windows draped in Damask silks. The furniture was so ornate that they dared not sit on the sofa for fear of ruining it. It was a vast change from the stark minimalism of their dormitory rooms at Hotchkiss.

The two twin-sized beds, separated by an antique gilded nightstand, seemed miniscule in comparison to the size and scale of the room. The bed dressings were gold, with rich jewel-toned colors of burgundy and green. At the head lay pillows bearing the royal crest.

Henry plopped his large teenage body down on one of them and yelped. "Crap, these are as hard as rock, way worse than at Hotchkiss. I can hardly fit, they are so small." Laying back, Henry looked around the room and said, "Ty, er, Charles, do we really have to live here?"

"I guess so. The king is supposed to live in Buckingham Palace. Isn't he?"

"Yeah, I guess so. But that means we're stuck in Yuckingham Palace." He sighed. "If we have to live here, I think we should at least put up some posters and get a TV. And for sure get rid of these awful beds and get some cool bunks like back in Hotchkiss."

Tyler was nodding. "Maybe they'd let us get a dog," he said hopefully. "You think?"

"Ty, darn it, Charles, you're the king, and kings can do anything they want and have anything they want. You just have to command it. You know, like in the movies. I've seen it."

"Yeah, right. But who do I command it to?"

"Damned if I know. We can ask Mom, if she's up to it."

"Let's go see."

They found their mother, now the Queen Mother, in a sitting room just adjacent to the royal bedroom. The room had a magnificent fireplace that glowed from a low fire set hours ago by a footman. Above the fireplace hung a magnificent portrait of the Empress Sophia surrounded by a beautiful hand-carved frame. Clearly it was a masterpiece and had been painted by none other than Hyacinthe Rigaud in 1698. It was ironic that of all the royals' portraits, it was the one of Empress Sophia that hung in the room the Queen Mother would occupy, for it was Sophia who had been appointed as the beginning of the modern succession line. In 1701, Parliament had passed the Act of Settlement that elected Sophia's heirs going forward as future kings and queens.

As Charles and Henry entered Liz's rooms, she put on a reassuring smile in an attempt to make the boys feel comfortable and safe. Although still confined to a wheelchair, she made light of the situation.

"Oh, how lovely, my boys!"

Charles stooped down to kiss his mother's cheek as Henry reached for her hand and pulled it close to his chest. It was a poignant moment for the three, who felt lost and betrayed by their fate. This was the first time they had been alone since the funeral. Moments passed in silence, mostly because they had very little to say. Broken hearts and scared people rarely do.

Liz broke the silence. "Well boys, I hope you are getting used to this place? Settling into your new room, I would suspect."

"Are you kidding?" Henry asked. "It looks like something out of a Frankenstein movie, except it's worse. Yuck!"

Charles quickly chimed in, fearing that if he said what he really thought it would make his mother feel even worse. "It's quite lovely, Mom, but pretty fancy, especially for boys."

Henry rolled his eyes. "Are you kidding? I'm living in a Richie Rich nightmare."

"I know you chose to share a room," Liz said. "But you do understand the palace has plenty of bedrooms and you need not share."

"No, thanks, I wouldn't want to stay alone in this mausoleum. It might even be haunted!" said Henry.

"There are no such thing as ghosts," Charles said in a hopeful tone.

"I wouldn't be so sure, Charlie! This place gives me the creeps. Even Grandpa Carnegie's old house in Westchester was less spooky."

"I'm glad we are alone, because we need to discuss some important things," Liz said, changing the subject. "First of all, we all have to set an example. We must learn to address Tyler as Charles, and certainly not

Charlie. We have to remember we are on display, not just to the people who work here in the palace, but to the entire world. Whatever you say or do will become national, even worldwide headlines. There is no privacy."

"Cripes," growled Henry. "We're screwed."

"Mom," Charles said. "What are we going to do? I can't be king, I'm having a hard time being a teenager!"

Liz grabbed Charles's hand and pulled him close. "Don't worry, son, I have been talking to some people who are here to help us get through this."

"How?"

"The most important thing is that you both continue your education. There are some fabulous schools here in England that will be able to prepare you for life. You know, I was schooled here too, and I have the fondest of memories. Some of the most important and prestigious schools would be thrilled to have the King of England and his brother in their stewardship. Schools like Eton or Saint Paul's. You most likely will have your choice of the lot."

"But I want to go back to Hotchkiss!" Henry demanded.

"Me too!" Charles said.

"I'm afraid that is impossible. You have a new life now, we all do, and we have obligations and responsibilities. Do you remember when your Dad was elected to the vice presidency? He told us all that our lives were going to be significantly changed. And he was right, but the changes, for the most part, were for the good."

"Yeah, but we still were able to go to Hotchkiss and do cool stuff. Now we have to live in a fancy museum and can't even fart without the world going nuts," Henry said.

"Henry, please stop with the vulgarity. You will still be able to do things, fabulous things, things that you can't even imagine now."

"Like fart in public?"

"No, you dork," Charles said as he punched his brother in the bicep. "You really are a jerk, aren't you?" Then he turned to Liz. "But seriously, Mother, how can I be the king and go to school at the same time?"

"In England, the law says that someone must be at least eighteen years old to serve as king. And when a chap isn't of age, the government appoints someone to act in their behalf until he is of age. They call that person a regent. Normally they would appoint me to be the regent, but because I'm too ill to serve, they must appoint someone else."

"Who?" both brothers said at once.

"Tradition, supported by law, dictates that the next in line to be the monarch is appointed regent, and if they can't or won't serve, then they appoint the next one in line. The next in line is actually you, Henry, but you are also under age. Following you comes a cousin known as Duke Edward, who for personal reasons has declined. And after Edward is his half-brother, another Duke named Richard. He has agreed to serve."

"So this guy Richard is a cousin?"

"Yes, Charles. He is a first cousin, once removed."

"What do you mean, removed?"

"That's just how they say it. It means there is a difference of one generation. So your father's first cousin is your first cousin, once removed."

"So Richard is going to be the king until I turn eighteen?" Charles asked.

"Not king, but regent. Someone who fills the job until you are ready. This is the law. But since it is vital that you finish your education, I think it would be best if Duke Richard remains regent until you complete university and are trained to reign."

"Yes! That means I don't have to worry about all this king stuff until later, much later."

"Not exactly, Charles. You see, you will still be the king, and therefore must always act in an exemplary manner and maintain the highest of standards and behavior. No exceptions. Remember, you are living in a fishbowl, a royal fishbowl, with the entire world waiting to see what you do next."

Henry poked Charles in the gut and laughed.

"Oh yeah," said Charles. "What about Henry?"

"Henry's responsibilities are none less than yours. According to the law of the land, Henry is next in line to succeed. So the same rules apply to him, no matter where you are and no matter what you are doing. I know you both have hundreds of other questions, but I'm getting tired now and must rest. Tomorrow I asked my Uncle Freddie to meet with us. He is a family member and a brilliant solicitor who will help us. He is very nice and we can trust him completely. Now come kiss me good night."

As the boys walked back to their room, Henry poked Charles in the back of the head and said, "Hey, jerk, you forgot to ask about the dog...duh."

"Shut up, Henry. And besides, you aren't supposed to hit the king."

"Oh yeah? Bite me, Charlie!"

CHAPTER 5
THE KNIGHT ON THE WHITE HORSE

L IZ, CHARLES, AND HENRY WAITED IN A SMALL STUDY JUST OFF ONE
of the palace's large halls. The room was filled with priceless
books neatly lined up on century-old carved oak shelves. Artwork by
celebrated artists lined the walls, and the room was strewn with tasteful and comfortable furniture that practically begged a person to curl
up with one of the books. The room was one of Liz's favorites, since
it was so inviting, and reminded her of the study she'd had at Hilltop
House in Westchester. Even the color palette, warm rusts and golds,
was the same.

The choice of room had been no accident. The last three days had
been hard on everyone, and Liz had wanted a place that felt safe. She
was still in pain, still in her wheelchair, and tired easily. She didn't have
nearly enough energy to manage the large household staff or deal with
the thousands of details that were involved in transitioning into their
new royal roles.

The boys, too, were having trouble—they had been fighting with
each other and with Liz almost nonstop for three days. First it was over
the dog they wanted, but it quickly grew beyond that, as the full weight

of the monarchy pressed down on them. Even something as simple as going for a walk in nearby St. James Park became a problem. They couldn't leave the palace without a heavy security detail, and whenever they tried, the mobs of photographers outside hounded them mercilessly, yelling horrible things about William, their beloved father, to get a reaction. Even the news of the Chernobyl meltdown wasn't enough to drive the press away from their interest in the new king.

Charles seemed dazed and in shock, and Liz worried more and more that he wouldn't be able to adjust to being king. Still, she secretly preferred his detachment to Henry's white-hot and ever-present anger. As far as Henry was concerned—and he had made this crystal clear— this whole monarchy business was nonsense and the joke was over. All he wanted was to go home, back to Connecticut, and back to his old room at Hotchkiss. He refused to even consider the possibility that this was their new home and their new life.

Worse yet was her growing sense of isolation and of being besieged. Buckingham Palace boasted a huge staff, so it wasn't as if they were alone. In fact, it seemed like every time she turned around, another footman or valet or maidservant was there, waiting to carry out her every order with ruthless perfection. The staff was polite, professional, and proper. They refused all attempts at small talk, and only allowed the barest of smiles at every joke. Henry had made it his mission to break through the staff's veneer of professionalism, and she had caught him more than once telling dirty jokes to a butler or maid, trying to draw them out. She had reprimanded him every time, setting off another round in the endless "I hate this place!" war with Henry.

Feeling hopeless and stuck, Liz had reached out for allies, and that explained why the three of them were tensely waiting in this inviting room together. Finally, the door opened and a tall, distinguished, and very patrician-looking man walked in. He wore a bespoke three-piece blue serge suit that must have cost thousands to tailor, a club tie and pocket square, and matching braces. His graying hair was neatly cut, and his horn-rim bifocals added a touch of slight humor to his thin and aristocratic features. Sir Frederick—Uncle Freddie to them—looked like someone whose advice would be sought and gladly taken. He had a strong yet gentle aura about him.

"Uncle Freddie!" Liz exclaimed, extending her hands to the distinguished gentleman. He kissed her hand lightly, then turned and bowed deeply to Charles and Henry.

"Your Majesty," he said to Charles, and Liz frowned as Henry smirked and rolled his eyes.

Charles had his hand out to shake, but then realized that Sir Frederick would follow the tradition of not touching the royal person and let his hand drop awkwardly.

"Boys," Liz began, "this is Sir Frederick Brighton. I asked him to come here today and give us a few moments of his time and hopefully help us."

The boys sized up their visitor, who seemed perfectly content to withstand the scrutiny in good humor. In fact, Liz suspected the boys had no idea who Sir Frederick Brighton really was. He was a title peer, educated at Eton and then Oxford and Cambridge. He had enjoyed a successful career as a solicitor before serving six terms in Parliament. After his retirement from Parliament, he still practiced law part time, and spent the remaining time at his ancestral estate, where Liz heard he bred foxhounds. Most importantly to Liz, however, was Sir Frederick's position as her uncle, godfather, and trusted friend. If anyone knew the ways of the aristocracy, and could be trusted, it would be Uncle Freddie.

After a moment, he seemed to pass inspection, and Charles relaxed and leaned back in his chair. Immediately, Uncle Freddie turned to Liz with a warm smile. She realized he had been waiting for a signal from the king that it was acceptable to talk.

"My dear Elizabeth," Uncle Freddie said in a clipped, very upper-class accent. "I'm so sorry."

"Thank you, Uncle Freddie, I appreciate your kind words and support. And how is Auntie Seibel?"

"Just the same, my dear. She putters around in the garden, has tea most afternoons with her lady friends, and is a voracious reader." Looking around at the room, he continued, "She'd fancy getting her hands on some of these beauties."

"And her health, Uncle Freddie?"

"Her health is good, and we are enjoying our grandchildren."

"Brilliant, that's just brilliant," Liz said. She was on the verge of continuing when a gentle knock on the door interrupted her. A uniformed butler came in bearing a silver tray with tea and a plate of the dry English cookies that Henry called "dog biscuits" every chance he got. She gave him a warning look as the butler set the tray down and backed out of the room, never turning his back on Charles.

"May I fix tea?" Sir Frederick said. "It would be my honor."

"Oh, um, of course," Liz said, feeling abashed as the older man—a titled peer—busied himself pouring tea and milk into the delicate and gold-rimmed tea cups. "As I was saying," Liz went on, "we're in desperate need of help, Uncle Freddie. This whole...series of events has been so unbelievable and difficult to process. To be honest, we're not sure where to begin or who we can trust."

Sir Frederick glanced up at her. "You can trust me, dear."

"I know!" she said. "Of course. But...I've been told a regent has been appointed for Charles, that it's necessary by law to have a regent ruling in his stead until he's 18. To be frank, we don't know who this man is and haven't met him yet."

"Mmm," Sir Frederick said, handing out the finished cups, his eyes darkening. "Yes, well, my dear, it's partly about that that I hastened to meet with you at your earliest invitation. You'll understand the succession committee's hands were bound by law and tradition. The Act of Settlement is clear on this point, and it's an unfortunate turn that Richard, Duke of Gloucester, is the only viable option."

"Unfortunate turn?" Liz said, worry in her voice.

"Well, let's just say Duke Richard is well known to many of us," Sir Frederick continued, carefully sipping his tea. "You'll forgive me for speaking frankly in front of Your Majesty, but I think it's warranted in this case. Before I came today, I placed some calls and did a bit of research, to confirm what I suspected. And I daresay the truth is worse than I'd suspected. Duke Richard was former head of British Intelligence. He has connections and moles throughout the government and the monarchy. It's highly possible that the palace staff here contains at least one, if not several, of Richard's agents."

"Agents?" Liz echoed. "Why would he need agents?"

"As insurance," Sir Frederick said. "A man like Richard...suffice it to say he's a dangerous man, always looking for an angle or upper hand. People who would know say that he is skilled in blackmail and utterly ruthless. He has a reputation for deceit, corruption, and downright thievery. I'm afraid he is not a good man, Elizabeth. Richard is far more vile than even I previously thought. Almost unilaterally, ***those whom*** I spoke with used the same word to describe him: loathsome! You and your family will need to be extremely careful in your dealing with him."

Henry, having not even touched his tea which he detested because it was so British, blurted out, "But why? What can he do? Doesn't he work for Tyler?"

"Tyler who? Oh, of course, you mean Charles. Well, yes and no," Sir Frederick said. "He is the regent, duly and legally appointed by Parliament. He is vested with all the powers of the monarchy."

"This is terrible news," Liz lamented.

"It isn't ideal," Sir Frederick said. "I spoke with the Prime Minister this morning, strictly off the record you understand, and Sir Owen assured me that Richard has given his word to act in your best interest. As of now, there's no indication that he has any other intention. But...I'm afraid that's a bit like trusting a snake to develop compassion. I shan't trust it for a second, and you shouldn't either."

"What can we do?" Liz said.

"The first priority should be your own health and strength," he said gravely. "This is vital, since as soon as you are able to serve, you can petition Parliament to revoke the appointment of Duke Richard as regent. You see, according to the Act of Settlement, the law that administers these things, the wife of a deceased monarch is named regent if a natural issue and heir is under age. Once the heir reaches the age of majority, 18 years old, he or she is then eligible to reign as Sovereign and the regency ends."

Liz sighed and tried to stop her voice from shaking. "I don't think I'll be well enough for some time," she said. "The doctors say I have a long recovery ahead of me. They aren't sure I'll ever walk again. I tire easily...and I'm...I'm not the person I once was." Tears spilled from her eyes, and Sir Frederick reached out and patted her hand while Charles and Henry looked on in despair.

"I understand," Sir Frederick said. "I really do. You've already shown such incredible strength in difficult circumstances. You are an inspiration to us all, to the world, already."

Liz smiled wanly and wiped her tears away. "Thank you. You have no idea how nice it is to hear that. But I'm afraid I have no idea what to do. Can you help us?"

"Absolutely," Sir Frederick answered at once. "You aren't in this alone. There are many of us who are on your side. In fact, I already took the liberty of making a few calls on your behalf. You are acquainted with Prince Cyril, Duke of Edinburgh?"

"Not intimately, no," Elizabeth said. "But of course we've met. As the late Queen Mary's second husband, I suppose he would be considered Charles and Henry's step-grandfather. We don't have too much to do with him, but he was kind and supportive at William's funeral. He seems like a warm and affectionate man and, I might add, very youthful for his age. Quite tall, I would say."

Sir Frederick smiled. "Yes. But you may not also be aware that, prior to marrying the late queen, he was the chief of her security—"

"The queen married her security guard?" Elizabeth said.

"Oh goodness no," Sir Frederick said. "The prince was no mere security guard. He came from an aristocratic family and went to all the right schools...quite bright, you know. He attended the Royal Academy Sandhurst, Britain's top military academy. It's rather our equivalent of West Point in the United States," he added with a nod to the boys, then he continued talking to Elizabeth. "I placed a call to the prince this morning and asked if he would be willing to provide a helping hand now and again. He was already well aware of the appointment of Sir Richard and could hardly wait until I finished the sentence before he offered his full and unwavering support."

"That's nice," Elizabeth said. "But I'm not sure I understand what he's offering."

"At the moment, nothing," Sir Frederick said. "But Cyril has a vast network of connections throughout the government and the security apparatus, as well as the monarchy. He has official access to virtually everything and can make requests to gain access to whatever he doesn't already have access to. More importantly, perhaps, he is beloved and widely respected by almost all who know him."

"I see."

"He can be an invaluable ally," Sir Frederick continued. "If you should need help, you shouldn't hesitate to reach out to either him or myself."

"It's a pity he can't be the regent," Liz said. "It would be so nice to have someone who has served as prince to help Tyler...sorry, Charles... and Henry adjust to their new roles."

"Quite so," Sir Frederick said, "but unfortunately the law is quite clear on this point, and Cyril is not in the line of succession, despite marrying the queen."

"I understand," Liz said. "And thank you, Uncle Freddie! I can't tell you how nice it is to feel like there is someone on our side! There's so much to learn, and we still have to figure out schooling for the boys."

"Indeed," he said. "I would of course suggest my alma mater, Eton, but there are any number of fine schools in the country that would be honored to educate the king."

"Mom—" Henry started, but Liz cut him off with a withering glare. Sir Frederick merely raised his eyebrows.

"In the meanwhile," Sir Frederick said, "there are a few last points of business I'd like to go over with you, things you will perhaps find helpful as you adjust to life in the palace. As the widow of the king and mother of the underage king, you are automatically granted the title of Queen Mother. That gives you the rights and protection of Buckingham Palace, considerable flexibility, and notable income. In short, you will be free from financial worry and automatically receive a security detail, plus have a royal secretary to attend to your business in running the royal household."

Liz frowned. "I'm not sure I'm up to running this place. I'm still very weak...and honestly, this is all mysterious to me."

"Of course, but you should know that as a member of the royal family, you have many people who are here to help and serve you. Perhaps you'd appreciate some background on the royal household. There are basically five departments. The first is the private secretary's office, which is charged with supporting the monarch in executing his duties as head of state. The current private secretary is the Right Honorable Sir Allister Combs. Sir Allister was appointed by the late Queen Mary. Since the entire monarchy has been in flux due to the recent circumstances, he has remained in office. It's a bit at odds, given today's realities, who would have the authority to appoint a new one. Clearly, Charles is entitled to, but given that he is under a regent, then perhaps it would be up to Richard, God forbid, to either keep Sir Allister or replace him.

"The second department is the master of the household. This department is in charge of all hospitality, catering, and housekeeping arrangements for official and personal entertaining at all the Royal residences. There are two branches to the household department, the general branch, or G branch for short, and the food branch, also known as the F branch. The general branch is responsible for the organization, running, and staffing of the ceremonial events and entertainment at all residences and special occasions abroad. The F branch is responsible for the preparation, cooking, and presentation of food for the royal family and employees at all royal residences."

He paused. "You look tired, dear. Are you feeling alright?"

"Yes," she said, and indeed her color had drained. "I'll manage."

"These two departments are the ones you will have the most contact with on a day-to-day basis. Anything you require, or preferences you may have, you can request of your personal secretary or any of the house staff."

"So I can have pizza any time I want?" Henry blurted out.

Sir Frederick smiled. "Indeed. That is one of the perks of being a member of the royal household."

"Awesome! How about parties, with girls, and maybe some fast cars?"

"Henry!" Liz interrupted. "This is serious. We need to focus on important things here."

"Well, what's not important about getting some girls in for a party?"

"Hush! Pay attention to Uncle Freddie."

"Yes. Well. The final three departments are concerned with the finances of the royal household and include the keeper of the privy purse, the Lord Chamberlain's office, and the royal collection department. The Lord Chamberlain is a part-time post and is designed to oversee the general operations of the royal household. The Lord Chamberlain also performs some ceremonial duties."

He stood up abruptly, seeing that Liz was beginning to blink rapidly. "And I believe that should be enough for today." He produced a small business card from inside his suit. "Here is my private line. Ring me any time, day or night, with whatever you need. That extends to you as well," he added, bowing slightly to the boys.

"Thank you so much," Liz said, taking the card. "I can't tell you how much this means to me."

"Of course. It is my pleasure," he said. "I shall go with one last piece of advice. You will meet with Sir Richard soon. Once again, I beg of you, be careful of him. Tell him no more than you need to and trust him with nothing!"

"We will," Liz said. "I promise."

CHAPTER 6
ETON BITES

THE DAY OF THEIR HASTILY ARRANGED TOUR OF ETON HAD FINALLY
arrived. Henry and Charles rode in a chauffeured Rover, with
Sir Frederick sitting in the passenger seat, while Henry moodily stared
out the window and Charles twisted his hands in his lap. Following
closely behind them was a second Rover filled with security personnel. Henry regularly turned back to give them gross and semi-obscene
hand gestures.

Outside, the lush late-summer beauty of Harmondsworth Moor
flashed by, lit by the afternoon sun. Since his coronation, Charles had
spent the vast majority of his time inside Buckingham Palace, hidden
away from London and the country he was supposed to lead. This
drive, through the suburbs of east London and then into the greens-
pace and the moor, was really his first sight of the countryside through
his new eyes—and it made his breath catch in his throat. Everywhere
he looked, all he saw was an immense, age-old history that he knew
almost nothing about. Back in Connecticut, the oldest buildings were
maybe a century old. Even Hotchkiss, where he and Henry had gone

to school before this whole thing started, had been founded in 1891, making it less than 100 years old.

Eton College, the school where they were currently headed, had been founded in 1441 by King Henry VI.

The thought made Charles almost physically ill. Charles had no idea how he was supposed to act or what he was supposed to do at a school that had been founded fifty years before Christopher Columbus had even sailed the ocean blue to discover his country. His old country, he corrected himself.

His mom had assured him that it wouldn't be difficult, that the people at Eton knew all about his situation and every care would be taken to make their time there easier. She had said this at the same meeting where she and Uncle Freddie had informed the brothers that the decision had been made for them to attend Eton. It wasn't a meeting Charles cared to dwell on. Henry's anger had been volcanic, and he'd used a few words that Charles didn't even realize Henry knew. But their mother wasn't going to be put off. She had said the decision was final and, quite simply, that was that. Despite Henry's sympathy and admiration for his mother and her situation, being sentenced to Eton only fueled the enormous chip now the size of Big Ben already on his shoulder.

The next step, she said, was a guided tour of Eton by none other than Uncle Freddie, who could hardly contain his excitement at the opportunity to show off his old school to "Your Majesty," a title that still made Charles feel like he wanted to curl up and disappear. It didn't help when he caught a glimpse of one of the London tabloids announcing the news that King Charles would be attending Eton with his brother, the Duke. As the school's sprawling campus came into focus, Charles felt like anything but British royalty. He felt like a fraud.

"Splendid, isn't it?" came Uncle Freddie's voice from the front seat, as the rolling hills and majestic buildings of the school came into view. "You lads are in for the experience of your lives. No doubt you'll come to agree this is the finest school in the world!"

"Pfft," Henry said under his breath. "This place's got nothing on Hotchkiss."

Charles shot Henry a warning look, then went back to fretting. If he was being honest with himself, Henry's attitude wasn't helping one bit. His normally cheerful brother was angry most of the time. When he wasn't angry, he was rude or sarcastic or somehow causing trouble. Henry had recently decided it was funny to rearrange things around the castle. He would take a priceless antique vase from one room and hide it in another, just to watch the staff scurry around when they realized it was missing and search high and far to find it. On one recent occasion, he had rearranged dozens of paintings in one of the palace's halls. This particular stunt had earned him a rebuke from their mother, who informed Henry that some of the pieces he had touched were priceless masterpieces from the greats, including Rembrandt and Monet.

Worse yet, news of Henry's antics had somehow leaked out of the castle and already the tabloids were having a field day with the "American Prince." Photos of both boys had somehow leaked out, and one in particular of Henry with no shirt was splashed all over the front pages. Charles had no idea how they got the picture, which came from his last school year at Hotchkiss, when he played lacrosse. "Girls Swoon for Hunky Prince," the headline screamed. There was endless speculation about him, from the ridiculous to the sublime...Did he have a girlfriend? What kind of music did he listen to? Was he a good student? And one of the most absurd: did he wear boxers or briefs? The media fueled the country's insatiable fascination for Henry, particularly among the English teenage girls.

If Henry had been hard to deal with before, once he realized he had become something of a sex symbol to millions of English girls, he was nearly impossible.

They turned off the A1 motorway and headed toward the school while Uncle Freddie filled them in for the third time on the school's history. Eton was one of England's leading "public schools" and steeped in tradition, he said. Attended by the famous and the powerful, it was a place reserved for the upper classes. As a single-sex boarding school, it fought fiercely against the pressures of the "ever-increasing feminization" of the public school system. The institution continued to be a holdout from the co-education trend of the times. Eton, he said, was frequently referred to as "the chief nurse of England's statesmen, and has graduated dozens of prime ministers and thousands of aristocrats. In short, the perfect place to educate a king."

Charles dutifully listened while Henry stuck his finger in his mouth and faked a gag.

"You said public school?" asked Henry, removing his finger from his throat. "I thought we were going to a private school."

"Well, Henry," Sir Fredrick explained, "in this country, a public school is really a private school. The term 'public' was first adopted by Eton College, which of course is a preparatory school, not a university. It refers to the fact that the school is open to the paying public, as opposed to a religious school, which generally is open only to members of a certain church."

Henry, clearly confused, asked, "So what do they call schools where regular kids go, not rich stiffs?"

Sir Fredrick paused, looked perplexed, before answering. "Truthfully, Henry, I have no idea. I don't know anyone who actually didn't attend a public school."

Nudging Charles, Henry filled in Sir Fredrick's pause: "That figures, Charlie, he wouldn't know those kinds of people." Poking his head out of the rear window like a dog trying to catch a breath of air, he grumbled, "Looks like an ivy-covered prison to me."

"Henry, shut up," Charles said. "Uncle Freddie went out of his way to make these arrangements. And besides, it's not a bad-looking place."

"Whatever. Hotchkiss was better."

"Please," Charles said. "There's no way Hotchkiss is a better school than this place."

"Says you," insisted Henry.

"You heard Mom," Charles said. "We have to give it a chance."

As the Rover pulled to a stop in front of one of the buildings, a small entourage emerged and briskly approached the vehicle. Charles saw with some horror that a red carpet had been laid down for their arrival.

The chauffeur, as well as the security team in the rear Rover, leaped out and dashed around the car, one of them opening the door for them and bowing as they slid out.

The entourage stopped, and the man in front bowed and introduced himself as the Honorable John Newborough, the long-time headmaster of Eton. Uncle Freddie greeted Newborough warmly and affectionately. Newborough's six-foot frame was bent with age and his thick hair was mostly gray, more from the weight of his awesome responsibilities than his sixty-something years on Earth.

"Your Majesty," he said, then turned to Henry. "Your Highness."

Charles, in yet another breach of royal protocol, ignorantly bowed in return, refusing the temptation to catch Henry's eye.

"If you'll please, we'll have tea in my private library," Newborough said. "Follow me."

He led them first through the Provost Garden. Dating back centuries, the garden was surrounded by high crenellated brick walls that were inlaid with numerous plaques containing names and dates of historical moments celebrated at Eton. Perennial flowers of all sorts were neatly planted in the traditional English garden style. Both large and small blossoming trees were sprinkled throughout, standing in stark contrast to the austere red brick walls and lush grass. Several small water features were intermingled, where wild ducks and native fish swam effortlessly, as their ancestors had for centuries.

As they walked toward the massive, ancient administration building on the far side of the garden, they passed by students and masters.

"Hey, Charlie, do you see what those guys are wearing?" Henry whispered. "Looks like a bunch of head waiters...and check out those stupid bow ties and colored vests! Cripes, maybe they are all fags here! And take a look at those haircuts! God, this place is spooky. They don't seriously think they can make me wear that, do they?"

Charles ignored his brother, hoping against hope the others hadn't heard him.

"And seriously, dude," Henry continued, "I mean, I know Mom said this was an all-boys school, but really? Not a single girl *anywhere* in sight!" Grabbing his crotch, he said, "I'm gonna be a virgin forever!"

"Shut up!" Charles hissed at his younger brother, after seeing Uncle Freddie turn his head back to glance at them, his eyebrows slightly raised.

They entered the administration building through a stout oaken door and walked down a gleaming hallway, with heavy oil paintings spaced every few feet. After passing through a series of more doors and high-ceilinged rooms, they came into a cozy and small library with a brick fireplace. Tea things had been laid on a table and the headmaster invited them all to sit down. A servant appeared as if from thin air and began to pour tea. As he attempted to fill Henry's cup, Henry blurted out, "No thanks, that stuff gives me the shits! Got any soda?"

The expressions on all faces but Henry's bespoke sheer astonishment. Did they really just hear that from the second-in-line to the throne of England? Did he really slur Britain's age-old national symbol of civility? Everyone chose to ignore what they'd just heard rather than deal with any kind of response, as if there could be one.

When the tea was poured, Newborough took a careful sip and then smiled and sighed. "I can't express what kind of honor it is to have you join our student body," he began. "You're no doubt aware that you're in good company. Kings and statesmen, and captains of industry, poets and Nobel Prize winners alike, have walked the very halls that you will. Eton will soon be your pride and joy, as it is for the thousands of alumni before you." He eyed Charles closely, perhaps hoping for a reaction, but the best Charles could muster was a faltering smile. He found that he suddenly had a lump in his throat. Newborough continued, "But I'm sure you two are anxious to be quit of us old codgers. I have arranged for a student-led tour of the campus."

Walking to the door, Newborough opened it and invited in two upperclassmen in school uniforms. The boys came in and stood still.

Henry leaned over and whispered into Charles's ear, "Tell the head waiter on the left, the one with the tailcoat and striped pants, that we want a table with a view."

"Quit it, Henry. You're acting like an ass."

"One of the things I think you'll like here at Eton," Newborough continued, "is our lack of class strata. All boys here, regardless of rank or status, are held in the same stead as every other boy. We understand your unique situation, so you'll likely be relieved to learn that no one here—Masters, deans, administrators, and fellow students— will be addressing you by your royal titles. That's right, gentlemen... many of them have titles too. The red carpet reception upon your arrival will be your last once you are an Etonian. Just as you won't be addressing any of them by their titles. Here, you'll simply be Charles and Henry." Newborough indicated the two waiting escorts. "So in that spirit, I'd like to introduce you to your student escorts. This here is Reginal Peel Arlington, house captain at Erskine House, and this chap here is Harley Ayscough, house captain of sports for Hampshire House, North."

Charles and Henry shook their hands.

Harley looked them over, then said in a thin, aristocratic voice, "Twins, yeah? You chaps look like you hopped from the pages of some American magazine."

"No, not twins, but just a year apart," Charles said. "Henry is sixteen and I am seventeen."

"Right then. Irish twins."

"Irish twins?" Henry said. "No, we're American, er...I mean, English, but raised in America."

"Irish twins doesn't mean you're Irish," Harley said with disdain. "It means you were born in the same year. You know, because those Irish Catholics breed like—"

"Gentlemen," Newborough interrupted. "Perhaps you should start your tour in the Great Hall, then the Refectory, and go from there."

"Yes, sir, right away."

The two older students exchanged a glance and turned to leave, with Henry and Charles trailing behind. As they left the room, Henry, whose best friend at Hotchkiss was an Irish kid from Boston, leaned over and whispered to Charles, "One more comment like that and that dude'll wish he had a twin, because I'll wreck the first version."

"Shh!" Charles whispered. "Are you serious? You can't get into a fight the first hour we're here!"

"Tell that to Limey McDickhead up there," Henry muttered, and Charles poked him hard in the ribs.

Harley and Reginal didn't bother to glance back as they led the two "Americans" out of the administration building and back onto the campus grounds. Charles had to admit it was a beautiful campus. The very air itself seemed to ooze history, and he couldn't help imagining other royalty actually walking these grounds. It wasn't a comforting thought, exactly.

"So," Reginal said over his shoulder, finally deigning to speak to them. "I saw your snaps all over the papers. How's that feel? You move here from America and you're teen idols inside of six weeks, and future bloody king to boot. Must be nice."

"Hey—" Henry started, but Charles put a hand on his arm. "Honestly," he said, "it's been a little overwhelming. There's a lot to learn, but we're trying. Also, I'm not actually American, although I was raised in America. We are British, born in South Africa."

"Right," Reginal said. "I read that." Charles noted with some satisfaction that a little of the sarcasm had drained out of Reginal's voice.

"Here we are," Harley announced, as they approached another ivy-covered building. "This is Erskine, one of the resident halls. Come through."

He pulled a heavy door open and they walked into a lobby, with stairs going up and hallways branching off.

"Oh my God," Henry said. "What is that smell?"

It was Reginal who laughed and answered. "We call it Eau de Eton. Four hundred years of jock sweat and oodles of money, mate. Get used to it. All the dorms smell like this."

"No way I'm gonna get used to that," Henry said.

Reginal shrugged, and some of his former hostility returned. "Suit yourself."

Henry looked like he was about ready to say something else obnoxious, so Charles inserted himself and said, "Yeah, our old school wasn't too fragrant either."

"Whatever," Henry grumbled.

The two older boys walked them through Erskine and showed them the rooms students lived in, the common areas, and the refectory where they ate. It all looked so old and even a little run down. Charles had a hard time believing this was really a top-flight school full of aristocrats, but Harley assured them the school was kept exactly as they wanted it. Tradition, he said, was very important, and it seemed like every inch of the school had some long story behind it or some tradition that dated back centuries, even down to a broken mirror in the bathroom that supposedly had been broken by a certain prince just after the war.

Throughout the tour, doors popped open and curious heads stuck out to get a look at them. Charles felt increasingly like a zoo animal, and realized he was going to have to adjust to it. No matter what the headmaster had said about their privacy and all the boys being on equal footing, obviously word had traveled fast among the students that the "American" teenage king was touring the school. Someone had even taped up one of the tabloids to a door, with a picture of him and the half-naked, jeans-clad Henry on the front, getting into a big black limousine. They had drawn a crude Union Jack over Charles's face.

He pretended he didn't see it, along with the dozens of curious boys who didn't bother to disguise their curiosity. He also silently prayed that Henry didn't see it—his brother was growing more surly by the minute, and Charles was sure he would say something terrible if he did.

By the time the tour was over, Charles was thoroughly exhausted and drained. Harley and Reginal led them back to the administration building and bid them farewell outside, then left them standing alone.

"Well," Henry said darkly, "this place sucks!"

Charles didn't have the energy to argue with him. "C'mon, let's just go find Uncle Freddie."

They found the older men sitting in a comfortable study and laughing uproariously about something or another. They immediately quieted down when Charles and Henry knocked, and again Charles felt like a hopeless outsider. Uncle Freddie rose and clapped Charles on the shoulder. "So, what did you think?"

"It's beautiful," he said. "And thank you, Headmaster, for the tour. It looks great."

Then they were all saying good-bye and finally on their way back to the Rover to go back to Buckingham Palace. As they walked, Henry leaned over and said, in a brutal, sarcastic, and mimicking whisper, "Thank you, Headmaster. I'll be sure to be a good trained monkey king! When do we get our costumes?

"You think I like this?" Charles hissed, his patience gone. "I didn't ask for any of this!"

"Yeah, well, you sure are along for the ride, like a good little brown-noser," Henry sneered.

"Screw you," Charles said.

"I don't know about you, but no way I'm staying here."

The ride back to the palace was quiet, with the boys in deep thought. Charles pondered if he ever could actually learn how to be a king here at Eton or anywhere else, and Henry fretted that he was about to be sentenced to two years of hard times in a place filled with and run by snobby assholes.

CHAPTER 7
THE ASCENSION OF TROUBLE

S IR RICHARD SAT IN HIS OFFICE AT THE HARTFORD HOUSE, THE OFFI-
cial residence of the Duke of Gloucester, thinking and planning.
He hadn't yet been formally approved as regent and there was much to
do, including figuring out when the right moment was to meet his new
charge. He had to officially meet with the royal family and the young
king for whom he was supposed to be caring. In truth, he had been
avoiding the meeting as he gathered information. For a man who lived
on information, it had been slowly dawning on him how little he knew
of how the British monarchy actually worked.

He could thank Sir Conrad Hampton-Smith for some of this education. Sir Hampton-Smith, who had just left his office minutes before,
was the Keeper of the Privy Purse and the man responsible for administering the Sovereign Grant. From this position, Sir Hampton-Smith
had a complete view of the finances of the royal household, something
that Sir Richard was keenly interested in.

It was clear from their first meeting that Sir Hampton-Smith
loathed Richard, and no wonder. Sir Hampton-Smith was exactly
the type Richard had enjoyed crushing throughout his career in

British intelligence. Aristocratic family, the best preparatory schools, degrees from Oxbridge, a country estate and tailor on Saville Row... his every movement, every word, dripped condescension. From their first meeting, Richard had idly wondered if he should put a tail onto Sir Hampton-Smith and see what turned up. More than half of these fools were perverts and fairies. The rest were invariably drug addicts and crooks. And at least a handful were outright sadists. It was more than likely that Richard could dig up information inside of a week that would compromise Hampton-Smith for the rest of his life.

But it turned out Richard hadn't needed to go that far—and this was another emerging lesson. As regent, Richard would have the statutory power to force Hampton-Smith to do his bidding, and if the man disagreed, Richard could fire him. Richard was only now beginning to appreciate the immense scope of his power as regent, and it sent his mind spinning with possibilities.

The content of his meetings with Hampton-Smith only inflamed his imagination. Over the course of a few days, Hampton-Smith had laid out the finances of the royal household, and they were staggering. The royal household had three main sources of income. The first was from properties, including Balmoral Castle and the Sandringham Estate, plus a bulging portfolio of investments. These holdings were worth an estimated £165 million and generated an estimated £8 million in annual income. The second source of the Crown's wealth was the Privy Purse/Duchy of Lancaster, which included more than 18,000 hectares of land in England and Wales. These, along with other assets, had been held in a trust since 1399 and were designed to provide income to the monarch, who also held the title Duke of Lancaster, and his family. These holdings generated another £4 million annually. Finally, there was the Sovereign Grant. This was a straightforward annual grant from the Royal Treasury—the taxpayers—to the monarchy. This money was used to maintain Buckingham Palace and Kensington Palace, as well as funding travel, entertainment, and investitures. The grant entitled the monarch 15% of the gross profit from the Crown Estate. The Crown Estate represented assets that had once been owned by the monarch but were historically turned over to the government in exchange for the Sovereign Grant. By law, the grant could never decline. It always had to be greater than it had been the year before. The previous year's income from the Sovereign Grant had totaled £10 million.

In all, Richard realized, the monarchy controlled several hundred million pounds sterling in assets and had an annual income of about £22 million.

And as regent, he would have access to all of it. What he didn't have quite yet was a plan to make sure that his access could never be interrupted—not in a year, not in ten years. It was this that had consumed his thoughts.

Then he had an idea.

———✦———

On the second Wednesday following the king's funeral, Prime Minister Sir Harold Linden arrived at his offices after a restless and sleepless night. He had been dreading this day ever since the king's funeral, for today was the day he had to swear in Richard, Duke of Gloucester, as regent. Parliament had dutifully approved the appointment—they had no choice really, and there were no further obstacles to the appointment.

At least none Sir Harold could find. In truth, he had spent the previous two weeks hoping against hope that something would turn up disqualifying the odious Sir Richard. He had discreetly asked several loyal retainers to send out feelers and see if they turned anything up that might be used to sink Richard. They returned with the worst possible news: it wasn't that Richard was free from blemish. Far from it. Rather, he seemed to have some kind of terrible grip on the people who could do him the most damage. They lived in fear of him. And British Intelligence appeared to be riddled with his agents and supporters, so they weren't to be trusted.

Over time, Sir Harold had come to view Richard as a bloated and foul spider sitting in the midst of a web that stretched throughout the government and would soon encompass the monarchy. And he, Sir Harold, was helpless to do anything about it. Turning, even temporarily, the reins of power over to the likes of Richard repulsed him. But it was Sir Harold's job to oversee the swearing in of the king's regent as dictated by law. The oath must be taken and subscribed to in the presences of the Privy Council, a formal body of advisors to the British monarch.

When the dreaded hour finally came, Richard left his office at 10 Downing Street and rode through a desultory rain to the Houses of Parliament and trudged inside, heading for the chamber to preside over the ceremony.

As the senior members of the House of Commons and House of Lords gathered, Richard soon entered the chamber accompanied by an entourage of aides and solicitors, more properly described as his flunkies, to witness the taking of the oath. He looked supremely satisfied, like a well-fed cat about to devour its prey.

Young King Charles and his visibly feeble mother in a wheelchair next entered and made their way into the great room. Charles, flanked to the right by Henry, personally pushed his mother's wheelchair down the long aisle following the sergeant-at-arms.

Sir Harold noted that the boy, Charles, looked pale and frightened. His heart went out to the young king, but there was nothing he could do.

The grand room, with ranks of stadium-like green leather seats surrounding the massive Speaker's table in the center of the chamber, was filled to capacity. Intricately carved chestnut woodwork adorned the walls and the enormous stained glass gothic windows were splattered with rain.

"Hear ye! Hear ye!" the sergeant-at-arms called as he led a procession of VIPs and royals toward the room's center. The sergeant wore a sword at his side; by tradition he was the only person allowed to carry a weapon of any variety in the chamber.

As the party reached the center of the room, the solicitor general extended a medieval Bible for Richard to place his hand upon. The holy book dated back to James VI's reign in 1603 and was a national treasure. It was removed from its place of rest at the Tower of London only for special occasions.

A hush fell over the chamber.

"By the grace of God and his majesty King Charles VII, I call to order this official taking of the Oath of Regency," Sir Harold said heavily. "Richard, Duke of Gloucester, please place your right hand on this holy book and raise your other."

Instantly Richard complied, placing his hand on the Holy Bible.

"Sir, are you here to freely and wholeheartedly accept the awesome duties of regent?" Sir Harold asked.

"Yes, sir, I am."

"Sir, are you willingly and without reservation prepared to take the Oath of the Realm as prescribed by the law of the land?"

"I am."

"So be it. Then please repeat after me. I, Richard, Duke of Gloucester, swear that I will be faithful and bear true allegiance to

King Charles VII, his heirs and successors according to law. So help me God."

Richard repeated the words.

"Further, I swear that I will truly and faithfully execute the office of regent, and that I will govern according to law and will, in all things, to the utmost of my power and ability, consult and maintain the safety, honor, and dignity of King Charles VII and the welfare of his people. So help me God."

Again, Richard spoke the words.

"Further, I swear that I will inviolably maintain and preserve in England and in Scotland the settlement of the true Protestant religion as established by law in England and as established in Scotland by the laws made in Scotland in prosecution of the Claim of Right, and particularly by an act entitled 'An Act for Securing the Protestant Religion and Presbyterian Church Government' and by the acts passed in the Parliament of both kingdoms for union of the two kingdoms, together with the government, worship, discipline, rights, and privileges of the Church of Scotland. So help me God."

Richard repeated the solemn oath. As the last words, "So help me God," crossed his lips, Sir Harold fancied he heard a sigh pass through the gathered dignitaries, barely audible but full of ill omen.

CHAPTER 8
FLIPPING OFF ETON

H ENRY ALSO HAD A PLAN, AND HE PUT IT INTO MOTION ALMOST FROM his first day at Eton. He knew that Charlie would have stopped him if he could, but it turned out that they had almost no contact. Charlie was in a class ahead of Henry and lived in a different dormitory. The brothers saw each other passing in the halls, at sports, and for dinner in the massive refectory, but that was about it. The rules and customs with regard to class placement prevented them from sharing a room and discouraged fraternizing between the class levels—third year boys stuck with their own and seniors likewise stuck with seniors.

Henry wouldn't have listened to his brother anyway. Even though they traveled in different circles, Henry heard plenty about his brother, the king. Officially, of course, every boy at Eton was on equal footing. As he heard over and over, "When everybody is somebody, then nobody is anybody." As far as Henry could tell, this referred to the fact that every other boy at the school came from the Duke of This or the Baron of That or whatever. He could never keep all the titles straight, and frankly didn't bother trying. From what he heard, though, this couldn't have been more different from Charles. It seemed his brother had thrown himself into this Eton thing and was doing his best to be a good Boy King. Henry had even overheard a few of these stuck-up twits complimenting his brother and looking forward to the day when Charles would be a real king instead of a student with a regent. They all figured it would be a good thing to know a king, and they were nothing more than suck-ups and ass-kissing social climbers.

If anything, all this talk did was reinforce Henry's low opinion of the place. He'd already lost his dad to this country, and his mom was infirm and sick. Now he was losing his brother. But he would be damned if he would lose himself. He got into the habit of humming "God Bless America" under his breath throughout the day.

Anyway, the way he figured it, he wouldn't be at Eton for all that long.

This was the mood he was in one Wednesday when he saw Charles making his way across the refectory toward his table. As usual, Henry was sitting alone.

"You mind?" Charles said.

Henry picked up the faint trace of an accent in his brother's voice. "No, go ahead."

"Great, thanks." Charles dropped his tray and sat down. He eyed the gray blob on his plate suspiciously. "Mystery meat night. Great."

"I figure it's gotta be horse meat, right? I mean, what else do you think they do with the old horses in this place?"

"Gross."

"So, how are things at Common Lane House?" Henry said. "I've been hearing things."

"Oh?" Charles said, raising his eyebrows. "Like what?"

"You know. Like you keep a line of women outside your door and run them in shifts."

Charles grinned. "Right. It's a bit of a problem, really. Traffic control is difficult. I've set up a queue system outside the door now."

Henry laughed, and it felt good to actually laugh with his brother, like they used to before Eton began trying to pull them apart. "You must be raw!"

Charles smiled. "Yeah, yeah. Anyway, I wanted to ask you something."

"What?"

Charles glanced around nervously and dropped his voice. "I heard some teachers talking. You know that cherry bomb in the third floor bathroom at the Westbury House? They think it was you."

"Me?" Henry said, his eyebrows raised in mock innocence. "Why, Charles," he drawled in a fake Southern accent, "wherever did you get that idea?"

"C'mon, Henry, for real. They were pissed about that. It caused thousands of pounds of damage to the plumbing and flooded two rooms so bad they aren't usable."

Henry chuckled.

"Where'd you get a cherry bomb anyway?"

"Seriously? Charles, stop being so prude. These guys act all proper and whatnot, but you can literally get anything at this school. And I mean anything, even a little punani. They may be ugly, but it's still punani!"

Charles frowned. "I'm worried about you, Henry. I'm worried you're getting in over your head. You were the one who spelled out ETON BITES in bleach on the quad too, weren't you?"

"Charlie, I'm shocked you would accuse me of that!" Henry said, still grinning.

"Henry, that's just stupid. Only Americans use that phrase. Literally every single person in this school knows it was you, and now they're going to have to resod the whole field."

"To be fair, though, it could have been you."

"Uh, no, it couldn't," Charles said. "Because I didn't do it."

"Well neither did I," Henry said, starting to get angry. "And you sure as hell can't prove I did."

Charles started to say something, then bit his words off. "Look, I don't care about proving it. And I don't care that you did it. At least while we're here, it seems like the press can't get to us, so it's not like an international incident or anything. But, Henry, you know what'll happen if you get caught doing one of these pranks, right? You know they'll kick you out, and it won't matter who you are."

Henry shrugged, and Charles leaned forward. In a tight, angry whisper, he said, "Are you really this selfish? It would break Mom's heart if you got kicked out of here, not to mention create an international scandal. This would be as bad as the *Challenger!*"

There was almost nothing Charlie could have said that would have hurt Henry more—this was like a punch right into his gut. But instantly, the guilt was replaced with the anger he kept on a low boil. "Yeah, well, guess what? Maybe it's breaking my heart that she sent me here."

Charles stared at him for a long time, then stood up. "I'm not hungry anymore. Be careful, Henry. Please."

"Love you too, bro," Henry shot back, and his older brother walked away.

It was a week later that Henry's housemaster and the head boy of his house showed up at his dorm room and informed him that he was to follow them immediately to meet with the headmaster and the disciplinary committee. Henry took off the headphones he'd been listening to and sauntered after them, determined not to let anyone see that his heart was hammering in his chest.

Before long, he was back in the administration building, standing in the foyer off one of the meeting halls, distracted by the shadows playing off the massively high ceilings and the medieval chandeliers. It was late afternoon, the light was failing, and the whole place looked ominous and dark.

The mousy secretary sitting at a nearby desk ignored him until a phone rang on her desk. She picked it up, listened, and then hung up without a word. She looked up. "Go in," she said. "They're ready for you."

Knocking softly on the intricately carved arched door, Henry pushed it open and entered a large room with an oval table around which were seated the headmaster, a few other adult officials, and half a dozen students dressed in the school's formal uniform. The disciplinary committee. Henry stood at semi-attention, facing them.

"Henry," said the headmaster. "I'm assuming you know many of the students seated here. I'd also like to introduce you to the Provost, Malcolm Handford, as well as the head of your house and the dean of your class, whom of course you already know. Provost Handford will be running this meeting. The rest of us are here as witnesses, and when the proceeding is finished, there will be a vote."

Henry nodded at the adults.

Handford indicated an empty chair at the head of the table, isolated from the rest. "You may sit there, if you please," he said in a clipped tight voice.

Henry sat down, fantasizing that this could very well be the electric chair. He had never felt more like a little boy, despite his outward appearance and antics.

"Young man, you do know why you are here this morning, do you not?" Handford asked.

"I have a pretty good idea," Henry drawled.

"A pretty good idea, say you?" Handford asked.

"Yeah, I mean yes sir."

"Yes sir indeed," Handford almost sneered, looking like he was enjoying himself almost a little too much. It was common knowledge that Handford viewed most of the young boys at school with disdain. Perhaps it was class envy, given that he was an Eton "charity boy" who made good but did not share the pedigree of most Etonians. Or more troubling, perhaps it was because of his rumored tendency to favor young men over the opposite sex, which he expressed as contempt for the male student body.

"I will take it upon myself to refresh your memory," Handford said, then addressing himself to the table, he withdrew a sheet of paper from a stack in front of him and pompously continued, "Headmaster, deans, and members of the committee, I am going to now read the list of egregious and ungentlemanly charges. I warn you they delineate bizarre and even perverted behavior that clearly demonstrated an intentional and obstinate desire to conduct one's self in a way that is unreasonable or unacceptable. These charges show a pattern of behavior that is in direct conflict with the rules of Eton and its code of conduct, despite repeated warnings received by Mr. Stuart, including from some of you sitting at this table."

The headmaster nodded gravely, and Handford went on, "Henry Stuart, a junior, enrolled in the school this year. Since his enrollment, he has been put on the Bill six times."

Here the Provost was referring to the tradition of charging a student money for repetitive bad behavior that required seeing the headmaster. In the old days, a boy might have been swiped, or beaten with a birch branch.

"When asked to pay up," Handford went on, "Mr. Stuart rendered payment in the form of pennies, hundreds and hundreds of them. AMERICAN pennies. It was a sign of his sheer contempt for the system.

"And that is just the beginning. Apparently, on more than ten occasions, Mr. Stuart succeeded in fouling food in the refectory by unscrewing salt and pepper shakers at the table and causing students to ruin their meals."

Henry smirked as he saw a few of the boys on the Disciplinary Committee look confused and shoot each other glances. Was this all they had?

Handford continued, "Then, three fortnights ago, Mr. Stuart was seen urinating out of his window onto fellow students, as well as their property and equipment. According to other accounts, this was just one of more than six or seven times his public exposure and urination has been witnessed."

OK, Henry thought, that sounded worse.

"Mr. Stuart has also been caught with pornographic material," Handford intoned, "in strict violation of the decency code. It was a magazine called *Hustler.*"

Again, Henry mentally shrugged. So what? Half of the mattresses in the school had copies of *Hustler* or even worse hidden underneath them. The thriving underground trade in dirty magazines was one of the school's worst-kept secrets.

"Three weeks ago, Mr. Stuart is alleged to have placed a dead fish in the hubcap of Dean Clayton's MG. It went for some time undiscovered, and the odor was so unbearable that the car is today still not drivable."

"Mr. Handford," the headmaster interrupted. "We have dealt with most of these frankly minor matters already."

"Of course, sir. But that is just prelude."

"Very well. Go on."

"Thank you, and I will do you the service of skipping over the constellation of other minor infractions, scores of them, that Mr. Stuart has committed and instead concentrate on the most serious. The first is an intentional act of vandalism that cost the school thousands of pounds. That is the matter of an explosive device that Mr. Stuart flushed down the toilet in the third floor of the Westbury House. The concussion exploded the water main, causing a flood on the second floor that rendered two rooms totally unusable. Much of the building was evacuated, and construction crews are still at work replacing the shattered section of pipe. It was only through the grace of God that no students were injured by the high-powered explosives."

Henry cringed. When he put it like that, it sounded much worse than it really was. For crying out loud, it was just a freaking cherry bomb, not an ICBM missile. Seriously!

"And finally, worst of all, Mr. Stuart is accused of smuggling young women into his dormitory room on multiple occasions. Some of the young women were daughters of faculty and others were shop girls and local inhabitants of the most common sort. Demonstrating sheer audacity, Mr. Stuart proudly displayed women's knickers on the door latch of his room while entertaining these females."

Henry hadn't thought this would be such a big deal—he was far from the only student who smuggled girls into his room—but judging from the horrified looks on the faces of the adults around the table, he could tell this was serious.

"Do you have proof of these infractions?" the dean asked.

"Of course, I have eyewitnesses to the comings and goings of these young ladies, as well as a written report from the housemaster at the time. May I continue?"

"Yes, do."

"In direct violation of school rules, Mr. Stuart has had a tattoo placed on his upper right bicep. Mr. Stuart's tattoo depicts a Cox Rooster wearing a crown sitting on a ruler measuring nine inches in length, with the word 'Niner' under it."

One of the boys on the Disciplinary Committee burst out laughing, but was quickly silenced with a scathing look from Handford. Tattoos, of course, were forbidden, but it was abundantly clear that they knew exactly what the tattoo meant. But clearly the Head did not, until a third-year proctor whispered into the Head's ear, vividly describing the relationship between the tattoo and Henry's masculine anatomy.

"And finally, headmaster, there is Mr. Stuart's pattern of conflict with other students. As you may be aware, Mr. Stuart is a member of the crew rowing red team, where his performance is exceptional by all accounts. It is one of the few areas at Eton where Mr. Stuart wins congratulations. However, Mr. Stuart is engaged in a rather contentious relationship with the captain of the blue rowing team, a senior who goes by the name of MacMillan. They, on occasion, have come to fisticuffs that required attention from the school nurse. The rivalry has resulted in bad blood among not only these two but the entire blue team. Prior to the last intramural competition between the blues and the reds, MacMillan attempted to retrieve his oar from the boat house storage cabinet. Apparently the oar was saturated with a milky-like substance that MacMillan didn't recognize at first. After a good measure of investigation, interviews with his boys, and Mr. Halifax, the crew coach, it was confirmed that the source of the unidentified fluid was Mr. Stuart, who apparently…shall we say… had his way with an oar and deposited—"

The headmaster raised his hand. "I think we get the picture here, Mr. Handford, no need to go into the details."

Henry had to fight back a smile at this one.

"Young man, please stand," the headmaster said. "Do you dispute any of these charges?"

"Um, not really."

Filled with disgust, the Head continued: "And you recognize that each of these charges recommends poorly against your character and shows a shocking degree of insolence? Yet you have nothing to say for yourself and your conduct?"

Henry shook his head, then decided he was about done with this whole proceeding. "To be fair, it was a cute oar, and I enjoyed every minute of it, but I don't suppose the oar did. And for the record, there were only three girls. Two of them were pretty much scags, with the exception of the third, Mr. Langford, my Latin teacher's daughter, who was a super scag and probably shouldn't count. Anyway, we just made out, nothing hardcore."

A shocked silence descended over the room, and the headmaster stared at Henry for an uncomfortably long time. Finally he said, "Mr. Stuart, I've been the headmaster of this school for longer than you've been alive. Much longer. I have seen and heard everything there can be to see and hear from boys like yourself. If you think your insolence is original, or daring, I can only assure you that it's neither. Indeed, it's a sign of your moral rot and low character that you would stand here and attempt to make light of behavior that, in reality, only reflects weakness and insecurity, and perhaps even deep-seated perversion."

Henry's anger was back in a flash. He knew his behavior was beyond reasonable, but it was his way of acting out his deep and nagging despair over his situation, not just at Eton, but in his life. "Maybe your school just sucks," he shot back. "Maybe all of you suck and as far as I'm concerned, you can all go—"

"Silence!" the headmaster roared, slamming his hand on the table. "That is quite enough, Mr. Stuart. Before we render a decision, I would say that it's your business if you'd like to bring shame on yourself and your family. But by God, you will not shame this school, and I can only hope that what transpires here today will encourage you to rethink your ways before you bring shame to the British monarchy."

The provost looked uncertainly at the headmaster. "Sir, shall we vote?"

"No, we shall not!" the headmaster said. "Because in fact, Mr. Stuart, I'm going to handle this myself, as perhaps I should have done already. You are expelled, Mr. Stuart, from Eton. By my personal order. For ungentlemanly behavior and conduct unbecoming an Etonian. My decision is final and cannot be appealed. I will be informing your uncle, Sir Frederick, myself. And as for you, your house head will escort you back to your room so you can collect your personal effects, and immediately escort you from the school grounds. We will have a cab waiting at the gates."

Henry stared defiantly back at the red-faced headmaster.

"Do you understand?"

"Yes."

"Yes, what?"

"Yes, sir!"

"Then our business is concluded. Mr. Stuart, be on your way..." The headmaster stood and indicated the Disciplinary Committee and gathered administrators. All of their mouths were hanging open in shock—none had seen the normally calm, politically savvy headmaster lose his temper this way, and of course every single person in the room was aware that Henry Stuart was second in line to the throne. In fact, they had all just witnessed the remarkable event of a schoolmaster dressing down a possible King of England.

"Gentlemen," the headmaster said, "I apologize for wasting your time today. And as for you, Mr. Stuart, get out of my sight."

There was more Henry wanted to say, but he bit his words off. He had wanted to get out of Eton, and he had done it. But Henry felt there was no reason for the headmaster to get so personal, and he was seething. It wasn't until he was almost back to his dorm, accompanied by the stony-faced house head, that his thoughts turned to his mother, brother, and Uncle Freddie. They would be horrified and hurt. He knew that. But dammit, they had forced him to come here. No one had asked him a single question about what he actually wanted, and he wasn't going to be turned into another upper-class squish like the rest of them.

No, from now on Henry Carnegie Bolin-Stuart was taking charge of his own life, no matter what price he had to pay.

CHAPTER 9
VICTIMS OF DESTINY

O N HIS WAY TO THE GATES FOR THE LAST TIME, HENRY BEGGED HIS house head for ten minutes so he could say good-bye to his brother in person. Under normal circumstances, the house head would never have agreed, but this was a request from a duke and brother to the king. He reluctantly agreed to "use the loo" for a few minutes, allowing Henry to race across the quad and into his brother's house. He knocked on the door and Charles called him in.

"Hey, bro," Henry said, finding Charles standing by his desk and nervously toying with a pen. "What's up?"

"That's a better question for you," Charles said. "They're saying you got called into the headmaster's office."

"Uh, well. Yeah. You might want to sit down for this. You're not going to like it," Henry said. "They're, uh, well, they sacked me. Expelled me. They threw the book at me and, like you said, I deserved it."

"You got expelled?" Charles said, aghast. "You jerk! I can't believe they expelled you. What are you thinking? I warned you!"

"Yeah, well, day late and a dollar short and all that. Anyway—"

"You know you're going to break Mom's heart with this? And disgrace the family. Uncle Freddie put his neck out for you."

Henry snorted. He couldn't believe Charles would think about Uncle Freddie at a time like this. "Who cares about that old goat, he's so uptight he wouldn't say shit if he had a mouth full of it!"

"Henry, you idiot, have you thought about this at all? Do you have any idea what's about to happen? Every single person in the country has their eyes on us. Our pictures are on every scandal sheet in London. We sneeze and a million people say, 'God bless you!' The press is going to lose it. Don't you get it? We're not just normal kids, like it or not." Charles choked up a little bit. "What do you think Dad would say about this? He died for us, and it's up to us to protect the family name. And Mom..." Charles trailed off.

It would have been easier for Henry if Charles had yelled at him or insulted him. But instead his older brother just looked heartbroken, and suddenly, all the rage that Henry had been carefully nursing since starting at Eton drained away. In its place, he was seized with regret and sorrow, and once it started there was no holding it back. Henry began to weep. Real tears. Tears of regret, sorrow, anxiety, and fear. The emotions poured out of him as he reached out to bury his head into his older brother's shoulder. From the outside, Henry looked like a man, but inwardly he was very much a young boy. One without a father and trapped in an inescapable alternate world.

Charles wept too, from the stinging and persistent grief that gnawed at his very being and the despair he saw in his mother's eyes. The two anguished boys lingered in their brotherly embrace.

In a low and sad voice, muffled because his head was buried in Charles's shoulder, Henry said, "I'm sorry, Charlie, I really am, but I just couldn't stand it another day. This place is so foreign to me and my heart is home, back in America. Not here. I want to go home."

"But, Henry, you are home. England is your home now. Mom and I are your family and we are here too."

Henry sobbed a few more times, then pulled back and wiped his face. He managed a watery smile but couldn't meet Charles's eyes. "I'm sorry. I just can't...and now I'm in here crying like a baby. Men aren't even supposed to cry."

"Yeah, they are," Charles said. "I saw Dad cry when he heard how badly Mom was injured in the attack, and again when he knew he wasn't going to be there to see us grow up. Men need to cry, it's only natural."

"You saw Dad cry? I didn't see that...you mean he knew he was going to die in the hospital?"

"I believe he did, but he was brave to the very end. He even sent me a note wishing me well and telling how much he loved us all."

Henry looked pensive. He felt raw and drained. "I miss him, Charles. I miss our old life. I just want to go back to America, back to Hotchkiss. Will you go with me?"

Charles shook his head. "You know I can't do that. Besides, I don't mind it here. I don't have a problem with Eton." He smiled a little. "Actually, I rather like it."

"Figures," Henry said. "You always were a stuffy sod."

The brothers smiled at each other, the storm passed.

"You think Mom'll let me go back?" Henry asked.

"I don't know. I'm not even sure how that would work. You're second in line here."

"Yeah, spare heir," Henry said with a trace of his old bitterness. "They'd have to put me in a straitjacket to make me be the king."

"You'll be alright," Charles said. "I know you will be. And if you do go back, I'll miss you. We've never lived apart, you know."

"Yeah, I know." Henry paused. "One thing's for sure. If I do go back, I'm not calling you Charles anymore. Screw that noise. Like I'll be your royal subject. You're Tyler to me, bro. Always have been. Always will be."

Charles grinned. "Fair. Now I guess you better go before they send security looking for you. You know, worried you're blowing something else up."

"Not a bad idea," Henry said. He gave his brother a quick hug and wiped his tear-stained cheeks. "Thanks, Tyler. I mean it. Thanks a lot."

And there it was. Charles and Henry, victims of destiny, one trying to embrace a new culture and learning how to be a king, and the other yearning to return to a life he loved and craved.

CHAPTER 10
WHEELS IN MOTION

SINCE TAKING THE OATH AS REGENT, SIR RICHARD HAD BEEN ON AN extraordinary run of good luck. First, both boys—the brat king and his obnoxious brother—were shipped off to Eton, far away from Buckingham and the real action. Although Richard highly doubted that the boy King Charles would have caused any real trouble at the palace, it was still nice to have free rein. Then, to make matters even better and without any interference from himself, the younger one, Henry, had gone and gotten himself kicked out of school!

It was almost too delightful to believe. At once, the palace had been consumed with this news. First, there was the inevitable avalanche of bad press to manage, which of course Richard exacerbated. On the one hand, he did everything he could in public to downplay the event. On the other, he worked the phones tirelessly, reaching out to his contacts throughout the tabloid media and sharing the more tawdry bits of gossip and insider info. Copulating with an oar? Personally kicked out by the headmaster in a fit of rage? The press gobbled up these tidbits like the jackals they were, and soon every royal subject around the world knew just how depraved these American interlopers really were. The word on the street was that a five thousand-pound bounty had been offered to anyone who could produce a picture of Henry's "Niner" tattoo and ten thousand for an actual picture of his extraordinary extremity.

Richard took special pleasure in some of the better headlines: "Prince Gets Sacked From Uppity Public School", "The American Prince Gets The Boot!", "Expulsion Exposed!", "Eton Expels Henry, the Piggy Prince, after Lewdness and Exhibitionism." And the most titillating of all, a quote provided by Eton's Provost: "Henry Has His Way with an Oar!"

No matter that the kingdom's youth seemed to find Henry some kind of folk hero, or that teenage girls reportedly collected pictures of the handsome (often clad in skin-tight jeans and shirtless) rebel prince. Sir Richard didn't give a fig what a bunch of silly teenagers thought. Rather, he played on the conservative, thoroughly British disapproval of the old codgers who gathered in pubs and clucked their tongues over the depravity of kids today. Hopefully, by the time he was done, the countryside would be thoroughly disenchanted with these Americans who would be kings.

Inside the palace, the effect of Henry's expulsion was electric. The Queen Mother, Elizabeth, was already weakened, and she retreated in near-seclusion at the news. Of course, Sir Richard appeared to help her, but again made sure that the worst details were whispered into the ailing woman's ears. He half expected her to drop dead of grief any day, a development that would have been more than welcome.

In the midst of all this chaos, while the country raged in debate about the propriety of the new king and his brother, Sir Richard put the wheels of his larger plan in motion. And this was now why he sat in his office, his fingers tapping impatiently, while he waited for his secretary to announce the arrival of Sir Melvyn Batton.

As far as Richard was concerned, Batton was a thoroughly wretched creature. A member of Parliament, Batton was like so many of the tattered nobility throughout the kingdom: broke. Yes, he had an ancestral title and the lands to prove it, plus a gaudy estate in the highlands, but being a noble didn't pay quite like it used to, and Batton's family's fortunes had been declining for a century. This fact had come to Richard's attention years ago, shortly after taking the position as head of M15, when he learned of an investigation into some sticky business involving Sir Batton. It had to do with a blatant conflict of interest related to insider trading on the London Stock Exchange. There was no question Batton was guilty and that public exposure of these crimes would destroy any shred of dignity Batton's family had left, not to mention leave him penniless and possibly jailed. When Sir Richard approached Batton with an offer to make the charges disappear, Batton had jumped at the chance. Ever since, he had been Richard's creature, helping Richard in everything from getting information on other members of Parliament to the treason trial of the short-lived King William, father of the current monarch.

Richard's phone rang with the announcement and he waited until Batton appeared in his door. He motioned to an empty chair and pointedly did not rise to shake Batton's hand.

"Melvyn," Richard said, leaning back and lacing his fingers across his belly, "we are pleased to see you."

The man actually jolted in shock. The royal "we" was reserved for the monarch. Richard knew his breach of etiquette was like a slap in the face to the sad, gray man in front of him. Bratton gathered his composure to choke out, "And you, sir, it's my pleasure to see you again."

"Melvyn, I have an opportunity for you which I think you must take."

"An opportunity, you say?" He looked positively ill. By experience and reputation, everyone knew that any opportunity Richard had to offer surely was one that would have benefited him far more than anyone else. As far as the "must take" part, there was little doubt that refusal was not an option.

"Yes," Richard continued. "You see, *we* have need to fill a very important post here at the palace. Well, it's actually two positions. I'm combining the office of Keeper of the Privy Purse and that of Private Secretary. The new position requires a person of the highest of sensitivities, and total loyalty to the regent and the king he represents."

"Indeed." The color was beginning to drain from Melvyn's face.

"This position would report directly to me, of course demanding total confidentiality and unquestioned allegiance."

A low whistle escaped from Sir Melvyn's lips. "I say, Private Secretary and Keeper! Serious positions with serious responsibilities. The scope of the position includes running, managing, and accounting for the financial and personal life of the monarch, his family, and their assets. I'm honored to be considered," he said. "But, sir, I'm not sure I'm up to the task. You know, my duties at Parliament and all that…"

"Melvyn, you don't seem to understand. I'm not offering you this job, I'm telling you to take it. Like it or not. You will be working for me and doing exactly what I say, no questions, no hesitation, and no argue the toss. Do you understand?"

Melvyn considered for a second, then said, "But there already is a Private Secretary and a Keeper, is there not? How do you plan on removing them?"

Richard leaned forward, noting with satisfaction that Sir Melvyn actually flinched. "Melvyn, I'm the regent, and I have fully vested power to do so. No one will have the authority to challenge their early bath and your appointment. It's as simple as that. So be it!" He snapped his fingers dramatically. "So do I have your sworn allegiance to accept the position and do exactly as directed?"

Sir Melvyn hesitated and a few beads of sweat appeared on his forehead. Richard knew from long experience in the intelligence business what was going on inside Melvyn's head. He was looking for a way out, any way out. But there wasn't going to be one. Both of them knew that Richard could destroy Sir Melvyn's life and family with a single phone call—a call he wouldn't hesitate to make.

All of the fight seemed to go out of Sir Melvyn as he slumped in his chair. "Very well," he said. "I'll do it."

Satisfied that the wheels were now in motion, Richard gloated, "Of course you will." Like a nanny lecturing her charge, he said, "Now, you're excused until I need you."

CHAPTER 11
A DREAM OF HOTCHKISS

HENRY HAD BEEN "HOME" FOR A WEEK. HE WAS ONLY DIMLY AWARE of the press frenzy going on outside the palace walls, and spent most of his time in his room playing Sega Genesis and waiting for his mom to make her decision. She had cried a lot at first. Sir Richard had made matters infinitely worse. The night Henry had told his mother he'd been expelled, Richard had been present in the room, almost like he had known what was about to happen.

"Go on," Liz had said, seemingly bracing herself.

"Well, it seems that they asked me to leave," Henry told her.

"Leave?" she echoed. "But…why?"

"Well, let's put it this way, the Head said that Eton and I were like oil and water, a bad combination that will never do."

"Perhaps Uncle Freddie can intervene and make this right," she had said desperately. "Maybe they can give you another chance? What do you say?"

"No chance. I want out of that hell hole."

This was where Richard had stepped in. He delicately cleared his throat and said, "I'm not sure they'd have him back, Your Majesty. After..." He left it hanging.

"After what?" she asked.

"Well, from what I hear, he was quite the disciplinary problem. I heard—"

"I was just fooling around!" Henry erupted, his eyes suddenly stinging with tears.

"I'm sure," Richard said. "I'll bet it was hilarious when you peed out of the window on the other chaps? Or perhaps it's not funny and you really are an...what's the word they used? Exhibitionist. Or deviant. I can't recall."

"Exhibitionist?" Elizabeth said. "Deviant? Is that what they charged you with? How could they?"

"It was the incident with the oar," Richard went on. "I'm sure you'll hear of it anyway, but he was caught masturbating on the crew captain's oar. Rather, he wasn't caught as much as he left evidence of a peculiarly personal nature."

Elizabeth's face drained of color and she sat still for a full minute before she raised her hand. "That will be enough, Richard. Please leave us."

"Of course," he said in an oily voice. "I'm sorry if I offended you, but perhaps it's best to hear it from a trusted ally instead of the press. The story of his expulsion is bad enough without their deviant exaggerations."

Henry couldn't take any more. He sprang to his feet. "You piece of crap," he said. "I'm sure you took great pleasure in embarrassing my mother and me just now. And for the record, I think you are the ugliest asshole who ever walked the Earth, and you stink like an unflushed toilet. Your name may be Richard, but you are really a dick."

Richard shook his head, his expression wounded. "Oh my. I'm sorry, Henry, but it does rather sound like they did the right thing at Eton. You can always trust a good school to recognize a bad apple."

Henry's eyes bulged, and if Liz hadn't rolled her chair between the two of them, he would have swung on Richard.

"Stop this immediately!" she said. "Richard, leave us, and Henry, you sit over there."

Richard walked briskly across the room toward the door. Just before he left, he turned around. "Now Henry, you listen to your mum and be a good little boy. No more of that masturbation stuff or you'll need glass. Oh, and don't forget to show your mother your tattoo. No doubt she'll read about it. You might as well come clean now, as if such a thing were possible from a foul-mannered pervert such as yourself. Really? A nine-incher!"

The door had slammed shut, leaving Henry stung with rage and shame. Since that scene, he'd managed to calm down, but the guilt continued to weigh on his chest like a stone. For her part, Elizabeth had been careful and kind. She had apologized more than once for the fact that he hadn't wanted any of this.

They were both trying to make the best of an impossible situation, so when the note arrived that his mother wanted to meet for tea, Henry wasn't sure if he should be excited or filled with dread. Long before the tea time, he left his room and roamed the palace, more than half hoping he was saying good-bye to Yuckingham Palace. Even in his funk, he had to admit it was a grand place. King George III had bought this residence from the estate of the original owner, Tory politician John Sheffield, the 3rd Earl of Mulgrave and Marquess of Normandy, later named Duke of Buckingham in 1703. Sheffield built Buckingham House for himself as a grand townhouse, but George III turned it into a palace and his official London residence. Remodeled several times since the original acquisition, the palace had 775 rooms.

As he entered yet another hall, he saw the reflections of thousands of crystal drops placed tier upon tier around the electric candles of the massive chandeliers. The red woolen carpets rolled on endlessly, with the royal crest prominently placed in the center; they were spotlessly clean, and looked as if they were laid just yesterday. He stood in the deserted splendor and wondered, "Why does all this mean absolutely nothing to me? Anybody else would be thrilled to have all this, but not me. This will never be home."

He turned and left, heading up the grand staircase to the private quarters and his mother's room.

In Liz's apartment, the tea was set, as always, in the bright stained glass bay window overlooking the palace garden. The window's ancient handmade glass diffused the streaming sunlight. Multiple royal crests adorned the window panes in a meticulous pattern, each depicting one of the great knights' houses. A silver service dating back more than a century, engraved with Queen Victoria's monogram, polished to perfection and looking brand new, laid in wait. A staff of pantry workers made certain of that.

A soft knock sounded at the door.

"Come in, Henry," she called.

Henry walked by the posted security men, entered, and walked toward his mother. She was sitting in her all-too-familiar wheelchair. It was a sad and pitiful sight—just a short time ago, she had been vital and active. A picture of his mother playing tennis and swimming with him and Charles flashed through his mind. But the picture he saw this day was one of an incapacitated and diminished woman, but one he loved very much.

"May I pour?" she asked as he sat across from her at a small round table dappled with sunlight.

"No, thank you, Mother. I'm not a tea drinker." Mentally, he translated this into, "It looks like cow piss and probably tastes worse."

"Something else?"

"No, I'm fine."

"At least have a sweet or a tea sandwich, you'll like them, dear."

The last thing Henry wanted was English tea. He'd had more English tea than he could stand. And besides, he was feeling a little queasy about this whole conversation. He could see her disappointment plain in her face, a sad and dark face that used to be the light in every room. His father's death and the enormity of her injuries had taken their toll. He hated adding to her misery.

Liz carefully poured herself a cup of tea and took a sip, then set the cup down and looked at him with a level gaze.

"Darling son," she started. "I know that life has dealt you a hand that is not anything like you expected and certainly did not deserve. The loss of your home in America and the pride you had for being a Carnegie, a heritage so cherished by all of us, was stolen in the blink of an eye. But as it turns out, that really wasn't our home or our heritage. Then, out of nowhere, the senseless killing of your father..." Liz stopped to regain her composure. "Yes, my Henry, I know how hard this is for you and your brother, and me too. But we have to go on. Go on living our lives, being the best we can in our new roles, setting the example and not being wrongdoers. We live in a fishbowl and there are forces that would just as soon see us fail and be destroyed rather than admired. It is our duty to walk the narrow and find solace and honor in serving our country and people."

"But they are not my people!" Henry said, a sudden sliver of fear lancing through him. What if she really wasn't going to let him go home?

"Yes, they are, Henry, they are as much your people as they were your father's. Someone a long time ago made some choices that allowed all of us to live a lie. We were deceived into thinking that we were someone else, but the truth be told, you are not an American, and you are not a Carnegie and never were. As hard as we wish differently, no matter how much it hurts, the truth must be told."

Henry bowed his head to hide his emotions and fast-forming tears. On an intellectual level he understood, but on an emotional level he just could not accept the reality of the situation. "Mom, I don't know what to do. I just want to go home, back to Hotchkiss, back to being Henry Carnegie, a kid who loved playing lacrosse and swimming in the pool with the guys, being a normal teenager! I wish that—"

Liz held up her hand to silence him. "Henry, it's not as simple as that."

"So you mean I'm stuck here doomed to be someone I don't want to be?" A hard edge of anger appeared in his voice.

A long silence drew out. Then she said, "You haven't thought this all the way through. You're in line for the throne here. You have unique security needs. And you are a British citizen. But—"

"Seriously?" he said. "Are you seriously telling me I'm stuck here?"

"Hear me out. Uncle Freddie came up with a compromise."

Henry looked suspicious. Uncle Freddie was the reason he got stuck at Eton in the first place.

"What kind of compromise?" he asked. "If it means going back to Eton or a place like that, forget it. I'd rather cut my throat."

"No, not exactly, but what do you say about going back to Hotchkiss to finish high school and then returning here to do your college? You know, like the other kids do, a term abroad?"

Henry had to take a deep breath. "Do you mean that…really?"

"It would be different than before," warned Liz. "You would likely be seen differently, and then there is the matter of security I mentioned, but you would be with your friends and back in America. But as I have said, you are never going to be an American."

"That sounds awesome," he said, then paused, "but why do I have to come back here to go to college? I want to stay and go to Harvard like Dad did. And I want Charlie to come too!"

"Slow down, Henry, one thing at a time. It is unfathomable that Charles could leave England. He's the king, and within the year will have to assume the throne. As for going to Harvard, let's contemplate that when the time comes. I'm not making any promises or commitments about college now. But I will say it's probable that you will have to do some higher education in Britain. It will be expected, and we can't ignore that."

Winning the Hotchkiss battle and going back to America was a major victory, and Henry knew he best not press his luck. "Okay. But you're serious about me going back to Hotchkiss, right?"

"Yes, I am serious. If the school will take you back, you may go. But remember, there will be some requirements and restrictions."

"YES! YES! Awesome!" Henry couldn't help it: he jumped up and pumped his arm in the gesture of victory. "Thank you, Mom! Thank you!"

Liz smiled but her eyes sparkled with tears. Her family would be separated, her boys split apart. But she knew it was the right thing to do. She also knew there was really no other good alternative, given

Henry's rebellious nature and strong will. To force him to remain in this life could destroy him.

The arrangements happened quickly after that. Uncle Freddie paved the way back into Hotchkiss for him and took a personal interest in arranging for a new permanent security detail. With the help of Prince Cyril, they recruited a very youthful looking and athletic chap barely out of the Royal Military Academy Sandhurst named Oliver Witherspoon. Although twenty-three years old, Ollie could easily pass for his late teens. Although Ollie looked cherubic, he was a trained killer and quite capable of protecting himself and his charge. He would pose as a student doing a post-graduate senior year of high school, assigned to room with Henry and be in his classes. No one at the school would be aware of Ollie's charade except the Headmaster and the dean of admissions.

CHAPTER 12
SIR RICHARD GOES ROGUE

WITH HENRY BACK IN AMERICA AND CHARLES AT ETON, RICHARD had the run of Buckingham Palace. Liz posed no threat to his plans—she spent most of her time in her room or the gardens and seemed totally unconcerned with any business of the monarchy that wasn't directly related to her sons. Richard assumed she was suffering from depression, which was fine with him. He made sure that a continuous supply of bad news and tawdry headlines leaked into her chambers, as an insurance policy.

Fortunately for him, there were plenty of bad headlines. The British tabloids were feasting on a steady supply of juicy tidbits. The fact that it was all fiction, leaked to reporters who feasted on negative anti-royal news, was only icing on the cake. Richard enjoyed watching Prince Cyril and Sir Frederick get enraged about "the leakers" and vow to hunt them down, knowing that nothing would ever come of it.

Meanwhile, Richard was free to operate with impunity. He set up a meeting with a longtime associate named Reginald Casey Jones, who he was waiting for at that very moment in a dark pub that smelled of centuries of beer.

Richard knew Jones would hate this place. Like so many rich bankers, Jones liked to pretend he was actual aristocracy. He wore bespoke suits from Saville Row, expensive Italian handmade shoes, and a pinky ring featuring a suspect family crest. Jones appeared in the tabloids often, surrounded by beautiful women and pictured on yachts in sparkling blue seas. But Richard knew for a fact that Jones planted many of those stories himself, calling up media outlets and using a fake name to "tip" them off. Richard knew the lyrics to that song better than "God Save The Queen."

In reality, Jones was a high-class hustler. He'd started his career in real estate, eventually amassing a fortune in commercial interests, mostly real estate throughout London. After that, he moved into foreign money markets—and this was where his genius really came out. Jones was doing things with currency exchange markets that few people even understood, and he was making a killing doing it.

Eventually, all of this activity came to the attention of regulatory authorities. Before long, the glowing stories about Jones's luck with the ladies gave way to stories about investigations into his business practices, including the mismanagement of 2,400 margin accounts. Under constant media scrutiny, Jones's whole empire began to teeter.

And this was precisely where Richard had come into the story. They'd been introduced through an acquaintance who told Jones that Richard—who was then rising in British Intelligence—might be able to help. Richard, who never let an opportunity to have someone owe him go, jumped at the chance. Calls were made. Quiet threats leveled. And the case against Jones evaporated.

A grateful Jones had told Richard that he would do anything to pay him back, and now Richard was ready to collect on his debt.

Jones entered the dark pub. As always, he was dressed in a resplendent suit. No doubt the stench of smoke in this place would send him running straight to the laundry.

"Richard," he said, spotting the other man and approaching the table. "Helluva place you picked to meet. Couldn't find somewhere a bit more posh?"

"Didn't want to be seen," Richard grumbled. He didn't rise to shake Jones's hand, a fact that the other man seemed to ignore.

"Right, right." Jones sat down and they waited in silence while a waitress came and he ordered a scotch, neat. After the drink arrived, Jones took a swallow, then carefully set it back down. "So, I'm assuming this isn't a social call."

"No." Richard shifted in his chair. The narrow arms were pinching his sides.

Jones wrinkled his nose, like he'd smelled something foul, suddenly realizing the odor was emanating from Richard. "I say, it's a bit close in here."

"To business," Richard said. "I have a question for you. Hypothetically, say. If one needed to get some money, say a large sum of money, in a place where nobody would find it or get hold of it, is that an area where you could be helpful?"

Jones smiled a wolfish smile. "Are you bloody kidding me? That's like licking a chop for me. I can make money disappear and reappear all day long. Puff, here today, gone tomorrow. It's my specialty. Hypothetically." He smirked.

"Brilliant," Richard said. "In that case, I have a...friend who is in need of exactly those types of services. I'm assuming there's a commission on this type of thing?"

Jones's smile grew. "Sir, any friend of yours is a friend of mine. No commission. Just that we'll be even. How much are we talking about?"

"I don't know exactly," Richard said. "A few million pounds at least. Maybe more."

Jones made a dismissive wave with his hand. "Child's play. Consider it done."

"Excellent." Richard paused. "And this can never come back to me. Under any circumstances. No matter who asks. No matter if the king himself asks. You understand?"

"Are you threatening me?" Jones asked, sounding somewhat surprised. "You must know I'm not a man who threatens easily. I said I'll take care of it, and I'll take care of it."

"Good. As long as we understand each other."

"I'd say we do."

"Then you may go. I'll be in touch soon," Richard said.

Jones left most of his drink on the table as he got up and walked out without looking back, glad to leave Richard's repulsive odor. Back at Buckingham Palace, Richard wasted no time calling Sir Melvyn to his offices, then waiting impatiently until the man actually showed. When he did, Sir Richard's instructions were simple: the royal family, the new king, was about to go on a spree of charitable spending. "To bolster his reputation, naturally," Sir Richard said.

Melvyn looked dubious but was wise enough to hold his tongue as Sir Richard slid a sheet of paper across the desk at him.

"This is a list of charities we are going to make large donations to," he said.

Melvyn picked it up and read a couple of them off. "The Royal British Foreign Legion? Worldwide Vision UK? I'm afraid I'm at a loss, sir."

Richard smiled. "Genius, if I must say so myself. Giving to a wide variety of good causes is nothing more than expected, a continuation of royal good will. But, Melvyn, take a better look. Every name on that list is fake. An ever-so-slight variation on the name of some existing charity. There is a Royal British Legion, of course, but not a Royal British Foreign Legion. And Worldwide Vision UK is actually World Vision UK."

Melvyn frowned. "I see...but then...I'm afraid I don't understand. You've made up names to sound like authentic charities?"

Richard rolled his eyes. "Precisely! It's a delicate two-step dance we're about to start. First we'll establish off-shore accounts in the names of these charities, then make rather sizeable donations. Surely no one will object, since they are almost identical to existing charities. And then, with the help of Reginald Jones, the charitable funds will be transferred from the original off-shore accounts into a second set of off-shore accounts. Jones told me that banks in a limited number of countries enjoy a status called qualified intermediary, which guarantees total international privacy and unreachability. He suggests that we start with a Swiss bank located in Geneva. The office of the regent should not be associated with this!"

"I see," Sir Melvyn said. "And my part in this?"

"You handle the transactions, working through Jones. The first accounts will be in Geneva. He'll give you the details. From there, you'll direct the wiring of the money to some sub-numbered accounts located in the Cayman Islands, one of the largest financial centers and a QI shelter nation. The movement from account to account will make tracing more difficult, if not impossible. Only one person has access to that account. Me."

"I see."

"So to begin," Sir Richard said, "I think the king is looking to make a substantial donation of, say, three million pounds disbursed among the top three or four charities on that list. Let's make it a test run, see how the system performs. Once it's up and running, we can accelerate the amount."

Sir Melvyn looked like he was on the edge of tears as he got up to rise from his chair.

"One more thing," Sir Richard said. "The press shall not hear about any of this. So far, you and I are the only ones aware of these donations, and it's going to stay that way. We have time on our side, Melvyn. Patience is a virtue in all things. If the press finds out before the right moment, I'll know it came from you and the consequences will be severe. Am I making myself clear?"

Sir Melvyn just gave him a horrified look.

"I said," Sir Richard said, leaning forward, "am I making myself clear?"

"Quite," Melvyn choked out.

"Excellent. Now, time to go to work! You may go."

CHAPTER 13
A STAR IS BORN

IT WAS A RAINY AFTERNOON WHEN HENRY FINALLY LEFT "YUCKINGHAM" to start his junior year at Hotchkiss. There was a tearful good-bye with his mother and brother Charles, who got leave from Eton to return to Buckingham for the farewell. A private lunch for Henry was held in a small and intimate dining room usually set aside for private meals with the family. The oval room had a table just big enough to accommodate Uncle Freddie, Aunt Cybele, Prince Cyril, Charles, Ollie Witherspoon, and Liz.

The Queen Mother, departing from a traditional English meal, had the cook prepare Henry's favorite: steaks of gigantic proportions and mountains of French fries served with America's all-time favorite, Heinz ketchup, a condiment almost unknown in the UK. The "feast" was followed by a bon voyage cake in the shape of a flag: the United Kingdom Friendship flag, half American and half Union Jack, artfully depicted in butter cream. Before lunch a bottle of champagne was opened and poured into Waterford flutes for a toast made by none other than the King of England and Henry's beloved brother, Charles: "Raise your glasses high for my brother Henry, my best friend, and my favorite cut-up. For he is on his way back to a place he loves and will flourish and grow. God bless Henry, you are the best!"

The small group clinked glasses and echoed the toast: "Godspeed Henry and cheerio."

When they set their glasses down, Henry came over and put his arm around his brother's shoulder. "Come," he said. "I've got something to say." He led Charles to a dimly lit corner.

"What's up?" Charles asked. "I'd know that look anywhere."

"I dunno," Henry said. "I'm just...I want to go, but now I'm not so sure it's the right thing to do. I mean, you'll still be stuck here, and Mom—"

"You don't have to worry about me," Charles said. "I'm going to be just fine. I don't mind Eton, and they say it's not bad to be king." Henry grinned at that. "And Mom too. She's getting better every day. This is what you want. You need to go. When the time is right, we'll be together again."

"You sure? I wanted to go so bad, and now I just feel guilty. You sure you don't hate me?"

"Henry, I could never hate you! You're my brother, we're blood! I want you to be happy. If going back to Hotchkiss is what it takes, I'm all in. I love you, bro."

Henry smiled and gave his brother a quick hug. "I love you too, man. And I swear, I'll pay you back for this. You have my word. You just have to ask, and I'll do it. Anything! No matter what, no matter when, no matter how hard it would be! I will never deny anything you ask. I owe you big time!"

"There's nothing to pay me back for," Charles said. "Just keep out of the papers, okay?"

"Alright, alright," Henry said. "Trust me, after all this, I'll keep a low profile."

At lunch, there was much light-hearted conversation, and they all thrilled to stories from Uncle Freddie and Prince Cyril about life in the monarchy and the British government. At quiet moments, Henry saw his mom stealing sad looks at him, or gazing out of the window with her eyes shining, but she covered it up quickly and put on a smile. Henry felt like there was so much he wanted to say, but every time he reached for words, the only thing he came up with was "Thank you," so he said it over and over again, along with "I'm sorry" to Uncle Freddie and Prince Cyril. They both batted away his apologies, saying that it was all done now and all was well.

After lunch, Liz insisted that Henry change into his new gray flannel slacks with a double-breasted blazer custom-made for him by Thurnbolt and Eden, one of London's finest tailors and holder of a Royal Warrant. Brass buttons embossed with his personal standard embellished the simple coat. The end result was the transformation of Henry into a handsome, well-dressed Englishman on his way to the "new world."

Then there was the final tearful waving as Henry and Ollie piled into a black limousine and finally headed for Heathrow. As Henry looked out the back window and watched Buckingham Palace fade into the distance, he yearned for the life that awaited him back "home" and yet was melancholy over the baggage he'd left behind.

—————

They were booked onto a British Airways jumbo jet. Henry and Ollie got the royal treatment—they were escorted onto the plane early by airline security and offered food and drinks long before anyone else was even allowed on. After sitting for a few minutes, Henry got up and announced he had to use the WC, so Ollie got up and promptly followed him toward the first-class bathrooms.

"For crying out loud," Henry barked. "Are you going to watch me take a leak? Are you gay?"

"No, man, I'm not gay and I'm not going to watch you," Ollie said. "I'm just going to be close by, you know, it's my job, so don't bust my chops."

Henry gave Ollie a look of annoyance, but instantly respected his willingness to stand his own, then entered the bathroom with his carry-on bag. As soon as the door was closed, Henry stripped down to his boxer briefs. He shoved the gray flannels and new blue blazer into his carry-on and removed a pair of his oldest jeans and a favorite long-sleeve Harvard T-shirt that his father had given him years ago. Henry had grown since he'd last worn this outfit: the shirt was baggy and fit fine, but the jeans were snug, to say the least. He had to struggle to button up the fly and suck in his well-defined abs to close the waist.

He exited the bathroom. When Ollie saw him heading back to the seats, he raised his eyebrows.

"Jeans tight enough, mate?" Ollie said. "You look like you can hardly breathe."

"I thought I told you to stop ogling me," Henry said. "Eyes off the merchandise."

Ollie laughed. "Fair enough. If you pass out, I'll make sure someone is available to give you mouth-to-mouth. Judging from the looks the stewardess gave you, I'm sure she'd be willing."

Henry rolled his eyes and leaned back in his chair, watching as other passengers started to file onto the plane and they got closer to actually taking off. Finally, Flight 1169 took off. As the plane lifted off,

Henry felt the invisible shackles of the British Empire falling away into the English Channel below. He was going back home at last.

Once in the air, Henry looked around the cabin. Lots of old people, some looking like Americans, others not, all on their way to New York for one reason or another. The cabin layout was two rows of seats side by side, slightly offset from each other and separated by an aisle. When the flight reached 35,000 feet, the seat belt sign rang off.

"Ladies and gentlemen, welcome to Flight 1169 nonstop to JFK International Airport, New York City. The captain has switched off the seat belt sign and you are free to move about the cabin. Dinner service will be offered in an hour's time and beverages will be forthcoming on a trolley."

Henry sighed. Seven hours to kill. He glanced at the window and saw that Ollie was curled up with a good book and seemed more relaxed now that he and his charge were safely on their way. His contemplation was interrupted by a female voice with a thick British accent that sounded like it was coming from right behind him.

"Crap, I'm arse over elbows all over this bloody plane. Blimey."

He turned around and saw a young woman on the floor, crawling around and looking for the contents of her upended purse. Looking down, he saw that some of her things had rolled under his seat. A small plastic circular case with numbers, or some sort of dial, printed on it contained what looked like pills. A pencil-like item marked Tampax, along with four lipsticks and a contraption that looked like an escargot holder apparently used to curl eyelashes, lay beside the case.

He was about to turn back and let her know he'd found some of her things when, to his utter surprise, her face appeared between his legs. She had somehow managed to crawl into his aisle and was just at that moment looking up at him. Worse yet, she was one of the most beautiful girls he'd ever seen, and her sudden proximity caused the blood to instantly rise to his face.

"Uh..." he stammered. "I, uh..."

"Nice view down here, love," the girl said. "You've got all my stuff between your legs." She laughed at her own dirty joke, then began scooping up her possessions and piling them into Henry's lap. "God. I'd be screwed if I lost these," she said, holding up her birth control pills. "Or should I say, I wouldn't screw if I lost these."

"Hey, who are you?" Ollie said, leaning over and frowning. "What are you doing down there? Get up right now."

"She's okay, Ollie," Henry stammered quickly. "No big deal."

"What the hell is she doing between your legs?"

"She's just collecting the stuff that fell out of her purse. Like I said, don't sweat it."

"Right," the girl said. "Don't sweat it, Ollie or whatever your name is. I'll be away in a jif." Mumbling under her breath, the girl let it slip out that she once had a cocker spaniel named Ollie.

A moment later, she had collected all of her things and was standing next to Henry's seat and looking down at him. She thrust her hand out. "My name is Star, Star Patterson."

"Your name is Star?" Henry said. "For real?"

"Of course, my mother gave it to me and I love it."

Henry could not take his eyes off this girl. Star was tall, but not too tall. Wearing a soft yellow sweater, she concealed what had to be the biggest breasts Henry had ever seen in person. Her blonde hair fell to her shoulders and danced loosely around her neck. She wore a short miniskirt, which better could be described as a big belt, and tall leather boots with silver buckles. She was dressed like Madonna, he thought, but way better looking. Most remarkable were her sapphire eyes that shone like stars. Henry was smitten.

"So, now that you know my name, what's yours?" she said.

"Uh...my...oh yeah, my name, it's Henry, Henry Stuart, but my friends call me Hank."

"You go to Harvard?" Star asked, nodding at his T-shirt.

"Not yet, I'm at Hotchkiss in Connecticut. But I want to go to Harvard when I'm done there."

"Nice," she said. "I hear it's a decent sort of place." Then she laughed at her own joke. "Well, nice meeting you, Hank. Maybe I'll see you around." She paused. "Unless, that is, you'd like to move back to my row? Seat next to me is open." She smiled suggestively.

Suddenly, there was nothing Henry wanted to do more than move back to Star's row. He glanced at Ollie, who sighed and rolled his eyes. Henry followed Star to her row, trying hard not to stare at her backside.

He took a seat and was instantly enveloped in the cloud of her perfume. It was hard to concentrate at first, but pretty soon he found out that Star had a wicked sense of humor and was unlike any girl he'd ever met. Not that there had been that many. She was forward and direct, and she swore like a sailor, and she wasn't afraid to tell the dirtiest stories without a shred of embarrassment. By English standards, Star would best be described as common, but for Henry that thought never crossed his pubescent mind. Henry, who had caused his fair share of trouble, couldn't imagine being as free and uninhibited as Star.

"So why are you going to New York?" he asked as the lights dimmed and darkness fell.

"I'm going to try out for a Broadway show. Starlight Express. I figure they'll have to take me, because of my name."

He laughed. "I guess so."

"Do you know the London show?" she asked. "It's at the Apollo Victoria Theatre on Wilton Road."

"No, I'm afraid not."

"Well, it's an Andrew Lloyd Webber show, and he wants to bring it to Broadway and I'm going to audition for it. But there's one problem, the whole show is done on roller-skates, and I'm not so keen about them."

"So is this your first trip to the United States?" Henry asked.

"Yes, and talk about luck! My agent bought me a coach ticket, but I charmed the pants off the counterman in the airport when I checked in. He upgraded me to first class! Cool, eh?"

"Yeah, sure."

"So," she said, "now you know all about me. What about you? How old are you?"

Henry thought for a moment. He figured this girl to be about 18 or 19, and he didn't want to appear like a kid. "Oh, I'm going to be 19 next month."

"Me too, 19 on the twenty-eighth."

Dinner was soon served. The stewardess assumed they were old enough to drink and served them a split of champagne, followed by two glasses of French white Burgundy. When the trays were cleared, Henry began to nod off. Star rested her head on his shoulder and the stewardess came by and covered them up with blankets. It was Henry's idea of heaven, and he soon drifted off, his head lolling back against the seat.

Around two-thirty in the morning, Henry jolted awake. He wasn't sure what had brought him awake, then realized: Star's hand had crept under his blanket. He glanced at her head, but it hadn't moved on his shoulder, and she still looked peaceful and asleep. The cabin was quiet around them, with just one reading light on a few rows up. The loud hum of the engines drowned out any sounds in the cabin—including

Henry's surprised gasp as, without twitching another muscle, Star began to unbutton Henry's skin-tight jeans. Stunned, he wondered if he was dreaming. This couldn't really be happening! But the reality of the situation soon became apparent. This was too good to be true. The most beautiful girl he had ever seen was playing find the pickle with him! It wasn't long before Star was past the outer banks of underwear and into the Tower of London where the family jewels resided.

Henry looked over to see what Ollie was up to, and was relieved to see him soundly dozing with his book propped up on his chest. He was certain that Ollie hadn't gotten wind of the blanket action going on in seat 4C.

Henry quickly yielded to Star's skilled hands. Arching back into the wide seat, the second in line to the British throne delivered a royal decree. Star opened her gorgeous eyes and smiled. She leaned into Henry's shoulder and reached up to his lips. They kissed deeply.

Ever so gently, Star tucked Henry back into his very saturated jeans. Groaning with satisfaction, he watched her draw her drenched hand out from under the blanket and bring it to her face, where she took an exaggerated deep breath as if to savor the very essence of Henry. "Nice," she said, then she laid her head back on his shoulder and closed her eyes.

Henry tried to sleep, but the intoxicating closeness of this girl was more than he could bear. It all seemed like some crazy dream, and he doubted even Charles, or his pals back at Hotchkiss, would believe this story. But he knew one thing for sure: he dreaded the arrival in New York, which would end this real life adolescent fantasy. Yet all too soon, the lights came on and the plane shook itself awake, as the captain announced they'd be landing in the US of A soon.

Henry had never been sadder to see a runway in his life.

"Say," Star said, all business now. "It's been nice, Hank. Maybe I'll see you around sometime. At Hotchkiss or someplace."

"Yeah, uh. That'd be great. How can I contact you?"

"I don't have an address yet, but give me yours and I'll be in touch." Star fished around her purse for a pen and produced a cocktail napkin. She wrote his contact information down and then ripped the napkin in half. She stuffed the half with his address down into her cleavage, then planted a cherry-red kiss on the other half and gave it to him. "Here," she said. "To remember me by."

And again, she laughed as he blushed and stammered.

CHAPTER 14
SUMMA CUM LAUDE

Eton College, June 1988

IN THE EARLY HOURS OF THE BREAKING DAY, CHARLES WALKED SLOWLY and deliberately through the Provost Garden at Eton. He had walked through this garden dozens of times since starting at Eton for his senior year, during fall, winter, and spring. The garden had never failed to impress him, but today it seemed more beautiful than ever. He sighed. That was the price of saying good-bye, he supposed. It was hard sometimes to appreciate a thing until it was almost gone, and now that he was planning to say good-bye to Eton, he realized how much he had come to appreciate this place. He felt it was the place where he had grown from a boy to a man—now more than six feet two inches and blessed with uncommonly good looks.

Eton was like a bubble in the midst of madness. Sometimes, he imagined that Eton existed under an actual glass dome. Just outside the dome, the entire empire waited for him, their multitude of faces pressed up against the glass. But while it was noisy out there, here at Eton it was quiet and peaceful, and Charles treasured the time he had spent getting to know his classmates, the patience they had shown help-ing him become more "British." Like his brother Henry, Charles had been raised uniquely American to the core, and while he was doing his best to act more English, he was still painfully aware every time he pronounced a word with a distinctive American twang or somehow yet again insulted the English sense of propriety.

One constant of this past year was missing Henry. The brothers had stayed in close touch, and Charles was grateful and happy to see that all of Henry's behavior "problems" had instantly resolved when he touched down on US soil. He had perfect grades, was a var-sity athlete, and had a girlfriend who sounded like a beauty queen. Charles smiled thinking about his younger (and now taller) brother. He was at that very moment probably somewhere over the Atlantic, on his way back to England for the graduation. They would see each other soon, and Henry had promised he had a big announcement for the family.

Then his smile slipped and the full weight of this weekend pressed on him again. Charles's days of anonymity and being sheltered were about to end. When he left the Provost Garden, he would be heading back to his cramped room at Eton to get ready to meet his mother and brother. Then, later, he would graduate with his class and head into an uncertain future. Mother wanted him to attend university, and Sir Richard even agreed. But Charles wasn't sure what came next—what should a new king do? Should he even attend university at all? Or should he skip that part and go straight for the throne?

The decision moment was approaching, and there was no way to stop it.

11:25 a.m. Eton Refectory

Eton's ancient hall stood ready for the proud parents on graduation day.

The tables had been laid with sweet rolls, breakfast cakes, and cus-
tard tarts. Gallons of hot tea and coffee filled huge silver urns. Fresh
flowers in tall Victorian silver vases from Eton's gardens dotted the
narrow antique tables like exclamation points. The medieval ambience
was enhanced by the dozens of flags depicting heraldry of different
knights of the realm, all hung high above in the arches. For this graduation, special attention to detail was made, because it wasn't every day
that Eton graduated a king.

Outside, the day was sunny and mild, not a hint of rain in sight.
Instead the campus had been engulfed in a storm of a different sort:
paparazzi swarmed the campus, and the reporters had no respect for
the press areas they'd been assigned. Photographers could be seen
stealing into every building, vying to get a shot of King Charles's dorm
room, pestering classmates for juicy bits of gossip and old photos, and
looking for ways to get onto the building roofs to take pictures. Security
guards on carts chased the press in every corner of the campus.

A gleaming silver Bentley limousine fitted out with Royal Standard
fender flags appeared behind a substantial police escort, making its
way slowly through the center of campus toward the great hall. The
campus seemed to hold its breath, the only sound the whirring of cameras as they competed to capture the moment. The Bentley stopped
outside the hall and the doors opened.

As if by magic, a wheelchair appeared from behind a nearby hedge
and rolled over to the car as the Queen Mother Elizabeth prepared to
head inside. Dressed for the occasion in the traditional black mourning

attire she had worn since the death of her husband, Liz was applauded by the bystanders. The fashion hungry press was quick to notice that her hat band was fashioned out of the Eton blue striped fabric usually reserved for the official school ties. Notes were hastily scribbled and more photos taken.

Henry next stepped from the limo, smiling. The cameras seemed to go into overdrive as the tall, young, and devastatingly handsome prince gave a quick wave and took over pushing his mom's wheelchair from the nurse. Countless girls, presumably sisters and daughters attending the ceremonies, squealed in delight to see Henry in real life. Watching from the crowd, the provost looked like he had bit into a sour lemon—Henry's escapades at Eton were still fresh in his memory. But if anyone else remembered—including the clapping headmaster—they didn't show it. Indeed, Henry was receiving a welcome befitting a rock star more than a prince.

The royal entourage proceeded to the refectory, where a receiving line waited. Eton officials took turns being acknowledged first by the Queen Mother and then Prince Henry, Duke of York.

The graduation ceremony followed morning tea. In an extraordinary departure from tradition, the keynote speaker was a student. Not just any student, but the King of England Charles VII. He had been cajoled into accepting the assignment by Uncle Freddie, who had been pressured by the entire Board of Governors. Charles agreed under the condition that no advanced public announcement be made, fearing it would create a media circus that would distract from the true meaning of the ceremony: honoring his fellow graduating class members. Further, he insisted that he file into the famous Eton Chapel with the rest of the graduates and be seated in the pews alphabetically, as if he were any of the other boys. The chapel had been built in the late *Gothic* or *Perpendicular* style and was a landmark at Eton. It had been commissioned by the school's founder, Henry VI.

When Charles entered the Chapel with the graduates, nearly at the end of the line as dictated by his surname Stuart, a murmur ran through the assembled crowd of families and undergraduates. He smiled at his mother and brother as he walked down the long aisle and headed for his pew, number 22. The ceremony was presided over by the headmaster, and numerous luminaries and alumni spoke. Finally, the chairman of the Board of Governors announced that the commencement speaker this year was a student and proceeded to formally introduce Charles, who rose and headed for the aisle.

The choir had been practicing under the direction of an Eton master for weeks, and had achieved an almost flawless rendition of the song that now rang out over the crowd as Charles headed toward the dais:

GOD SAVE OUR GRACIOUS KING:

LONG LIVE OUR NOBLE KING,

GOD SAVE THE KING;

SEND HIM VICTORIOUS,

HAPPY AND GLORIOUS;

LONG TO REIGN OVER US,

GOD SAVE THE KING.

Ignoring the long-standing anonymity policy, the entire student body, clad in traditional collegiate graduation regalia and standing for the anthem, recognized their king as he walked through their midst with a respectful bow. When Charles arrived at the front row of the assemblage, he bowed his head in a sign of his respect and even awe at the circumstances. A pair of school honor guards escorted him onto the dais.

The podium centered on the dais was exquisitely adorned with flowers and ferns. The Royal Standard flag, flanked by dozens of Union Jacks, decorated the stage. The headmaster, Honorable John Newborough, walked to the podium, tapped the mic, and spoke: "Your royal highnesses Queen Mother, His Royal Highness Prince Henry, lords and ladies, your lordship Reverend Father, ladies and gentlemen, Etonians, friends and family, may I present His Majesty King Charles."

Charles got up and approached the podium. Before he began speaking, he took a moment to survey the crowd, perhaps seeing the people awaiting his words as subjects for the first time in his life. Press observers later noted this moment, and at least one headline proclaimed, "A KING IS MADE!" Other reporters noted that Charles didn't have any notes as he stood preparing to address his class. Finally, when the moment seemed like it couldn't contain any more suspense and tension, Charles leaned forward and began to speak directly from his heart in a slightly proper and painstakingly acquired English accent.

Charles began by recalling his journey. One filled with unexpected twists and turns, secrets and surprises, heartbreak and triumph. He spoke of how he would pledge his life to serve his people, dedicating his every moment to making Britain a place of pride, prosperity, and respectability. As he concluded his remarks, he looked directly into the faces of his audience and said, "While I am not the king you expected, I shall be the king you will remember as the one who learned to love a nation, a people, and a way of life, embracing it with vigor and passion. Beginning as a stranger in a strange land, I have come to love and cherish this great country. My country. Now, I commend my fellow Etonians to go forward into an awaiting world ready to share your ambition, genius, and love of country.

"I end my time at Eton College with the greatest of pride and humility. That I walked amongst the finest and have come to learn from the brightest. It has been a journey well-traveled.

"My time here, like yours, will be long remembered. It has been the beginning, not the end, of our life's journey. A journey that will take us to many places and teach lessons far beyond any learned in books. As for me, I know that destiny has taken me down a path I could never have chosen. I can only pray that I will be worthy of the task and earn the respect and admiration of the people of this great nation. I pledge to you all my allegiance to God and country, and dedicate my reign to serving this great empire and its people."

As he completed his speech, he turned toward the dais's steps and paused. He glanced in wonderment out over the sea of Etonians surrounded by their loved ones, and saw the admiration, compassion, and even love on their faces, some with tears in their eyes. At that moment Charles knew that he was their sovereign. He felt it in his soul, deep within, and knew he never could allow himself to fall short of their expectations.

Descending the stairs, he once again paused, this time in front of his mother and brother, both seated to the right of the headmaster. He leaned over and kissed his mother's forehead and whispered, "I love you, Mum, you are my inspiration."

As he requested, Charles was treated just as all the other boys were and received his diploma in alphabetical turn, seventy-eighth in a class of 118. Like all the other graduates, Charles's name was called out: "Charles Carnegie Bolin-Stuart." He approached the dais and the headmaster gave the chairman of the board Charles's diploma for presentation. The chairman handed the young man his diploma, shook his hand, and again departed from Eton's long-standing tradition of royal anonymity when he bowed slightly and whispered: "Congratulations, Your Majesty."

As the men shook hands, Henry extemporaneously rose and loudly shouted: "Hip hip hooray!"

The audience spontaneously joined Henry, jumping to their feet and yelling, "Hip hip hooray!" three more times.

CHAPTER 15
THE CRIMSON SURPRISE

AFTER THE GRADUATION CEREMONY, THERE WAS AN ENDLESS LINE OF people wanting to meet the king and his handsome brother, followed by no less than three receptions at various houses around campus. Charles and Henry did their best to keep up with the stream of names and titles coming at them, and they bowed until their backs were sore, but it was tiring work for the both of them. Henry, still uncomfortable with his role as a prince and younger brother to the king, kept up a steady supply of quiet jokes he muttered under his breath, and Charles did his best not to laugh out loud in some lord or lady's face and start a national incident.

"I say," Henry muttered at one point in a put-on English accent, "King Charles, you've become quite the little diplomat."

"Shhh!" Charles hissed, but he was smiling nonetheless.

Finally, after dusk gave way to early evening, the boys noticed their mother was visibly exhausted and announced they would be retiring to the family's nearby rooms. The group included Charles, Henry, Liz, Uncle Freddie, and Prince Cyril. They piled into matching Bentleys, into a cocoon of silence and comfortable leather after hours of entertaining.

"Whew!" Henry said, leaning back and stretching his long legs out in front of him. "Man! If that's what it's like to be king, I'm glad it's you and not me, bro. I couldn't handle that."

"I'm just worried I'll mess up someone's name next time I see them."

"Ah, no biggie. Just call everybody My Royal Subject. They won't say anything. You're the king!"

"Ha ha, yeah right," Charles said.

They were staying at a local estate, Hardwick Abby, an Elizabethan masterpiece owned by a wealthy benefactor. When the limos arrived, they got out and found that everything had been set up for them. A table of biscuits and finger sandwiches was next to a sideboard laid out with cordials and refreshments. Fresh-cut flowers bloomed from every surface.

Hardwick Abby sat high on a bluff overlooking a massive land grant given to an earl's family centuries ago. Boasting more than four hundred rooms, it was one of the largest estates under private ownership outside of the monarchy. The grandeur was equal to any of the royal residences, and kept in pristine order by an army of housemen and servants.

"Whose place is this?" Henry asked as they filed in, while their drivers began unloading bags.

"It belongs to the Earl of Plymouth," Uncle Freddie answered. "He was only too happy to accommodate us."

"Nice place," Henry said.

"I'm sure the majordomo will be happy to relate its history, if you'd like a tour," Uncle Freddie said.

"Uh oh. No, thanks. I'll pass."

Prince Cyril and Uncle Freddie found this uproariously funny for some reason.

After they had all settled into their rooms—one more magnificent than the other, with the boys in separate rooms—they met again in the downstairs salon. Liz looked drained, with bags under her eyes, so she cut straight to the business at hand: "Henry dear, you've been making us wait all day. Now please, out with it. What is this announcement you've been dying to make?"

Henry grinned and stood up. "Well, I know this is Big Chuck's day and all, but I wanted to tell you in person. Since I got back to Hotchkiss, I've been taking extra credits every semester, so I'm scheduled to graduate a term early, after next fall term."

There was some light applause, but Henry held his hand out. "That's not the news! After I graduate...hold on...I need to get something." He darted from the room and returned holding something behind his back. "Anyway, after I graduate," he moved his hand from behind his back and unfurled a familiar crimson and gray T-shirt, "I'll be starting Harvard for the winter term!"

The T-shirt was the same well-worn one he had been wearing on the plane ride over to the States, given to him by his father years ago.

There was a silence in the room as the news settled in. Finally, Charles broke the silence: "Bravo! That's great! You're going to Dad's school!"

"Yep," Henry said. "They accepted me on an early admit. I'd like to say it's because of my movie star good looks and grades, but they seemed pretty excited that my brother is the King of England and I'm, or at least was, a Carnegie." He laughed lightly.

"Henry," Liz began, then took a deep breath, "I'm very proud, of course, but...I thought we had discussed that you would come back here, to England, for university?"

"Well, we did," he said. "I know. But Mom, seriously, I don't want to go to school here. My life is back in the States. And, I mean, Dad went to Harvard. It's obviously a good school—"

"No one is disputing the quality of a Harvard education," Uncle Freddie put in smoothly. "Only that there are...other considerations here. Having the Duke of York with an American education attend an American college would be highly irregular."

Henry nodded, and for once didn't make a wise remark. The last year on his own had matured him. "I know. I can appreciate that. But the fact is, this is my life. I'll be an adult soon, and this is what I want."

He said it in such a final way that there was no real response to it. Henry was making it clear that he wasn't asking permission. Finally, Liz sighed and rolled her eyes over a gentle smile. "Henry, dear, you really are your grandfather's grandchild. He was as stubborn as an ox, just like you. It appears you're not asking for my permission, but I can see how much this means to you. So go ahead and study hard and make us proud. But do please remember to visit your mother every so often."

Henry broke into a huge grin and crossed the room in three big steps to lean over and give his mother a nearly crushing hug.

"Thank you, Mom! I really appreciate it." He turned to Charles. "And you too. Thanks for your support, bro. It means the world to me."

"We'll miss seeing you," Charles said.

"Yeah, yeah, but I'll visit a lot." Henry picked up one of the cookies off the silver tray and wolfed it down in a single bite.

CHAPTER 16
A ROYAL CHRISTMAS

EVEN AFTER HE WENT BACK TO START AT HARVARD, HENRY WAS AS good as his word. He arrived back in England at Christmastime to celebrate the holiday with his family at the Sandringham Estate on the Norfolk Coast Area.

Charles, now a freshman at the University of Cambridge, would meet his brother there. He first got there at the palatial estate in the late afternoon to find it ablaze with Christmas decorations and lights. Without waiting for the driver to get his bags, or his security detail to scope out the place, Charles bounded from the back of his limousine and went inside. He found Liz in a comfortable and warm salon, sitting before a roaring fire.

"Mother," Charles called out as he was announced by the faithful butler, McKinsey. "Happy Christmas, Mother, Happy Christmas!" Charles was careful to use the British greeting rather than the typical American "Merry Christmas." He wanted his mother to know how hard he was working to assimilate the British culture and traditions.

"Oh dear, Happy Christmas to you, dear Charles," Liz answered. "You are looking quite well. I'm thrilled you are here so that my holiday can begin. But of course we must wait for your brother Henry, mustn't we? He should be right along. McKinsey sent a car to the train station to collect him."

"He took the train?"

"Yes, dear. Well, you know Henry; he hates a fuss, and all that special treatment. He's so headstrong about things like that. Never wants any attention or recognition of his place in the royal family. He calls it un-American."

"Well, I guess that sounds just like Henry...but Mother, how are you? Are you feeling any better? You look well..." But Charles couldn't quite finish the sentence. In truth, his mother looked even more tired and defeated than she had just a few months before. Instead of making steady progress, it seemed she was lucky to maintain her remaining health. The thought crossed his mind that she might never get up from the wheelchair again, but he pushed it away and kept a smile on his face.

"I'm alright, dear," she said. "I have my good days and bad, but I am feeling better now that my boys will be home for the holidays."

"Mother, I love being here at Sandringham for Christmas," he said.

"Well, you know it's traditional that the royal family spends the holidays here. I wanted to keep that tradition alive, even if it is a new one for all of us. The people expect that. But I did keep the guest list small. I...it's hard for me to entertain too much lately." She paused, then smiled brightly and changed the topic. "Did you see the tree in the great hall?"

"I did, it is massive and so beautiful. I really fancy it. Where on earth did they find such a tree?"

Liz raised her eyebrows. "Was that a trace of British accent I heard?" she said. "I believe it was!" Charles blushed but didn't answer, so she went on, "I'm not quite sure where the tree comes from, but

I'm pretty sure it is fresher fir. They are the most fragrant, wouldn't you say?"

"Right, you can smell the fresh pine scent everywhere. It looks like every room is decked out with greens and flowers and bows."

"We tried to make the old place as festive as possible. I'm glad you noticed!"

There was a light tapping at the door and McKinsey stepped in. "Mum, it's Prince Henry."

A second later, Henry bolted into the room like a hamster that had been released from his cage. He embraced his mother. "Mom, Merry Christmas. Merry Christmas to you too, Charles."

Liz returned the hug, lingering just a bit longer. She had missed her baby and had not seen him for many months. "My God, Henry, you've grown even more!"

Henry grinned, then shouldered up to his older brother and looked down his nose at Charles. "Just an inch or two...an inch or two bigger than Charlie, that is!"

Charles snorted. "I think you might be a bit off, maybe we should fetch a yardstick and get a proper measurement, 'cause I think we are just about equal."

"Woah, Charlie! Sounds like Cambridge finally got to you. When did you start talking like that?"

"Blimey! What are you talking about?"

"Blimey? What the hell? You sound like Elton John!"

Liz laughed and waved at them. "Boys, you mustn't needle each other now! I do believe you are both the most handsome lads in all Britain."

"How about in America?" joked Henry.

"There too," she answered. "But Henry, you must know I'm frightfully upset with you."

"About what?"

"About your refusal to go to university here in Britain, of course! Remember, when we arranged for you to return to Hotchkiss, we also agreed that going to college in the United States was not a promise? Then without any discussion you got yourself, and God only knows how, to skip a semester at Hotchkiss and get an acceptance to Harvard."

Henry waved her concern away. "Aw, Ma, you know how much I wanted to be like Dad and go to Harvard."

"So, dear, are you saying you go right from Hotchkiss to Harvard after the holidays?"

"Well, yeah. Isn't that cool?"

"What about graduation from Hotchkiss?"

"Oh, that. Well, they don't have graduation mid-term, no commencement ceremony or anything like that."

"Henry, you know how much I wanted to see you walk down that aisle, just like Charles did. It's what every mother wants to see…It's—"

"It's no big deal really," Henry interrupted. "I won't even know the kids in that class…it is the one before mine. And besides, I wanted to avoid all the hoopla that would surely have happened if you and Charlie showed up. The press in the States is ten times worse than here. You remember how it was at Eton when Charles graduated? Trust me, I did us all a favor."

"Well, Henry, it wasn't a favor for me, I wanted to see my baby graduate. Promise you won't take that away from me when you finish Harvard!"

Henry looked pained and promised quickly, then turned to Charles. "So what's Cambridge like? Full of tight-assed somebodies?"

"Not at all, Henry," Charles said. "The place is fine, and I'm really into it. I am taking courses in history, English, and philosophy, all quite keen. I'm also enrolled in Officer Training Corps (OTC). It's kind of military training for future officers."

"So is that what future kings study? Don't have courses in throne sitting, or maybe decree making?" laughed Henry.

"You know, Henry, you really are a twit," Charles said, grinning. "So, Mr. Big Shot, what are you taking up at Harvard? Space?"

"Good one, Charlie, but no. Just for your information, I'm taking business and pre-law. You know, like Dad."

"You can't be like Dad, only I can."

"Yeah, why not?"

Charles leaned forward and said, "Because he was king, and now I am."

"Ha! You can have it! But that was a good one. I've been underestimating you, Charlie."

Liz interrupted their banter to talk about the Christmas plans at Sandringham, especially the Christmas lunch. This event had been attended by the royal family and guests for decades at this estate. Gifts would be opened on Christmas Eve, and the staff was allowed to have their own holiday on Boxing Day, December 26th.

"And as I mentioned, the guest list for the Christmas lunch is small," Liz said.

"Who's coming?" Charles asked.

"Other than we three, it will be Prince Cyril, Uncle Freddie and Aunt Cybele, your Uncle John and his wife and children, cousins Philip, Hartley, and Margaret, along with their wives and children. I love to have children at the table, it makes everything so magical, especially at Christmas. I remember when you were children and we celebrated in Westchester, it was…" A single tear rolled down Liz's cheek and she dotted it away with her handkerchief. The boys gave her a moment of silence, until she smiled wanly. "I'm sorry. Forgive me. It's just, sometimes the memory comes back so strong and I miss your father terribly. I always loved Christmas at Westchester, with the special dishes prepared by cook and the family together, you boys so excited about your gifts and your grandfather visiting. I just...it's hard to be alone."

Real tears flowed down Liz's sullen cheeks. Charles went to his mother and hugged her. "Mum, we all have those same memories and miss Dad as much as you do."

"Yes, Charles, I know." Sitting up a bit stiffer in her wheelchair, Liz gained control of herself and resolved not to let melancholy ruin Christmas. "Now boys, let's get down to business. How about we open a few early Christmas gifts?"

"Right on!" Henry gave the old thumbs-up. "Let the fun begin!"

"Thumbs up?" Charles said. "Really? That's crass and so——"

"So what?" Henry said. "Yankee?"

"Boys, come." Liz wheeled herself toward the door as the boys fought off each other to have the privilege of pushing their mother's chair. Charles won and was rewarded with yet another one of Henry's royal gooses.

"Boys, haven't you outgrown such shenanigans?"

Chiming in, they replied in unison, "Never!"

As the trio walked toward the Great Hall, Liz went on. "I forgot to mention that I invited Prince Edward, but he declined. He's a lovely chap, but seems a bit preoccupied. I hear he does a wonderful job at the Ministry of Art and encourages young artists."

Henry leaned in and whispered to his brother, "Yeah, I bet he likes to encourage young artists, pretty boys, no doubt, probably a few at a time." Henry popped his finger in his cheek and made a crude gesture.

Charles laughed in a short burst. "Still a rube, I see." Turning back to his mother, Charles said, "How about Richard?"

"He's very busy, but I asked him to stop by after the luncheon to make an appearance. He said he would."

"Richard!" Henry barked. "He's a total jerk and I can't stand him."

"Henry," Charles said, "he's been fairly invisible over the last few years. He's given me some guidance and has arranged to stay on as regent until I finish university and some military training."

"Are you kidding me?" Henry said. "Remember that Grandpapa Cyril said not to trust him and watch every move he makes?"

"Yes, Henry," Liz chimed in, "we all have Richard's colors. But he is serving as regent, and until Charles is ready, we will have him in our lives. Although he is obnoxious, he seems to be handling the demands of the job. He's turned out to be very charitably minded. I'm told he's greatly expanded the royal giving."

"Charitable? I'll bet." Henry added, "Does he still stink?"

"Oh Henry, please, the man has a condition," Liz said. "Now, let's all put personalities and politics aside and enjoy the holiday."

"Fine, Mother, we'll be good little boys," Henry quipped.

———•—•———

Christmas fell on Sunday that year, and the day dawned clear and bright, with a chill in the air and a light snow falling. Excitement ran high that morning as guests began to arrive and prepare for the royal Christmas lunch.

The table glistened with golden flatware service, gold-rimmed Waterford crystal stemware, and a series of floral arrangements in fifteenth-century vases. Candles in mammoth candelabra, adorned with holly and ivy, bathed the table in a warm and welcoming radiance. Traditional Christmas crackers had been placed at each place setting.

Charles sat at the head of the table with the Queen Mother directly to his left. Henry sat to the right of the king, and next to him sat Prince Cyril, the boys' step-grandfather. The other guests were seated according to title and rank.

Luncheon was served at precisely 11:45. A traditional Christmas goose, three of them actually, supplied by local Sandringham estate farmers, were roasted to a golden brown and presented on a massive silver tray. The fowl was surrounded by grilled parsnips, carrots, and Brussels sprouts arranged upon a lush bed of deep green curly kale. The palace executive chef, who had traveled to Sandringham with the family, was charged with the official carving. A wide variety of carved cold meats were beautifully displayed on the sideboard, along with other local and imported delicacies. Centered on the sideboard and adorned with a necklace of cranberries was a boar's head, replete with a juicy red apple protruding from its mouth.

Nudged by his mother, Henry rose from his seat to propose the traditional holiday toast to the king. "Hear, hear! Let us raise our glasses and wish Charles, our sovereign, a happy and blessed Christmas and long, successful reign! May he enjoy health and the love and support of all his subjects."

The guests, now standing around the table, raised their glasses and saluted Charles.

Thoroughly embarrassed by the attention, Charles stood and acknowledged the kind words: "Thank you for your sincere wishes. I am grateful to be here with you and share the holidays. My wish for this day is the complete recovery of my wonderful mother."

An explosion of Christmas crackers followed, and some of the guests donned the silly tissue paper hats that had been carefully tucked inside.

As the meal wound down, a flamed Christmas pudding with brandy butter was passed around the table by footmen.

The guests soon finished their dessert and the Queen Mother clinked her glass. "Shall we retire into the Great Hall for some holiday music and singing of the carols?" she asked.

"Brilliant!" responded Uncle Freddie. "Aunt Cybele, will you play the piano for us?"

The group filed out of the dining room and headed to the hall.

On the way to the hall, McKinsey caught Charles's eye and motioned him over. He whispered in Charles's ear, "Sir, Duke Richard has arrived and would like to join the family."

It was appropriate protocol that when Charles was in residence, the chief butler would address him as the head of household and not the Queen Mother. These subtleties were ingrained into the English in service.

Charles glanced over to his mother, who nodded and whispered, "Show him in to the library, please."

"Thank you, McKinsey. Please show Duke Richard into the library."

"Of course, as you please, sir."

Liz and the boys excused themselves from the rest of the family and headed toward the library. They walked in to find Richard laying back on an elegant chair, his bulk spread out. At once, his terrible body odor assailed their nostrils.

"Richard," Charles said formally. "Happy Christmas. My mother and brother wish you the best for the season, as do I."

"Thank you, Charles, and the same to all of you." Addressing Charles by his first name was a clear sign of disrespect for his position, but Charles let it pass by without comment.

They exchanged more stiff Christmas greetings, and finally Charles worked the conversation around to Richard's charitable work.

"So Richard, it seems you have been particularly active in the promotion of some worthwhile charities. Tell us about them."

Richard covered his surprise at the question, then smiled his oily smile. "Yes, Charles, we are being quite active in those efforts. After all, it's the right thing to do for the people of the realm and, for that matter, the world."

"Certainly. So, which charities do you fancy the most?"

"Hmm, well, there are so many different ones, those for children, the elderly, and the infirm, and of course there are the arts and antiquities. We try to diversify the giving to reach a wide segment of those most in need and those serving the public's interests."

"How much money has been distributed so far this year?" Henry asked.

"That's hard to say," Richard said, with a visible effort not to sneer at Henry. "You see, there are so many and the amount of the contributions varies."

"So you don't know?"

"Of course we know, Henry. It's all documented in the records. But as far as the exact amount, we would have to get back to you on that."

"I'd like that, Richard, please do," said Charles.

"Really, Charles, you need not concern yourself about such matters," Richard said with an edge in his voice. "As regent, I have the best interests of the monarch in mind and act accordingly."

"Is that so?" Henry said. "You don't exactly have a stellar reputation for that. And with all due respect, I wouldn't trust you to feed the pigs out back on the farm."

Richard was too smooth to let his expression change, but his neck colored red with rage.

Before the confrontation deepened, Liz rang a bell to call McKinsey and break the tension. "Thank you, Richard," she said, "we do so appreciate you coming by, but I'm afraid I'm frightfully tired and need a nap. McKinsey will escort you out."

This dismissal was unmistakable and Richard heaved himself to his feet. His face was a careful mask but underneath, Charles saw only anger. McKinsey appeared and Richard muttered only the flimsiest of good-byes on his way out.

"That was weird," Henry said. "Why'd the guy even come here at all? I mean, he obviously can't stand us. And I really wouldn't trust him as far as I can throw him, which obviously isn't far. I mean, seriously, he must weigh—"

"Henry," Liz interrupted, "it's not seemly to comment on people's weight. And yes, we are all aware of Richard's shortcomings, but he is the duly appointed regent and we must tolerate him until Charles is ready for the throne, after university, as we all agreed. For now, we have to grin and bear it. Truth is, while you are both away, Richard is virtually invisible. I think we can all manage."

"I don't know, Mother," Henry said, "I still think he's up to something."

CHAPTER 17
STAR-STUDDED NIGHTS

ENRY TOOK A DEEP BREATH AND EXHALED, HIS BREATH FOGGY IN the crisp air of Cambridge, Massachusetts. This was only his second January at Harvard, but he had already quickly grown to love the place, with its imposing buildings and air of studious intellectualism. The first big snow had fallen shortly after he returned from England and he had spent a few hours that night walking the campus through the pristine snowfall. He often imagined his dad walking these same sidewalks, and it made him smile. It made him feel closer to his dad than he had in a long time—his mother said that William had loved his time at Harvard. This was something that Henry felt he shared alone with his father, which made it all the more special. Charles could be king, but at least Henry had this connection.

The days since he'd returned to the States had been hectic. He had moved from Hotchkiss to Harvard's VIP residence hall, River House. The hall was a prewar building that had been given as a gift to Harvard by the family of Theodore Roosevelt, twenty-sixth President of the United States and a graduate of Harvard. The ivy-covered structure blended into the campus that was already blessed with many beautiful buildings, some dating back to the earliest days in America. In fact, Harvard was home to many US presidents—and just a few months before, had elected another Harvard man as president.

A high red brick wall, topped with a daunting wrought iron fence and menacing spikes much like sharp spears, surrounded the River House property, so visitors had to enter through an imposing set of iron gates into a courtyard. Vehicular traffic passed through a rear gate that was monitored by both campus police and Boston's finest.

From the outside, it was virtually impossible to detect the intense security that protected River House. Every square inch of the wall and courtyard was under round-the-clock surveillance, and there was a guard detail on duty at all times. Henry had heard there was a small armory in the basement and hardened rooms that were designed to protect occupants against all kinds of security breaches.

On this afternoon, he and Ollie were just finishing unloading boxes from a truck and carrying them inside. In his typical self-sufficient manner, Henry had rejected a courier service and opted to rent a truck and move himself. Ollie had tried insisting that Henry should wait inside while he unloaded, but Henry wouldn't hear of it. There was no way he was going to sit around while someone else unloaded his stuff.

"Well," Henry said, setting a box down in the living room of his new apartment, "here we are. Home sweet home, eh?"

"Not bad," Ollie said appreciatively.

"Right? Two bedrooms, our own terrace with a view of the Charles River, and private bathrooms. Thank God for that. My nose would die if I had to share a bathroom with you all year."

"Like you're fresh as a daisy?" Ollie said, practicing his near-perfect American accent. He looked around the apartment carefully. "But still, from a professional point of view, I'd say it's an improvement.

Fourth floor, keyed elevator, lots of security, and no windows facing other buildings. And the neighbor. I checked him out. He's a South African poet, a Fulbright scholar. Building staff says he hardly ever leaves his room, and has only one regular visitor, another guy, South African friend of his I reckon."

"A poet? Have you met him?"

"No. Like I said, a near recluse."

"Huh. Poet…you think he's gay? You know, poets and all that?"

"Who knows? You can find out, though. They have a view of the terrace, so go out there and give a flash of the old wanker and see if they come knocking."

"Gross, Ollie. You're just jealous."

"Doubt it, mate," Ollie said. He nodded toward a small maid's room off the kitchen. "I'll take that room, by the way. Has its own bathroom and an outside entrance. I'll be out of sight, but still nearby, and it's a good emergency exit if we need it."

"An emergency exit?" Henry scoffed. "C'mon, man, it's not like we really have anything to worry about. Besides, why would you want to stay there? There's two perfectly good bedrooms. Take one of them."

"No, thanks," Ollie said. "Too far out of the way. I need to see and hear what's going on here. And as for whether or not we need security, it doesn't matter. My job is to make sure you never need it."

Henry shrugged. He had long ago given up arguing with Ollie about security matters. It was generally a futile endeavor.

After they moved in, Henry settled into an easy routine of classes, hanging out with Ollie…and seeing Star as often as possible. After their chance encounter on the airplane—an episode that Henry knew he wouldn't forget no matter how long he lived— Star was a regular at

Hotchkiss, especially on the weekends, making Henry a happy chap. When Henry moved to Harvard, Star followed her man.

It hadn't looked like she would at first. In February, Henry had been seriously bummed out that she was headed to New York to audition for some acting job. But only two days later, his phone rang and Star announced that she needed help. Turned out she was moving to Cambridge in between auditions. She had a job offer to nanny for an English couple who lived somewhere on Commonwealth Avenue. She said they were giving her free lodging, but not much else. Truth is, Star almost never talked about her background, her family, or anything else about herself. If Henry brought it up, she just distracted him (something she was *very* good at) or refused outright to answer any questions. Henry assumed there was some bad or painful stuff in her family history and didn't want to press too much.

Besides, if he was being honest with himself, he didn't press any further because he didn't really want to get involved in whatever was going on with Star and her complicated family life or whatever. No, their relationship was almost strictly physical—and they both seemed happy to keep it that way. She didn't seem to care one way or the other about Henry's schooling, his grades or classes, or even the fact that his brother was the King of England. She never asked if he had other girlfriends and never even asked to meet his friends. Instead, she liked to show up late at night, sometimes a little tipsy, and do things to Henry that were probably illegal in certain states. Or at least they should be.

Star visited their River House apartment only a few days after they settled in.

Ollie let her in and went back to his room, his finger stuck in the book he had been reading.

"God," she said, walking into Henry's room. He looked up from his desk, where he'd been doing homework. As always, he was struck again by just how very hot Star was and how, even in the dead of winter, she still managed to find clothes that hugged her every curve in the best way possible. "This place is like a palace! How'd you get this place?"

"Don't know exactly," Henry said. "My grandfather went here, though. Gave lots of money. And my dad went here too. You know. Legacy benefits and all."

"Right, right, whatever," she said. Then she eyed the king-size bed and launched herself across the room at it. She landed with a thud and a squeal. "Nice springs!" she said, then rolled onto her stomach. "This looks like fun. What do you say we give it a test run?"

She wasn't even done with her sentence before Henry was out of his chair and heading for the bed. As always, their chemistry was instant and electric. She was tugging on his jeans seconds later, while he stripped off his shirt and she murmured the things he loved to hear. Star worshipped his body and let him know it.

"I'm going to break this bed in properly and you bloody best love every second of it," she said. "So lie back and relax. You're all mine."

She blew warm breath in his ear, her hand already working on Mr. Niner.

Henry responded like a hungry animal. He pulled off Star's form-fitting sweater and her perfect breasts swung free. He could not resist placing his lips on them, alternately kissing and caressing them gently.

"Hank, you are making me crazy. I want you."

Her words were like fuel on a fire, igniting their love-making. Reaching down, he pulled on Star's skin-tight jeans until she kicked them off and lay only in her underwear. He rubbed the length of his body along her, as somehow both of their remaining clothes seemed to vanish in a whisper of cloth and urgency. Throughout, Star's hands worked on him non-stop.

"Star, you are amazing, don't stop, don't!"

"I've not yet begun, and neither have you."

Rolling over to sit on top of Henry, Star massaged his inner thighs, slowly working her way upward. He laid back and closed his eyes in ecstasy as she leaned over him, tickling his abs with her breasts and her breath. She kissed his neck, then slowly traveled down, nibbling on his chest and stomach. When she reached "the best part of Hank," she virtually consumed him.

He groaned, but she wasn't ready for the finale yet. In a split second, she rolled over and pulled Henry with her.

"Hank, I want to feel you inside of me. All of you."

Henry gladly complied. Slowly, he began the ancient ritual of consummation.

Star winced at first and then moaned as Henry entered her willing body. "Oh, my God, you are amazing."

Star reached back and grasped Henry at the small of his back, lifting her legs into the air. She pulled him closer, allowing her to feel him deep within. Matching Star's efforts, Henry thrust and then froze in place to prolong the euphoria. He tried to keep his mind focused on the need to preserve the moment. Then, almost involuntarily, Henry began to accelerate his body's motion until he thought his heart would explode.

Finally, when both lovers were on the brink and soaked in sweat, Henry closed his eyes, tossed his head back, and released a throaty moan while he erupted as only a youthful lover can. At that very moment Star succumbed.

After catching their breath, the couple embraced each other and lay quiet until Star broke the silence.

"Hank, I don't think I've ever enjoyed anyone so much. You are the most spectacular lover ever."

Henry smiled, shaking his head clear from the fog she always left him in. "I'm hungry. You wanna take a shower and then get something to eat?"

She poked him in the stomach. "You're so romantic. Let's."

The couple showered, dressed, and went for a long walk that ended up at Boston's famous North End. This was a neighborhood settled by Italian emigrants at the turn of the century and filled with ethnic restaurants, bakeries, and some very questionable characters. Frozen in time, the North End might have well been in Italy.

"Hank, isn't this where the Mafia lives?

"I heard something like that, but it's supposedly one of the safest tourist spots in Boston."

They walked until they came to a long line outside a bakery. The winter air smelled of fresh bread and hot coffee.

"This must be a good place, look at the long line. Wanna get something?"

"Sure, what do they have?" Henry asked.

"It's a bakery, silly. What do you think they have? Bakery stuff."

He grinned at her as they got in line. When they entered the store, Henry looked around in wonder. He had never seen anything like this. They walked up to the tall counter on top of the expansive glass cases filled with every kind of confection imaginable. The server, a buxom redhead, barked in her undeniable Boston accent: "Hey you kids, are you looking or buying?"

"Buying," Henry said.

"So what's it going to be, I got a line out the door and they all are just as hungry as you." Then she stopped and looked more closely at him. "Hey kid, you look kinda familiar. Did I see you on TV somewhere?"

"No," Henry said.

"C'mon, you sure? Hey! I know. You look like that prince of England kid. Anyone ever tell you that before? That you look like that prince of England?"

"Uh, no. Not really."

"C'mon," she pressed. "I gotta brain that never forgets a face. And I swear that's you."

"Nope," Henry said.

"Huh. I think you're pullin' my leg, and I gotta lotta leg to pull!" She laughed at her own bawdy joke. "Now, what will it be? I ain't got all day."

Star pointed to a freshly filled tray of extra-large cannoli with white cream on the ends. "What are they?"

"Jesus, you two. Where the hell have you two been all your life? They're frickin' cannoli, our house specialty."

Star leaned over and whispered to Henry. "I like those, Hank. They remind me of your—"

"Star!" he said, blushing.

"I'm just saying," she said. "I'll bet you I can get an entire one in my mouth all at once."

Henry was blushing bright red as he said to the clerk: "OK, lady, we'll take two of those, what did you call them, cannoli?"

As the server grabbed the pastries to wrap, she laughingly said, "You got it, Your Highness."

As they left the store, Henry was eagerly waiting to see if Star made good on her boast.

CHAPTER 18
INTRIGUE AT BUCKINGHAM

WITH HENRY SAFELY INSTALLED AT HARVARD AND CHARLES AT Cambridge, Liz found that she had more time on her hands than she knew what to do with. As the winter bloomed into spring and then summer, she was less content than before to simply sit in her rooms and stare moodily out the window. It preyed on her mind that neither of her boys was coming home for the summer. Henry claimed that he had some type of commitment in the States—although Liz wasn't sure of its exact nature—and Charles had signed up for a summer officer training program in the British military. Liz didn't know what to make of this either, but Charles was set on it. As he explained in one of his lengthy letters home, he felt that it was important and necessary that he serve Britain in the armed forces, to show the people that he was willing to "do the hard work" of being king and demonstrate his patriotism. She supposed this meant he would be entering the military after graduating. This wasn't entirely unheard of—most of the modern princes had spent some time in the military—but with the low-grade rebellion in Northern Ireland still going strong, she wasn't overly keen that her oldest son might find himself in harm's way. After all, she had already lost her husband to an IRA terrorist.

Gradually, as the weather improved, Liz felt some of the black cloud that had hovered over her for such a long time now beginning to lift. It was as if life was breathed back into her a little bit, and she found herself laughing more often and starting to once again look forward to things she used to enjoy. She even began going to therapy more regularly, no matter how much it hurt, and fantasized that maybe one day she would get up and walk again. It pained her to see herself in a mirror lately. She looked so wan, prematurely graying and old, confined in her wheelchair with her face wasted away. Her William would barely recognize her.

As her spirits lifted, she began to prowl around the palace more freely. It wasn't exactly easy. Buckingham Palace was a very old building and hadn't been designed for easy access with a wheelchair. She became intimately familiar with the back halls and loading elevators she used to navigate the tremendous residence, and it wasn't uncommon for her to surprise palace employees catching a smoke in an out-of-the-way place. They always looked horrified and begged the Queen Mum's pardon, but she laughed it off and only gently chided them. Mostly, she was surprised how few of the staff she recognized lately.

The construction didn't help either. She had barely any contact with Sir Richard, but apparently he had started some type of renovation project. Liz often found workers in white gloves handling the priceless antiquities and artwork that hung from every wall and inhabited every shelf and cabinet. Liz knew the artistic wealth of the empire was immense, with countless masterpieces spread among the royal homes. There were works from da Vinci, Reynolds, Rembrandt, El Greco, Van Gogh, and Michelangelo, among others. Some of the best of these hung in Buckingham. Liz had recently sent a message to Richard, asking to meet with him so she could get a better idea of what his renovation plans were. She knew she had been negligent in her duties as steward of Buckingham, so she felt she should at least come up to speed when work was done to the palace itself.

Another consequence of her improving mood and energy: she began to seek out social company once again, and she regularly invited Uncle Freddie or Prince Cyril to the palace for tea or a light meal. She had grown much closer to Prince Cyril in particular. She had always known he was a good man whose loyalty to the crown could never be questioned, but she was only lately getting to know his tender and compassionate side. She had begun to view the dapper old gentleman as a sort of father figure.

One spring afternoon, she invited Cyril over and met him in her favorite garden room. The tall windows gave a lovely view of Buckingham's grounds and, beyond that, the bustle and energy of London on a sunny and warm day.

"My dear," Cyril said as he swept into the room. "You're looking radiant. How are you feeling?"

She smiled. "You old liar. But thank you. I'm feeling better these days."

"How nice to hear! And the boys?"

"Good, I suppose," she said. "I don't hear from Charles very often. Not nearly as often as I'd like, and much less often than his brother. And I suspect he's leaving much out of his letters. He seems to be getting very good grades. Says he has all As. I suppose he's like his father like that, a natural intellect. Come to think of it, a natural athlete too."

"Yes, a credit to his family," Cyril agreed.

"Still, I know so little about his day-to-day life," she said. "Does he have a girlfriend? Who are his friends? Is he in a finals club? I wouldn't know!"

Cyril patted her hand.

She smiled. "I'm not too angry, though. I have my spies. His security detail, Ollie, is a fine chap and a good one for sending back reports. Reading between the lines, it does seem that Henry has a female friend, even if he doesn't want to admit it to his mother!"

"Only natural, I suppose," Cyril said.

"Yes, I suppose. And Charles, well, no doubt you've heard he's signed up for the officer training corps this summer. He's such a thoughtful and sweet boy. It's hard for me to imagine him as a soldier. But I do respect the impulse that led him to sign up. He feels that he has a lot to prove!"

"Yes, I guess he would."

"He's also apparently discovered a love of advanced maths. He says he's in advanced calculus! Oh, I remember how difficult a time I had at school with maths, much less calculus."

Cyril laughed. "Me too! Calculus was the only course I did not ace at Sandhurst. I had a dreadful professor from someplace like India, or maybe it was Pakistan; you know those people are really good in mathematics. At any rate, I could barely understand what form of the King's English he spoke, which made matters worse. But bright he was and learn I did, painfully, I might add." He paused, then asked, "And Richard? How are things here at the palace with Richard?"

"I suppose well," she answered. "He is a very private man and seems to have built up some sort of little army that keep guard of his apartments here at the palace. I can't imagine why he would need such a detail, but it's his business, I guess. As far as I can see, he's limited his job to the charitable giving he incessantly talks about and now this renovation at the palace. Otherwise, it seems he's content to keep himself away and out of sight."

"A renovation? At the palace?" Prince Cyril's eyebrows raised.

"Why, yes. Surely you saw the workers?"

"I suppose, but didn't know what to make of it exactly." He frowned.

"What is it?" she asked.

"Well, I lived here for many years, you remember. A renovation at the palace is a substantial undertaking. I'm just...surprised that I hadn't heard anything about it."

"You think this is something we should worry about?" she asked, feeling guilty again that she had spent so long in her rooms, removed from the daily life of the palace.

"Oh no," Cyril reassured her. "I'm certain there's nothing to worry about, although I might place a discreet query or two."

Liz smiled at him. "You're such a dear."

After a delightful conversation and tea, Prince Cyril left Liz in her sun-drenched garden room and strolled slowly down the carpeted hall. Yet he hardly noticed the exquisite artwork at every turn or enjoyed the familiarity of the palace he loved so much. In truth, his mind was disquieted, and he was silently berating himself. He had come to see Liz this lovely afternoon to have a difficult conversation with her, but then he hadn't been able to bring himself to ruin her mood or disturb her peace, especially after her mention of Sir Richard's "renovation."

In fact, he had received some disquieting news about Sir Richard recently, and he wasn't quite sure what to make of it. Prince Cyril didn't advertise the fact, but he had his own network of people embedded through the monarchy's security services. And of course, it helped to be a prince when it came to enlisting people to his cause. It also helped that Cyril was the picture of discretion. Liz had said nothing to him this afternoon that he didn't know already. He knew, for example, that Henry was engaged in a torrid, almost purely physical relationship with an English beauty named Star. Ollie had confirmed as much and described the relationship as "skin deep, if you know what I mean." Apparently, it had been going on for some time and, judging from the pictures he saw, Prince Cyril could hardly blame Henry for his narrow interest in the girl.

He also knew that Charles had enlisted over the summer, signing up for the officer training corps with a commitment to enlist in the service after graduation. Cyril drew on his contacts within the military to check up on Charles and found, to no surprise, that Charles was a capable and exceedingly eager recruit. He did everything that was asked of him cheerfully, then volunteered for more. When asked for a candid opinion, one of his superiors remarked, "The bloke seems like he's trying too hard." Cyril wasn't surprised about this either. He had a lot of respect for Charles, and appreciated the difficult spot he'd been put in, but there was little question in Cyril's mind that Charles was a bit like a deer in front of headlights and likely scared witless.

He withheld these observations from Liz for the same reason he didn't relate his news about Sir Richard: the woman seemed happier this afternoon than she had in months. Why bring her down when Cyril himself felt that he could handle any situation that arose and never bother the Queen Mother? And there was the matter of the sensitive nature of the allegations he'd only just heard about Sir Richard.

The story had come from a junior agent Cyril had recruited to keep an eye on Sir Richard, Jamie Gorden. Gorden was one of a handful of young men Cyril had personally chosen, based on their loyalty and competence. He had no doubt that what Jamie told him was true, and that it could present a major problem on multiple fronts. Cyril remembered the conversation well. He had met Jamie in his personal salon the previous Sunday after an urgent request from the young agent.

Jamie had arrived precisely on time and had looked nervous as Cyril's butler ushered him into the room.

"Sir," he stammered. "I'm sorry to disturb your Sunday. But...I'm afraid there's been a development with the subject known as Predator that you should know about as soon as possible."

Cyril had encouraged the young man to sit down and have a brandy to calm his nerves. Jamie had declined.

"Alright then," Cyril had said. "If it helps you at all, I'm familiar through long experience with Predator. No need to gloss over the gory details, if you take my meaning."

Jamie flushed. "Right then." He produced a few typewritten pages from an inside pocket of his jacket. "You don't mind if I read it directly, sir? I have an eyewitness account."

"Please go on." Cyril was calm on the outside, but wrestling with a growing sense of dread. The young man in his salon looked positively mortified.

Jamie cleared his throat and began to read.

"On Monday last, I...that's Agent Greenstreet, sir," Jamie interrupted himself, then continued, "I observed several men and women, all appearing to be between the ages of 16 and 23, arrive at a town house rented by Predator located at Lancaster Mews, South East. It was approximately 2100 hours. They arrived in two separate motor cars. I noticed that they were rather heavily intoxicated, demonstrating a good deal of instability and behaving in a rowdy manner. I was able to mingle in with the group and entered the residence with them. We were shown into a large drawing room on the first floor. I managed to slip into the shadows unobserved and secured a position to remain unseen.

"A maid clad in only the lower part of her uniform passed what appeared to be illicit drugs in the form of marijuana and hallucinogens, as well as a powder I suspected was cocaine. I observed Predator circulating among the participants. He was provocative in his actions, groping the young women, and in at least one case, a young man. Loud music blared from a wireless, and soon the party turned more intense as the guests shed their clothing and engaged in copulation and other sexual activities, some more extreme than traditional and definitely considered illegal in the commonwealth." Jamie looked up, and Cyril motioned him to continue. "Predator took great care in observing and in at least two instances participated in group sex with two or more participants."

Cyril made an exclamation of disgust and Jamie stopped again. "Shall I continue?" questioned the young agent.

"Yes, do."

"At approximately 0100 hours, the party began to disperse. When there were only a few people left, Predator physically restrained one young woman. She appeared to be underage, perhaps 15 or 16 years of age. He forced her onto her knees and instigated genital/oral contact. When he was finished, he invited three of the remaining males to engage in the same behavior, despite clear protestations from the young woman. Afterward, the four men—"

"Enough," Cyril said. "Good Lord, the man is a bloody pervert." He took a deep, shaky breath. "Thank you, Jamie. That will be all. And thank you for bringing this to my attention. You were right to do so."

"There is more, sir, a lot more." Jamie paused. "To be frank, sir, what the agent witnessed is a crime. This man should be prosecuted!"

Cyril sighed. "Yes, I don't doubt it. But for now, I need you to continue your work. And please, leave that report here. I'll read the rest later."

But later had never come. After Jamie had left, Cyril couldn't bring himself to read what he could only assume was a graphic account of rape. It wasn't a sense of propriety that caused him to avoid the report. Rather, he was afraid that if he read it, his next move might be to load a pistol and seek out Sir Richard himself, or perhaps empower some of the men in his employ to visit Sir Richard for a little bare-knuckled therapy. There was no way the regent could be arrested—he knew that—but there were other ways of dispensing justice. For now, after seeing Liz in higher spirits, he knew that Richard's justice would have to wait, but when it came, Cyril vowed that it would rain down on Richard like an avenging hurricane.

CHAPTER 19
DOUBLE TIMING

Henry's time at Harvard passed in a blur of classes and visions of Star draped over his mattress in every position. As he moved into harder and harder classes, Henry discovered—almost to his own surprise—that he enjoyed his classwork and school in general. Not only that, he was good at it. After his searing experience of getting kicked out of Eton, he had sometimes wondered if all those terrible things the headmaster said about him had been true. In his lonelier and darker moments, he worried that maybe he was too angry, that he really was a deviant of some sort or at least a major behavior problem. But as he built on a string of straight As at Harvard, Henry began to see a deeper truth: the angry person he had been at Eton was not his real self. That was only a temporary persona, one that had been forced on him by circumstances.

In reality, Henry found himself growing more focused all the time. By his sophomore year, he was taking more than a full load of classes and still hungry for more. His advisor actually told him to slow down—"I'm worried you'll burn out"—but Henry felt like he was just getting started. At this rate, he expected to graduate with his undergraduate degree in three years and go straight to Harvard Law School. He liked the idea that he and Charles would graduate at the same time, even if Charlie had already announced he was planning to enlist in the British military.

At the same time he felt his own power growing, he was beginning to wonder about what was going on with him and Star. Sure, it had been pretty great, but after all this time, Henry was starting to feel like he wanted more out of a girlfriend than an insatiable sex goddess. Of course, his objections didn't last long once Star actually showed up and worked her magic on Mr. Niner.

Henry's living conditions at River House remained pretty much the same, except that he lost his roommate. Now, after years together, Ollie announced it was time to give up his "high class babysitting" job. It was a hard blow for Henry, who had come to view Ollie almost like a brother. Henry had virtually grown up with Ollie, from his prep school days at Hotchkiss to his "senior" year at Harvard.

It was a sorrowful departure when the day finally came to say good-bye. Henry found Ollie in the living room, his bags packed and his little cubby hole off the kitchen cleaned out. No more soccer pictures on the wall, no more dirty tea cups on the nightstand next to his narrow bed.

"Hey," Henry said. "So this is it, huh? You're out of here?"

"Yeah," Ollie said. "Need to catch a cab for the airport. Should be here any minute. I'll bet you'll be glad to be quit of me, eh? No more foul smelling tea!"

"No kidding!" Henry said, who had still never cultivated a taste for English tea. "I can't believe you've lived here for, what, four years and you still drink that crap. It makes me seriously question your taste."

Ollie laughed. They'd had this familiar argument on and off since Hotchkiss, and there was a comfort for both of them in falling into a familiar rut. It made it easier to say good-bye.

Then Ollie's face grew serious. "Before I go, though, I want to tell you something."

"Uh oh. If you're about to tell me you've been lusting after my body all these years, please spare me."

"No, no. There's not that much whiskey in the world," Ollie said. "But seriously, I wanted to tell you it's been a real pleasure seeing you grow into one of the finest young men I know. You are an outstanding credit to your family and your country...both of them. And you are wicked smart, one of the smartest. I know you will take the world. I will miss you more than you could know, and I will always be there for you no matter what or where. Just call me."

Henry shuffled uncomfortably for a second, then he suddenly grinned. "Aw man, you're gonna make me cry and I hate crying. But seriously, you know you're my man, right? I know this was work for you, but still...you're like my brother over here. I'll never forget that."

Henry was taken aback to see Ollie tear up. "I appreciate that. You know...you're a frankly lousy Brit, I don't mind saying, so this might be hard for you to understand. But I was raised to love the crown and the king, and...well, there's no other way to say it. You've treated me as an equal all this time, and you're practically the king, second in line to the throne. And...I just have to say, it moves me more than you know to hear you say that."

Now Henry really was embarrassed. He still thought of himself as a regular American and had never adopted the British sense of class, no matter what his "official" position was. "It's okay," he mumbled. "Seriously."

"Julian will be here soon," Ollie said, tactfully changing the subject. "He's the new guy. Comes highly recommended, very qualified. But if he gets out of line, you let me know directly and I'll be back here and kick his arse."

"Right."

Ollie dug into his message bag and removed a small trinket. "Here. I want you to have this. It's something that my dad gave me when I enlisted."

"What is it?"

"It's kind of a lucky charm. A keepsake."

"Ollie, I can't take this, it looks valuable. No—"

"Yes you can, and don't argue. You know you can't win an argument with me. Keep it. It will bring you luck and you'll need as much as you can get."

"Why would I need luck more than you?"

"Sometimes you really boggle the mind. Didn't I just say you were the second in line to the throne? There are people out there who don't wish you well. You or your brother. Let's just say there's a rich history of killing English kings and successors."

"Oh please. I'm not worried about it," Henry said.

"You should be."

The intercom buzzed and the deskman announced the arrival of Ollie's cab. "Well," Ollie said, "that's my ride. Take care and keep in touch."

The two young men shook hands and then embraced, then Ollie turned to go.

———

Julian Lancaster moved in just hours after Ollie left. Unlike Ollie, Julian did not blend into the atmosphere. He was tall, thin, and wiry, and at least to Henry, he looked a little nervous, like he was ready to spring into action at any second.

After introducing himself, one of his first questions was, "How secure is this place?"

"Uh, very secure," Henry said. "I think. But you know, feel free to do whatever you need to do. I've been here for four years now with no problem."

"Right," Julian said. "Don't mind if I check it out myself."

Henry watched in amazement as Julian then did an incredibly thorough sweep of the apartment. The guy was actually lifting up lamps, like he was looking for bugs or something. Henry kept his mouth shut, but found it a little amusing. Anyway, Henry figured he'd be graduating soon enough, so Julian's assignment would be pretty short. If the guy was kind of paranoid, it wasn't like they'd be living together for long.

Over the next few days, they settled into a routine. Henry stayed busy with his immense class load and Julian busied himself getting to know the neighborhood, mastering several games on Henry's Nintendo, and ogling Star every time she came over. Unlike Ollie, Julian didn't seem to feel it necessary to trail along behind Henry on his way to class, which seemed strange to Henry, considering how thoroughly he had searched the apartment. But Henry didn't mind. He liked walking to class alone and was happy to let Julian do whatever it was that Julian was doing.

This explained why Julian was surprised to arrive home alone one afternoon and realize someone was in the apartment. His training kicked in immediately—as far as he knew, no one else had a key to the place for obvious security reasons—and he followed the noises to the bathroom. He stood outside the door and listened, then realized he was hearing sloshing noises and off-key female singing. Star.

Julian smiled, then without any warning opened the door in a rush and barged into the steamy bathroom.

Star was in the tub, surrounded by heaps of glistening white bubbles. When she saw him, to her credit she didn't scream, but startled and then smiled.

"What the hell are you doing in here?" Julian demanded, already aroused by the sight of the beautiful girl in the tub. He wished a few of the strategically placed bubbles would disappear. "I thought you were an intruder!" he lied. "How'd you get in?"

"I have a key," she said coyly.

"No one's supposed to have the key here!"

"Henry gave it to me, silly. Years ago."

"Humph," Julian said. "Well, you're going to have to give it back to me. And leave. You can't be here when no one is home."

"Oh, don't be such a grouch. But if you really want it back…fine."

And then she did exactly what Julian was desperately hoping for: she stood up. The water and bubbles slid down her flawless skin, and he was instantly and painfully aroused. Star used her hands to scoop away more bubbles, then she stepped out of the tub to stand in front of him totally naked.

"Can a girl get a towel?" she asked, raising her eyebrows at him.

"Uh, what?"

"I need a towel," she said. "Behind you. Unless you want to keep staring at me."

"Um."

She smiled. "Fine. I'll get it." She leaned toward him, her breast actually brushing his arm as she reached for the towel hanging from the door.

Julian's hand acted on its own, he swore, but he stroked her breast and ran a rough finger over her nipple, which instantly responded. She pulled back, now holding the towel but making no effort to cover herself.

"My, my," she said. "You're awfully forward. And from the looks of it," she glanced down at the bulge in his pants, "you're all backed up."

Suddenly Julian found himself sweating. He'd been lusting after Star since the first time he saw her, but he knew this was highly inappropriate. But...his mind was clouded and he couldn't seem to think straight as he stared at her. He could think of nothing more than pursuing this provocative opportunity.

"You know what, I think you need some help," Star said. "Come here."

She grabbed his hand and led him out of the bathroom and into Henry's bedroom. By the time they got to the bed, every last thought of resistance had crumbled and Julian let himself be pushed into sitting on the bed while Star knelt in front of him and undid his jeans and released him, then lowered her head to inhale him, her wet blonde hair falling down her back.

Julian bucked his hips to meet her. He was less than gentle with her, but Star didn't protest and seemed to grow more heated and urgent the harder he pushed against her. Finally, he couldn't take it any more and, standing up, he picked Star up bodily and tossed her down on the bed. She squealed with delight as he tore off his clothes, revealing a physique that had been toned by hundreds of hours in the gym, and fell heavily onto her.

Her nails raked his back, unnecessarily encouraging him, as he pinned her down with his body weight and plunged into her. He was a strong, muscular man who used his physicality to his advantage. Star allowed Julian to have his way, every which way, going limp as he used her body to satisfy himself. Afterward, she laid in sweaty satisfaction as he withdrew and collapsed on the bed next to her.

"Jesus," he breathed. "You're some bird, you know that?"

"Mmm," she said. "I like a man who knows how to control me."

"Blimey, there's plenty more where that came from. The things I'll do to you—"

They both froze at the sound of noises in the hall, then a jangling of keys. Then Henry's voice rang out through the apartment. "Julian? Yo, Julian? You home?"

Star giggled and jumped up from the bed, then slammed Henry's bedroom door and locked it.

A second later, he was knocking on the door. "Julian? Are you in there?"

"No, baby," Star breathed. "It's just me. Preparing a little surprise for you!"

"Oh." Henry actually sounded annoyed, and Julian wondered at the man's sanity. He couldn't help a stab of jealousy either, at the thought that this trollop was ready to service Henry only minutes after he had finished with her. This thought made him rise again in sudden urgency, and he wanted to throw Star face down on the bed and go at it again.

She saw him and gave him a wicked grin. "Not now, lover boy," she whispered. "You better get your clothes and go out that window! And no peeking in here! There's plenty to go around."

A minute later, Julian was out the window, then creeping to the terrace, so he could sneak out and come back in. He wanted to look in and see if Star really was as wanton as she suggested, but he resisted the urge. Instead, he started planning ways to make Star pay for doing this to him. Next time.

CHAPTER 20
UP IN SMOKE

RICHARD WAS A PATIENT MAN—IT WAS A TRAIT THAT HAD SERVED him very well over the years. He knew from experience that even the smartest opponent would eventually make a mistake, that even the goodest of goody-two-shoes would stray from the straight and narrow if they had enough time. Oftentimes, in his job, it was just a matter of waiting patiently, like a spider in a web, until his prey made a mistake, and then capitalizing on it.

So far, everything had been going according exactly to his plan. With Sir Melvyn and Jones's help, he had managed to siphon off millions of pounds from the Royal Treasury and set up a nice fat account in the Cayman Islands. He had even made solid progress on his plans for the renovation. Of course, he had known that any work on Buckingham Palace would raise red flags, so he wasn't surprised when his sources told him that Prince Cyril had been sniffing around, asking all manner of questions about what was going on. Back then, the work had been totally legitimate, all by his plan. Finally, as the months went on and the work continued in its very slow way, Prince Cyril got bored of asking about it and eventually his interest drifted away. With attention shifted away, Richard was ready to put the second part of his plan in motion—because it turned out that diverting a few million pounds here and there wasn't enough after all. If he wanted a big score, he'd have to think bigger.

And now, after all these years of waiting while the Yankee brat king went through Eton and finished up at Cambridge, he was running out of time. Worse yet, his source in America told him that the younger pretender, Henry, was hurrying through Harvard and would graduate a year ahead of schedule. Richard couldn't be certain there wasn't a plan here, that both the king and the spare wouldn't show up in London together and ruin everything.

And this was why he was on the phone to his secret weapon in the States.

"That's not going to happen," Badger assured him over a crackling phone line from Boston to London. "I'm telling you, Henry's not moving back to England. He bloody hates it."

"How do you know for certain?" Richard pressed.

"I just do. I've overheard him say it a dozen times."

"Not good enough," Richard answered.

"Well, I don't know what else you want me to say. That's all there is to it."

"I'm not sure you understand me," Richard said in his oily voice. "Like I said, I want to know everything that's going on, and you will call me if there is something that I need to know...got that? You're not there on vacation. And I sent you plenty of money to spread around if need be. You're there to do a job for me. And I know you want to do a good job, because if you don't, your father could wind up doing some very hard time up there in Brixton prison and I'll bring you back here to work for me. I fear he might not survive, given his frailties...get my drift? As long as you are doing a good job for me, your father will be protected. Understand? Now piss off."

He hung up and leaned back. For the thousandth time, he wondered if Badger would screw this up. He didn't think he had anything to worry about. Richard had met Badger at one of his parties after Richard had framed Badger's father for malicious manslaughter and he was sentenced to 35 years in prison. Badger had approached Richard and unsuccessfully pleaded for him to intervene. Realizing that Badger might be useful in the future, he made a deal to provide "easy time" for the father while he was in jail, and maybe someday pull strings for a pardon.

A knock sounded at his door. His secretary stuck her head in and announced that Sir Melvyn was waiting for their weekly meeting. He told her to show the wretch in and waited while Melvyn came in and sat down. As usual, the man looked positively gray and totally mortified, which was exactly how Richard wanted him to feel.

"Melvyn," Richard said. "You're late."

"Sorry, sir," he said, setting an elegant alligator bag at his feet. "Traffic."

"Right. So, let's get to it. I want to see the state of accounts, then I'll need your help on something else."

Melvyn visibly swallowed. "Of course." He opened the bag and withdrew a ledger. Opening it slowly, he said, "Sir, the latest transfers are confirmed. I also have posted the updated figures from the portfolio statements and produced a summary for your review. There are about 984,000 pounds in transit. Once those funds arrive in the Caymans and are added to the accounts there, now in the amount of 7,234,090 pounds, at that point the grand total of funds will be 8,218,090 pounds."

"Is that it?" Richard demanded. "I would have thought by now we would have more...a lot more!"

"Sir, we have to be cautious. The amount of money we are moving around is great, and we don't want to be too hasty and perhaps catch someone's attention."

"Rubbish! Listen, Melvyn, I don't have a lifetime to do this. Charles is finishing university soon and doing a stint with the military—we think. But he'll be back here before long and take the throne. This isn't to mention his brother in America, who seems to be in a bloody awful hurry to get out of school for some reason. Fact is, if Charles were to walk in here tomorrow, and the grand sum of our efforts is just over 8 million pounds, then this was all for nothing! There's much, much bigger fish out there."

"Hmm," Melvyn managed, with no other comment.

"So, onto the next. Where are you at with finding capable and discreet artists?"

Now Melvyn looked even more miserable.

"There are two excellent artists who are capable of duplicating the masterpieces you have identified for, shall we say, replacement," Melvyn said. "Each are trustworthy, perhaps a poor choice of words, but what I mean is that they are in no position to expose anyone, especially themselves. The very fact that they are unapprehended felons gives one consolation that they won't be running to the authorities anytime soon. Insurance, if you will. They are ready to begin working at any time."

"Excellent. Then I believe you know what to do next."

Richard couldn't keep the excitement from his voice. This plan of his had been hatched years before and was the reason he'd invited workers into Buckingham Palace and staged an elaborate ruse to throw Prince Cyril and all the others off the scent. The idea had come to him while walking around the palace and seeing the art as if for the first time. A single masterpiece, sold to the right buyer, would make as much money in an afternoon as they had been able to skim from fake charities in two years.

"Yes, sir," Sir Melvyn answered.

"I want these forgeries to be perfect!" Richard said. "Our men can begin actually removing the originals at any time, so the artists can get to work. When the new fakes come back in, they have to fool all but the most expert eyes."

Sir Melvyn seemed to chew on his next words. Finally, he spit it out. "Sir, if I may, I understand your plan here. But to be frank, sir, there's no way forgeries of the world's great art hanging in Buckingham Palace will be missed. Someone will know, and sooner than later. I strongly urge you to reconsider this."

Richard was about to blow up, but instead took several deep breaths and forced himself to consider the truth of Sir Melvyn's words. This was a nagging doubt with him as well, he couldn't deny it. Yes, there was a very good chance that someone would notice a forgery hanging in Buckingham Palace, even the most meticulous of forgeries. And on the scale he was planning on doing it, there would be so many ways to be discovered. Whether he liked it or not, the simpering Melvyn had a good point.

"Sir—"

"Shut up," Richard snapped. "I'm trying to think."

The silence drew out while Richard considered the problem from every angle. Then a lightbulb went off in his head. "I'm afraid you have a valid point, so a change of plans. We'll remove the paintings as planned, but forget the forgeries. You can tell your boys their services won't be needed."

Visible relief flooded Sir Melvyn's face.

"Instead, there will be an accident."

"Excuse me?"

"You see, we will put the paintings in storage during the renovation. While they are in storage—secure storage, mind you, under armed guard of course—there will be a fire that will destroy the whole bloody building. And all the art along with it."

"I'm sorry, I don't follow," Melvyn said, looking genuinely confused.

"Don't be thick, Melvyn. If the paintings are destroyed, we don't have to worry about forgeries. Or at least good ones."

"But sir, surely you don't mean to burn countless irreplaceable masterworks?"

"You're so dimwitted it's a wonder you can wipe your own arse," Richard sneered. "No, of course we're not going to burn tens of millions of pounds' worth of artwork! We're going to burn a building of fakes, Melvyn. Bad fakes. Any fakes. Meanwhile, I'll see what I can do about finding some eager buyers for the originals."

"Sir," Melvyn said, then stopped and seemed to choke up before he burst out, "You can't be serious! That's beyond the pale and profoundly greedy. It's utterly unconscionable to rob the country of so many treasures. I...I...I'm not sure I can abide by that extraordinary violation of the people and—"

"Rubbish! Don't you start going soft on me, Melvyn. You are talking to the man who could ruin you, your wife, your family, your career and even your bloody dog in a blink of an eye. I own your miserable hide, and you bloody well better get used to it. Don't give me any guff. You'll do just as I say!"

Melvyn seemed to be shrinking in the chair. Richard marveled that Melvyn really and truly seemed to lack in any sort of backbone.

"Well?" Richard pushed. "Out with it!"

"Sir," Melvyn said, "please, please reconsider this. It's an assault on the very history of our country. These are not just valuable masterpieces, but the very thread that connects generations and centuries of antiquity, the very core of Britishness. I implore you to—"

"Enough," Richard cut him off.

Melvyn bit off his next word, but his brow creased with a new concern. "But sir, the palace collection includes works from Picasso. Monet. Da Vinci. You won't be able to sell these at all. Anyone who would be interested would surely recognize them as stolen from the British Crown."

Richard actually laughed out loud. "Melvyn, you really are a fool. What you don't know about the world could fill libraries. Do you really doubt there are Russian oligarchs or Arab princes who wouldn't jump at the chance to buy a painting from the royal collection, no matter how they got it? No, there are plenty of Middle Eastern buyers out there who will leap at the chance to have such a trophy buried away in one of their ghastly palaces. These towelheads are all crooks to begin with. You'll see. They'll take as many as they can, load them on their private jets, and cheerio Gainesboro and the rest of the lot!"

"I...I'm speechless."

"Good. Now you can go. Have the men start to remove the best of the lot from the palace at the earliest possible moment. No one will ask questions. The palace has been under renovations for too long." Richard laughed at his own cleverness. "And be quick about it! I want the whole thing sorted out as quickly as possible."

Without another word, Melvyn got up and left Richard's office.

CHAPTER 21
ADVICE FROM THE DEVIL

LIKE EVERYTHING ELSE IN ENGLAND, THE GRADUATION CEREMONY AT Cambridge was steeped in tradition. Part of the proceedings were in Latin, and Charles had learned that some of the ceremony dated back 800 years. He sat in the Senate House with the rest of his class, watching the elaborate ceremony playing out and gnawing on his lip. When it came time, the Praelector came and took his hand, leading him across the packed room to the Chair, where the university vice-chancellor sat resplendent in his red robes and shawl.

Charles knew, of course, that he could have asked for special recognition during the ceremony. As king, he didn't have to submit himself to the standard protocol of a Cambridge graduate. Yet once again, he felt that it was important to take the same steps as the other students, to show that he planned to live among the people of Britain, not hover above them as a detached and distanced "American king."

They stopped in front of the Chair, and the elderly vice-chancellor looked up at him from where he was sitting. The old man was smiling.

In a deep and commanding voice, the Praelector voiced the words that were music to every Cambridge graduate, beginning, "Dignissima domina, domina procancellaria et tota..." and on to the end. Just as it had been done for centuries previously, much of the ceremony was conducted in Latin.

When the sentence was done, the vice-chancellor reached out for Charles's hand. Without hesitation, Charles grabbed the older man's hand and knelt, as was customary for a Cambridge graduate. A slightly shocked whisper slithered through the Senior Senate chamber. The king was kneeling! Charles had known this would cause whispering, but he was determined and had cleared it with the vice-chancellor first.

The vice-chancellor first intoned his ceremonial sentence in Latin, and then switched to English: "By the authority committed to me, I admit you to the degree of political science in the name of the Father and of the Son and of the Holy Spirit."

Before this moment, Charles hadn't known what to expect, what he would feel. He had been at Cambridge for four years now, and like any college student, everything was building up to this moment. In truth, he hadn't expected to feel much—and if he did, he expected it would be a gnawing sense of anxiety. Cambridge, like Eton before it, had been a carefully cultivated oasis for him. He had mixed easily with the sons and daughters of English nobility, celebrities, and super rich. He had worked hard to understand more of the country he was supposed to lead, and still cringed occasionally when he heard a broad American vowel creep into his speech. He had participated in student activities when he could, although he hadn't made close friends.

Charles had come to view his graduation as another box he needed to check off on the long path to feeling like a proper king. Which made it more surprising to him when a wash of emotion swept over him as the vice-chancellor actually conferred his degree. At that moment, Charles felt a sense of pride and belonging—to Cambridge, to England—stronger than he had experienced yet. His eyes welled up with emotion, and as he walked to the door to receive his actual degree in the next room, he spared a glance into the audience. His mother, the Queen Mother, sat in her wheelchair in a specially cleared place for her, alongside Uncle Freddie and Prince Cyril and a group of notables and relatives they had brought along. There was no press allowed inside the august chamber, so for one long second, Charles could believe that he was a regular college graduate with his proud family looking on as he achieved one of life's major milestones.

He missed his father.

He also missed his brother. Through one of life's crueler quirks, Henry's graduation from Harvard was the same weekend as Charles's graduation from Cambridge. Their mother had been tearfully conflicted for months about it, saying that she couldn't tolerate missing another of Henry's graduations but also that it was inconceivable that the Queen Mother not attend the king's graduation from Cambridge. Henry had laughed it off and assured his mother and Charles that he was content to walk alone, that he might not even attend the ceremony. "I'm not really into that kind of stuff," he said. "You know that. Seriously, it doesn't mean anything to me." Charles believed his brother, but he also felt like the worst brother alive that he couldn't be there to support Henry after his brilliant academic career. His little brother had sailed through Harvard with near-perfect grades and graduated in three years, magna cum laude. He had been accepted on early admission into Harvard Law and planned to start with almost no break. Charles and Henry had stayed in touch, of course, but it was hard to really know what was going on from across the Atlantic, and Charles worried that he wasn't being a very good brother. It usually ended up falling on Henry to assure him that everything was fine, that Henry knew how his older brother felt and understood the pressure on him. And after all, there would still be a Harvard Law graduation to come.

These thoughts and emotions all swirled in Charles's head as he, like all Cambridge graduates, walked through the Doctor's door of the Senate House into the next room, where an official waited to hand him his degree. "Your Majesty," the man said as he pressed a leather-bound folder into Charles's hands with his actual degree. Charles, still too emotional to say much of anything, just nodded in response and took a minute to open the binder and get a look at his degree.

He stopped short. The degree had been awarded to "Charles Bolin-Stuart."

Charles. It hit him hard.

He had been known as Charles for five years now, since his memorable coronation as King Charles. His classmates had called him Charles. His relatives here in England, even his mother had switched over to calling him Charles.

Everyone except Henry, who still for the most part called him the name he was born with: Tyler.

He stared at his new name on the diploma, and all of a sudden, he felt like a fake. Who was King Charles anyway? King Charles wasn't even a real person, just a name they gave him because someone thought it was a good idea. King Charles had been king of the United Kingdom for five years now and had spent all of his time hiding in a bubble of elite schools, afraid to show his face in public lest someone realize that their king was really just a teenager who forgot his own name sometimes.

Frustration welled up in Charles. Why did it always come down to this? When would he ever shake this doubt that gnawed at him, this sense that he could never measure up to the role he had been thrust into?

In that moment, Charles experienced a surge of surprising gratitude to the last person on earth he should be thinking about at a time like this: his regent, Sir Richard. He knew that his brother held a low opinion of Richard, along with his mother and brother and everyone else he loved. He didn't doubt for a second that Richard was every bit the odious scoundrel everyone said, and his odor really was foul. But Richard had provided Charles with sound advice not too long ago: not only did he agree with Charles's decision to join the military, he had counseled Charles to show that he really was "one of the lads," as he said. "Don't shirk any duty," he had told Charles. "There's no sense in pretending you were born into the throne. You'll have to earn it. And that means you'll have to show the doubters and the critics that you can rise to it. You'll have to work twice as hard, be twice the king they suspect. A people's king, truly, one who is not afraid to risk for his country."

Charles had been mulling over those words since Richard spoke them—it was like the regent had glimpsed the conflict in Charles's heart and spoken directly to it. Charles had agreed wholeheartedly, and now, standing with his diploma and feeling transparent, Charles finally and completely committed to his next step. Yes, he was going to enlist as planned, but he was going to turn down any offer of "champagne duty" or a largely ceremonial role. No, Charles was going to volunteer for the hardest service there was. He would go through boot camp like a regular soldier, and then he would ask for the most dangerous duty the service would allow for him. He would show every single subject that their king was willing to work hard and take risks for the country. He would earn the throne.

CHAPTER 22
BOSTON LEGAL

SINCE HIS EARLY DAYS AT HOTCHKISS, TEACHERS AND PROFESSORS HAD been telling Henry to "wait for the next school, that's when it would get really hard." In middle school, they told him that high school would be hard. His prep school career was interrupted by his short and disastrous experience at Eton, but after he returned to Hotchkiss and news got out that he'd been accepted to Harvard his senior year, his teachers all warned him that college would really be where the rubber met the road. Then, after completing pre-law in three years magna cum laude and getting into Harvard Law, he'd been virtually buried under an avalanche of people warning him that law school was really, seriously hard.

For once, they were right.

Henry's first year at law school was unlike anything he'd ever experienced. The course work was more than just demanding: it was an avalanche of information that cascaded into his tired brain day after day after day. He learned to speak an entirely different language, one rich with the arcana of law, and he studied the intricate details of thousands of cases going back hundreds of years, then was forced to connect them all in a theoretical framework that was supposed to explain how

American jurisprudence worked. It was exhausting and never-ending, and his professors and classmates were merciless. Harvard Law was the most competitive place Henry had ever experienced, with students all angling for the best classes, positioning themselves to slide from law school into white-shoe law firms, where they would happily work 80- or 100-hour weeks as junior associates for years until they earned the golden ticket: partner.

And yet. As hard as it was, Henry quickly adjusted to the increased work load. For maybe the first time in his life, he was forced to reach deep inside himself to see what kind of internal reserves he had. While his classmates gulped coffee by the potful (and many didn't stop at coffee, but spent whole nights buried in law books while popping amphetamines or even doing lines of cocaine), Henry relied on discipline. He maintained a strict schedule, up at dawn to run and hit the gym, then classes and studying, sometimes in Harvard's ornate library on his own and sometimes with groups of students. Throughout this baptism by fire in one of the best law schools in the world, Henry learned something he had always suspected but had never tested before: he was strong. When he reached inside for strength, he found it. And instead of floundering in his early months, like so many of his baggy-eyed and strung-out classmates, Henry actually thrived. He felt like a fine Italian sports car that had finally been let loose on a deserted Interstate, allowed to push itself to its maximum performance.

As good as school was going, not everything was perfect. Star had become something of a problem lately. Henry and Star had been involved now for years, long enough that they had fallen into a pattern. But with the new demands on his time, he saw less of her than ever before—and found himself not missing her all that much. He actually would have been happy if she had eased herself out of the picture, but it seemed like she was coming around the River Street apartment more often than ever. He was getting used to coming home and finding her already there, sitting in the living room and reading some trashy magazine. Henry was just glad Julian was around—he didn't put it past Star to search his room when he wasn't home, looking for who knows what. At least with Julian at home to keep an eye on her when he wasn't around, he didn't have to worry about anything strange going on. He knew he would have to deal with her sooner or later, but...if he was being totally honest with himself, he didn't really have time to find a new girlfriend just then, and Star was really good at taking care of his physical needs. If anything, she'd grown even more sexually insatiable over the past few months.

Until then, Henry's plan was to stay focused on school. As part of the requirements to earn his degree, Henry needed to either author and publish a thesis or prepare a mock case law study as if it were going to trial. Henry opted for the case law study and requested Professor Preston Copeland Greenway, Harvard's most eminent law scholar and internationally recognized as one of the most learned and influential authorities of the law. Not surprisingly, Professor Greenway readily agreed to take on Henry as his protégé. After all, Henry was not only a superior student, but the mere association with someone of Henry's stature would add a welcome addition to Greenway's curriculum vitae: "Mentor and advisor to the Royal Family."

Henry had their first meeting in the cubby of an office that Professor Greenway called his "little hole in the wall." Even though by rank and tenure he was entitled to a far more palatial work space, Greenway liked the cubby's intimacy and the unpretentious image it telegraphed. "Less is more," he often taunted his colleagues. Besides, in the bitterly cold Boston winters, it was easier to keep his office warm and toasty like he liked it.

On the day of their appointed meeting, Henry knocked on the frosted glass door of Greenway's office. "Professor, may I come in?"

"Of course, Henry, please sit down," the professor said. "Just move those books over there and clear out a spot. My assistant has been on vacation and the place is a mess."

"Thank you, Professor." Henry set the stack of books on the floor and sat down, balancing one ankle on a knee and getting right down to business. "Thank you for taking me on. I really appreciate it. I, uh, have an idea about which case I want to pursue for my project, pending your approval of course. I looked at a lot of possibilities, some very compelling, but I wanted to do something different. My case isn't really a case, exactly. It's more like something that should have been a case, in my opinion, and I think there are some really interesting legal questions involved. But more than that, I have a personal connection to the matter."

"Interesting. Tell me more."

"So you know who I am and who my family is—"

"Of course. And I must say, you've done a marvelous job of keeping all that on the back burner and not capitalizing on the notoriety and preferential treatment that certainly would be yours if you allowed it. That's one of the things I most admire about you."

Henry blushed, but accepted the compliment. "When my father was Vice President of the United States, he was known as William Carnegie. I don't know if you've heard the whole story, but it was in the news. His...our...world exploded when he learned that he wasn't who he, and everyone else around him, thought he was. That he wasn't really the biological son of Ambassador Carnegie but was actually the son of the queen of England, born in secrecy and given away to the Ambassador and his wife to raise as their own."

"I remember it well," Greenway said. "There was a lot of tricky law involved on both sides of the pond, if I remember correctly. It took a four-hundred-year-old English law to install your father on the throne over there, while over here the Carnegie Trust used the news to cut him out. Fertile legal territory certainly, and on a personal note, I was very sorry to hear about your father's assassination. I don't know if you knew this or not, but I knew your father. He went through a class or two of mine when I was an assistant professor. Excellent student, like yourself. A very good man."

"Yes, thank you for the kind words about him," Henry said. "But... it's actually part of that story that I want to use as my project. I was too young when it all happened to really know what was going on. I just knew that something bad financially had happened to my family and that we had to move to England as my father became king. It was traumatic for my parents, and us too, I guess. But lately, I've been doing some research and asking some questions. Like you said, the Carnegie Trust moved pretty fast to cut him out once this news broke. It was surprising to my parents, of course, because the trust had been a strong ally to my family. But my dad had bigger fish to fry in England and apparently chose not to pursue legal action."

"Understandable," Greenway said.

"So, that's my idea. I want to build the hypothetical case that I think my father could have brought against the Carnegie Trust for my project. I've looked into this a little bit and I think there was a good case. I think if my father had chosen to pursue legal action, he might have prevailed. He was raised as a Carnegie son and grandson. There was never any question in the family that my father was a Carnegie and we were all Carnegies, with a trust that measured in the billions of dollars. I think the trust was clearly motivated by greed when they acted against him."

Greenway laced his hands over his belly and leaned back in his chair. "Interesting. So what do you want to do exactly?"

"I want to do a mock trial. I'll investigate this like a real case and prosecute a theoretical case against the trust that they had no standing to oust my family. I was hoping...well, I was hoping we could get an independent judge to review the arguments and render an opinion, just like a real case."

Greenway nodded and considered this for a second, then he startled Henry by laughing out loud. "My goodness, Henry, that's got to be one of the most interesting mock trial ideas I've heard in my career! Bravo! And for the record, I agree that there are some very interesting legal questions involved that would make an excellent project." He leaned forward. "But I don't think you're thinking big enough here. Why don't you take this to its logical conclusion and follow through?"

Henry frowned. "I'm sorry, sir. I don't understand what you mean."

"Why a mock trial? You have standing to bring a real suit against the trust. Based on your reading, do you really think you could prevail?"

"Well," Henry said, choosing his words carefully. "I don't really know, to be honest. There's a lot of research I'd need to do, and...I mean, I'm sure they wouldn't cooperate."

Greenway waved that concern away. "All the more reason to pursue it for real. As part of a real discovery process, you'd have the ability to subpoena records, depose witnesses, and get testimony under oath."

"Yeah, I mean, obviously that would be helpful. But...wouldn't it actually cost a fortune to do all that? I was just going to put together a hypothetical brief. But deposing people? Especially people with very deep pockets? I don't know."

"Of course. First, the reason I propose this at all is because, to be frank with you, when I read the original story, I had the same thought and have long wondered why your father didn't pursue it. I think you are on more solid ground here than even you suspect. Second, there are very specific laws that protect heirs, and that includes you. Finally, yes, this kind of thing would be expensive…for most people. But Henry, don't forget where you are! This place is swimming with lawyers. I'm sure if we put out some feelers we could find a half-dozen professors here who would be happy to work on this pro bono."

"But why? Why would anyone do that?"

"Well, Henry, first there is the obvious answer. Your family is a well-known and historic family, not to even mention that you are second in line for the throne and your brother is a sitting King of England. I'm sure there are people here who would be happy to do this just for proximity."

Henry squirmed in his seat. He hated trading on his name and family history for anything.

"But second, as I mentioned, this case is not unknown to us. Your father was a Harvard Law graduate, Henry. In some ways, that's more motivating than who he was. This is a close-knit tribe here, and I'm not the only one who thinks your dad was likely railroaded at a moment of extreme vulnerability. Why, Henry, I suspect there's a small army of Harvard litigators that would jump at the chance to take down your tormentors and have some fun in the process."

"Really? You think so? But…what if we lose?"

Greenway laughed. "My boy, I'm going to give you the first real-world lesson in the law right here, right now. If you agree that we should pursue this for real, you'll have a chance to do the investigation you're talking about, and you'll have to prepare your arguments and question witnesses and do all of the things that so-called real lawyers do. For the class and credit, you understand. But at the end of the day, when a real suit is filed, I suspect the Carnegie Trust will do what most often happens in these cases."

"What's that?"

"They'll settle!"

"Oh," Henry said, his thoughts racing with all of these new possibilities. "To be honest, Professor, I don't know if I really care about a settlement. I mean, I'm more interested in justice here and—"

"Yes, yes. Another quick lesson: don't start counting the spoils of war before the first battle. But I am serious. I like your idea, Henry, and think it's worth pursuing for real. I'd be happy to work with you and see about rounding up some sharks."

"Wow," Henry said. "That's...incredible. I mean, I really, really appreciate it."

"Of course," Greenway said. "So it's agreed?"

"Yes! Definitely!"

"Excellent. Now, let's get started."

CHAPTER 23
THE SET UP

C HARLES WAS BONE TIRED AS HE DRAGGED HIMSELF INTO THE BAR-racks phone room to call his mother. He had just finished his infantry training at Catterick Garrison, a grueling 26-week marathon of physical tests, military readiness training, operational security, and force protection drills that often started in the pre-dawn and lasted until long after the moon had risen. Charles had been offered the shorter 10-week officer's training, but he had refused. He was adamant: he would go through infantry with the rest of the lads and only assume a command after he had proven himself, not only to the men he would lead, but to himself as well!

Now that he was done, he was made a Company commander and put in charge of a select group of men. Some special considerations had been made—he still had personal security, and the men in his company had been carefully vetted and approved to serve under the king—but Charles was satisfied that his men and hopefully the nation at large had seen the effort he'd put in.

The phone rang three times before Liz picked up, and he pictured her sitting in her favorite salon with the sun streaming through the big windows and the garden beyond, London bustling just beyond the palace grounds.

"Mum," he said.

"Charles!" she said. "What a lovely surprise! And how very British you sound. I almost didn't recognize you."

"Thanks. I think living in the barracks has improved my accent somewhat," he said. "At least I hope so."

"I should think so." She paused. "So I hear you've finished your training?"

"Yes. And not a day too soon. If I have to run one more kilometer in full gear, I'll probably keel over."

"Don't say that!"

"I'm joking. Truth is, I'm more fit than I've ever been. If it came to it, I'm sure I could show Henry a thing or two." She laughed, and he continued, "You sound good, Mum. Cheerful."

"Yes. Well, I have been going to therapy. They've even got me up and around now a little bit, although not for long. And outside of this cursed renovation that never seems to end, the palace has been peaceful. It suits me."

"Glad to hear it."

"So," she drew it out, sounding nervous to go on, "Uncle Freddie tells me you've got your assignment? Where shall you be going?"

"The north," he answered promptly. "Up by Belfast."

"What?" She sounded horrified. "Why on Earth would they send you up there? After...those animals killed your father! And I don't care if it's safer now. You have no place being anywhere near the Troubles. I'll call Cyril and we'll—"

"I requested the post, Mum," Charles said in a heavy voice.

There was a long silence. "Why, Charles? Why would you do that?"

"I want to serve for real. It matters, to me and to the people."

"Matters to you?" she echoed. "Charlie, is this about…revenge? You're not going up there to get some kind of revenge, are you?"

"No," he said. "It's about acting like a king."

"Acting like a king? You don't have to act like a king, Charles. You *are* the king. By definition, anything you do is acting like a king."

"You see it that way, but not everyone does." He paused. "I'm hoping you can support me in this, Mum. I need you to support me."

She sighed and, even over the long-distance line, he could hear the tears in her voice. "Of course I support you, Charles. Of course. I just wish…" But she let it trail off. Then she said, "Be safe. Please."

"Of course. My men are good men. We'll be safe."

—•—

Sir Richard didn't need to actually hear the conversation between King Charles and his mother to know what was going on. He didn't have to eavesdrop or listen to playback from a bugged phone. Rather, the young king had called him personally after he graduated from basic training and asked his advice. Richard couldn't believe his good fortune—the boy wanted to volunteer for the "front lines," as he said, and wanted to know what Richard thought about it.

"Your Majesty," Richard had oozed, "I think it's brave and will show the nation exactly what type of king you will be. I applaud you, and I'm sure the country will as well."

Charles had thanked him profusely, then hung up and prepared to call the Queen Mother and break the news.

As soon as he'd hung up, Richard was on the phone again to his sources in Operation Banner, the long-running operation in Ireland under the command of the British Army. It had taken only minutes to learn where Charles's company would be deployed and only slightly longer to dig up the name of a trusted contact in regiment command, a Colonel Ashley McIntosh at 4th Army Regiment headquarters. As he dialed, Richard recalled the circumstances that made the colonel vulnerable. It seemed that some military materiel had gone missing and ended up somewhere in Libya. Richard, who was actually on the other end of that transaction with the Libyans, knew all about the colonel's willingness to profit from the sale of the munitions under his command. Once the transfer was completed, Richard had cause to blackmail the colonel, allowing him to benefit twice.

"Colonel McIntosh's office, Sergeant Rutgers speaking."

"I'd like to speak to the colonel, put me through," Richard said.

"Of course, but I need to know who's calling. It's procedure, you know."

Fortunately, he and the colonel had set up a code name known to his staff so he would be put through without true identification or delay. "Sergeant, this is Mr. Black calling."

"Right, sir. I'll put you right through. Straight away."

Three rings later the colonel abruptly answered. "Colonel McIntosh here."

"Colonel, it's Mr. Black."

"Mr. Black, of course, how may I help you, sir?" He sounded thoroughly deflated.

"Colonel, your help is required," Richard said. "It's my understanding that a certain company commander is about to be assigned to a battalion under your command. I expect you know who I'm talking about."

"Blimey," McIntosh said. "News travels fast. I just heard myself. But yes, his company is due here in the next week or so."

"Good. Now, he's going to request difficult duty. I want to make sure he gets that assignment. I trust you can make that happen?"

There was a pause.

"McIntosh," Richard said, "I'm sure I don't need to remind you what happens to ranking officers who are convicted of selling British war materiel to terrorists. Life in prison would be a mercy."

In a very stiff voice, McIntosh said, "I understand, but I'm not sure you do. This particular commander has friends in very high places. I've already been instructed in no uncertain terms that he is not to be placed in harm's way."

"By who?"

"The prince, Prince Cyril."

Richard snorted. "Look, McIntosh, if you think that old man can do worse damage to you than I can, you're delusional. Make sure he gets the assignment he wants, and if anyone complains, you tell them the king himself made the order."

"Yes, sir," McIntosh said.

"Also," Richard went on, "I need someone in his company I can rely on. I want eyes on the ground. Someone who can report to me exactly what's going on, when and where the unit will be assigned."

"You can't be serious!" McIntosh said. "Those are operational details, and this is no ordinary commander! Releasing that kind of information is treason!"

"I think you know I'm serious."

"Anyway, it's not possible," McIntosh said. "The men in his command have been personally selected by the brigadier general. They are all elite recruits, men of impeccable backgrounds and courage. There's no one."

"Not acceptable," Richard said. "You need to find someone and you need to do it now. I don't care how. But I expect a name and contact before the company deploys. Am I understood?"

"Yes, sir," McIntosh answered in a voice dripping with venom. "Understood."

"Good."

Richard rang off and grinned. This was going even better than he'd expected. Charles was like a steer racing toward the abattoir under his own power. Richard had dreamt of finding an opportunity to actually rid himself of this king, but he hadn't seriously believed it would be possible. No accidental death would suffice. But a combat death? It was almost more than he could bear. The king would become an instant martyr, beloved. His mother would be heartbroken, of course, so she would be neutralized. And Richard suspected he didn't have anything to worry about with Henry. According to Badger, Henry lived with his nose in a book and was thoroughly involved in law school. American law school, which of course was useless here in the United Kingdom. Richard would bet a sizable chunk of his hidden fortune that Henry would be glad to never set foot in England again after his brother was gunned down by the same terrorists who'd killed his father.

No, the path to the throne would be clear for him.

The thought of it caused a stir in Richard's groin. Without hesitation, before the aphrodisiac of power could wear off, he picked up his phone to his private attaché. "I need a girl," he said simply. "Make that two girls. I want those two I saw in SoHo. Dressed like schoolgirls. Pay them well for their trouble and send them to me at once."

"Yes, sir. Right away."

"And this time, I don't want them warned. You understand?"

There was a longer pause, during which Richard wondered if it was time to find a new attaché. Then, "Yes, sir. No warning."

Richard hung up abruptly and began to look forward to the exercise of raw power.

CHAPTER 24
THE CARNEGIE JOURNALS

AFTER WEEKS OF EXTENSIVE RESEARCH, HENRY MET WITH PROFESSOR Greenway to review the status of his case study on a chilly, rainy day in Boston. The heat poured out of the oversized radiator under the palladium window in the professor's office when Henry, soaked to the core, arrived for the 2:30 meeting.

"Boy, it's raining cats and dogs out there, this weather bites," he said. Then he caught himself and rephrased, "I mean, it's bad."

Professor Greenway smiled. "If weather could only bite...it would keep a battalion of lawyers busy every day of the year, suing mother nature," he said. Henry laughed as he sat down and started unpacking his materials. Already a hard worker, he had poured himself into this project with a zeal that surprised even him. It wasn't only because he knew that Greenway had assembled what might be one of the finest legal teams in the country for him—although it certainly helped to know that he was backed up by multiple litigators who had argued cases in front of the U.S. Supreme Court. His enthusiasm also fed on his direct relationship to this case. In fact, the deeper he had gone and the more he learned about exactly what happened, the more convinced he became that they were really onto something.

"You look like it's your birthday," Professor Greenway observed, watching Henry laying out papers on the table. "Tell me, what do you have to make you look so thrilled?"

Henry had organized everything into stacks, just like he had practiced in his apartment at the kitchen table. He was treating this like a real presentation and wanted to nail it.

"So," he began, "it looks like this. The Carnegie Trust is administered by a board of directors, usually four at any given time, depending on the expiration dates of their terms. They are all handpicked by the chairman, Mr. Paul Whitman. I have their resumes in this binder, if you'd care to look at them. As an aside, the trust gave more than a million dollars to Harvard last year, and as you know, there are two buildings on campus with the Carnegie name on them."

"Yes, the Russian Research Center and the Library for Fine Arts and Antiquity, I believe are both funded by Carnegie money."

Henry paused. "We don't have to worry about that, right? I mean, if we go after the trust, can they pull strings here at the university?"

"I wouldn't think so," Greenway said. "We'd raise a holy stink if they tried it. It's also worth noting they'd be in the wrong. My philosophy is that you have to do what's right, regardless of the politics."

"Okay, good." Henry glanced down at the paper in his hand and continued, "According to public records, each board member gets an honorarium, travel expenses, and administrative support, such as secretarial assistance and the like."

"Do we have a number on that?"

"Not an exact number, Professor, but it looks like from the available records that the board is paid approximately four million dollars collectively. It isn't clear as to how much each individual member gets."

"So it's safe to assume a million each, all in?"

"That probably is pretty close to the right number. Now, the current reported assets under trust management is more difficult to determine, since it is made up of a huge portfolio including stocks, bonds, debentures, buildings, residences, aircraft, and other tangible assets. I'm estimating between \$4 billion and \$6 billion. However, back when my father was still a beneficiary, the number would be less: \$3 billion."

"A lot of money."

"Right," Henry agreed. "The rationale they used to cut my father out was thanks to Fillmore Blair Carnegie's will. In his will, Fillmore specially prohibited any benefit to anyone who was not a blood relative. Apparently, he was afraid of his descendants marrying gold diggers or lining up a string of divorces with million-dollar settlements. My father was raised by Fillmore Carnegie's son, the Ambassador and my grandfather. When the news broke that my father was not a 'true' Carnegie but just someone they took and raised as their own, and there was no bloodline between my father and the Carnegie family, they interpreted it in the most narrow way possible to exclude him."

Greenway nodded. This was the most well-known part of the story. "Yes, true enough. Have you examined the actual will or trust documents yet? Those will be critical to our effort."

Henry grimaced. "No, not yet. That's not too easily accomplished, it turns out. We filed for full disclosure of those documents under the premise that my father, and consequently, my brother Charles and myself, were treated like blood relatives and should de facto considered to be heirs."

"I imagine the trust didn't find that very compelling, considering they used exactly the same argument against your father."

"They didn't comment on that specifically. They just refused to hand anything over or cooperate in any way. They've been ordered twice now by Judge Lowenstein in the second district court to comply, but they're dragging their feet."

"They won't be able to hold out forever," Greenway advised. "The second district is a federal court and has far more authority than state. Judge Lowenstein…I know of him. He is very astute and clear thinking, even though he's a Yalie. If he's ordered release of the documents, you can be assured he will get them."

"Okay, good," Henry said. "I mean, it feels like we can't go much further until we get the will and the trust documents."

Greenway closed his eyes and thought for a second. "Perhaps, but perhaps not."

"What do you mean?"

"Well," Greenway said, "let's step back and take a look at what's happening here. The trust made a bold move when they cut your father off. You'd think they would have solid legal advice here, that they would have anticipated your father would fight back and they'd have a legal case essentially ready to go. Yet when you come sniffing around and asking perfectly reasonable questions, they suddenly clam up and act like they've never even considered the idea. Why is that? At this present moment, we don't know, but we do know that they are acting like people with something to hide. If they were 100 percent confident in their situation, they would have come back at us with both barrels blazing. Instead, they hunkered down and are playing deaf, dumb, and blind."

"Okay, I see that. But…I'm not sure what we can do about it."

"We can go fishing," Greenway said. "Let's see if Judge Lowenstein will allow us to subpoena their financials just to see if there is anything irregular. Our request could be substantiated by the notion that should the plaintiff prevail, he would be entitled to know if there were any reachable assets and any irregularities. We could also ask for depositions of all four of the board members to see what they know, or don't know. Lowenstein is no fool, and he may deny the asset disclosure on the grounds it's a bit premature since you haven't yet won the case. That's okay. Just asking for this kind of information will make the trust nervous. It will show them you're serious and you want to see the numbers. We'll see just how nervous by how they respond. If they throw up a fog of objections, they're regular, garden-league nervous and that's a bad sign for us. But if they immediately offer to settle and pay you off in an effort to call off the dogs, well, that means they're plenty nervous. That would be a sign that we're really onto something here and they know it."

"Errr. I guess so."

"Why don't you leave your binder here and I'll take a good look at it? Maybe something will pop out."

"Great. Meantime I'll work on getting the documents and any relevant information. I think I'll call my mother too and see if she has anything she can add. Then, if it's all right with you, can I call you for an appointment?"

"Of course, call any time."

As Henry stood to leave, he stretched out his arm and shook Professor Greenway's hand. "Thank you, sir, you have no idea how much I appreciate your help."

"You are most welcome, young man."

Henry headed immediately for home, but was surprised to run into Star in the hall leading to his door. "Hey," he said. "You just leaving?"

"Uh, yeah," she said, tugging at her clothes. "Sorry I missed you, baby. I waited but you never showed up and now I've got something to do."

"Right, okay." He looked at her more closely, like he was seeing her for the first time. "You okay? Something seems off."

Henry wondered if it had anything to do with the guy who lived next door, the South African poet. He had been hanging out on his terrace lately, and not too long ago, it looked like someone had tried to break into Henry's apartment. Of course they hadn't made it in— security was far too tight for that—but he half suspected his mysterious neighbor.

"I'm fine," Star said, an annoyed look flashing across her pretty features. "Anyway, I can't help it when you're not around. Later!" She waved at him almost sarcastically and barreled past, leaving him in the hallway looking after her. Henry watched until she disappeared, then stood there thinking for a minute. He didn't mind Star showing up at his place when he wasn't around—in some ways it was easier because he didn't have to bother tracking her down and calling her. She just showed up, the way a feral cat will sometimes come around the back door looking for food, except in her case it was almost always looking for sex.

And yet...if he had to say where exactly she was headed to just now, he would have no idea. Actually, for that matter, he realized he had no idea what she did for work anymore. She couldn't possibly still be nannying for the rich couple—their baby would be school age by now. Nor did he know anything about her family, come to think of it. She told funny and bawdy stories about her school days, before she moved to the States, but said almost nothing about her family except to grimace and drop dark hints. Henry had always assumed there was some kind of terrible secret in her family history, that something had happened to her somewhere along the way. But now he wasn't so sure. It would be more accurate to say that he knew nothing about her at all, really, except for her almost supernatural sexual skills.

He sighed. Someday soon he was going to have to deal with the Star problem. Just not today. And besides, Mr. Niner was in no mood to go solo any time soon.

He turned the key and went into his apartment, to find Julian just emerging from the bathroom in a towel. Steam from his recent shower billowed into the hallway.

"Cheerio," Julian said. "How's it going?"

"Fine. I just ran into Star in the hallway. Was she here long?"

Julian cocked his head and thought about it. "Not really, no. I tell you, though, you keep feeding that girl and she'll keep coming around."

Henry smiled inwardly. It was like Julian had read his thoughts.

Alone in his room a few minutes later, Henry placed a call and waited for a few rings until it was answered by the very proper voice of his mother's personal secretary. A second later, he heard his mother's voice. "Henry!" she said. "What a pleasant surprise!"

"Hey, Mom. How you doing?"

"Oh, fine, fine. Prince Cyril was just here, visiting for tea, but he had to leave early. He got himself upset over the renovations here at the palace. Apparently on the way in, he passed through the South Gallery and found some men packing up and moving the art-work. You remember the South Gallery. It was the one with the real masterpieces. They call it the Musculum Devolvunt Magistrorum. Latin for the Gallery of Masters. The most precious and important pieces of the Royal art collection are so beautifully displayed there. I often wish that I was up to visiting it more often. I so enjoy the genius that it took to create the masterpieces."

"Yeah, I don't actually remember, but I know there's a lot of valuable art there."

Liz laughed lightly. "That's an understatement, Henry. Oh dear, I'm sorry, I'm sure you didn't call here to ask me about the work at the palace."

"Er, no, actually I need your help." Henry proceeded to fill her in on his project. When he got to the part about the trust, he heard a sharp intake of breath.

"Oh, Henry, they treated your poor father with such indifference and disrespect," she said. "They refused to recognize that he was a victim of a mean trick and turned him out virtually penurious. A vile sort, those trustees."

"Right. My sentiments completely. Now I'm trying to make right a very serious wrong. I have lots of help from my professors here at Harvard and they think we have a good chance to make the trust accountable for their cold-heartedness and maybe even get some restitution."

"That would be long overdue. But how can I help?"

"The thing is, they used the fact that Dad wasn't a blood relative to cut him out," Henry said. "Obviously that means me and Tyler, according to them, aren't blood relatives either. So as of right now, we're trying to establish that Grandpa, who was a Carnegie by blood, considered us blood relatives."

"Of course he did! You know your grandfather loved you very much! Don't tell Charles, but you always were his favorite!"

"Mom! I mean, that's great, but...we need something more."

"Hmm," Liz said. "Well, let me think. Have you looked in his journals? There might be something there."

"Journals? No. I didn't even know he had journals."

"Oh yes, your grandfather was a habitual chronicler of everything. He kept detailed notes. I often saw him writing in it late at night."

"Huh," Henry said. "Do you know where they are now?"

"I really couldn't say. But I do know that your father turned boxes and boxes of your grandfather's records over to his attorney. Let's see, I think his name was Paul something, I only met him a couple of times when your father was Vice President."

A stone dropped into Henry's gut as he pictured the head of the Carnegie Trust. "Was his name Paul Whitman?"

"Yes, I fancy that was his name."

"Why would he give Whitman his journals?"

"Indeed, why would he? Let me think a minute. Now I recall. Your grandfather wanted Mr. Whitman to write a biography about him and he thought he should have all of the material as documentation for his research."

"Did Mr. Whitman ever write the bio?"

"Not to my knowledge."

"Do you think he still has the material?"

"Henry, I have no idea, that was a while back and the part of my life I want to forget. Mr. Whitman was less than sympathetic to our situation and hardly charitable."

"Yeah, well..." Henry stopped, realizing he didn't want to upset her any further by reminding her of the fact that Mr. Whitman was now running the trust. "Thanks, Mom. Seriously. This is big. I really appreciate it."

"Of course! Now, when are you coming to see us? Charles is in Belfast still, but I'm sure he would arrange a leave to come see you. Please tell me you're coming soon!"

"As soon as I can, Mom."

"Please do. I miss you so," she said.

"Yeah, me too. I gotta go now," he said. "Love you."

He hung up the phone with his mind spinning. Whitman was in possession of his grandfather's journals and never said a word about it. If he hadn't just left Greenway's office and it hadn't been still pouring rain, he would have run straight back to his professor with this news.

CHAPTER 25
LONG NIGHTS, BITTER STRUGGLES

SECOND LIEUTENANT CHARLES BOLIN-STUART, KING OF ENGLAND, adjusted to military life with just a few bumps.

He headed a platoon of sixteen men who spent most nights hunting down IRA terrorists. It was a dangerous job, but one that had to be done. Charles had hardened up during his military training and, with considerable effort, was up for the job. It was extraordinarily unusual that such an important figure would be assigned to this degree of "hands on" military maneuvers, and under normal circumstances it would never be allowed. But Charles had fought hard for the post.

Once in his post, Charles found himself turning more and more often to his right-hand man, an experienced military sergeant called Percival Thompson, who had been handpicked for him by his commanding officer under the direction of Sir Richard. Charles had come to trust Thompson's instincts and judgment, despite the obvious differences between the two men. First and most obvious, Thompson was a commoner who spoke with a broad Liverpool accent. His parents were greengrocers and he had only a minimal amount of higher education, most of which was obtained during his time in the Royal Army. With a shock of auburn hair topping his military crew cut and bulging, tattooed arms, Thompson looked like any of the lads who could be found hanging around the snooker halls in Liverpool.

To Charles, who had spent virtually all of his time in England either cloistered in Eton or Cambridge, his relationship with the likes of Thompson was like a breath of fresh air. It wasn't that he had disliked the upper-class boys in Eton or the scions of rich families at Cambridge. Instead, he was keenly aware that, to rule effectively, he would need the support of men like Thompson. And perhaps more fundamentally, Thompson reminded him of certain traits that ran through his own family. His rugged individualism, courage, and strength recalled Charles's grandfather and even his brother, Henry.

It didn't take long for the other men in the platoon to see the depth of admiration Charles had for his sergeant and respond to it. Here was a king who didn't act like a king, but volunteered for the worst duties readily and ate and lived with them day in and day out, who treated a common sergeant from Liverpool with respect and dignity. Charles took point on dangerous patrols and never gave an order he wouldn't follow himself, even though he could easily have arranged to have any cushy post he'd wanted instead of walking the dangerous streets of Belfast side by side with chaps from poor councils and housing projects.

One evening while on patrol, Sergeant Thompson, Charles, and the platoon lay in wait for some IRA soldiers to return to their safe house. It was boring but tense, and the men often talked to ease the stress.

"Sergeant, what's it like back in Liverpool?" Charles asked. "Do you have a family there?"

"Yes, sir. Not a wife and kids, but a mum and dad and two siblings, a brother and sister."

"That's great, I have a mum and a brother. He's off in America going to school."

Thompson chuckled lightly, and Charles realized that of course Thompson knew about his family. Who in England didn't? "Right," he said.

"Are you going to make a career out of the Army?"

"Not sure, sir. A lot depends on how things go. I'm just hoping to get out of this place alive before one of these bloody Micks punches my clock."

"What would you do after the Army, then?" Charles asked.

"Don't know. Maybe go to school and learn something useful. I know I don't want to go back to Liverpool and run my father's shop. You can barely make a decent living doing that. That's not for me, I'll leave that for my brother. And besides, there's plenty in Liverpool I don't mind leaving forever."

The lights of a small lorry appeared at the end of the street. It seemed to be slowing as it approached the suspected safe house. Suddenly, the men grew anxious and the air snapped with tension.

"This is it," whispered Thomas into the radio. "Get set."

The men cocked and loaded their weapons. An advance man jumped out in front of the lorry and yelled, "Halt!" The driver did not swerve and aimed to run down the trooper, even as the boot of the lorry opened and men poured out, firing their weapons. But they were no match for the seasoned troops, and it was obvious they were outnumbered and outgunned within a minute. Thompson barked an order for the IRA operatives to drop their weapons and raise their hands. Most of them immediately followed the order, except for one bloke who suddenly bolted away. Two soldiers raced after him and apprehended him.

"Lieutenant, sir, we have this under control," Thompson told Charles over the radio.

With the situation under control, Charles hopped on the running board of a waiting personnel truck and rode up the street to where the IRA terrorists were lying on the ground, surrounded by the men of his platoon. He jumped off the side and walked up to Thompson. "Pile them into the truck and get them back to headquarters for questioning."

"Yes, sir, at once." Thompson pulled the nearest prisoner up from the ground and gave him a shove toward the transport. "Get a move on," he snarled. The man tripped and fell, unable to break his fall because his hands were bound with a zip cuff. Thompson took two long steps toward him and kicked the prisoner hard in the gut, then the groin. The terrorist didn't cry out, but grunted in pain. "Get up, you bloody Irish scum, or I'll introduce you to your maker."

"Whoa," Charles said. "Easy, Thompson. This is just a kid." He was right. The IRA soldier couldn't have been over nineteen years old. His red beard was just starting to grow in.

"Kid?" Thompson said. "With all due respect, sir, he's an IRA pig and they will kill you no matter how old they are."

"These men are our captives now and we have the duty and responsibility to treat them with respect and dignity. The same that you would want our men to have if the situation was in reverse."

"Sir, they are rubbish, and rubbish don't get no respect! And if this was the other way around, we'd all be dead by now. They don't take prisoners, they kill them."

Charles knew that Thompson was right. He had spent weeks on the streets now, chasing down IRA foot soldiers and thugs, seeing the aftermath of their attacks. Yet he also recognized that not all Irish were the problem, a point that sometimes was lost on the men under his command, who often spoke of the Irish as if they were all sub-human, murdering terrorists. As an American, Charles hadn't been raised to "take sides" in the long-standing battles between the Irish and the English. In fact, Americans were pretty much unaware of the "Troubles" altogether.

"That will be all, Sergeant," he said. "Now let's get these guests of His Majesty processed. Do you understand?"

"Yes, sir, I completely understand." From his tone, though, Charles could sense that Thompson's understanding was only skin deep. The burly sergeant eyed the IRA soldier at his feet distastefully, then hauled the prisoner back to his feet and loaded him into the transport.

CHAPTER 26
NEEDLES IN HAYSTACKS

HENRY WAS MORE THAN READY FOR HIS NEXT MEETING WITH Professor Greenway. He was not only excited to pass along the news of the journals, but also to meet the newest member of the legal team, Professor Boris Haverman.

Like Greenway, Professor Haverman was a renowned member of Harvard's law faculty. His specialty was trusts and wills. He had been studying the financial documents that finally arrived after being subpoenaed from the Carnegie Trust. In anticipation of this meeting, Haverman had meticulously poured through literally pounds of case studies and legal opinions. He was especially interested in those rulings made by Judge Aaron Lowenstein.

On his way to the meeting, Henry decided to make a stop and bring everyone a treat. Since Star had introduced him to cannolis from the iconic Mike's Pastries, he couldn't get enough. Every time he saw one, he laughed to himself, recalling when Star said they reminded her of Mr. Niner and how he had dared her to put an entire one in her mouth—then watched in amazement as she actually did it.

Henry arrived right on time to meet with Professors Greenway and Haverman.

"Preston, have we received all of the documents now?" Haverman asked Professor Greenway.

Henry, not used to hearing Greenway addressed by his first name, listened intently.

"Yes," Greenway answered. "It wasn't easy prying them out of the trust, but I believe we have everything now."

"Good. So let's start with the trust documents first. Clearly, the trust documents are in order. They were drafted by the law firm of Cavanaugh, Wolf, Whitman and Smith, one of the best in the country. Attorney and senior partner Paul Whitman was the principal author of the trust, as well as acting as Fillmore and his son Harrington Carnegie's personal attorney."

Greenway picked up the thread. "Although Whitman occasionally consulted with William Carnegie, he did not act in the capacity of legal counsel. The documents call for a board of trustees, not to exceed four, to administer the trust. Henry, do you have the trustees' resumes?"

"Yes, Professor Greenway, I have resumes of all of the current members, as well as those who served during my father's lifetime. All of the current trustees were appointed after my father left the United States and went to Great Britain," Henry added.

"Ah, I remember that from our last meeting. It's interesting that all of them were replaced after your father left. Not sure if that is meaningful, but we will look at each of those trustees to see what we can see," Professor Greenway said. Then turning to Haverman, he continued, "Boris, what interests me the most is the underling will, which the trust is relying on for direction. It was an unconventional one, not drafted by Cavanaugh, Wolf, Whitman and Smith, or for that matter by any attorney. It was handwritten by Fillmore Blair Carnegie himself. As you recall, Henry said his father told him that Fillmore Carnegie was a bit of a maverick and trusted virtually no one, especially lawyers. Poor misguided man."

"Ha ha, Preston," Haverman laughed. "Good defense of our vocation. But you are right, it was unconventional to say the least, but from my review it is totally legitimate and sustainable. Many such documents are legitimate and binding. Sad to say, one doesn't need an attorney to write their will."

Reaching for a copy of the will, Greenway said, "Let's see it again."

Haverman produced a single sheet of paper with looping, precise handwriting on it and a large, scrawled signature. He handed it to Greenway, who shook his head slightly as he skimmed it. "Imagine a man of such vast holdings today producing a one-page, handwritten will," he said. "It's mind-boggling."

"Yes," Haverman agreed.

Reading aloud, Greenway related the part of the will that concerned their case: "It is my desire and decree as my last will and testament that no one may inherit or have benefit from my estate, inclusive of my property, money, businesses, investments, or any other tangible or intangible assets unless they have Carnegie blood flowing through their veins. No wife, no ex-wife, nor paramour of a decedent thereof may have stake in or access to this legacy, which is solely intended for those raised by Carnegies with Carnegie blood. There will be no exception, under any circumstance to alter or subjugate this, my fervent and final degree."

He shook his head. "It's rudimentary, but you can't get much clearer than that. What do you think, Boris?"

"Exactly my opinion. It's not legalese, but it's certainly clear and enforceable. There is no indication that the author was not of sound mind and body, as they say. To my mind, he comes across as he likely was: a Victorian and rugged individualist, a man who was clearly concerned about protecting his family from gold diggers. What do you say, Henry? Thoughts?"

Henry, flattered by being asked for an informed opinion by such eminent legal authorities, could do nothing more than nod his head in agreement.

"Okay," Greenway said, "so let's set aside the question of the trust documents and will for a moment. We can all agree that the trust was properly formed and written, and the will is a clear expression of Fillmore's wish that only people raised by Carnegies and with Carnegie blood should benefit from the trust. Boris, you took a deposition from Paul Whitman, the drafter of the trust and executor of this will, did you not?"

"I deposed Mr. Whitman in New York," Haverman answered. "He recounted a conversation he had with William Carnegie when he discovered that he was not the birth child of Ambassador Carnegie."

"And? Anything more helpful there?"

Boris rifled through a pile of folders until he found the right one and removed a stack of paper. "Here it is, the deposition of Paul Whitman. I'll read that part verbatim:

Boris Haverman: "Mr. Whitman, can you tell me about any discussions you had with William Carnegie with respect to the matter at hand: his claim on the Carnegie Trust?"

Paul Whitman: "As you all well know, there is something called Client Privilege, but given that William Carnegie was not actually my client and that he is no longer living, I will be able to accommodate and answer the question. I recall a meeting

William and I had in late 1985. It was held at the vice presidential residence located in Washington DC. At which time William disclosed the results of certain DNA testing."

Boris Haverman: "At that meeting, did you discuss any concern regarding the eligibility of William and his heirs for benefits from the Carnegie Trust?"

Paul Whitman: "Yes sir, it was discussed."

Boris Haverman: "Can you be more explicit about that discussion?"

Paul Whitman: "Of course. First I told William that I was shocked beyond words to learn of this situation. I told him I was totally unaware of any irregularities about his birth circumstances and his real birth parents. I explained that I had spent countless hours with both Ambassador Carnegie and his father and grantor of the trust, Fillmore, not only as their attorney but as their personal advisor and friend. I told William no one ever uttered a single word of the apparent charade that was perpetrated by the Ambassador and his wife, Fiona."

Boris Haverman: "Was the Ambassador's father, Fillmore Carnegie, aware of the charade, as you called it?"

Paul Whitman: "Not possible. He was deceased at the time of the revelation about William's birth. As far as I know, the Ambassador never revealed any of this to his father. But I can't say that with certainty, since it never was discussed."

Boris Haverman: "What specifically did you say about the trust to William Carnegie at that meeting?"

Paul Whitman: "I explained that given that he, William, was clearly not a blood relative of Fillmore Carnegie, or for that matter Ambassador Carnegie, any benefit from the Carnegie Family Trust would no longer be permitted by the trust."

Boris Haverman: "Did you outright exclude William and his family from benefits at that moment?"

Paul Whitman: "Well, not exactly. I explained that I would call a board meeting and present the facts. Then they would vote. This probably would give him about a week to get his affairs in order. I told William that many of the board members were powerful people, all with vested interests in various charitable institutions which the trust generously supports. Given that, I explained that I was positive that the board would gladly strip away any inheritance in order to allow more money to remain in the trust for their discretionary disposal. Naturally William was distraught."

Boris Haverman: "Was there anything else that you discussed?"

Paul Whitman: "I don't recall if I specially mentioned this or not, but I do recall thinking at the time, how would a court of law view an inheritance to a legally nonexistent person named in a trust? In other words, since William was neither natural born to the Ambassador and his wife, nor legally adopted, an argument could be made that he was *persona non grata* in the eyes of the trust as well as the law with respect to any right of inheritance and probably even citizenship.

"I advised him, given that he was not even an American citizen, to resign as Vice President before a possible impeachment. I also indicated to William that even though I was a close acquaintance, I was not his lawyer, and therefore could not give him any legal advice, even informally. You see, I felt it could constitute a conflict of interest due to the fact that I was the chairman of the board of the Carnegie Trust and had a fiduciary responsibility to it. It was devastating news to deliver to such a wonderful young man and dear friend."

Haverman looked up. "And there it is."

"Very interesting, Boris," Greenway said. "Whitman may well be right about the court being unwilling to recognize William. That is what this case will be all about."

"Agreed," Haverman said. "There is no clear case law that covers a situation quite like this. Clearly, William, and for that matter Henry here, were raised to be Carnegies, by Carnegies, so that meets one of Fillmore's criteria. Unfortunately, neither William, Charles, nor Henry are actually blood relatives to the trust's grantor, Fillmore Carnegie. That's the sticky wicket."

"Have we seen Ambassador Carnegie's will?" Greenway asked.

"Yes, we have it here. Basically it is pretty standard, with one exception. Apparently the Ambassador understood that William was not legally his son, so in his will he bequeaths everything to his surviving spouse and then, to quote, 'to the person known to me as William Carnegie.' He clearly omits reference to 'his issue' as offspring are commonly identified in wills. Very interesting wording. But the point is almost moot, since the vast majority of assets that benefited the Ambassador were not personal, but were held in the Carnegie Trust."

"You're right, but it does go to show how William was regarded by the Ambassador."

"What about William's will, what did that say?"

"William's will was also standard fare. It bequeathed everything to his wife, Elizabeth, and his sons—Tyler, who is now King Charles of England, and of course Henry here. Like his father, William held virtually no assets in his name. He had donated all of his earned income as governor, and later Vice President, to charity, since he had no need for such small amounts of money. He was lavishly cared for by the trust, which provided residences, automobiles, and covered every conceivable expense for him and his family. With respect to whatever assets he might have had, once he became king, they are irrelevant to this case. I can guarantee you it would be far more complicated to figure that out, and certainly not in our purview.

"When Henry's father was disenfranchised from the trust, they confiscated all the assets purchased with trust money," Haverman continued. "The trust had the audacity to claw back and demand forfeiture of all assets given to William by his father if they were purchased with Carnegie Trust money, including real estate, automobiles, and even jewelry given to both he and his wife. William was left practically penniless. The administrator of this clawback effort was none other than Paul Whitman, chairman of the Carnegie Trust."

"Incredible," Greenway remarked, shaking his head. "What a blow to such a great man."

"I remember it," Henry chimed in. "It was a terrible time for my father and mother. They even took my mother's engagement ring. It broke her heart. But they were strong and literally picked up and moved to England to pursue their newly discovered destiny."

The room remained silent for the next few seconds, each man lost in his own thoughts.

"So," Haverman said, "that's where we're at. Right now, it looks like Whitman and the trust are on pretty solid ground. It's hard to argue with a will that's so clear. We'll need something else."

Professor Greenway looked at Henry. "You were planning to talk to your mother. Did she have anything to add?"

This was Henry's cue and he excitedly took up the thread. "Yes, actually. I think. Or at least I hope. But before I get there, I did some more in-depth checking on the current Carnegie Trustees. It's an interesting group of people who are all in one way or another tied to Paul

Whitman. There is a tangled web of interrelated business dealings and relationships. On the surface, it all looks pretty much above board, but look a little closer and it has the earmarks of flagrant cronyism and incestuous behavior. As we know from our previous meetings, the trustees are all generously remunerated via honorariums and handsomely reimbursed for expenses."

"Yes, it was $4 million for the board, correct?" Greenway observed, likely for Haverman's benefit.

"Yes," Henry said, "but I suspect that's peanuts compared to what they are probably siphoning off in the form of business contracts with the trust. Adding insult to injury, the trust is represented by the law firm Cavanaugh, Wolf, Whitman and Smith, which is paid millions of dollars a year in legal fees. As you probably already put together, the Whitman in the firm's name is Paul Whitman, the very same one who is the chairman of the trust and doling out mega bucks to his friends on the board."

"And these board members, what is their relationship to Whitman?"

"That's interesting too. Two of the four are actually related to Mr. Whitman. One is his brother-in-law and the other is a law partner in his firm who happens to be married to Whitman's youngest daughter. Oh yeah, and his daughter is vice president of a brokerage firm that manages the Carnegie Trust's portfolio, collecting huge commissions and a hefty retainer. The two remaining trustees are both CEOs of companies of which Mr. Whitman holds a seat on the board, and the Carnegie Trust portfolio holds major positions in their stock."

"Well, if that isn't a conflict of interest I don't know what is. All very cozy," Haverman said. "But I'm not sure it means there is anything illegal going on. Lots of family trusts have interlocking directors, and as long as they are not public corporations it is all very legal. But the spirit of the trust must not be violated. By their very nature, charitable trusts are set up to help others, not the directors. But one would be naive to think it doesn't happen."

"Do you think this is material in our case?" Henry asked.

"Maybe. Maybe not. It could go to careless and self-serving management of the trust's funds or an ulterior motive to keep control of the money and, in your father's case, not wanting to dilute the assets by giving him any kind of distribution. In other words, the more money the trust controlled, the more they could spend on their own pet projects and handsomely remunerate themselves. It remains to see how Judge Lowenstein rules. He may or may not take this blatant example of conflict of interest into account."

"Right now, that leaves us with two major angles," Greenway said. "The first is that you and Charles clearly meet the first of Fillmore's conditions, that you were raised by Carnegies. The second is that the trust's current management is rife with conflicts of interest. It's better, but still...we need more."

"I know," Henry said. "And here's where my mom comes in. It seems that we need to find some mitigating factor, either with the will's stipulation or at least how it's been interpreted. When I talked to my mom, she mentioned that my grandfather kept meticulous journals where he chronicled everything about his life and particularly about the family."

"A journal?" Greenway said, sounding a little doubtful. "I'm not sure—"

"Not so fast," Haverman interjected. "I think Henry might be onto something here. Something we should at least pursue. A journal or diary can often shed light on a decedent's frame of mind in inheritance cases. There is a decent body of case law supporting the notion that judges will consider later writings in interpreting a will or trust. Let's say these journals show that Harrington had every intention of altering the family trust structure to William's benefit, which of course he would not have been entitled to do under his own father's mandate and the irrevocability nature of the trust. However, the journals could show in what regard Harrington held William, like a true son and heir, which was also supported in his own will with the language 'to the person known to me as William Carnegie.' The evidence of this thought process might influence the judge's thinking and ultimate ruling with respect to William and his legitimate heirs."

"But we don't know that," Greenway said. "It could just as easily be a fishing diary. Henry, did your mother mention how we can get these journals? Does she have them in storage somewhere?"

"Uh, well, that's where it gets interesting," Henry said. "It turns out my grandfather gave them to someone he trusted to hold before his death. He was interested in having a biography written."

"Who?" Greenway asked.

"Paul Whitman," Henry said.

Both professors said in unison, "Paul Whitman?"

"Yes. As far as she knows, he still has them."

Greenway took a second to absorb this new information. "I think we should have those journals," he said. "Henry, we need to subpoena them right away and see what they say. Maybe my esteemed colleague here is right and we'll find something that strengthens the case."

"I'm on it, Professor," Henry said. "I'll request a subpoena from Judge Lowenstein and have it served ASAP."

CHAPTER 27
FOR BETTER OR WORSE,
BUT MOSTLY WORSE

As usual, Sir Melvyn looked like something that had been dragged through traffic as he entered Richard's office for their regular meeting. Richard actually enjoyed the tortured look on Sir Melvyn's face—it was fun to have a former Member of Parliament squirming under his thumb. But with Charles moving through his deployment, they had important business.

"Sit," he ordered Melvyn, and the other man dropped miserably into his usual chair. "I see the art has been taken out of the North Gallery. What is its status?"

"It was transported to a storage facility that is totally secure. It is guarded twenty-four/seven by your men, as well as electrically protected with state-of-the-art security devices."

"What do the guards know?" Richard asked.

"They have not been allowed into the storage area, which is sealed. The men have no idea what is in the facility. Those who actually transported the art were foreign contractors and totally controllable."

"Who here at the Palace knows the location of the site?"

"Just you and myself, none others."

"And what about the art in the other galleries?"

"The plan is the same. Next week, the art in the South Gallery will be removed, as will art in two other palace locations. All of the paintings will be stored in the off-site facility."

"Are the renovations moving along?"

"Yes, but as you directed, it will be a very prolonged process. It will continue to drag on for as long as we need."

"Smashing. By the time anyone figures this scheme out, the paintings will be long gone. Now let's discuss the evacuation of the art to Switzerland. I have already contacted some international art dealers, all with dubious reputations, and instructed them to test the waters for possible buyers. They will need color photographs and the pedigree of each of the paintings. Arrange for that immediately."

"Of course, sir. I believe the palace historian has all that on file. The documentation should be available to you."

"Once they get details, these art dealers can start shopping the paintings around, all very hush hush, of course. When can we begin the relocations to Switzerland?"

Sir Melvyn looked at his notes. "This will be a complicated process. I know you didn't want to bother with the forgeries, but I think it's necessary to have at least something done so there will be charred remains. Most of the original frames on the masterpieces will be removed and left to burn in the fire, along with forgeries. We opted not to contract highly skilled forgers; that would be unnecessary since the art will be burned. The artists we did hire will use paint that will closely forensically match the paint that was used in the originals."

Richard's eyebrows went up. "For a man of limited intellect, Melvyn, I'm impressed. So it will match in the inevitable forensic investigation."

"Yes, sir."

"Bravo. I'm convinced. So we'll need forgeries, then?"

"Yes. It helps that the paintings aren't insured as well. Because it's impossible to insure something that's priceless. There won't be an insurance investigation to deal with, only the internal investigation. I'm assuming we'll be able to find 'friendly' investigators who won't look too closely."

"Not a problem," Richard said. "I can have some pretty convincing credentials made up and give them to a couple of my men."

"That will work. The investigator's findings will be rendered to you, and of course you will accept them as authentic."

"Right. So when do we switch the forgeries for the originals?"

"Not for some time. The artists will have to first produce them, which will take a little bit even though they don't have to be perfect. Also, we aren't having them produced in the United Kingdom. Too risky. So once the reproductions are ready and flown to the UK, they will be transported. Several vans will drive directly into the storage area and a team of non-English foreign workers will switch frames, leave the forgeries, and load the van with the originals. We will make certain that when the switch is arranged, no guards will be scheduled."

"Tell me about the fire."

"The fire must be carefully planned. We have two options, spontaneous combustion or arson. Both have advantages and both have risks."

"Suppose a troubled and malicious guard should be accused of setting the blaze? Or better yet, this arsonist happens to get killed in the fire or perhaps shot dead by one of the other guards as he flees the scene? I should think that would deflect any suspicion from a fire like this."

"Are you serious? Shoot one of your own men? I can have no part of that."

"Shut up, you twit. You'll do as you are bloody well told. I have just the man in mind to do the shooting, and you can pick which guard will be the patsy."

"Sir, I will not! I refuse to do that. I will not be your executioner."

Richard leaned forward as Melvyn shrunk back in his seat. "You will, because if you don't you will be a ruined man. Maybe you could be the one in the fire, burned to a crisp."

Melvyn paled and his lips trembled, but he didn't say anything in response.

Richard, taking Melvyn's silence as acceptance, moved on. "Do you have the book of accounts?"

Fishing into his bag, Melvyn produced the ledger. "Yes. It's all here. As of Friday last, we have transferred 11.6 million pounds to the Cayman accounts and have 480,000 pounds in transit. There is another payment from the Privy Purse coming in a fortnight, at which time we will make additional transfers."

"Brilliant. I want to get as much into those accounts as possible. Leave me the ledger, I want to look it over."

"Very well." Melvyn slid the ledger across the desk and Richard picked it up. Leafing through it, he said, "In the meantime, I've been in regular touch with Badger, my mole in America. Badger is keeping a close eye on Henry's comings and goings. Henry apparently is on to some lawsuit with the Carnegie Trust, but the details at this point are sketchy. I'm not sure if it's an academic exercise or the real thing. Badger listens in on every word and will report back."

"A lawsuit? Does that affect us?"

"I don't know, but anything that sod is up to is of interest. He's part of my master plan. I'm not worried...with Badger's constant surveillance and eavesdropping, I will be tipped off well in advance.

"As for Charles, he's right where he needs to be," Richard continued. "He's in the thick of things, and with any luck will soon become a war hero, whenever I decide. I have this patsy, some sergeant, practically sleeping with him, and when I say, he will do whatever needs to be done. We may need your help too."

"But, sir...you can't be—"

"Not now, Melvyn," Richard said. "Spare me your bleating for now." Richard rose from his chair, sending a wave of noxious body odor rolling across the desk and signaling the end of the meeting. "That will be all, Melvyn, now get out. And bloody hell, leave that ledger, like I said."

———•◆•———

Melvyn left Sir Richard's office and headed for the exits, leaving Richard's stink behind. He walked outside into the soggy London air and was engulfed in the sounds of the city. He dismissed his driver and opted to walk, hoping to clear his tormented brain and assaulted nostrils. As he walked through the palace gates, he saw the usual throngs of tourists looking for a glimpse inside and the mass of Londoners going about their daily business. In the park, young couples walked hand in hand and children ran around under the trees.

Now on foot, he found himself wandering the city streets, his brief-case dangling from his hand like a weight. His feet seemed to guide him on their own, past the city's famous sights that, at one point in his life, had comforted and inspired him.

Melvyn wasn't always a person of questionable character. He'd had a remarkable career, starting in the village where he grew up. His father was a magistrate and his mum the daughter of a royal land grantee. Melvyn rose through the ranks of politics and ran for Parliament at the age of thirty-nine. His run was unsuccessful, but his second attempt four years later proved to be a winner.

In the august chamber, Melvyn managed to get appointed to some influential committees after proving himself a true conservative. It was during his third term that Melvyn came to know Richard, who at the time was heading MI5. Melvyn's committee was investigating a number of issues regarding the "overreach" of MI5 in obtaining sensitive information from members of Parliament and certain public enterprises. In an effort to prevent unfavorable information from being made public, Richard quietly approached Melvyn with a proposition. As consideration for being less than transparent with the committee's findings pinpointing MI5 and its director's questionable actions, Richard arranged to put up Melvyn for knighthood.

As a knight of the realm, Sir Melvyn Batton's sphere of influence and career skyrocketed—as did his vulnerability to human flaws and his feelings of invincibility and entitlement. It wasn't too long before Sir Melvyn began engaging in some risky business. He frequently dabbled with insider information, making investments that were shaky at best. Losses mounted, which created more reckless behavior.

It wasn't long before Richard pounced.

First Richard gained Melvyn's indebtedness by intervening in an investigation by the UK's Central Bank that was looking into some serious margin overreaches. Using his considerable influence and some arm twisting and intimidation, Richard managed to have the probe squashed.

Next Richard arranged to entrap Melvyn into a scandal involving some women who made their living in a less than honorable way. He first invited Melvyn to a special night at an underground brothel, then organized a raid of the same brothel. Melvyn was arrested literally with his pants down. Richard quickly arranged to have all charges dropped and the record expunged, but it came at a steep cost.

By the end of his third term, Melvyn was totally corrupted by greed and power and so over his head with debt, multiple scandals, and infidelity that he contemplated suicide. He was drinking heavily and self-medicating with prescription drugs. When Richard approached him and offered to protect him and make his problems go away for good, Melvyn agreed to whatever conditions Richard placed on him.

Melvyn stopped walking and looked up. He found himself outside the Marlborough Club in central London, where he'd long held a membership. He went inside, ordered himself a 40-year-old brandy from the bar, and found a deserted chair to sink into.

He recalled his recent conversation with Richard and how, little by little, he had allowed himself to be sucked into a treacherous world. He was now a co-conspirator to crimes he never imagined he would commit. Larceny, extortion, murder, and high treason. He was a party to the wholesale pilfering of the Royal purse and the blatant theft of priceless artwork that rightly belonged not just to the Monarchy, but to the people of Britain. And now Richard was hinting of assassinating a king and his younger brother. The thought made Melvyn physically ill. He didn't know Charles or Henry, but like every Briton he knew their story. Those two innocent boys had already paid a huge price by having their father snatched away from them when they were so young.

Melvyn's eyes teared up as he realized that he had been derailed from reality for so long now that it was almost impossible to recognize it even when it seized his consciousness.

A voice broke his train of thought. It was that of one of the footman. "Sir Melvyn, may I fetch you another drink?" Melvyn looked up and saw the face of a young man, the one they called Ian, about the age of his own son. He was smiling broadly in anticipation of a reply.

"Ian, isn't it?"

"Yes sir, thank you for remembering. Now is there anything that you will be requiring?"

"No, Ian, I'm quite fine. Wait a minute. I have a question. Has your father ever disappointed you or made you feel ashamed that he was your father?"

The puzzled lad thought for a moment and said, "Sir, I could never be ashamed of my dad, no matter what he had done or said. I love him no matter what. He's my mate, not just my father."

"Even if he did something terrible or maybe against the law?"

"You mean like if he robbed the Bank of England? Bloody no. I'd still love him. I'd say to all who asked: my dad is my dad, for better or worse!"

It was at that moment Sir Melvyn realized what he must do...for better or worse.

CHAPTER 28
FLUSHING OUT THE ENEMY

THE MAIN PHONE LINE RANG AT PAUL WHITMAN'S OFFICE ON PARK Avenue.

"Cavanaugh, Wolf, Whitman and Smith, how may I help you?"

"This is Henry Carnegie Stuart. I'd like to speak to Mr. Whitman."

"One moment please…"

Elevator music played as Henry impatiently waited.

Two rings later, another voice answered: "Mr. Whitman's office, this is Candace. How may I help you?"

"This is Henry Carnegie Stuart. I'd like to speak to Paul Whitman."

"Of course…one moment, please, and I'll see if he is available."

After a chilling silence, this time with no music, the gravelly voice of an elderly man came on.

"This is Paul Whitman. How are you, my boy?"

"Oh, just fine, Mr. Whitman. I was hoping to set up an appointment with you sometime next week, perhaps Monday or Tuesday?"

"And the nature of your visit, Henry?"

"I'd like to discuss some issues relative to the circumstances surrounding my great-grandfather's trust and the subsequent disposition of said with respect to my father."

"My, my, dear Henry, you are really sounding like a lawyer. I guess Harvard has done its job. Have you sat for the bar yet?"

"No, Mr. Whitman, I have not. I will be ready to sit by June or July. But I'm calling to discuss the case study I'm working on."

"You do know, Henry, that I am totally aware of that. Some of your associates, I believe a Professor Greenway and his team, deposed me on this matter. But I must, with all due respect, correct your statement. Fillmore Blair Carnegie was not your great-grandfather and Harrington Carnegie was not legally your grandfather. William Carnegie was indeed your father, but not related to either of the elder Carnegies. I know you thought of them as grandparents, but the truth be told, they were not. As a result of that reality, your father, you, and your brother are specifically excluded from any benefit provided by the Carnegie Trust."

"Yes, I'm aware of that, in fact, I've read the trust's position on that several times."

"So then why do you need to see me?"

"I have a few questions that we, Professor Greenway and the others, want to review with you as the Attorney of Record for the Carnegie Trust."

"Questions? Like what?"

"Well, if you don't mind, we prefer to present that to you in person, say next Monday or Tuesday? You name the time."

"Very well. But I'm out of the office this weekend and won't be back from Palm Beach until Monday night, so it will have to be Tuesday. Say around eleven?"

"That will work for us."

Paul Whitman paused and then continued, "When I was a young lawyer years ago, I worked for Fillmore Carnegie, who established the trust in question. He was a bit of a bird, very eccentric and totally unpredictable and trusted very few people, especially lawyers. Fortunately, he allowed me and my senior partners to establish a very tight irrevocable trust. He made millions, which turned into billions. The bottom line, my dear Henry, is you're probably barking up the wrong tree. I'm sure your questions have all been asked and answered before. However, I'm willing to hear anything you have to say."

"Thank you, Mr. Whitman. We will be seeing you on Tuesday, eleven a.m. sharp."

"Indeed you will."

Henry hung up, hoping that was a bit of worry he'd heard in Whitman's voice.

<hr />

When the appointed time came, Henry and his lawyers, accompanied by Julian, found themselves on Park Avenue, heading for the offices of Cavanaugh, Wolf, Whitman and Smith. The offices were nothing short of spectacular. Taking up the forty-ninth, fiftieth, and fifty-first floors of a neo-classical limestone building, the partners were supported by hundreds of staff.

Henry, Julian, and Professors Greenway and Haverman passed through the massive street level lobby and bellied up to the reception desk. Their names were cleared in an instant. The visitors were given a sticky name tag, which they were instructed to place on their jackets.

"Please proceed to the forty-ninth floor, you will be met from there," directed the Wackenhut security guard.

As the three walked toward the elevator bank, Henry reminded Professor Greenway that the judge had yet to issue a subpoena for the journals. He had hoped it would have been served by now, but due to an overloaded court schedule, the request had not been processed.

"Don't worry, Henry, we'll wing it without that subpoena for now. The idea here is to chum the water a little bit."

Like a silver bullet train, the express elevator raced the foursome up, opening its doors and announcing, "Forty-ninth floor. Please watch the elevator doors as you exit." The small entourage walked down the broad corridor toward a pair of two-story etched glass doors. Artfully etched into the thick glass panels was the name "Cavanaugh, Wolf, Whitman and Smith." As the men entered, a large custom-built reception desk came into view. Behind this one-of-a-kind marvel and beneath the firm's silver-lettered sign sat another one-of-a-kind: a receptionist who must have been hired out of central casting. Her blonde hair was pulled back into a sophisticated knot. Her features were so refined and her bearing so correct that she was captivating. Later, the professors agreed that she looked like the legendary Eva Peron.

When she smiled at the approaching men, her face lit up. Henry was mesmerized.

In a clipped British accent, she welcomed the men. "Good morning, gentlemen. I'm Samantha, and you must be Mr. Carnegie Stuart and Professors Greenway and Haverman and Mr. Julian Cox?"

Still awestruck by the sheer and simple beauty of this woman, the men could do nothing more than nod in unison.

"Mr. Whitman is expecting you, gentlemen, so if you wouldn't mind, I'll have someone take you to his office."

The visitors again nodded in unison. The momentary wait gave them a chance to look around the splendid reception area. The two-story room was flanked by an imposing staircase that seemed more like a sculpture than stairs. It floated above the reception room, which was arranged in a series of small sitting areas, each with handcrafted sofas in soft kid leather.

"Boris," Greenway whispered, "do you see that painting over there?"

"The one over that table, with all those colors? Yeah, I do."

"That's Picasso's 'The Woman of Algiers,' and if it's the original, I have no doubt it's worth a small fortune. And the table looks like an original Florence Knoll…another masterpiece."

"How do you know that?"

"My wife teaches art history and she has dragged me to so many lectures and museums that I actually learned about this stuff. Like, see that other painting, it's another Picasso and just as valuable as the first one."

"I tell you, Preston, we sure missed the boat. Teaching lawyers don't have Picassos or the salaries to go along with them."

"I guess not," said Professor Greenway.

While the professors were eyeing the art, Henry was eyeing Samantha—and his gaze did not go unnoticed. He had all he could do to keep from drooling. He figured that she must be twenty-one or twenty-two, no more than that, and she was put together as well as anyone could be. Star was hot, but Samantha was a perfect example of a lady and, in her own way, totally sensuous without a hint of promiscuity. Her tailored dress, so simple and sophisticated, was fitted to her body to show how much a woman she really was. And Samantha's face was striking, with only a touch of lipstick that shone like translucent rose-tinted pearl.

Henry did not escape Samantha's scrutiny either. She looked him over from head to toe and thought he was a fine-looking lad. American, no doubt, given his appearance, his tight jeans, preppy sports coat, Harvard tie, and cropped brown hair. He had a kind face, almost like a little boy, and yet he was handsome and even sexy, now that she thought about it. Unconsciously, she shrugged off the little tingle that seemed to work its way into her consciousness.

Another gorgeous young woman appeared, walking down the floating staircase. As she approached, she said, "Hello, I'm Vanessa, will you follow me? Mr. Whitman is ready to see you."

As the men ascended the staircase, Henry turned to have a last look at Samantha, but she was gone, replaced by yet another very attractive young woman. Henry thought, "Boy, I can't wait to be a lawyer in a firm like this. I'll die a happy man."

Within minutes, Vanessa had dropped them at Mr. Whitman's office door. Paul Whitman stood to greet them. Now in his late seventies, the graying but refined lawyer smiled broadly as he welcomed the group. His $4,000 custom-made Baroni Italian suit was tailored to perfection and his Hermes orange tie was clipped with a gold tie bar. His bearing and appearance screamed money, power, and success.

"Gentlemen, please be seated." He pointed to a conversational grouping at the north end of his enormous fiftieth-floor corner office. Paul walked slowly to join them, just the hint of an arthritic limp that to date had not impeded his early morning jogs in Central Park or afternoon squash at his club.

The floor-to-ceiling glass windows allowed the incredible cityscape to act as living wall murals. To the east, there was a panoramic view of Central Park, and to the south Henry saw many iconic skyscrapers: the Empire State Building, the Chrysler building, and the Waldorf-Astoria

Hotel. Behind Paul's desk hung another contemporary masterpiece, an explosion of color by Paul Klee, the acclaimed Swiss-German painter. The remaining office walls were painted in a dark chocolate brown that was set off by the almost white Berber carpet and mahogany brown leather seating.

"Let's get started. First, I want to say that I am friend, not foe. I represent two generations of Carnegies and consider both of them not just clients but friends, close friends. As for Henry here, I am more than sympathetic to his cause and the totally unfair charade that was perpetrated against his father. No doubt one of the most shocking states of affairs I've known in my lifetime. That being said, I really don't have much more than what I have already stated in my deposition."

Professor Greenway took the lead. "Thank you, Mr. Whitman. Henry appreciates your sensitivity to the situation and certainly your commiseration. But having studied at great length and in great detail the facts of the case, we feel that perhaps there could be a different outcome given some previously undisclosed information."

"And what might that be?"

"It seems that Fillmore Carnegie handwrote his will, apparently without benefit of legal counsel, yet still perfectly sustainable, but shall we say, not in traditional legal format," Greenway said.

"Yes, that's correct...nothing new there, we are all aware of that. And as you say, perfectly sustainable."

"Right, so we thought it would be instructive to revisit the will more closely." Greenway removed a copy of the will from his briefcase and read parts of it aloud.

"As noted," he said, "Fillmore Carnegie's will states only two conditions to be a beneficiary. They were: to have had Carnegie blood running through their veins and to be raised by Carnegies. Now I'm sure you would concede that Henry here, and his brother, were raised in part by Ambassador Carnegie. For years the boys resided in a number of his estates, as well as traveled extensively with him. The Ambassador even participated in their schooling, paying their tuition. In fact, he was intimately involved and intimately familiar with almost every aspect of their rearing."

Whitman frowned slightly. "Well, on a broad interpretation one might conclude that the Ambassador had involvement in the boy's upbringing, but that would be a stretch to say 'intimately involved' as far as I'm concerned."

"Certainly understandable from your point of view, Mr. Whitman. But from our point of view it's more than clear that Ambassador Carnegie was omnipresent and fully engaged in the boy's rearing for years. Document evidence will substantiate that."

Choosing not to argue the point further, Whitman simply shrugged off the notion. "Yes, but what of it? Even if that is the case, the other point stipulates that only blood relatives are beneficiaries. As we've stated many times, William was not a blood relative, so therefore his children are not blood relatives either and are thus not entitled to any proceedings from the trust."

Greenway put the will away and sat for a moment, letting an uncomfortable silence draw out.

"On that point, we believe there is a new avenue to pursue," he finally said.

"A new avenue?" Whitman said. "What new avenue?"

Instead of answering, Greenway said, "We appreciate your cooperation thus far, but it's noted that we've had to subpoena this firm to obtain documents and then you've only met the barest request."

"Why would we do otherwise? I'm afraid I'm not following where you're leading here."

"Mr. Whitman," Haverman added, "please be advised that should this matter come to litigation, the plaintiff in this case, Henry, will be represented by Professor Greenway, myself, and three other senior law associates at Harvard. Pro bono, of course."

"I see. That would be an impressive legal team. One that money couldn't buy. But I'm afraid I'm still confused. There is no matter to come to litigation. The facts of his will aren't in dispute."

Greenway took back over again. "Mr. Whitman, to save us time and effort, are there any other documents that might weigh into this matter that you haven't disclosed, but that might be of concern in the matter of a contested will?"

Whitman hesitated. "Other documents?"

"Yes. Anything that might shed light on the relationship between Harrington, who of course managed the trust, and William or his children? Correspondence? Journals?"

Henry watched Whitman's face closely. He'd read about all the ways people show they're lying when they are talking, but Whitman was far too experienced to give anything away. His face was a perfect mask of composure as he said, "No, I don't believe there are. And it should be noted that Harrington's ability to modify the original trust is very much in question given its irrevocability. The will establishing the trust is very clear."

"Noted of course," Greenway said. "Fortunately, my colleague Haverman here is an expert in inheritance law and would be able to help us all understand the legal protections afforded to heirs. A rather complicated area of law, if I understand correctly. Yes, Boris?"

"Very much so," Haverman said. "You'd be surprised how robust protections are for heirs and how trust law empowers them."

Whitman didn't respond, but his mouth drew into a thin line. Henry tried not to smile.

"Well, that should be enough for today," Greenway said. "Thank you. And of course, thank you for your time. We appreciate it."

Whitman looked confused as the meeting ended with a round of handshaking. As they left, Henry and the professors walked down the staircase and into the lobby. He looked to see if Samantha was there and saw that she was not. He could not help himself from walking over to the desk and asking, "Where did Samantha go?"

"Oh, she was just filling in while I was on break. Is there something I can help you with?"

Henry just shook his head and walked toward the elevators where the professors were waiting. He thought he would not soon forget Samantha, for her image was etched in his mind.

The men were silent on the elevator ride down. Henry waited until they were on the street to ask, "Well? Did that go well?"

Greenway shrugged. "Hard to say right now. The important point is that we've planted a seed of doubt in his mind. Right now, he's probably rushing to those journals to find out if we know something he doesn't know. And he's wondering how we found out about them. At this point, all we're aiming to do is get him off balance, willing to deal. It's the best we can hope for with the hand we've got."

"Got it," Henry said. He wanted to ask more, but he didn't want to look ignorant. He didn't really see how this strategy was going to help them, but he decided he would have to just trust the superior wisdom of his professors for now. In the meantime, since they were in the city, Greenway suggested lunch at his favorite deli. Henry and Haverman agreed enthusiastically.

CHAPTER 29
COURAGE BEYOND QUESTION

CHARLES'S QUARTERS WERE SPARSE BUT COMFORTABLE. HE HAD A private room with a shared latrine, a cot, a small desk and lamp, a wardrobe, and a dresser. A picture of his mother when she was younger and Henry in a simple brass frame was the room's only decoration. His men billeted in the same structure lived just above his room in a large open bay, their bunks lined up in rows. Adjacent to his room was a small alcove that housed a single armed guard who was charged with his personal security. Down the hall from Charles's room and the other officer's quarters was the enlisted men's day room where the men were able to play cards, snooker, or just hang out. Officers, on the other hand, were entitled to go to the officer's mess hall, which was fitted out to vaguely resemble a men's club and more gentrified than the enlisted men's day room.

Rather than hang out with the officers, Charles spent much of his time in his room. After weeks of patrols, he had witnessed the Irish situation up close and begun to absorb the enormity and reality of the conflict most people just called the Troubles. To learn more, Charles spent many evenings immersed in books, reading about the history of the conflict between the IRA and the British government. Rooted in years of hatred and distrust mostly based on religious and ethnic discrimination, it seemed so foolish to him that civilized societies would engage in such brutality and atrocities. Still American in his core, Charles believed that all people should be free to practice whatever faith, or lack of faith, they wanted and that all men were created equal. He resolved that once he became a true reigning king, he would devote himself to finding peace between the factions.

His dreams of peace, however, had to be tucked away during his nightly missions to seek out and arrest IRA leaders. The fighters were more guerillas than soldiers and sought to avoid open conflict with the better armed and equipped British soldiers at all costs. They moved safe houses constantly and spent their days acting as innocent milkmen or shop boys, only to don black balaclavas at night and hit the streets with Molotov cocktails and AK-47s they bought from Libya. Every night was dangerous, and Charles and his platoon arrested hundreds of foot soldiers. The prisoners were interrogated and then shipped off to grim prisons, but it seemed like there was a never-ending supply of more. It broke his heart to see mere children, many in their teens, trucked off to the most dire of internment facilities where he knew they probably would be brutalized.

Charles's social life was pretty much put aside. There were the infrequent times he would visit London to see his mother and make some token official appearances, usually arranged by Richard. On his occasional visits to the Belfast officer's club, he mixed freely with his fellow officers and shared a pint or two. It wasn't a very posh club, but it was nice enough and Charles liked seeing the other officers. The place had the dark and smoky vibe of a neighborhood pub. It was a place you would not be embarrassed to bring a date for a drink or to have some fish and chips.

One evening, a captain who was sitting at the bar with an attractive young woman approached Charles as he entered.

"Excuse me, sir, may I introduce myself? I'm Captain Morgan Fairfield, and I believe we were at university together," the captain said.

"Really?" Charles said. "Brilliant. I think I remember seeing you, but I'm embarrassed to say I recall nothing more."

"Well, sir, I guess we ran in different circles. I was at Joslin House and a cricket player, and you were into tennis and circulated in a totally different crowd."

"Right."

"May I introduce my friend? Sir, this is Beatrice Grandton, she's up from London."

Charles turned to the young woman standing with Fairfield. "How do you do, Miss Grandton?" he said. "Very pleased to make your acquaintance. But...why on earth have you come to such a dangerous place, with all this terrorist business going on? One would think you'd stay in London, safe and sound."

She laughed. "I wouldn't be very good at my job if I did that, now would I? I'm a journalist with the BBC. We're doing a series on IRA terrorism."

"Ah, I see," he said. "So you and Morgan go way back?"

"Not exactly, we met during my last visit to Belfast. He was assigned to me as a liaison officer and we hit it off. Friends, you know."

Charles studied Beatrice. She had the tone of an educated Londoner, but it was ever so slightly different from the puffed-up aristocratic class Charles had come to know at Eton and Cambridge. At first glance, she was pretty but not gorgeous. Her features were refined, but not cover-girl perfect. Her dirty blonde hair, streaked with highlights and obviously cut and styled by a skilled beautician at one of Oxford Street's posh salons, became her. Her red dress was simple but elegant. A deep V neck showed just enough of her cleavage to pique interest but not elicit vulgar stares.

"You have an unusual accent," he said. "You're British? Or are you from somewhere else?"

"Keen observation. Yes, I do have a bit of an accent, mostly because I was born British but raised and educated in the United States. My father was president of an English brokerage firm and ran the New York office."

"Ah, I thought so. So we are both hybrids: you born here with a noticeable American accent and I born in the US, trying to have an English one."

They both laughed at the irony of it all.

Charles ordered a round of drinks. "So you're a reporter?" he said.

"Yes. I majored in journalism at Bryn Mawr College. I'm on assignment, my third here in Belfast. I'm doing some human interest stories on the victims of the struggle...both sides. You know, for the first time it feels like peace is in the air, and after so many years of anarchy and destruction, the BBC wanted to emphasize the horror of the struggle and the need for all parties to end this senseless killing."

Charles nodded in agreement. "I lost my father to the idiocy of the politics and the unconscionable conduct by ideologues in both camps. No one knows the pain of this more than me and my family."

The drinks arrived and Beatrice raised her glass. "Peace in our time."

"Indeed!" The threesome clinked glasses and chorused: "Cheers, to peace in our times."

The group sat together until midnight, long past the time Charles would normally have left. Morgan escorted Beatrice back to her hotel, and Charles returned to his lonely room. As he walked the dark streets, his thoughts turned to the events of the day. There were no missions planned, so he hadn't worried about his men. He wondered if it was time for him to end his military career, return to London, and take his rightful place. Although officially he had three months left to serve in Ireland, he could prevail upon his commanding officer, Colonel McIntosh, to abbreviate his tour of duty.

As he turned into the courtyard of his billet, his mind turned to Beatrice. She was a very lovely girl, he thought. Smart, educated, and fun. But rather than make him feel better, this knowledge only depressed him. It occurred to Charles that he had not been allowed a single day to do just what he wanted since his early teen years. In a way, he envied Henry for this. Henry had always been able to do exactly what he wanted, consequences be damned. But for Charles, as the eldest, it wasn't that easy, and he had borne up under the pressure of Eton, then Cambridge, and now the military in an effort to prove that he could handle the burden that had fallen to him.

If he could do anything he wanted right now, he would have asked for Beatrice's phone number. He was still berating himself for letting the opportunity slip by when he reached the door to his room and went inside. Why was it almost as hard to ask for a girl's phone number as it was to be king?

As he prepared for bed, Charles pushed these thoughts from his mind and berated himself for feeling self-pity. It was true that much had been asked of him, but much had also been given to him, and he was afraid it was ungrateful of him to deny that. Tomorrow would be another day, and there would be more missions—and, he promised himself, if he saw Beatrice again, he would seize the opportunity.

The next three missions were particularly dangerous, with two late-night ambushes from rooftop snipers on two consecutive nights.

The men took cover and then searched the slightly seedy neighborhood, but they never got close to the shooter. Word got out quickly that the IRA had a new marksman among them, words that were sure to strike fear in any British soldier's heart. They weren't afraid to deal with IRA terrorists in any sort of open combat, but the snipers were the worst and inflicted by far the most casualties. An effective sniper was like a ghost that haunted them.

As the men tore through buildings and smashed down doors, Charles also found himself growing more and more morally conflicted. He was just beginning to embrace the British patriotism that was still foreign to him, but his deeper understanding of the conflict and his essentially American nature made it all seem so pointless. What were they fighting for exactly? He wasn't sure he could say. Hurt feelings? Old grudges? Which church was right? Who knew? He surely didn't.

With a night off, Charles headed for the officer's club, hoping he might run into Beatrice. When he arrived, he was disappointed to see that she was nowhere to be found. However, he did see Captain Fairfield in the corner.

Crossing the dark, loud, smoky room, he came tableside to Fairfield. "Hi, how are you, Captain?"

Fairfield sprung to his feet in a show of respect even though he militarily outranked Charles.

"Sir, pleased to see you again. Won't you join me?"

"I'd enjoy that, thank you."

The two officers relaxed and chatted freely for the better part of an hour. Fairfield observed that it was incredible that Charles, his king, was so nonchalant and approachable.

As the night wound down, Charles finally worked around to asking about Beatrice. "Have you seen her around?"

"Not really," Fairfield said. "She's getting ready to return to London within the next day or two. Her news special is going to air nationally and she needs to get back to the studio."

"I see. Are you by any chance interested in her, you know, on a personal level? Like, do you go out with her or something?"

"Blimey, me. I'd say not, sir! I think my old lady would have none of that."

"So you're married?"

"Very much so, sir. Happily, at that, with two young lads to boot."

"That's great!" Charles said, a little more enthusiastically than he intended. He tried to cover it up, saying, "I mean, about you being married and having a couple of sons and all. Just brilliant." He cleared his throat nervously. "So...I'd like to contact Beatrice. Do you happen to have her phone number?"

The captain fished into his breast pocket with two fingers and broke into a broad grin. "I can do better than that. I have her card with all the contact information." He handed over a business card.

"Fantastic! And thanks a lot."

"Sir—"

"Please, Captain," Charles interrupted, "call me Charles and I'd like to call you Morgan, if that is okay with you?"

"I'd be honored, thank you, sir...er, Charles." Morgan hesitated and then continued, "Not that my opinion counts, but I think Beatrice Grandton is first class. She's not hung up on her looks or celebrity. You know she is a hit on BBC? Anyway, she is really into helping people and is one of the most sincere people I've ever met. Good thing I'm happily married or I'd be tempted myself."

"You know, Captain...er, Morgan, I got that impression right away. Do you think she would like me?"

"Bloody hell! Are you kidding? You are the perfect bloke, handsome, smart, brave, and I'm sure it would help that you're king of our country! My God, man, I hope you don't mind my saying, but you're a dream come true for any girl. My only concern would be that she might be a bit intimidated by it all. Who wouldn't be?"

Charles was embarrassed but a little pleased about Morgan's reaction. It seemed he'd won over at least one British fan. "Well," he said, "we'll just have to see about that!"

"Trust me, sir...Charles. You're a bloody bloke!"

CHAPTER 30
CHOOSING RIGHT OR WRONG

ALTHOUGH IT CAME LATER THAN HENRY HAD HOPED, JUDGE Lowenstein finally issued the subpoena for his grandfather's journals. It read:

SUBPOENA DUCES TEC

You are hereby commanded to produce for inspection and/or copying on or before Wednesday next no later than eleven-forty five AM, Eastern Standard time, to the Second Circuit Court to His Honorable Aaron Lowenstein's court clerk located at 74 Monroe Street in the City of New York in the county of New York, any and all documents, records, Journals, and other tangible material which are in your possession or under your control relating to certain journals and communications of the late Ambassador Harrington Carnegie...

The court document was served to Paul Whitman at his Park Avenue office.

Whitman sat at his desk, absorbing the meaning of the subpoena. Greenway and Haverman had asked him about journals at the end of their last meeting. At the time, he had played dumb, but the subpoena sent a shiver of fear through him. If there was one thing Whitman hated, it was not having all the information he needed. He recognized this was a fishing expedition on their part—but he also knew that sometimes fishing expeditions actually landed fish.

He called Leon Peck, a partner in the firm, into his office.

Leon was many years Paul's junior, but as bright as they come. He had gone to Princeton and Columbia and served a stint as a Supreme Court clerk. Being married to an ancestor of the Rockefellers didn't hurt him in the "connection business" and helped explain why he had been made a full partner at the firm within the first three years of his employment. Very few lawyers achieved a partnership in a white shoe firm like Whitman's after such a short tenure. Leon belonged to more clubs than most people have in their golf bag, a game at which he incidentally boasted a handicap of four.

Tall and almost gaunt, Leon had all the earmarks of a compulsive jogger. His long legs and huge feet anchored his skeletal body. His thin blond hair was parted and combed forward to hide an increasingly aggressive receding hairline. Despite his appearance, he was usually the smartest man in the room, and he never failed to make sure everyone realized it.

"Leon, take a look at this subpoena from Judge Lowenstein."

Leon slipped on his frameless glasses and took the document from Whitman. "Hmm, I see they are looking for some journals and anything else that we might have that's not presently proffered. What do you know about the journals they are referring to?"

"They are journals that Ambassador Carnegie kept on pretty much a daily basis. He wanted to chronicle his life so that someone, preferably me, could use them to write his biography."

"Ah, modest man, was he? Obviously thought his life was worthy of a biography."

"It really was, Leon. He was a brilliant and accomplished man who built an empire on top of an already massive one created by his father. He was a statesman and master politician, although he never held any elected office."

"I see. Do you know where the journals are now?"

Paul stood up and walked to the back wall of his office, where a floor-to-ceiling bar was attached to the wall. The unit was custom-built in a rich zebra wood and so highly polished that Whitman could see his own image in the wood. The glass shelves were filled with Baccarat crystal barware and matching decanters, all filled with various kinds of liquor. He reached below the marble bar top and pressed a secret button. The entire bar unit slid to the left, revealing a pair of stainless steel vault doors.

"Impressive, Paul," Leon said. "I've heard you had something like that, but never knew it was so cool."

"It's a lot more than cool. It's virtually impenetrable. I even had them build a massive concrete shroud around the safe so it's totally fire and earthquake proof. Cost a pretty half million. Don't worry...I billed the Carnegie Trust for it, since we keep all their records for them."

The men entered the room-size vault. The whirl of an exhaust fan pierced the tomb-like silence. Paul and Leon walked toward the far wall, where sturdy stainless steel shelves held what appeared to be leather binders. They were lined up, one and sometimes two journals for every year, beginning from the Ambassador's college years.

Picking one up, Leon leafed through it and then turned to Paul. "These are Xerox copies. Where are the originals?"

"They're in the Carnegie library in upstate New York."

"He had a personal library? Do you mean in his home?"

"No, no. Not his home, and it really isn't a personal library per se. It's part of the New York State Historical Society, which he heavily endowed. He sat on the board and donated millions of dollars, as well as a lot of his personal effects. You know, antiques, famous people's letters, artwork, and lots of photos of him with world dignitaries. After the Ambassador died, they took possession of the original journals. Later they made copies, which they sent to me, thinking that I would use them to write a biography. Probably on the instructions of the Ambassador. The society periodically reaches out to the trust for funding and never fails to mention that they remain keepers of the Ambassador's legacy."

"So the original journals are upstate and publicly available?"

"Exactly. The NYHS has a major facility in upstate New York, in Cooperstown. The Ambassador was great friends with the Anheuser-Busch people, who were another huge benefactor of the Historical Society and practically owned the town."

Back in the day, the "New York Four Hundred" would have their private rail cars bring their entire family and staff up for the summer to escape the city heat. They built mega homes and heavily endowed the arts to build museums and summer stock theaters, even an opera house. Then the rich and famous would encourage artists and actors to make a pilgrimage to the sleepy little village to entertain their friends and family on a grand scale.

"The Ambassador's father had a camp along the lake," Whitman said. "Camps are what they call estates up there. Hundreds of acres, lakes, and horses, the whole country gentry bit. He called it Carnegie Camp Bliss. All very understated, but big bucks."

"Cooperstown, the Baseball Hall of Fame...that Cooperstown?" Leon asked.

"The very one, Leon. Lots of big money there."

"I always wondered how the Baseball Hall of Fame ended up there," Leon mused.

"Well, Leon, as I understand it, back in 1939 one of the million-aires, a guy named Stephen Clark, was trying to revive the area by bringing in tourists. Like so many other rural towns, Cooperstown had been seriously affected by the Great Depression, which decimated its tourist industry. Clark owned a grand hotel there and he wanted to create a draw for visitors, so he funded a Hall of Fame."

"Interesting, I never knew that."

"It's probably one of the few things you don't know," Whitman joked.

Leon gave an awkward smile, then nodded back at the journal in his hands. "So from the subpoena, I think it's safe to say they know about the existence of these."

"I think so," Whitman answered. "Although I'm not quite sure how they learned of it. Maybe someone in the family. They asked me about them last time we met. It was clear they were trying to rattle me."

"What'd you say?"

"I told them the truth," Whitman said. "I said I don't have the journals. I left out that I have copies."

"So you don't think they already have them?"

Whitman shrugged. "I'd say no. I think they're fishing."

Leon skimmed a few pages, then looked back up. "Let's set aside the question of possession of the journals. Is there anything in these journals that might help their case?"

"Honestly, Leon, I have no idea. I've never even read a single word of them. There are more than seventy of them, and at this point it would be impossible to read and scrutinize every word in time to respond to the court order." Leon raised his eyebrows, and Whitman continued, "After Henry's father, William, left for Britain after all that nasty business, there really were no Carnegies left in the United States. I was the sole executor of the Ambassador's estate and chairman of the Carnegie Trust. There were no other legitimate heirs according to the old man Carnegie's will, so the trust took total control of all the assets and made all the decisions."

Leon rubbed his forehead. "You say you have never read the contents of these copies?"

"I've never had time to even think about them," Whitman answered. "I can say with certainty that no one has touched these copies since the day they were placed in this vault and I am the only one who has access."

"Any idea who made the copies?"

"The Historical Society. I vaguely recall that they were delivered to me by a courier." Grabbing one of the binders, Paul thumbed to the last page. "Oh look, there's a stamped insignia. NYHS: Cooperstown New York-Reproduction Department."

"Ah, so it was done in-house," Leon said. "Not much help there, so that leaves us back where we started. We have to assume they know the journals exist, they obviously at least suspect you have them, and we have no idea if there's anything in here that might make a material difference in their case." Whitman nodded somewhat miserably. "Then I have to ask, Paul, what's at stake here? Give me the worst case."

"Worst case is that, well, there is something in these journals that reflects on Henry's claim to a legitimate heir to the Carnegie fortune, or at least opens a legal door. They have Boris Haverman on their team. A worldwide expert in inheritance law, and in his pre-Harvard teaching days, a superstar litigator with an almost flawless success record. I'm confident that the original will is solid, but if Harrington expressed a desire to include William as an heir in the trust...Haverman could turn a tiny loophole into a case big enough to drive a truck through. And I'd say that Henry and his brother make sympathetic plaintiffs, to say the least. Worst case scenario is that their claim is found to have legal merit."

"Then what?"

"The total control of the trust falls to the trustees. However, a legitimate heir has the power to change the trustees, the legal representation, and the chairman of the board. I would imagine that should Henry prevail, he would be deemed legitimate heir. Given our history, he would be nothing less than hostile to all who were involved, including this firm. As you know, the trust is our firm's largest client and accounts for more than 25 percent of our gross billings. Losing that business would be catastrophic to the firm, not only financially but it could ruin our reputation. In addition, the trustees are all handpicked by me and have material interest in the affairs and business of the trust."

"Can we speak candidly and off the record, Paul?"

"Of course. We are in the most secure place in New York City."

"Indeed. Paul, you have to make a big decision here. Either turn over these documents as demanded by the court, or not. The subpoena doesn't distinguish between copies and originals and there's no question these copies would fall under the subpoena. If you disavow knowledge of their whereabouts and turn nothing over, there is a slim possibility that the plaintiff could track the originals down and find them in Cooperstown. Conversely, if you turn them over, the court may find something in them circumstantially supporting the plaintiff's claim that the Ambassador considered him family, if not legally, but certainly by actions and intent, thus implicitly challenging the narrow interpretation and basic tenets of the trust. If so ruled, this firm and all your fellow trustees will be out in the cold."

Leon paused as Whitman digested this, leafing through more journal pages without really seeing them.

"And Paul," Leon said gently. "I know I don't need to tell you this, but...if you deny that you have these and don't honor the subpoena and they are later discovered, that's a criminal act." He let his words hang in the air a second, then took a breath and went on. "I would also be concerned that if there is, and I say IF in capital letters, scrutiny on the trust's operation that turns up anything less than exemplary actions by the trustees, there could be serious legal and reputational ramifications, personally and corporately. In other words, the board better make Mother Teresa look like a shady lady if there is a great deal of scrutiny."

Whitman coughed nervously. "Yes," he said. "Well, as I mentioned, the appointment of trustees is left up to the chairman, which in this case is me. And...let's just say Henry's team already knows the trust structure and who the trustees are. We were ordered to provide that information by Judge Lowenstein some weeks ago."

"And?"

"Let's just say that I'm not sure an outside investigation would be kind to us. One might find that a couple of the trustees were interrelated and had proprietary interests in directing trust assets or placement of business."

"Are you saying you hired relatives?" Leon asked, not totally successful in keeping the shock out of his voice.

"Qualified relatives, but yes. Some of my relatives serve on the trust board."

Leon shook his head. "That's not good, Paul. Not a good way to start this."

"I know."

"So…what are you going to do? As your lawyer, I'd have to advise you to turn over the journals and hope the chips fall your way. Anything else could leave you open to serious consequences."

Paul stared at the journal for a long time. "I don't know," he said honestly. "Right now, I just don't know."

Paul knew Leon was right, and he idly leafed through a few of the journals later that night, unable to sleep. Surely the subpoena covered copies, and it was a criminal act to defy the subpoena and claim he didn't have them. And yet he'd been unable to decide what to do. Whitman had known the elder Carnegie well, and reading his crisp, intelligent writing was like having the old man speaking directly into his ear. Whitman was surprised to find himself so moved, full of regret for the things that had to come to pass and even missing a man he had come to admire as one of the truly great men he had known.

But that didn't change his problem, and there was nothing he saw in his glance at the journals that helped. With dozens of binders, there was no way he could read them all, and for all he knew, the Ambassador had directly addressed the trust somewhere in all of these thousands of pages.

He rolled over in his king-sized bed and looked at his clock. It was 5:45 a.m. Muted sunlight peeked through the heavy velvet drapes that tried unsuccessfully to prolong the room's darkness. Paul's wife, Lucille, was away visiting their son and his family in Palm Beach.

Whitman realized full well that the Carnegie Trust had made his life pretty comfortable for decades. A seven-figure salary plus millions in legal fees, both from the trust, allowed him to keep a Park Avenue duplex, a rambling oceanfront Hamptons beach house, and a luxurious gated estate in Palm Beach, Florida. It was a really good life, courtesy of Carnegie money.

Paul stepped out of bed and walked into his oversized beige and brown marble bathroom. The gleaming brass faucets and floor-to-ceiling glass shower enclosure were nothing short of opulent. By New York City standards, this bathroom was the size of a bedroom. He looked into the mammoth mirror over the double sinks and saw the reflection of a troubled man. Whitman had no illusions about the ordeal he was facing. Even if he was on totally solid legal ground, he realized how it would look to have the trust battling Henry in public. Henry was not just another heir trying to squeeze some funds out of a regular family trust. He was the Prince of York, brother to the sitting King of England and second to the throne, and the son of a murdered "Carnegie." There was no way the press could resist that type of story; they would flock to it like moths to a candle. And once they did…Whitman could only imagine the headlines once they found out the trust employed a solid percentage of his family.

Then again…if Henry was victorious or managed to somehow convince Judge Lowenstein of his claims, it was a certainty that Whitman and his firm would be frozen out.

Those damn journals! For the thousandth time, Whitman desperately wished he knew what was in them and if they could somehow influence the proceedings. He sighed. Even if there wasn't anything direct, Whitman knew what a good lawyer—especially a world-class lawyer like Haverman—could do with thousands of pages of direct personal reflections. In a way, it almost didn't matter what was in the journals. If it came down to a legal street fight, it was very likely that control of the trust could be tied up in court for years.

The choice to comply and surrender the documents or not was not an easy one, but must be made and made today. Paul finished dressing and slowly descended the striking staircase leading to the main floor of his apartment. Pausing on the landing halfway down, he peered through a massive two-story Palladian window illuminating the staircase. The window framed a panoramic view of Central Park and the cityscape of Park Avenue. Paul took a deep breath and feared the wrong outcome to this situation could end his own personal *la dolce vita.*

He walked into the impressive foyer and into the breakfast room. Their housekeeper of thirty years had breakfast laid out. Paul sipped his hot coffee, closed his eyes, and with great trepidation made his high-risk decision. He would stonewall and deny the whereabouts of the Ambassador's journals.

It was a risk he must take, even though it tugged at his very core to betray his sacred oath as an officer of the court by lying. Should the lie be found out, it would mean disgrace and certain disbarment. But there was almost no choice, and Paul told himself there were only two people who knew of the whereabouts of the copies of the journals: himself and Leon Peck. Neither would tell. He was reasonably certain that no one would have knowledge that the originals were tucked away in an obscure library in Cooperstown, New York. He was certain the historical society had no reason to be in contact with the plaintiff and his attorneys.

Paul took another deep breath and swallowed hard. He would roll the dice and hope the odds were in his favor.

CHAPTER 31
WHO'S LOOKING NOW?

THE SUN FLOODED THE ROOF TERRACE AT RIVER HOUSE. IT WAS PAR-
ticularly warm, so Star was taking advantage of Henry's absence
and working on her tan. She knew he would be away meeting with
some professor all afternoon for whatever this case was he was so
excited about. Star found the details of the case boring, but she followed along anyway.

At the moment, though, she couldn't have cared less about Henry
or his case. Instead, she was watching the guy next door through her
eyelashes while she stretched out in her itsy bitsy bikini. The same
South African guy still lived next door, and she'd caught him peeping
at her more than once. Sometimes she wondered if he was more than
casually interested in both she and Henry. He almost seemed to be
watching and listening. Odd, after all this time, that he was still there
and yet a total stranger, a particularly nosy one at that. But then she
chalked it all up to being a bit too paranoid. After all, he was probably
just getting off on her, and who cared? He was young and not bad looking, but pretty formal and a bit stiff for her liking. He frequently had
another guy around too, and sometimes she'd seen them both at the

window. Today, she was going to give him the show she knew he was dying to see and rolled over again onto her stomach, then arched her back and rolled back onto her back, like a cat preening in the sun.

She could almost feel his excited eyes on her body and she loved it. Drops of sweat rolled down her from her neck over her bare breasts and down her flat, firm stomach to her waist, puddling at the top of her bikini bottom.

She was considering stripping her bikini bottom off completely when a shadow fell over her and she opened her eyes. She gave a sigh of relief. It was Julian, standing in her sun and grinning down at her. He made no move to hide where he was looking and let his eyes linger on her body.

"Blimey, what do we have here?" he said. "Sleeping beauty? Bloody no, it looks more like Pandora's Box!"

"Go on, you bloke, get out of here, I'm enjoying a bit of the sun."

"I expect you are," he said. "But I know something you would enjoy a lot more than a bit of sun."

"I don't think so, not today."

Julian leaned over, using his size to block out the sun and looming over her. "Why not? You like it every day usually. In every way."

"Not when Aunt Flo and Cousin Red are in town," she said.

Julian looked confused. "What are you on about? Who the hell are bloody Aunt Flo and Cousin Red? And where are they?"

"Don't you know anything? It's my period."

Julian laughed, a bit disappointed. "Your period, eh? I certainly hope you don't have a sore throat too. That would really ruin my day."

Star raised her eyebrows at him, knowing full well the jest. "You're a bad bloke, Julian."

Julian straddled her chaise lounge so his crotch hung just over her. "Go on, baby. How about you stop talking and put that mouth to better use?"

Star did as she was told and reached up to unfasten his pants. She considered saying no, but only because she knew it would provoke Julian to further demands and, if she resisted hard enough, he would likely pick her up and take her inside where she would have little choice but to submit. Star had never been in a relationship like this one before. Julian was common and lacked any sort of refinement. With her, he made it clear what he wanted and, after that first time, what he expected her to do. And she always did it. She liked it, she liked his raw hungry masculinity and the sheer power of his knotted muscles and long body. She liked that he commanded her and that there were no limits to his imagination. If she objected to one of his ideas, he would wear her down until she gave in. After their encounters, she often found herself shaking and dreaming about it for days afterward.

Now it didn't matter if the South African was watching any more. Star did what he'd asked and pleasured him with her mouth and hands, shamelessly and out on the terrace in broad daylight. Soon the moment of truth arrived and Julian emitted a soft, almost animalistic groan as he released a flood of pent-up lust.

"Good for you, baby," he muttered, then he reached down and pulled her up so he could wrap his arms around her and kiss her. The couple lingered in their embrace, exploring each other's bodies.

"I'm not done with you yet," he said. "Let's go in and shower. We can play drop the soap. And don't worry about Aunt Flo and Cousin Red. I'll be using the back door!"

Star put her hands on his stomach. "You're a pig," she said into his chest. "But I love it."

"Of course you do. Now let's go."

———•———

Henry arrived home several hours later to find Star napping alone in his room and Julian gone somewhere. As he walked into the bedroom, Star stirred. "Hi. Home early?"

"Yeah, we had a good meeting with the legal team. You know I finished my classes up last week. All that remains is the completion of my case study thesis and I'm done."

"That's smashing, Henry, it's been a long road and I'm glad you are now at the end. I'm proud of you too."

"Where's Julian? I thought we'd go play racquetball."

"He went to the store, should be back in a bit."

"Oh well, I'm tired anyway. How about I go get showered and we can all go out for Chinese later, whaddya say?"

"Chinese? Brilliant. I'd love that."

Henry walked into the bathroom and stripped down. As he entered the shower, he paused to reflect on whether the ever-ready Star had turned into more of a sexual habit than a relationship. He would have expected that, after all this time, a bond or deeper connection would have developed between them, but it hadn't. In reality, he felt like the distance came from her, not him. Her life away from Henry was still opaque to him. She came and went when she wanted with no explanation, she only seemed to barely be pursuing a career in theater, and he'd never heard a word about any friends she had outside of Henry's circle of acquaintances.

The glow of romance, the kind that eventually develops into love, seemed out of reach—not because he didn't want it, but because the basic elements for it remained absent. They had no trust, little respect it seemed, and even less mutual admiration. Star was beautiful and insatiable, but it was increasingly hard for him to admire a girl he felt he barely knew. He wondered if maybe he was just growing up, leaving his adolescent instincts behind and beginning to seek something more than gratification. And now that he was about to graduate law school...

As he soaped his body, he glanced down and smiled. He knew one thing for sure: that Mr. Niner had no complaints, much less any intentions of giving up the girl of his dreams no matter what Henry thought.

CHAPTER 32
GET THE SHOW ON THE ROAD

RICHARD WATCHED THE CITY FLASH BY FROM THE WINDOW OF HIS limousine without really seeing the buildings. Like always, he was turning over his plans in his head, probing for weaknesses and potential problems. The fresh air flowing in through the driver's window—which he kept open to help get rid of his overpowering body odor, thanks to his trimethylaminuria—helped keep Richard's head clear and sharp.

His plans so far had been proceeding well, but things were coming to a head sooner than he'd expected. Earlier that week, he had received a call from Colonel McIntosh, Charles's commanding officer in Belfast. McIntosh had advised Richard that Charles had submitted a request asking for an early release from his command and to have his active duty tour status changed to inactive. Apparently, Charles was done playing soldier and ready to return to London to take over the throne.

Richard had naturally ordered McIntosh to deny the request, and then he himself had talked to Charles and suggested that an early release wouldn't look good. It would look like Charles was pulling strings to get special treatment, he said, and ordinary people would resent it. Just as Richard, a master manipulator, had known he would, Charles had agreed. But still…this meant that Richard had only about 85 days to complete his plans. Once Charles returned to Buckingham and filled that empty throne, Richard would be removed as regent and everything would end.

That wasn't acceptable.

The limo pulled up to the abandoned estate where he had agreed to meet Sir Melvyn. Richard exited the car as fast as his bulk would allow and waddled up to the door. He entered and found Melvyn standing by the dormant fireplace in the entry hall. The house was dark, damp, and empty and smelled almost as badly as Richard.

"Where can we sit?" Richard wheezed, dispensing with any pleasantries.

Melvyn pointed the way to the dusty drawing room just off the hall. "In here, sir."

The two entered the once splendid room and Melvyn removed some dust covers from the upholstered chairs. The room was dark and dank and had apparently been out of service for some time.

Richard fell into one of the chairs, which groaned under his weight. "Let me get down to business, Melvyn," he said. "We have a lot to do and a very short time."

Melvyn sat on a nearby dusty chair and listened.

"Charles has requested to be discharged so he can return to London and assume his role. I was able to defer it, but not for long. He means to come back here, and that means we must act now."

"I see."

"First we must siphon off as much money as possible and get it into the untraceable accounts in the Caymans. Can you tell me how much we have now?"

Melvyn opened the updated ledger and read the balances: "It looks like we have 375,000 pounds in transit and 14 million secure in Cayman."

"And what can be added in the next two or three months?"

"Probably something in the neighborhood of 475,000."

"No chance of more?"

"Sir, that is a fortune and I don't think bleeding the purse for more would do anything but arouse notice, something you certainly don't want to do."

"Right, okay. Now how about the motherload...the art? One piece alone can fetch enough to make the Cayman stash look like chicken feed!"

"The fakes are just about completed, another two or three weeks at most. I have the men in Poland lined up and ready to fly here on a private aircraft any time we are ready. They will replace the paintings with the fakes, leaving their frames, and fly the originals to Switzerland. As for the fire, as you know, I'm not onboard for framing and then killing one of the guards. That's out."

"Look Melvyn, I'm the one who decides what's in and what's not. However, as much as I hate to admit it, you have a point. I think it would be less complicated if the fire was an accident, with no perpetrators. There would be no questions from surviving relatives and formal inquiries. It can get messy when someone dies, bloody relatives and stuff."

Melvyn heaved a sigh of relief. "As for the fire, it will be set up to look like spontaneous combustion caused by unknown chemicals being used in an abutting storage area. All very professional."

"Who's going to do it and are they traceable?"

"I found two pyromaniacs from Morocco who will be more than glad to do the deed, and of course are totally unaware of the motive. All they will know is that they can start a fire, pick up some loot, and get away with it. That's what they are all about. After the fire, you can arrange to have them deported through your MI5 connections. Once out of the country, you'll never hear from them again."

"Superb. See what you can do when you set your mind to it?" Richard paused, then plunged into the more delicate part of his message. "Now to deal with the Charles problem. I have a good man on the inside with Charles. From what I understand, they're almost best mates. According to this man, part of the reason Charles wants to get back to London is thanks to a BBC reporter he has the hots for. At first, I wondered if this woman could come in handy, but her background is unfortunately spotless. This means that Charles needs to become a war hero sooner than later."

Melvyn visibly shuddered at the thought. "How do you know you can trust this man of yours?"

"Oh, I have no doubt he'll do what we want when the time comes. Let's just say there are some skeletons in his closet. Seems he has a passion for little girls and sometimes little boys too. Apparently, there's quite a dossier on him. I've read it, and some of the things in there would curl your tender toes, Melvyn. And put him on the inside for the rest of his life. I'm sure you must know what they do to pedophiles in prison, don't you? They make it bloody hell. Most of them don't live though their sentence."

Melvyn just shook his head in disgust, and Richard went on, "So yes, that plan is in motion now. I'm not sure exactly when and how yet, but it will be soon and it will have to look like a casualty of war."

Melvyn couldn't even bring himself to nod.

"And that leaves only Henry as the last obstacle. My sources in Boston say he's about to graduate and is consumed with some case against the Carnegie Trust, which apparently cut his father off and turned the family out without a penny. If he were to somehow prevail in this effort, he would suddenly gain access to billions of dollars. This worries me. If he has that kind of money, there is no telling what he will do. So it looks like Henry has to be neutralized. Any suggestions?"

Melvyn shook his head miserably. "None whatsoever."

"Hmm, I thought you wouldn't. Well, I'll have to speak to Badger. There might be some ideas there."

"I hear what you are saying, and your intentions are clear, but I'm not sure I can be party to any of it," Melvyn said, sitting up straighter. "Not when it comes to killing people or ruining their lives. You must understand that is not in me and it shouldn't be part of any decent human being. If—"

"Oh, shut up," Richard said. "Don't bore me. It's far too late for you to change anything, Melvyn. Forget your original crimes. Do you really think I'm stupid enough to have my fingerprints on the looting of the royal treasury or the plans to steal the royal artwork? As far as an investigation would be concerned, that was the sole work of...you. And once all that came out, I'm sure the press would soon get wind of your other problems. You are a disgusting excuse for a man, one not worth his salt in any measure. A bloody train wreck. Do you understand?"

Melvyn sat stunned through Sir Richard's tirade, his face growing whiter by the second.

Richard heaved himself up out of his chair to stand in front of Melvyn. "I said DO YOU UNDERSTAND?"

Moved to tears, Melvyn whispered, "Yes, I understand, completely."

"Good. Don't ever forget it."

CHAPTER 33
I Want to Hold Your Hand

S OMEONE FINALLY ANSWERED AFTER FOUR RINGS: "GOOD MORNING, BBC World News Headquarters, how may I direct your call?"

Charles, nervously gripping Beatrice's business card in one hand and the phone in the other, said, "Yes, I'd like Extension 294, Miss Grandton's office."

"One moment please and I'll connect you."

The phone went silent for a moment and then rang repeatedly before being answered.

"Beatrice Grandton speaking."

"Ah, yes, Beatrice? Is that you?"

"Yes, it is, may I ask who is calling?"

"It's Charles," he stammered, "do you remember me? We met in Belfast with Captain Morgan Fairfield."

"Charles?" she said, "you say I met you in Belfast? With who?"

"Captain Fairfield, Morgan Fairfield, at the officer's club?"

"Oh, that Charles, the Charles who is also king of the country?" She laughed lightly and he realized she'd been playing with him. "Of course I remember you! How are you? Where are you?"

"I'm still in Belfast, still doing my bit for God and country."

"Brilliant. Are you safe?"

"At least for now I am. Our missions are very dangerous, and I have to mind my way and protect my men and all that."

"Of course, I've been there and seen what's going on. A bloody shame and so senseless."

"Yes, it is a pity." He paused to gather his courage and blurt out the question he was dying to ask, but at the last minute he chickened out and instead said, "The reason I'm calling is to ask when your TV special will be airing. Morgan told me that you returned to London to host it live and I don't want to miss it."

"Oh, that's really nice of you. It will be aired in London next Monday at 8:00 p.m. I'm not sure which channel it will be on in Belfast. But I can check for you if you like."

"Yes, I like that very much. Shall I hold?"

"Right, please do. I'll be back directly." Beatrice jumped up from her desk and walked over to the station manager's office just across the room. "Pardon me, Burt, is my special airing in Belfast? If so, what station?"

Burt, the burly station manager, looked up and curtly asked, "Who wants to know?"

"Oh, it's just the King of England. He's on the phone and is inquiring."

"I say! The King of England? Please spare me. I'll bet he just can't wait to see your show, ha ha."

"Come on, Burt, stop harassing me. Do you know or not?"

"Let me check." Burt opened the broadcast program file and ran his finger down the list of affiliate stations. "Ah, yes, here it is. Tell his majesty that it will be airing at 9 p.m. Belfast time, BBC Channel 4. Or if he prefers, we can do a command performance for him...tell him to bring along the Prime Minister and the Queen Mum too."

Beatrice thanked Burt, briskly walked back to her desk, and told Charles the particulars.

"Do you have any plans to come back to Belfast anytime soon?" he asked.

"Not sure, Charles. There is some talk of doing a follow up on this special. Sort of a second look, but it's not certain yet."

"Well, if you do get back, please let me know. I'd, uh, enjoy seeing you again. We can hang out at the club and maybe catch some of that gourmet Irish cooking, if there is such a thing!"

The line went silent for long enough that Charles started to worry. Then she said, "Are you asking me out, Charles?"

He was totally taken aback by Beatrice's forwardness. Charles was far from practiced with women. He was embarrassed by the fact that he really had no experience to speak of, unlike the epic carnal episodes of his brother Henry. Charles stumbled into an awkward reply: "Oh no, uh, I mean, yes, well, I mean if you are around and have nothing better to do, then I thought that we'd—"

"Charles, relax," she said. "I'd love to have dinner with you, and when I get back to Belfast, we must certainly make it a date."

"Perfect, I'd fancy that."

The couple rang off after Charles gave Beatrice his phone number, leaving Charles feeling more satisfied with himself than he had in a long time. He realized this was the first time he had done something on his own in years. Calling Beatrice wasn't arranged for him, or expected or monitored. It had nothing to do with being "king," and sometimes Charles felt like that was all he ever did: prepare to be king.

———◆———

The next morning, Beatrice sat at a table at the weekly meeting of the editorial staff and the producers of her show. She brought up the topic of doing another special in Belfast.

"Well, Bea," said Josh Donavan, the executive producer. "It's a bit early to commit to that. After all, your first show hasn't aired and there are no ratings to base a second shot at the subject."

"Ratings rule, of course," Beatrice said. "But there's something you don't know. One of the reasons I want to go back to Belfast is that I have made an excellent contact who can give me a very special perspective into both the military and political points of view from the very top of the government. It could be unique and revealing."

"Who is the excellent contact?" Josh said, sounding bored.

Beatrice coyly looked up from her notes as if she had been checking for the name in them. "It's a friend of mine, his name is Charles."

"Charles who?"

Enjoying the tease, Beatrice continued, "Well, I'm not sure. I think he uses Seventh."

"Seventh? Weird surname for a bloke," Josh fired back.

"Well, he has several last names," she said. "But he often goes by his title, His Majesty Charles VII."

Dead silence filled the room. "Are you shitting me?" Josh finally said, starting to rub his hands together like he'd won a lottery. "King Charles, the boy king? The one from America? That Charles?"

"Christ, he called here the other day but I thought you were pulling my chain," said Burt, the station manager.

"Indeed, that Charles," Beatrice said. "By the way, he's no longer a boy, but a handsome and brave lieutenant serving in his majesty's Royal Army."

"He's serving in his own army!" Josh said. "Tell us more. Everything."

When Beatrice finished relating her brief encounter with Charles, you could practically hear the wheels spinning as a room full of media professionals contemplated this news.

"Beatrice, pack your bags the minute your special is over. You are going to Belfast and latching on to this story like a dog on a bone. It looks like you have exclusive access to someone who's never given an interview, or for that matter, someone no one has ever met. Aside from his coronation, he's been virtually invisible, vanished into who knows where."

"Yes!" chimed in a staffer named Courtney. "There's a million questions I'd like to ask him. He's like a secret king. I'll bet it would be the interview of the year, maybe the decade!"

"Not to mention that every twenty-something woman in the country would tune in!" said a young female intern. "He's hot!"

Everyone laughed, until Josh took control of the meeting again. "Vince," he said, pointing to the head of the video department. "Get the best video guy we've got and send him along with Beatrice." He pointed to another producer, "Merle, you go too, and make sure we have the best written copy. Peter—"

"Wait a minute! Wait a minute!" Beatrice interrupted. "Let's not put the cart before the horse. We mustn't spook Charles. He's a bit shy, and if we all show up like a flock of vultures it won't work. Let me go and develop the relationship, and then we will see what he is willing to do, or more importantly, what he is not willing to do."

Josh sat down and reluctantly agreed. "You're right, Beatrice. Let's play it cool. You call the shots and we'll follow your lead."

<hr />

Beatrice's special on Belfast aired the day after her meeting and it was a huge success. It was aired nationwide as well as throughout most of the British Commonwealth. Among the most important of the millions of viewers was Charles, who watched alone in his billet. He was still torn on the legitimacy of the struggle and the efficacy of the factions, but he was also a partisan if only because he was king of the country supporting actual combat. He found the show difficult to watch in parts—with scenes of bombings and shootings flashing across his screen—but he was mesmerized by Beatrice. She looked even more beautiful on TV than she did in person. As the program ended and the credits rolled, Charles hoped he would see Beatrice again.

He didn't have to wait long. Two days after the airing of the special, Beatrice arrived back in Belfast and called him. Rather than going to her hotel, the couple arranged to meet at the officer's club for drinks.

Charles arrived first. As always, an armed security man shadowed him and sat nearby. Charles, dressed in civilian clothes, nervously sat at the bar, and ordered a gin and tonic. His good looks were uncommon, but other than that he fit into the bar crowd as just another bloke. Within a few minutes, he spotted Beatrice at the entrance. She was even more attractive than he remembered. Blue! She was wearing blue! How could she know that was his favorite color? Of course she couldn't have, but it was a good omen as far as he was concerned.

Like a shy schoolboy, Charles rushed up to her. "Hi, you look beautiful, thank you for coming."

"Oh, you are so sweet, thank you for noticing," she said. "And thank you for asking me out."

They sat together at the bar, enjoying cocktails just like so many other officers and their girls did night after night. Charles, who was pretty much a novice at dating, found it far less challenging to engage in conversation than he'd expected.

After a second round of drinks Charles said, "Beatrice, are you hungry?"

"Starved, I haven't eaten all day except for a cup of tea and biscuit at four."

"Great. I hope you don't mind, but they don't exactly have gourmet restaurants around here, although they do have a pub that serves a wonderful steak and ale pie. What do you say?"

"Lovely, I'm in."

"It's called the Duke of York, on Cornmarket Square. Do you know it?"

"No, I don't. But I do know that you have a brother and he *is* the Duke of York."

"You mean Henry? You know, I never connected that before. How did you?"

"Charles, I'm in the news business, it's my job to know things like that."

"So that means you must know everything about me too?"

"A lot," she laughed. "But not the kind of things I want to know."

"Such as?"

"Like what kind of person you are. What you think and what you believe in. How you feel and what you want in life. Do you pray? What do you hope for? Those are the kinds of things I want to know. In short, you as a person, not an icon."

Charles laughed out loud at the suggestion that he was an icon. "Wow, that's pretty heavy, an icon. May I ask why you need to know all this?"

"Well, it's my personality, I'm inquisitive by nature. I see something in you that I just genuinely like and want to know more."

The couple strolled the few blocks, discreetly followed by the guard, to the pub and took a table in the corner. A waiter approached. "Evening folks, get ya a pint of Gat to start?"

"Not for me," Beatrice answered. "I'll stick with white wine."

"And for the gent?"

"Oh, Guinness, I mean Gat, is fine for me."

The couple ordered the house specialty of steak and ale pie and washed it down with a couple more drinks and lots of conversation. Charles found himself being honest with Beatrice, much more than he was with almost anyone else. He confessed that he felt like a victim of destiny and that the whole thing still seemed like a dream to him, a bad one at that. He even told her about his father and how much he missed him.

Gradually, as he loosened up, so did she. She told him about her wonderful family and her father's successful business career, about her days at Bryn Mawr College in Pennsylvania followed by a year at Oxford. She talked about the daily struggle she and many women faced in the chauvinistic broadcast business. Beatrice shared her hope that one day she would settle down and raise a family, but only after she met her career goals and found the right chap.

The evening ended far too soon for both of them. As Charles walked Beatrice back to her hotel, he took her arm and turned to her. "I hope we can be together again. When are you leaving Ireland?"

"I have a few more days here, how about you?"

"I applied for an early out, but it was denied, so I'm here for a couple of more months, maybe three at the most."

"Denied? Isn't that strange? I'd think you would have a little pull on something like that."

"Well, it's about completing my commitment here. I understand that it is important to set an example and not cop out on the others. Duty is duty, especially for someone like me."

"Well, you will be careful, things here get very nasty."

The Fitzwilliam Hotel came into sight as they turned the corner.

"Beatrice, I hope you had as good of a time as I did!"

"I did, honestly, it was a really nice night. Thank you."

"No, thank you. I know you're not going to believe this, but it's been one of the best nights I've had since I left America. No kidding."

"Thank you for that too. Charles, you are an amazing man and I know you will someday be revered and loved by the people. I know I don't know you well, but I can already tell. You have what it takes to be not only a king, but a man of the people, one with integrity and sincerity. That's a rare gift. You have something else too, Charles."

"What's that?"

"You have a good heart, one that would be easily loved and a kindness and innocence rarely seen. It's more than refreshing…it's inspiring."

Charles blushed as he stared into her eyes and wondered if he was already falling for her. "Will you see me again?"

"That would be lovely!" she said. "What would work for you?"

"Not tomorrow night, there's a mission." He grimaced. "Whoops, I shouldn't have said that. It's always hush-hush, you won't say anything, will you?

"Of course not, Charles."

"Good. Now about next time, would Sunday be okay?"

"Yes, I'd fancy that. I'll look forward to it."

Charles was far too shy to kiss Beatrice good night so he simply grasped her hand and tenderly covered it with his other one. "Good night, I'll see you Sunday, let's make a day of it...a picnic lunch and then dinner too!"

CHAPTER 34
BLOOD COUNTS

"MMM, BABY, DO YOU *HAVE* TO LEAVE SO EARLY?"

Star was reaching for Henry and pulling him back down into bed as he tried to get up. It was just past dawn and he was distracted by the thought of his long day ahead with Professors Greenway and Haverman. Still, when he looked down at her groping for him, he figured he could spare a few minutes. Like so many times before, Henry and his best friend Mr. Niner answered Star's early morning call.

When they were done, he jogged to the shower and emerged minutes later from the steaming bathroom in his standard uniform: skin tight jeans and a Harvard tee. He was out the door with the early morning light still pink in the sky and a truly gorgeous morning. This was rare in New England, and he took his time to enjoy it as he walked to Greenway's building on campus. Julian, having become comfortable with Henry's solo romps about the campus, stayed home, hoping again that Star was getting ready for an encore with the lead's stand-in.

When he arrived, Haverman was already there with Greenway, both of them drinking some of the terrible sludge that Professor

Greenway called coffee and brewed up in an ancient pot that Henry had never seen washed. Greenway looked up as Henry came in.

"Come in, my boy," he said. "We just started, you haven't missed anything."

Sheepishly smiling, Henry said: "I'm sorry I'm late, but something came up this morning and I had to—"

"You're not late, Henry, we're early. So just sit down and relax. Some coffee?"

Henry glanced at his watch. He was actually late, but he realized that Professor Greenway was excusing his tardiness so he wouldn't feel guilty about it. It was just the kind of thing a loving parent would do.

"Thank you, sir, but no thanks on the coffee."

As Henry sat down, Greenway and Haverman picked up the conversation they were having. "At this point, we hopefully have Whitman rattled a little bit, but...I don't know how strong our position really is. I really wish we had those journals. I'm convinced they'd speak directly at least to one of the will's requirements, that William was raised as a Carnegie, and wouldn't be surprised if there was something in there that would be grounds to modify the original trustee's narrow interpretation."

Haverman grimaced. "You're right of course, Preston, but you saw Whitman's answer to the judge. He says he doesn't have them."

"Do you think he's lying?" Henry said. "Do you think he has them or knows where they are and is just stonewalling to protect himself or others?"

"Who knows? It would be a serious violation for a member of the bar to knowingly hide subpoenaed material. Such a serious action, if proven, could get Whitman disbarred and criminal charges brought against him. I can't imagine he'd be that stupid. But he certainly wouldn't be the first to flagrantly scoff the law."

Henry uttered a short, bitter laugh. "Professor, Paul Whitman was in a position to do a lot more for my father then he did. When my father's true birth situation was revealed, Paul Whitman was the first one my father told—and he was the first one to drop my father like a hot potato. He did nothing to help and, in fact, I'm told that it almost seemed like he felt he was being handed an opportunity to take control of the Carnegie money and trust. Based on his own history, I would not put anything past Paul Whitman or his conflicted band of trustees."

Greenway and Haverman looked at each other. "Henry," Greenway said, "if we win this case, there will likely be a substantial monetary reward for you. Even if we don't win outright, you are likely in a position to force a substantial settlement from Whitman. Wouldn't that be enough? Or are you looking to avenge your family and make accountable the persons who were responsible?"

Henry didn't answer right away. His speech had caught him by surprise and he hadn't expected his anger to well up so forcefully. It reminded him of the deep-seated anger he had felt at his father's funeral, or when he was stuck at Eton against his wishes. He took a deep breath to calm himself.

"I don't know, Professor," he said honestly. "I can't just let Paul Whitman and his kind get away with this. It's dishonest, and it hurt my family."

Professor Haverman cleared his throat. "We understand, Henry. I'm sure you've heard that in many cases, the cover-up is worse than the crime. For what it's worth, I tend to agree with you about Whitman. Something smells fishy with his answer. If he is lying about those journals, or has destroyed them, and we can prove it, he will pay the price for his crime. As for revenge, your motivations are totally irrelevant to the case. We either win this thing on our own merits, and the merits of the case, or justice isn't served. It's that simple."

"Thank you," Henry said. "I really appreciate it."

"We're doing the right thing," Professor Greenway added. "No question about it. Now, let's just see what Judge Lowenstein has to say."

———•———

Three weeks later, Henry found himself in a suit and tie, sitting at a table in front of Judge Lowenstein in the New York City Second District Court. He was surprisingly nervous about the outcome of today's session, in part because neither Greenway nor Haverman had any real sense of what was going to happen.

Prior to that day's court session, both Henry and Whitman had agreed to a bench trial in lieu of a jury trial, knowing that if the results were unsatisfactory either party could appeal. All of the evidence and depositions had been duly submitted and reviewed by the judge. The parties gathered in the small downtown second district courtroom precisely at 9:45 a.m.

"All rise!" barked the court bailiff. "For the Honorable Judge Aaron Lowenstein."

Judge Lowenstein entered, looked around his courtroom, and took his chair behind the bench. Lowenstein was a well-respected man of the bench. His reputation was spotless and his jurisprudence learned. Small in frame, slightly balding and bespectacled, His Honor was in his late sixties and looked more academic than Wall Street.

"Be seated, gentlemen," he said. "Professor Greenway, please proceed."

Professor Greenway stood up and cleared his throat before he addressed the judge. "Your Honor," he began, "in summary, we are presenting our claim as a simple one. There should be no doubt or question as to the validity of my client's eligibility to be the full and undisputed heir to the Carnegie estate and Trust based on, as I said, a simple and clear statement of facts. In his own hand the originator of the Carnegie Trust, Fillmore Blair Carnegie, wrote in the simplest and clearest of terms the qualifiers to be a beneficiary. And I quote, in part from the actual handwritten document:

It is my desire and decree as my last will and testament that no one may inherit or have benefit from my estate, inclusive of my property, money, businesses, investments or any other tangible or intangible assets unless they have Carnegie blood flowing through their veins. No wife, no ex-wife, nor paramour of a decedent thereof may have stake in or access to this legacy which is solely intended for those raised by Carnegies with Carnegie blood. There will be no exception, under any circumstance to alter or sub-jugate, this, my fervent and final degree.

Greenway paused for effect and then reiterated, "The aforesaid mentioned, the mandate set forth in Fillmore Carnegie's last will and testament were just two simple tenets. First, that a trust beneficiary must have Carnegie blood running through their veins and, secondly, that they be raised by Carnegies. We are focusing our present effort on the second tenet, that the plaintiff was raised by Carnegies.

"In the case of Henry Carnegie Bolin-Stuart, the plaintiff, obviously he was raised by his birth parents, said William Carnegie and his wife Elizabeth, neither of them Carnegies. However, we have presented clear and documented evidence that the plaintiff was also raised by Ambassador Carnegie himself. There is substantial existing evidence to support this, and we believe there is even more compelling evidence that has yet to come to light.

"We are aware that the deceased Ambassador kept meticulous journals that no doubt would reflect on his paternal feelings toward Henry, a boy he clearly cherished. And perhaps even reference in said journals his intention to alter or amend or make other provisions for his beloved grandchild contradictory to the trust's disenfranchisement language. These journals were entrusted to Paul Whitman, chairman of the board of the Carnegie Trust and one of the defendants." Greenway paused again. "Mr. Whitman currently claims he does not know the whereabouts of these journals, although they were allegedly under his exclusive guardianship as Ambassador Carnegie's attorney."

He let an accusatory silence draw out, then continued, "Nonetheless, based on admitted affidavits by eyewitnesses and photographic evidence, Ambassador Carnegie had material and constant association with the plaintiff in the form of regular cohabiting, innumerable travel excursions, and frequent participation in his rearing. This participation took the form of attending many of the plaintiff's school events, birthdays, holidays, extended vacations, visits, and the like. So clearly, the plaintiff was raised by Carnegies in the truest sense of the word. Having established meeting that criterion, we ask the court to find accordingly and confirm that the plaintiff was raised by Carnegies."

The judge did not comment, but simply made some notes on his legal pad. He looked up, giving the signal for Greenway to proceed.

"And now, Your Honor, we turn to the will's remaining qualifier, the one addressing Carnegie blood running through the plaintiff's veins. It was on this point that the trust originally stripped the plaintiff's father of his beneficiary status with the trust. The trust moved forward on this single provision, namely the blood relative requirement that, in fact, should not necessarily have been the single basis for total disfranchising of William Carnegie, or for that matter his son the plaintiff. The trustees grouped the exclusion of wives, paramours, and others into the same status as those raised by Carnegies. Fillmore Carnegie did not intend to exclude family members or those persons treated, recognized, and raised as Carnegies—be it blood or not. The creator clearly was exempting only third parties from attempting to benefit from the trust and in fact specially allowed those raised by Carnegies to inherit as proffered in the second tenet of his will."

Greenway stepped back from the bench and gave a reassuring glance to Henry. "That is all for now, Your Honor."

Judge Lowenstein paused in thought and began slowly. "Thank you, counselor. That was very concise and enlightening." He glanced at the defendant's table, where some of the highest-priced lawyers in the country sat without expression, something they were well paid to do. "Gentlemen, are you ready to proceed?"

"Yes, Your Honor. We are." These words were spoken by Leon Peck, who was the lead attorney representing the defendant. Peck was looking especially skeletal as he rose and addressed the judge.

"Your Honor, pursuant to our proffered brief, we are in serious disagreement with the plaintiff's supposition. It is our clear contention that the most important of the criteria set forth in Fillmore Blair Carnegie's last will and testament has not been met. To suggest otherwise is laughable! That criteria being the requirement that Carnegie blood is running through a beneficiary's veins. The plaintiffs appear to be arguing that the intent of the will's creator differs from his actual words, that his lack of Carnegie blood is a mere technicality. Your Honor, notwithstanding the observation that the law relies upon technicalities for precision, our contention is that it could not be more clear what the will's creator intended, and could not equally be more clear that neither William nor the plaintiff meet this requirement. We are asking you to dismiss this case."

The judge regarded Peck calmly for a few minutes. "Thank you," he finally said. "Do you dispute the plaintiff's claim that he was raised by Carnegies, as a Carnegie?"

"Your Honor, there is no way to accurately divine intentions in this case," Peck said firmly.

"But if we could, would it reflect on the plaintiff's status as a Carnegie family member?"

"No, Your Honor, we don't believe it would."

The judge paused again, then continued, "I see, thank you. Well, gentlemen, thank you for your time today. Before we adjourn, however, I would like to point out that I did in fact request that the trust and Mr. Whitman specifically turn over the journals, as they might have a material bearing on the case. I still believe those journals might be important. I would urge the defendant to continue to fervently look for the missing evidence and, should it be found, deliver it to this court immediately. That withstanding, I will review all the facts and documents of the case as we know them now and issue a written judgment. Meantime, I strongly encourage both parties to meet and negotiate an amicable solution prior to my ruling. If you can resolve this matter, please notify the court's clerk immediately. We stand adjourned."

"All rise!" shouted out the bailiff as Judge Lowenstein left the courtroom.

The Harvard contingent walked toward the door and Professor Greenway extended his hand to Henry. "Well, Henry, how did you like your first case?"

"It was awesome, Professor, I can't believe my case study idea turned into a full-fledged legal action in a real court. Thank you! How do you think we did?"

"I'm not sure…one can never be. The court is fickle. But I think his line of questioning really didn't give much of a hint into his thinking. My gut tells me this is no shoo-in and I'm not sure we are in a particularly strong position. From the expression on the judge's face, I'd say we have an outside chance of prevailing…but who knows?"

"How long do you think it will take to get the ruling?" Henry asked.

"One can never predict that, but usually it's a few weeks. But there is no set rule. The judge could get lazy and go on vacation, or just put it aside for a while."

"Yikes!" Henry said.

"You said it, Henry. Now, let's go get a good German dinner at Luchow's. I'm buying."

As they left, Professor Greenway put his arm around Henry and pulled him close, signaling how fond he was of this incredibly bright and unassuming young man.

The trip back to Boston was a quiet one. The professors kept their noses buried in the pages of material they used to prepare for the hearing, re-litigating it over and over in their heads. Henry stared out the window, looking at the landscape rushing by as the Metro reached one hundred miles an hour. Professor Greenway finally looked up and spoke as he tapped his pen on the binder containing Paul Whitman's deposition. "Clearly, it is in our best interests to find those journals before we get Lowenstein's ruling, after which it will be too late," he said. "I'm convinced with the addition of that evidence, our case would be much more compelling. It will be like the Ambassador speaking from the grave in support of Henry's importance to him and how he thought of Henry as his own flesh and blood."

Haverman nodded in agreement. "I think so too, and it sounds like the judge agreed. Any ideas how we could find them?"

"Henry, your mother told you about the journals and that she thought that Paul Whitman had them, right?" Greenway said.

"Yes, Professor."

"Further, your mother said something about Whitman writing his biography, but to her knowledge he never did. The Ambassador was a pretty famous man, with close connections to presidents, congressmen, and celebrities."

"He knew everybody," Henry confirmed. "Once he even had Michael Jackson sing at his house. When my father ran for vice president, the Ambassador took us all to the White House to meet the sitting president. I even got to see the Oval Office and sit at the president's desk. It was pretty cool."

"Well, someone that connected and famous must have had lots of mementos…you know, gifts from important people, autographs, and maybe even pictures of their grandson sitting at the president's desk. So where are they?"

"I have no idea," Henry answered. "When we moved to England, just about everything we had, including personal items, was left behind. The trust claimed ownership of all valuable assets since they were purchased by trust money and they no longer belonged to us. They even took my mother's jewelry and our cars. It was devastating."

"Henry, have you considered getting in touch with the State Department?" Greenway asked. "Maybe someone there who knew the Ambassador and would be willing to help us. We might get a lead."

"That's a great idea!" Henry said. "But I don't know anyone at the State Department."

"Try starting with the British Embassy," Haverman said.

"British Embassy?" Henry said, confused. "Why would I call them?"

"It's safe to assume the British ambassador has contacts throughout the State Department, and he'll only be too happy to help."

"Why would he want to help me?" Henry asked.

Professor Greenway burst out laughing. "Charming! Henry, you never cease to amaze me. Did you forget you are the Prince of York?"

"Oh. That." Henry looked down to hide his blushing. "I hate pulling strings like that."

"Only because you're the best kind of person," Greenway said warmly. "But in this case, I think it's worth it."

"Right."

The next morning, Henry called the British Embassy and was pleasantly surprised how quickly he was put straight through to the ambassador, a Sir Arthur Arnold Sturbridge who sounded exactly like the stuffy snobs Henry had escaped at Eton. Still, Sturbridge virtually tripped over himself in his haste to help Henry and immediately suggested that Henry make the trip to Washington, DC to visit the embassy in person and assured Henry he would contact his friends at the State Department to help in any way that he could. He even offered to send the official embassy Lear jet to pick up Henry and was mortified when Henry insisted on taking the Metro train. In the end, Henry prevailed, and set up a date for Julian and him to take the train to Washington and start their hunt for the missing journals.

CHAPTER 35
THE WAY YOU LOOK TONIGHT

C HARLES WALKED OUT OF HIS ROOM AND SAW SERGEANT THOMPSON sitting on the front stoop of their billet having a smoke.

"Thompson, mind if I join you?" he said.

Jumping to his feet, Thompson promptly replied, "Sir, not at all, but it would be most irregular, wouldn't it?"

Charles waved off the concern. "Please! Sit."

The two men sat quietly for a few minutes. The sergeant offered his commanding officer a cigarette, but Charles refused and gazed out at the beautiful Irish night.

"Sir, I have to say that it is really amazing to me that you would sit on a stoop with a mere commoner, being that you are who you are, you know..." Thompson trailed off.

"Sergeant, you have to understand something. I was raised just like any other kid in a place where anyone can sit on a stoop with anyone else. Then my whole world was turned upside down, and I ended up being a bloody king. I didn't choose that, it chose me. I might add, the price has been high. There is no free lunch with any of this. This is who

I am, just another bloke like you, who likes to sit on a stoop and chat with anyone he chooses."

"That sounds so common, especially for a king."

"Well, Thompson, maybe it is. Maybe I'm the commoner's king. I sort of like that idea. Don't you?"

"I'm not so sure. In Britain, we are all taught to hold the Royals on a pedestal, look up to them and almost worship them."

"Ha ha. Save your worshiping for God. He's the only one who deserves it. And as far as pedestals go, I prefer a stoop. Just like this one. Now let's change the subject. I'll be going home soon. It's been a long time and I'm ready to get back and start my life. How about you? When is your tour up?"

"Well, sir, it's another six months, and God willing I'll get out of here alive. You know, it makes me laugh to hear you. You sound like any Tommy Atkins wanting to go home and pick up where they left off."

"Who's Tommy Atkins?"

"Whoops. Sorry, sir. That's what we enlisted men call a typical soldier in the army. Much like the Yanks used GI Joe. But like I was saying, you aren't exactly going back to pump petrol or drive a lorry. You're going home to be a bloody king! That's unreal to somebody like me."

Charles laughed. "It's even more unreal to me." A comfortable silence developed between them, until Charles said, "Sorry, Sergeant, I have to go now and get ready. I'm seeing Beatrice later and want to be all spiffed up. See ya."

"Good night, sir, and thank you."

"For what?"

"I don't know...I guess just for being such a regular chap."

The two men parted as friends, a fact that caused a guilty lump to swell in Thompson's chest.

When Charles arrived at the Fitzwilliam hotel, Beatrice was waiting for him in the modest lobby, sitting by the fire. Charles paused and watched the glow of the fire on her beautiful face. She was so lovely. "I think I'm in love with her," he thought.

The thought seemed to come out of nowhere and startled him, but deep down he knew it was true. He had recently begun to count down the days when his service commitment would be over and he could go back to London, where Beatrice lived. It was the first time in his entire life he was able to make his own plans, and he was excited about it. He was at last ready to move on and maybe, just maybe, have someone like Beatrice at his side. He'd even allowed himself to think about marrying her. She was a perfect match for him. She was intelligent, kind, understanding, and funny. His mother would be relieved to also find out that Beatrice was a British subject, came from an aristocratic family, and was baptized and confirmed in the Church of England—a definite must for any future queen as dictated in the Act of Settlement.

Beatrice looked up from her seat and her face lit up. He crossed the room quickly and leaned down to kiss her cheek. "How are you?" he asked.

She leaned up from her chair and kissed him back and grabbed his hand. "Oh Charles, I'm fine, and so glad to see you. I've missed you and really worry when you are not nearby."

"Worry about what? There's nothing to worry about."

"Oh no, not much. How about those crazed IRA who would love to put a bullet in any Englishman they could? When you are on those missions, I'm sick with worry."

"Oh that! Let's not dwell on it. How about we get a good meal and maybe some dancing too?"

"Dancing? I didn't know you like to dance."

"Well, I really don't like it that much, not much experience at it, but it gives me a chance to hold you close and feel our hearts beating as one."

"Oh, how sweet, Charles. You are so sweet. I can't believe how gentle and caring you are."

After an intimate dinner at a local spot, the couple danced to the music of a sole piano player who tickled the keys and sang an old-fashioned tune, "The Way You Look Tonight". Holding each other tightly, they were able to put all their cares and concerns aside. At least for a few moments. The lyrics engulfed the room and Charles whispered the words in Beatrice's ear:

OH BUT YOU'RE LOVELY

WITH YOUR SMILE SO WARM

AND YOUR CHEEKS SO SOFT

THERE IS NOTHING FOR ME, BUT TO LOVE YOU

JUST THE WAY YOU LOOK TONIGHT.

Afterward, the couple walked hand-in-hand back to the hotel. Spontaneously, Charles took Beatrice in his arms and kissed her deeply. "You know I've fallen in love with you and I hope you love me too."

"I do, really, and I'm frightened by it. I've never known love before. We live in such a dangerous time and place, and I fear our love could be snuffed out in a split second." Beatrice shuddered and Charles held her close.

"Don't worry. This will soon be over and we can return home to the safety and sanity of another world. You and me. That is, if you'll have me? I come with a lot of baggage."

"Baggage? Whatever do you mean?"

"Like having a duty beyond the military one. Like never having a single second of privacy or peace of mind. Like having to always to be noble and wise, even though I am not. That kind of baggage."

Beatrice looked deep into Charles's eyes. "Then I'll be your porter. I will gladly help you carry your baggage with pride and dignity and yes, love, the kind that you can count on until we are taken from each other by death. I do love you and never forget it!"

Charles was seized with a deep happiness and kissed her again, thinking that this moment would forever change his life.

———•——•———

Not far away from the spot where Charles and Beatrice held each other and kissed, Sergeant Thompson picked up a phone in a remote call-box and placed a call to Colonel McIntosh.

"Sir, this is Sergeant Thompson," he said when McIntosh picked up the phone.

"Right, Sergeant, go on."

"Sir, I just wanted to update you on the situation here on the ground. It seems that our lieutenant is anxious to get out of here. He's come to counting the days, and the way I hear it, he's going to be out of here pretty soon. It seems he's taken to a BBC correspondent, Beatrice something or another. He's talking about a future with her." Thompson paused. "You know, Colonel, this lieutenant, he's a decent sort."

"Not for you to decide," McIntosh snapped. "Thank you for the report. It may be time to act. I'll be back to you in 24 hours."

McIntosh was as good as his word. The next morning, Thompson received the message: it was time to make King Charles a war hero. As soon as he got the message, Thompson started on an almost full bottle of Jameson's Reserve and drank until he blacked out.

CHAPTER 36
SEEKING WITH SAM

HENRY AND JULIAN CREATED QUITE A STIR WHEN THEY ARRIVED AT 3100 Massachusetts Avenue NW, where the British Embassy was located in a pretty red brick building with two chimneys poking up that looked somehow English to Henry. From the moment they hopped out of the cab at the embassy gates and sauntered toward the entrance, phones were ringing off the hook throughout the building as the British delegation furiously tried to stick to protocol and prepare for a visit from the royal prince.

On the way in, Henry stopped and glanced at a bronze statue of a portly and familiar man with one hand raised and his fingers spread in the V for victory salute.

"It's Churchill, isn't it?" he asked.

"Bloody right," Julian said. "It's a famous statue. Did you know you have something in common with him?"

"Me? Are you kidding? He's one of the most famous men of the century. What the hell could I possibly have in common with him?"

"His mother was American and his father was British. You have the opposite pedigree. Your mum was British and your dad American, or at least raised American, so you're both hybrids."

"Frankly, Julian, I don't really know who the hell I am most of the time...and by the way, where'd you learn that, about Churchill?"

"In school, mate. One of the few days I was awake. That's not the only thing interesting about the statue, though. It was put here in 1965. See how he's standing?"

Henry shrugged. "Sure."

"See how one foot is forward to the other?

"Yeah."

"Well, as you know, embassies have exclusive sovereignty in the country they are located. That sovereignty only applies to the actual piece of land owned or leased by the embassy. So when we go through the gates, we are actually entering Great Britain, where British sovereignty rules. In 1963, in recognition of his leadership and our special alliance with the United States, Churchill was made an honorary American citizen."

"I thought you said his mother was an American. Wouldn't he automatically have been a citizen?"

"He was a special case. Apparently, there was some debate on whether his mother had forfeited her citizenship or not. When the controversy came to light, Congress stepped in and reconfirmed Churchill's American citizenship and made it permanent. So when they placed the statue, they wanted to show that Churchill really belonged to the United States as well as Britain. He's got one foot on US soil, just over the line of embassy property, and the other foot on British soil."

Henry regarded the statue, thinking that whether he liked it or not, he kind of understood how Churchill felt. "That's pretty cool. Learn something new every day."

"Aye. Let's hope that's not all we learn today."

They continued in through the gates, toward the building, and Julian filled in Henry with more detail. It turned out there was a good reason the building looked English: it had been designed by Sir Edwin Lutyens and was his only building ever built in the US.

A guard previously tipped off about Henry's visit recognized him as he entered the grand lobby, respectfully bowing to Henry as he walked by. In the lobby, they were greeted with the sight of Ambassador Sturbridge rushing down the elaborate staircase to greet them, then slowing when he saw them and walking at a more dignified pace. To Henry, the ambassador looked like he'd just gotten finished telling someone off.

"Your Royal Highness," Sturbridge said, bowing from the neck. "Welcome home. It's indeed an honor to welcome you to the embassy."

Henry was meticulously dressed in a well-fitted blue suit, a Christmas gift from his mother, and a Harvard tie. He looked around for a moment, confused, then realized that Sturbridge was welcoming him "home," back to British soil. Henry smiled, quickly reached out, and grabbed the ambassador's hand to shake it.

"Thanks!" he said. "And thanks for having us."

The ambassador looked scandalized and it took Henry another second to figure out why: they weren't supposed to shake hands. His smile only grew—as far as he was concerned, the Brits had a lot of silly rules and he had no plans to follow any of them.

"Sir, may I suggest we retire to my office?" Sturbridge said.

"Of course, I'd like to get this business done as soon as possible."

The next forty-five minutes was spent with Henry filling in the blanks not covered in his earlier phone conversation with the ambassador. "So you see, Sir Arthur, that's the situation," he concluded. "I was hoping you could give me some ideas on how to proceed."

Sir Arthur nodded. "Of course, Your Highness. After we spoke on the phone, my office made several inquiries at the State Department and I believe we've located a historian who will be more than willing to help you. Sounded like a decent chap. I hope it's acceptable to you, but knowing that this is a time sensitive matter, I've taken the liberty of setting up an appointment with her for first thing tomorrow morning."

Henry nodded appreciatively. "Wow, thanks. I really appreciate that."

"Of course, Your Highness. Now, I'll be happy to have someone escort you to your rooms, and please don't hesitate to ask if there's anything else we can do for you. We serve tea promptly at three, and we've arranged for dinner at seven. I'm afraid on such short notice, it will be embassy staff, nothing formal or diplomatic."

"Uh, yeah, dinner sounds good. But I think I'll skip the tea. Truth is, I can't stand the stuff."

Sir Arthur gave a small and pinched smile, as if the idea of the Prince of York not liking tea actually caused him physical pain. And that AMERICAN accent! "Of course, Your Highness. Now, to your rooms!" He pressed a button on an intercom on his desk, gave a brief order, and a man appeared in the office almost magically. "Heathcliff," Sir Arthur said, "please escort His Royal Highness to his quarters."

Heathcliff was a male version of the Ambassador's secretary. A prim and proper lifetime bureaucrat who worked hard at looking efficient and important.

Henry and Julian followed him along a winding and twisty path through the embassy, passing halls, beautiful public areas, and various offices filled with embassy personnel. As they turned into a small reception room, Henry saw a familiar figure walking toward them. He stared at the woman for a good ten seconds but still couldn't quite place the face. He knew he had seen her before, but couldn't remember where. As they passed each other, they exchanged smiles and continued on.

"Who was that, she looked so familiar but I can't place the face?" Henry asked Healthcliff.

"Oh, that is the ambassador's niece," Heathcliff answered. "She's in the States for an internship or something like that in New York City, I believe. She spends time here at the embassy now and then, helping out here and there. She's quite lovely, isn't she?"

"What's her name?"

"Samantha, Samantha Smythe."

"Oh my God, it's her!" Henry exclaimed, a light bulb going off in his head.

"Who you talking about, mate?" Julian said.

"The girl in Paul Whitman's office, in New York," Henry said. "You know, the one at the front desk, the gorgeous one."

"Oh yeah, her. She is gorgeous." Julian paused and frowned. "But why is she here? You don't suppose Paul Whitman has something to do with this? You know, keeping tabs on you?"

"God, I hope not," Henry said. "But there's no way he could know I was coming here...no way. Maybe it's just a coincidence. And besides, she's the ambassador's niece. She's not going to do Paul Whitman's bidding."

Julian grunted, and Henry could see he wasn't totally convinced. Still, he felt like he needed to meet her.

"Heathcliff," Henry said, "do you think you could have Miss Smythe meet me somewhere in the embassy? I'd like to talk with her."

"Of course, sir. I will organize that as soon as possible. She probably would fancy meeting Your Highness."

"See if you could set up something for this afternoon around five. Maybe for drinks?"

Heathcliff nodded as the men arrived at their rooms. Julian's room was just down the hall from Henry's and a bit more austere, although neither room was very large or splendid. Henry was happy, however. The accommodations suited him just fine and he was more than happy they had refused the ambassador's offer of putting him up in the royal apartments.

Henry arrived in the blue parlor room on the second floor of the embassy just before five o'clock. He was a little nervous because he had never done anything like this before. For the last six years, he had been totally committed to being with Star, even as it had grown more habitual and routine. It was strange to think that a primarily sexual relationship with such a hot girl could be boring, but there it was. Henry was mostly bored with Star, but Star had a magic that Mr. Niner could not resist even if he wanted to.

The parlor was smartly appointed in blue damask silk with an enormous crystal chandelier. The burning fireplace emitted welcoming warmth, which set the stage for a very cozy meeting. Over the fireplace hung an original Gainesboro, a striking and vividly executed image of a young boy and his dog.

Henry paced around the empty parlor, waiting and thinking about Samantha, wondering if she'd remember him. He heard the click of high heels coming down the corridor and turned toward the door, his heart actually beating faster. Samantha came in, carrying herself gracefully and looking very classy, with her blonde hair swept up and a perfectly tasteful dress accenting her amazing body.

"Good evening, Your Royal Highness, I'm Samantha Smythe," she said, giving a small bow. "I understand you wanted to meet me." Then she did a double take. "Wait, don't I know you? Have we met before?"

Grinning broadly, Henry said, "Yes, we have, but it was in a different place."

"Where? Sir."

"The reception area of Cavanaugh, Wolf, Whitman and Smith law offices. I was in to see Paul Whitman with my professors from Harvard."

"Oh my God, now I remember. That's right. How could I forget? You caused quite a stir."

"Oh yeah?" Henry said. "I hope it was the good kind. But...seriously, let's start out right. I'm going to call you Samantha and you are going to call me Henry. Got that?"

"Yes, but I must admit it's a bit awkward, you know, being who you are...well, I'm not sure I can...It's most irregular..."

"Well, Henry is who I am."

Samantha gave him a small smile. "As you wish, then. It shall be Henry!"

A proper English butler appeared and took their drink requests. Samantha had a Pimm's Cup and Henry a Bud Light, if they had one.

"How very American," Samantha said. "You'll no doubt scandalize the Keeper of the Spirits with that request."

"Who?"

"Oh silly, the bartender..."

Henry laughed. "What can I say? I don't mind causing a scandal now and then."

"So I've heard," she said.

"Oh? What have you heard?"

"You had quite the famous career at Eton," she said. "I read all about it, as did every young girl in England, probably in the world. Your pictures were most becoming!"

Henry squirmed a little, remembering some of the more lurid details of that period of his life. He imagined this beautiful girl reading about the incident with the oar and felt himself blushing.

"Oh goodness," she said, "I've made you blush."

"Uh, yeah, sorry. Just, um—"

"Dear me," she said. "I should be apologizing to you! But you do blush adorably."

Henry grimaced as the blush faded. "Very funny."

The couple chatted the typical small talk newly introduced couples do. Henry finally got around to asking Samantha why she was in Paul Whitman's office and if she was a receptionist.

"No, I'm not a receptionist, not that there is anything wrong with being one, mind you. I was just filling in while Heather was on break. I am in law school and doing an internship at Cavanaugh, Wolf, Whitman and Smith. My uncle Arthur arranged it. I come to DC on my days off to spend time with him. He's my favorite uncle and a recent widower so I like giving him company. I get to meet so many interesting people here and learn lots of different things. Since my aunt died, Uncle Arthur often asks me to be his dinner partner at official events. You know, it's exciting to be around an embassy. I'm seriously considering finishing law school and trying to enter diplomatic service."

"You're going to be a lawyer! That's great. Me too. That's why I was in Whitman's office in the first place. I'm doing a case study for law school. It's turned into an actual case. Paul Whitman and the Carnegie Trust are defendants. Actually, that's why I'm here too. I'm following up a lead for some missing documents. I'd like to tell you all about it, but should I be concerned about a conflict of interest given that you are at Whitman's firm?"

"No need to worry about that. I finished up last Monday and will be moving back to DC."

Samantha listened intently as Henry related the whole story, ending with why he was now in Washington.

"I have a great idea, Samantha," he said as he finished the story. "Your uncle offered to have an embassy person accompany Julian and me around town in pursuit of the journals. What do you say? You want to lend a hand?"

"I'm here for a few more days before going back to New York to pack, and I have nothing special that I must do, so if you're good with it and Uncle Arthur is, I'm in. It will be brilliant."

"Great, we'll start tomorrow morning."

CHAPTER 37
CAPTURED

I T WAS EARLY ON A DAMP WEDNESDAY AFTERNOON WHEN BEATRICE AND her cameraman, a talented young man named Jake, were returning from a shoot. The pair had been at St. Mary's orphanage just out-side of Belfast filming the child victims of the Troubles and both were depressed and quiet as Jake guided the unmarked BBC van through the open farmland a dozen kilometers from the narrow cobblestone streets of Belfast. Beatrice was still processing the images she had seen: children with burn and shrapnel injuries and orphans who had lost their parents. All of this bloodshed, and for what?

Her attention jerked back to the road as Jake swerved to avoid a lorry that had seemed to materialize directly in front of them.

"What the hell?" he yelled. "That bloke did that on purpose! What are they thinking?"

Even as he fought the steering wheel, Beatrice grabbed onto the dashboard and saw that he wouldn't be able to recover in time. Their van skidded off the road and into a shallow ditch.

"Damn it!" Jake said. "I'm going to go give——"

He stopped in mid-sentence as a man bearing a machine gun with a black mask over his face jumped out of the lorry. IRA. He waved wildly at them in the van and screamed, "Get out of the bloody van, NOW!"

More fighters poured out of the lorry behind him, fanning out and covering the van with their weapons. One of the lads yelled to the band's leader. "Shall we kill them now, Seamus?"

Stunned and frightened, neither Jake nor Beatrice moved. The group leader opened the door, reached in, and yanked Jake out of the driver's seat. Turning to Beatrice, he yelled, "I told you to get out of the goddamn van now! Do it, little lady, or I'll put a bullet through that posh little head of yours."

Beatrice raised her hands and got out slowly. She knew that highway robbery was common in Northern Ireland, driven by persistent short-ages of money and food. She tried to catch Jake's eye and willed him to cooperate with the foot soldiers as the leader approached her and grabbed her purse, while others roughly frisked Jake and took his wallet.

Seamus rifled through her stuff, then whistled softly when he found her BBC credentials. "So you're a reporter?" he growled.

She was too scared to do anything other than nod.

"Well that changes things a touch," he said, then pulled out a radio and turned his back to call his superiors. Nearby, a group of three soldiers were starting to taunt and push Jake. He stumbled between them, and one landed a nasty, cracking blow on Jake's shoulder with the butt of his gun. Jake cried out in pain.

"Leave him be!" Beatrice screamed. "He didn't do anything to you!"

They ignored her as another one hit Jake between his shoulder blades and the cameraman went down. Immediately, the circle closed on him, their feet kicking and guns thudding into his body. Jake tried to curl into a fetal position, but the blows were suddenly coming fast and furious and Beatrice saw blood running down his face.

"Stop it!" she yelled. "You're hurting him!"

This time they stopped. "Get up, you limey prick," one of them growled.

Jake raised himself slowly to his hands and knees, blood running from his nose, and then started to stand up. Before he could even raise himself, another vicious blow landed on his head and sent him back down again. He groaned in agony and stayed down.

Beatrice made a run for him, but the leader suddenly turned around and grabbed her arm in an iron fist. She cried out in pain.

Seamus yelled to the men: "Dylan said we can do whatever we want to the bloke. But take the girl with us."

A cold shiver of fear ran through Beatrice at those words. Once they had her off the street, they could do anything to her, and she'd heard plenty of stories about what the IRA did to captives, especially women. She began to cry as the IRA soldiers advanced on Jake again and began kicking him harder than before. He was hardly moving now, barely bothering to protect himself, and the sound of fists and hard metal thudding into his flesh mingled with the heavy breathing of the soldiers as they worked Jake over. A tall Irish boy, just a teenager, appeared, looming over Jake with a tire iron.

"This is for my friends," he said. "A bit of your own medicine."

He smashed the tire iron into Jake's rib. Beatrice heard a rib shatter and Jake, who was almost unconscious, jerked wide awake and bellowed in pain. His cry was cut short by another smashing blow from the tire iron, then another. Jake sagged against the pavement as the kid handed the tire iron to another IRA soldier. "You have a go," the kid said. "For your brother, Connor. Least you can do."

The one named Connor grabbed the iron and Beatrice watched in numb horror as he took careful aim at Jake's groin, then smashed him three times. Jake was totally unconscious now and his body only twitched under the sadistic blows.

"That will fix this scrawny little limey arsehole," Connor said. "He won't be making any more British babies anytime soon with a broken dick."

"Alright," the leader bellowed, his hand still gripping Beatrice's arm. "Time to go! Grab what you can from him and let's get out of here!"

The young soldier roughly searched Jake's pockets and took some paper money, then removed his watch and a silver cigarette lighter. He tried pulling a gold ring off Jake's pinky finger, but it was stuck.

"Come on!" the leader said. "On the road in one minute!"

"I can't get his ring!" the soldier cried out.

"Here," Connor said. "Try this." He handed a field knife to the soldier, who made a quick slash at Jake's finger, severing it from his hand, then held the ring aloft.

"Got it!"

Beatrice screamed in horror as the rebel tossed the severed finger into the bush. Her shock was so profound that it was almost like she watched herself being roughly blindfolded and pushed into the back of the lorry. This floating, non-Beatrice watched as the young soldier who had extracted the ring from Jake's finger had one final insult: he stood over Jake's battered and bleeding body and sent a thick stream of urine splashing onto her cameraman. "Piss on you," he said, "and the whole lot of you!"

And then it was dark and Beatrice had nothing left but the stink of sweat, the darkness of the blindfold, and the rough hands as they grabbed her and threw her into a lorry, which then took off careening toward the narrow city streets. She didn't know how long it had been before the lorry skidded to a stop and they grabbed her again and pushed her along, stumbling on some hard surface like concrete. Then she was inside, passing through a door, and knocked her shins on a stair. Around her, men laughed and joked. She smelled cigarette smoke. As she was pushed up a flight of stairs, she heard a man down below saying, "I hope we get a taste of that bitch before too long. She's a fine looking one."

Beatrice thought, "They're going to rape me before they kill me." She tried to summon her courage, but all she found was terror.

The blindfold was ripped from her eyes as she was shoved through a door into a small bedroom with a single high window and an old iron bed. The terror bloomed inside of her at the sight of the bed. It was coming now.

"Get on the bed," a voice commanded her, and she recognized it was coming from the leader of the group.

Her legs wouldn't obey and she stood dumbly inside the room, until he shoved her and she stumbled forward, then sprawled across the bed. As if in a movie, she saw herself from above, looking down on the girl half on, half off the bed, her eyes glazed with terror. This detached Beatrice felt sorry for the girl down there.

The leader crossed the room and Beatrice hardly moved as he reached for her. But instead of tearing off her clothes, he produced a set of handcuffs and quickly handcuffed her to the bed, then stood back. "You'll stay here until we get back," he said. "And don't bother screaming. Anyone who can hear you around here has no interest in helping you." He turned to leave, then faced her again. "And don't you dare piss on that bed. If you need a piss, there's a pot under the bed."

And then he was gone and Beatrice was left handcuffed to the bed, with nothing to do but pray. Without trying, an image of Charles rose up in her mind, him grabbing her and saying he loved her. Hot tears washed down her cheeks, and she said, "Oh, Charles, I'm so sorry!" without knowing exactly what she was sorry for.

———•———

Miles away from where Beatrice sobbed in her prison, a British patrol van skidded to a stop on an empty road next to the deserted BBC lorry. Soldiers climbed out carefully, their weapons at the ready, and scanned the area.

"Sergeant!" one of the men cried out. "There's a chap over here, in the ditch! He's hurt badly."

Two soldiers walked over and peered into the trench. "Bloody hell, is he alive?" one asked.

First Lieutenant Charles Stuart, the patrol's leader, stepped down into the trench and put his fingers on Jake's neck to check the man's vitals. He winced from the smell of urine and blood. Jake didn't move at the touch, but Charles was relieved to see his chest rising slightly. "Yes, he's alive, Sergeant, radio for an ambulance," Charles barked out. "I'll check his pockets for an ID. Maybe we can find out who this poor bloke is. Corporal, go search that van and see what you can find."

A corporal headed for the unmarked BBC van 1 and climbed inside. He checked the glove box and found the vehicle's registration. He emerged a moment later carrying a purse. "Here, sir," he said. "I found this. And it looks like the van is registered to the BBC."

"The BBC?" Charles said, his heart skipping a beat. "Did you say it was registered to the BBC?"

"Yes, sir."

Charles grabbed the purse and looked at it. He did his best to recall what type of purse Beatrice carried, but he couldn't remember. He rushed over to the ditch, where the men rolled Jake on his side and were administering field first aid. When they moved him, he came awake with a scream of pain as his broken ribs were jostled.

Charles knelt down beside the terrified cameraman, who was sipping water from a canteen and barely conscious, his eyes sinking.

"I'm a British soldier," Charles said. "You're safe now. Can you tell me what happened?"

"IRA," Jake whispered. "Ran us off the road."

"Us? Is there someone else?"

Jake nodded. "My reporter. Beatrice Grandton."

"Where is she?" Charles demanded.

"They took her. After they beat me."

"Where? Do you know? Did you hear any names? Any identifying information?"

Jake seemed to nod off and Charles and his corporal exchanged a worried glance.

"Go easy on him, sir," the corporal said. "The man is in shock."

"They've got Beatrice!" Charles retorted. "You! Wake up!"

Jake's eyes opened with effort and he struggled to focus on Charles.

"Time is of the essence," Charles stressed. "We need anything you can give us. We'll go get her."

"I heard names. Seamus is the pack leader. They called a bloke named Dylan, maybe the commander. One called Aedan, I think. That's all."

Charles heard someone behind him and saw a young medic jogging toward them with a black emergency medicine kit. The medic jumped down into the ditch as Jake's eyes began to close again.

"This'll help," the medic said. "Don't move him yet, though. Wait till we get a board in here."

He produced an ampoule of morphine and injected Jake with a large dose, enough to put him out, and his body slumped. Before the other medics could even catch up with their trauma board to lift Jake out of the ditch, Charles was running back toward his van and calling for his men.

CHAPTER 38
VALENTINE'S DAY

HENRY WOKE UP AND, BY HABIT, GLANCED AT THE SPACE NEXT TO HIM in the bed, expecting to see Star. When he saw the space was empty, he remembered: he was in Washington, DC, embarking on a hunt for his grandfather's journals with Julian and Samantha Smythe. The thought of her brought a smile to his face, and as he jumped up and headed for the shower, he realized it had been years since Star had made him feel that good. Physically, Star rang his bell, over and over and as often as she could, but there hadn't been any kind of connection in a long time.

This realization had been growing in him for a while, but it really hit home that morning as he stood under the hot shower water. Star was just a habit at this point, not a real relationship. He had managed to convince himself otherwise, partly because of her insatiable appetite for Mr. Niner and partly because of her endless interest in every aspect of his life. She seemed to want to know every detail of where he went and how he spent his time. For a long time, he'd thought she was jealous, but that couldn't be it. He had been strictly monogamous all this time (something he was quite sure she couldn't say). No, in reality, he figured it was more that Star was a little obsessed with him. As good as that felt for his ego, he realized it was empty and hollow.

On the other hand, he was actively looking forward to getting to know Samantha better. She was beautiful, yes, but that wasn't it. She was intelligent and kind-hearted, and she had something going on. The girl wanted to be a lawyer and knew her way around the corridors of power. She was formidable and challenging, and Henry liked that.

A knock at the door interrupted his thoughts as he toweled off in front of the bathroom mirror. Expecting it to be Julian, he wrapped the towel around his waist, hastened to the door, and flung it open. "Come on in."

His mouth fell open. It was Samantha.

"Maybe I will," she said, smiling.

Henry yelped. "Oh my God! What are you doing here?"

"Were you expecting someone else?" she asked, her eyes straying down his body.

"Yes. No. I mean, I thought you were Julian."

"Well, clearly I'm not."

"Yeah, I can see that. Uh, hold on. Give me a minute and I'll get dressed and we can get out of here." Embarrassed, he raced back to the bathroom and shut the door so he could take a few deep breaths and dress in privacy. Through the door, he heard Samantha come into his room and shut the door.

"So," she said through the door, "I've arranged for a car and driver. It will be just you, Julian, and me. We have an appointment at the US Department of State with a Ms. Clair Anne Miles, chief historian. Not sure how helpful he will be, but it's a start."

"Great, thanks for doing that. Errrr…could you do me another favor?"

"Of course, what would that be?"

"Hand me my boxers and jeans. Oh, and the blue shirt too."

Thoroughly amused at the thought of a hunky Henry hiding behind the loo door, she crossed the room and fetched the unmentionables, along with the shirt and well-fitting jeans, and slightly opened the bathroom door. "There you go, Your Highness!"

Henry emerged from the bathroom dressed and ready to go slay the dragons. He reached for a finely tailored blue blazer hanging off the back of the desk chair and slipped it on over his broad shoulders. "Done."

"Very professional," Samantha said, laughing and arching her eyebrows. "You know, I've only seen you out of those jeans once."

They started at each other, then both of them burst out laughing. "Er," she said, "I didn't mean it like that. I meant—"

"Sure, sure," an amused Henry said. "I know what you meant. Now stop feasting your eyes on me and let's go."

She looked shocked for a second, then realized he was kidding and laughed. "Fair. I'm ready."

———◆———

Clair Anne Miles, the official historian for the State Department, sat across her cluttered desk at the Department of State and listened to their story politely. She didn't take any notes, Henry noticed, and gave it hardly a second of thought before she said, "I'm not sure I can be much help, I'm afraid. I would know if we had possession of the Ambassador's journals, and I'm quite sure we don't."

"Oh," Henry said, disappointed. "Well, thanks. I guess—"

"Wait," Miles said. "Let me check something." She turned on a large computer on her desk. "They just gave us these new desktop computers. I've hardly figured out how to turn it on yet—hard to believe they'll be much help in actually getting work done—but let's give it a whirl and see what it can do."

"What it can do?" Samantha said.

Miles was typing gingerly now, staring at the screen like it might bite her. "Old employment records. Maybe there's someone who worked at State during the Ambassador's service that might be able to help." They waited while she tapped away some more. Then she raised her eyebrows. "Well, look at this. Turns out the Ambassador had an executive assistant, one Marion Valentine. She must be rather elderly by now, since this was a while ago. It looks like she terminated her service with the Department of State just about the same time the Ambassador left. Perhaps she went with him? I have a forwarding address, but who knows if she is still there, or even still alive. I'll jot it down for you. 321 East 53rd Street, New York City. Apartment 14F. There's a phone number too, probably not operative by now." She pushed a button. "Now let's see if this thing really prints."

The printer on her desk whirred to life and a few pages scrolled out. She tore them off, then tore off the hole-punched guides along the side and handed them to Samantha. "There you go," she said.

Samantha thanked Miles as they got up to leave and headed for the embassy. It was a quick drive, and once they were back, Samantha suggested that she should make the call from a basement conference room. "I'm good at getting information out of people. Lots of practice at Cavanaugh, Wolf, Whitman and Smith."

"Sure, that would be great. And thanks."

Samantha dialed the number and got a recording. She was about to hang up, when she stopped suddenly and snapped her fingers for a piece of paper and a pen. She wrote "646" down, then hung up.

"What?" Henry said.

"Number was disconnected, but said I should try it with a new area code." She dialed the new number and they all waited as the phone rang on the other side. Within three rings, someone answered. It was the voice of an elderly woman. "Hello?"

"Hello. My name is Samantha Smythe, calling from the British Embassy in Washington, DC. Are you Miss Marion Valentine?"

"No, I'm not. Who are you again?"

"I'm Samantha Smythe, from the British Embassy in Washington."

"I see, dear, but how can I help you? Marion is not here."

"Oh dear, is she well?"

"Very, despite the aches and pains of old age and being a bit hard of hearing. For her age, she is doing way better than most of us."

"Brilliant, but I'm so disappointed. You see, I wanted to give her something we found in the embassy's files that we thought she'd like to have. It's a letter of accommodation from the then-serving British Ambassador. It was very complimentary of Miss Valentine. It looks like it was never sent out." Samantha paused and held up her hand to Henry with her fingers crossed.

"I see, I'm Marion's sister, Beverly. Mrs. Beverly Samoni. Marion is on a cruise and won't be back for a couple of weeks. It will have to wait until then. But I am sure she would be thrilled to have the letter as a memento. You know she saves everything."

"Oh! A cruise, how lovely. Where did she go?"

"Marion is on the QE2 doing a Caribbean route. All those exotic islands, you know."

"That sounds smashing, really smashing. Thank you for helping."

"Of course. And Marion will be happy to hear from you, no doubt. Just call back in a few weeks."

"Of course," Samantha said, hanging up.

Henry gave her a thumbs-up. "Nice! You're pretty quick on your feet. Now, let's get the QE2's itinerary so we can track her down. We don't have three weeks to wait."

After some bureaucratic bobbing and weaving, Samantha reached the right person in the Ministry of Travel, London office. She learned that the QE2 was at sea and due to arrive in Turks and Caicos, a British possession, at 7:45 the next morning. She also confirmed that a Miss Marion Valentine, age eighty-four, was aboard in Cabin 1249, Deck C, traveling as a solo passenger on an American passport.

Henry paced around the room, trying to figure out what he would do next. He ruled out reaching Marion by phone. Her sister said she was hard of hearing, so a phone conversation would be, at best, difficult. Besides, his story was pretty far-fetched. It was the kind of thing that needed to be done in person. "Samantha, is your uncle in?"

"I believe so, I'll check if you like."

"Please, and if he is I'd like to talk to him."

Within minutes of Samantha's call, Sir Arthur arrived in the basement conference room. Henry filled him in on their mission, then made his request. "I'd like to borrow that Learjet you wanted to send to pick me up in Boston. I need to see someone in Turks and Caicos tomorrow morning. It's the only way I can get there in time. "

"The Lear? You mean the aircraft?"

"Yes, the very one. Can you arrange that? I will be traveling with Julian and Samantha. If all goes well, we will be back the very same day."

Sir Arthur could do little more than grant this request from the Prince of York, next in line to the throne. "I will have someone check to see where the plane is now and if it could be organized."

Things moved fast from there, and Julian, Samantha, and Henry boarded the British-registered Learjet 35A at 3 a.m. the next morning.

The flight time was just over four hours to Providenciales International Airport. The aircraft was well fitted out with luxurious cream-colored leather seating. Britain's three-lion crest was embossed on the head-rests. Plush carpeting, deep enough to sink into, covered the passenger cabin. Given the early hour, the passengers settled down for a few winks. Samantha sat next to Henry, and as she dozed her head fell onto his shoulder. Henry placed his head next to hers and inhaled the scent of her clean, perfumed blonde hair. He soon joined her in sleep.

Right on time, the plane landed at Turks and Caicos. They were met by a small contingent from the local government who, as a matter of protocol, had been tipped off by the British Embassy that a Royal was going to be on the island. After a few niceties, they were whisked into a waiting sedan and headed for the port and the arrival of the QE2. The majestic ship soon pulled into the harbor, sparkling white in the clean, tropical morning sun. The ship was far too large to dock at the small port, so they had to take a tender out to meet the big cruise ship. Once aboard, Harry walked up to the concierge desk and asked to be connected to Miss Valentine's state room. The phone was answered immediately.

"Hello?"

"Hello, is this Miss Marion Valentine?"

"What?"

Henry remembered she was a bit deaf and said in a much louder voice, "Is this Miss Marion Valentine?"

"Why, yes it is. How may I help you?"

Using his old identity, one she would recognize, Henry carefully articulated: "I don't think you know me, but my name is Henry Carnegie. I am Ambassador Carnegie's grandson."

"I'm sorry, young man, I am a bit hard of hearing. Could you say who you are again?"

"Of course. I don't think you know me, but my name is Henry Carnegie. I am Ambassador Carnegie's grandson."

"Oh my goodness, Henry! Of course I know you. I haven't seen you since you were a mere child. Where are you?"

"I'm right here on the QE2, in the lobby. I was wondering if I could have a word with you, privately. It's important."

"Of course, dear, I'll be right up. You said the lobby? Which one, you know this ship is enormous, and I have a devil of a time finding my way around."

"I'll wait for you by the concierge's desk, Deck A."

Although Marion Valentine was well into her eighties, she was as healthy and spry as a woman decades younger. She arrived on the lobby deck looking fresh and dressed sharply, with tasteful makeup and jewelry that befitted a dignified woman of her age.

Henry, seeing the elderly woman walking toward him, asked, "Miss Valentine?"

"Yes, dear, and you are little Henry? Oh my, not so little any more, I'd say. And who is the beautiful young woman? Your wife? I say, Henry, you've done well."

Samantha blushed and smiled as Henry answered. "No, Samantha is not my wife, just a good friend helping me out with a big problem. You see, Miss Valentine, I was hoping you could provide me with some information about Ambassador Carnegie's personal effects."

"Of course I'd be glad to help you in any way I can. You know, working with the Ambassador was the best time of my life. He was a wonderful man, such a gentleman, and so intelligent. Always treating me with such respect and professionalism."

"That's great," Henry said. "He was a great man. Um, did you know that my grandfather kept a journal?"

"Of course," she said. "He was almost manic about writing something every day, no matter how busy or tired he was or where he would be. He took great pride in this. You know, he had wonderful penmanship. The Ambassador told me many times that he was hoping that someone would use his notations and write a biography. Is that what you're up to now?"

"Perhaps," Henry said. "But...the journals seem to have gone missing. It's very important I find them. Do you know where they are?"

"Hmm, it has been a while, and my memory isn't always the best these days. Comes with age, along with some other not-so-charming deficits. Let me think. When the Ambassador left the State Department and returned to run his business, I left with him. He moved me to New York and I worked with him until his death.

"Your father was vice president when the Ambassador died. We were all so proud of him, especially the Ambassador. After his death, I remember packing up things and putting them in storage. As for the journals, I don't recall packing them up at all. I know the Ambassador wanted someone to have them so they could write that biography, but I just can't recall who."

"Could it have been Paul Whitman, the Ambassador's lawyer?"

"Wait, I think it was him! But we didn't send him the journals. I'm sure of it. They might have been brought to the house in Westchester, but of course that house has been sold long since and the contents auctioned off or donated."

Henry started to feel like this was a waste of time and his heart sunk. But he hadn't come all this way to give up so easily. "Donated? To who? Was there a charity maybe, or a museum?"

"Hmm," she said. "Now you're really asking me to think back. There was a museum in upstate New York, near the Ambassador's summer camp. I do recall that a truckload of material was sent there, but I don't know what was in the truck."

"Could it have been the journals? What museum?"

"Yes, it could have been the journals, but maybe not. I'm sorry to say I don't remember the name of the museum. Only that it was in Cooperstown, New York. Maybe you could try looking there?"

"I will!" Henry said, feeling hopeful again. "Thank you! You've been terrific."

"Anytime," Marion said. "Your family means a great deal to me, and I was so sorry to read about your father's murder." She stopped suddenly and her face clouded over. She put a hand on Henry's shoulder. "I'm sorry. I didn't mean to be so harsh. Good luck, Henry. I'll pray for you."

"Thank you," he said, already plotting their next move, this time to Cooperstown.

CHAPTER 39
DESPERATE!

C HARLES COULD HARDLY HEAR HIS OWN THOUGHTS OVER THE BLOOD pounding in his head. They had taken Beatrice. At that very moment, she was being held by Irish terrorists. God only knew what kind of hell she was enduring, and Charles found himself wishing and hoping against hope that she was taken by the "good" type of IRA.

As a seasoned fighter in the Troubles, Charles had learned there were several kinds of fighters in the IRA. There were the true patriots who fought for a free Ireland and were motivated by ideals. This type made it a point to try to win hearts and minds as well as battles. They planned for the day Ireland would be free and they would need to govern. And then there were the opportunists, the thieves and criminals, and the psychopaths who were attracted to any kind of violence and war. These bands were little more than hooligans and oftentimes couldn't even be controlled by the IRA itself. They used the war as an excuse to roam the streets at night, often in drunken stupors, looking to murder, rob, and rape.

Please, Charles sent up a silent prayer, please let it be the Irish patriots who have her.

"Thompson," he barked as his platoon converged on the van. "Radio this into headquarters and make a report. Time is critical. We need to get the word out to the informants and spies. We're looking for a group led by Seamus, with a leader named Dylan and an Aedan. Hurry!"

The sergeant hopped to the command as Charles issued rapid orders to the rest of the men to gear up and get ready to canvas the city. He didn't know where they were going yet, but he planned to break down the door of every known IRA safe house and assembly hall he could find, to rush every pub where they met and round up every military age male. Tonight, he vowed, they would fall on the IRA like a hammer and get Beatrice back. The sense of purpose and mission felt good—it helped him push back the fear and sadness that, once again, everything he loved was under threat.

They spent the next several hours breaking doors and shaking people down, with no luck. Charles was becoming increasingly desperate, the fear blossoming into terror, when Thompson's radio crackled. He answered it and listened intently, then turned to Charles. "Sir, a call came in from a Patty Murray to HQ just now. Murray, one of ours, said he was at the Chat and Chew and overheard a few young IRA soldiers bragging about beating up a BBC reporter. Said they had a female reporter stashed in a house on Langston Road. Said the lads sounded like they were getting liquored up and looking forward to a little..." Pausing, Thompson changed their words to spare Charles and finished with, "An assault, sir."

Charles, who had commandeered the wheel from the driver, was already turning the van toward Langston Road before Thompson could finish thanking the intelligence officer on the other end of the radio. The officer told them that there was a suspected safe house at 5 Langston. The mood inside the van was quiet and tense as Charles killed the running lights, and his men slipped into operational readiness out of habit. Weapons were loaded with fresh clips and helmets and straps checked and tightened.

They glided to a stop two houses down from the dilapidated Victorian house at 5 Langston Road. Charles didn't see anyone on the front porch, but knew that, if the information was correct, there were already eyes on them. They had only minutes before the rebel soldiers inside could prepare a defense, or worse yet, slip out an escape hatch with Beatrice and vanish. He gave brief orders, got an affirmative reply from his men, and then jumped from the van at a dead sprint with his gun drawn and Thompson behind him.

They covered the ground quickly and the two men pounded up the steps onto the porch. There were two IRA men on the porch, both snoring loudly and clearly drunk. British soldiers leaped onto them and quickly handcuffed them.

"Captain," Thompson whispered. "You stay here! I'm going in first!"

Before Charles could respond or even order otherwise, Thompson sent the door crashing back against its splintered frame with a mighty kick and leapt into the darkness beyond. Charles was one step behind, his gun still out and his eyes adjusting to the dim room. Instantly, his nose was assaulted with the stink of men, whiskey, and filth. Clearly this was a safe house and not somebody's residence. The furniture was sparse and rundown, and boxes of ammunition and grenades were stacked up the walls. The room was empty. Thompson cupped a hand to his ear and pointed at the ceiling. Charles heard it too: there were voices coming from upstairs.

Thompson led the way, with Charles behind him, as they crept up the stairs to the second-floor landing. The other men from the platoon were now fanning out through the first floor, but they didn't find anyone.

As they neared the top of the stairs, Charles saw a hall with several closed doors. A strip of light showed under one door and he clearly heard a voice say, "Shut up, Aedan, I'm going first. I called it."

"No way, you dolt. I'm as horny as a toad. Move over, mate."

Thompson and Charles locked eyes, then Thompson signaled for permission to go in first, with Charles covering him. Charles nodded and they crept into position on either side of the door. Inside, the men were arguing in loud, drunken voices. Charles couldn't hear Beatrice.

Thompson nodded, then held up three fingers to countdown. When he got to one, he swung into the hallway and kicked the door open, then rolled into the room. Charles waited a heartbeat in case there was any fire, then followed his sergeant into a tiny bedroom. He saw Beatrice still bound to the filthy bed, and a man standing over her with his trousers down around his knees. A second man stood nearby, watching.

Both whirled around. The one with his trousers down said, "What the—"

But his sentence was cut off by a vicious blow to the face from Thompson's rifle. He crumpled to the floor.

"LOOK OUT!" Beatrice screamed as Thompson turned to the second man and dispatched him with another thundering blow of his rifle stock.

Charles followed Beatrice's eyes and saw it: a third man in the corner, bringing his pistol to bear on Thompson. Charles instantly, instinctively raised his revolver and fired three quick shots in rapid succession. Each of them found their mark: a perfect group in the man's chest. He fell without uttering a sound and thudded to the floor.

"Blimey," Thompson said. "You killed him."

"I sure to Christ hope so," answered Lieutenant Charles Stuart, holstering his pistol and running to embrace Beatrice.

CHAPTER 40
CROSSING THE LINE

RICHARD SUMMONED SIR MELVYN FOR A WALK IN THE PARK. IT WAS the perfect location to ensure complete privacy, away from any prying eyes and ears. As they approached a park bench, Richard told Melvyn to sit down. "Melvyn, I got some work for you. But first, let's talk about those bloody paintings. My villa in Switzerland still isn't ready for the paintings. Those uptight Swiss technicians can't get the security system to meet the specifications and are taking entirely too long. It could be another couple of weeks…blimey. I'd sack them all and tell them to sod off, but then I'd have to start all over again with a different lot. I don't want to delay the fire any longer, since what I'm going to tell you next will cause a great deal of turmoil, a lot more than any fire."

"What's that, sir?" Melvyn said, dejectedly.

"Steady on, Melvyn, I'm getting to that, but first things first. It's time to get the Polacks to move the fake art to the hangar as we planned and have those firebugs burn the blinkin' storage place down. Right away, you understand? Post guards 24/7 around the hangar and make sure no one goes in."

Sir Melvyn nodded.

"Now on to the more important piece of business." Richard leaned forward, his eyes lit with excitement. Sir Melvyn inched back, driven away from the smell and the closeness of his loathsome handler. "Let's talk Charles first. Remember Shaun McCabe, the IRA bloke who threw the hand grenade at William? You know, the one you visited in prison, who later testified at William's treason trial?"

"How could I forget! A killer and traitor. Pure scum."

"That scum Mick owes us his life," Richard said. "We let him get away after the trial and the assassination. He's been on the run ever since, but some of my people have been keeping track of him and actually have helped him out now and again. I've kept him alive and around, thinking that someday he could be useful again. Well, today is the day. He's the ace in the hole, Melvyn."

Richard pulled out a piece of paper from his vest pocket and handed it to Sir Melvyn. "This is how to contact him. You will tell him the plan."

"What plan?"

Richard then detailed the deadly scheme he'd concocted for Charles's elimination. Sir Melvyn listened intently, his face becoming whiter and whiter as Richard talked.

"So you see, my dear Melvyn, that will take care of Charles. Now for Henry. We have been in touch with my mole, Badger, in Boston. Badger has been instructed to arrange a fatal accident for Henry. Badger will have no option but to comply with my order, or otherwise there will be painful consequences to the family. Once that accident takes place, the throne will be mine."

Melvyn swallowed and dabbed at the film of sweat that had appeared on his forehead. He was overwhelmed with the evil of this wretched but deranged Richard. How could Richard possibly believe he could get away with killing a king and his heir, and then high jacking national treasures worth billions of pounds? There would be no escape for either of them. Melvyn was finally convinced beyond a doubt that Richard had crossed the line over to insanity. "Sir," he began, then faltered. "Are you committed to this course of action? I mean, it's… beyond treason, sir. It's…diabolical."

Sir Richard laughed. "Diabolical, is it? Yes, I do believe it is. Now shut up and get to work, Melvyn. By the time we're done, you might be a counselor to the king. Me."

The meeting ended and Sir Melvyn left in total despair.

CHAPTER 41
THE PROPOSAL

AFTER THE IRA KIDNAPPING, CHARLES HATED EVERY MINUTE HE WAS separated from Beatrice. The image of her bound to that filthy bed, and how she was moments away from being violated by a gang of Irish hoodlums, haunted him until he could actually lay eyes on her and see that she was safe. No matter what else he was doing—brushing his teeth, going on dangerous night missions, or reading in his room—a clock in his brain was counting down hours until he could see her again.

At the same time, his conscience pricked him. He had killed a man. Charles had taken a life. He knew it was the right thing to do, that it was unavoidable. But the fact remained: Charles was a killer now, and even though he felt it was completely justified and the morally right thing to do, taking a life weighed on him more heavily than he would have imagined. It was hard to fathom how his fellow soldiers coped with such a nagging moral struggle. But for him, it was a burden he would carry the rest of his life. Still, he knew he would do exactly the same thing again, without hesitation, when it came to protecting the love of his life.

With all of this going on, Charles came to view Beatrice's little room at the Fitzwilliam Hotel as a safe harbor. It was the only place where he felt he could truly be himself and relax. It was the only place where he felt the weight of his title and his awesome responsibility slip off his shoulders. On one of their regular nights, Charles arrived a bit late. He bolted up the stairs, passing the reception desk at breakneck speed.

"Take it easy, love," a cheeky hotel desk clerk yelled after him, "you'll break your wee neck on those steps. You've got all night, don't you?"

Charles ignored her and took the steps two at a time, then rushed down the hall to room 212. He knocked softly.

"It's me, Charles. Are you there?"

Beatrice rushed to the door and opened wide. A beguiling grin split her face when she saw him. "Come in. I've been waiting for you. It seems like forever."

"Sorry, Bea. I was detained at the regiment. I hate being late, especially when it comes to seeing you."

"Oh, Charles, ever since that horrible incident I worry endlessly about your safety, and mine too. Every time there's a knock on the door or a strange man in the street looking at me, I fret. If it wasn't for you being here, I would have obeyed my producer's order and left a long time ago. But I just want to be near you. Somehow I think being here makes you safer. I know that's weird, but it just does." She took his hand. "I'll forgive you, Lieutenant, for being late, but the price is a kiss."

Charles was only too happy to close the door with his foot as he stepped into her arms. "That's a steep price. Where shall I start?"

"Here," she said, placing her open lips on his.

Charles pressed his strong frame against the woman who he had come to cherish and kissed her back, deeply and passionately. Pulling their lips apart for just a second, Beatrice spoke softly in his ear. "I love it when in the middle of our kiss I can feel you smiling. It speaks to my heart."

"I have a lot to smile about. You make me the happiest guy in the world. I never knew I could feel so much in so short a time. My life has been one tragedy after another, until now." Charles kissed her again, this time more intensely, stirring him to his core.

The couple made their way toward the bed as Charles removed his uniform jacket and let it drop to the floor, while he loosened his tie. He turned his attention to the tiny buttons that fastened the front of Beatrice's Laura Ashley dress. As he unbuttoned each one, he became more and more excited. Within seconds, the well-tailored dress was no longer on, and Charles was feasting his eyes on this most beautiful woman. Immersed in the light flowery fragrance of her perfume, a mix of jasmine and rose she called Joy, Charles thought it was a perfect name. For it was joy that he felt, and joy that Beatrice had brought into his life. He kissed her neck and then her shoulders, shuddering in anticipation.

Beatrice helped Charles out of his shirt, then his trousers and the rest of it, leaving him standing totally naked, clearly ready to demonstrate in the most intimate of ways his love for her. They sat on the edge of the old iron bed and wrapped their arms around each other. Gazing into each other's eyes, they slowly reclined onto the rickety bed. Charles's hands lightly caressed Beatrice's naked body. She put her arms around Charles's neck and drew him close.

"Bea," Charles whispered. "I've never felt anything like this. You make me feel whole and loved and…I don't know…just wonderful. I can only hope I make you feel the same. If I don't, then I consider myself a failure."

"Oh my God, Charles, that is the nicest thing anyone has ever said to me. And you are hardly a failure, since I feel exactly the same towards you. We are bound together not just physically, but in every other way."

Their passion rose as Charles entered his sweet Beatrice. She softly spoke into his ear as they gently rocked to the rhythm of their desire and quenched their thirst for one another. "Charles, I love you, and I want you now and forever."

"I love you too, and you shall have me forever, as I will you."

The lovemaking went on until he could wait no longer, pulled Beatrice tightly toward him, and culminated. When they were finished, Charles rolled over and kissed Beatrice's shoulder. "That was wonderful. You know I really do love you?"

"Yes, I know, you mentioned it a few dozen times this evening, but as far as I'm concerned I'll never get tired of hearing it. I promise it will never be taken for granted. And just so you know, I love you too."

Charles spent the night in the shabby room. When the couple woke the next morning, they lay in each other's arms, silently, each lost in their own thoughts and the closeness they felt. Beatrice spoke first: "Charles, when you go back to London, will you be as free to see me as you are now?"

"Of course, Bea."

"How about after you take your place on the throne, what then?"

"Nothing will change. You will be there, right next to me."

"I hope you mean that, because I don't know what I would do without you. By sheer chance, you came into my life and then saved it. Now I feel it would be no life at all if you weren't part of it. I am worried that things will get very complicated once you get back to London. You will have so much on your plate, and the powers will be pulling you in all different directions. I'm nervous that maybe I will not be part of it all."

"Bea, you are all of it! No one will ever get in between you and me." Charles propped himself up on his elbow, looked into Beatrice's eyes, and kissed her tenderly. When he finished, he leapt off the bed, knelt at her side, and asked, "Beatrice Grandton, will you marry me? Will you be my wife? Will you be my queen?"

Beatrice sprung up and gave her answer: "Yes, yes, and yes! I will marry you and be the best wife in the world. You are my best friend, my confidant, and my lover. I could never ask for more."

Reaching over to the nightstand, Charles grabbed his keys. He removed the assorted keys, leaving only the simple metal ring. He slipped the makeshift engagement ring on Beatrice's finger and said, "I had something a little more impressive in mind when it came to an engagement ring, but I hope this will do for now. I just didn't want to miss this moment. I promise you something much grander will follow."

"Charles, I think this is better than all the crown jewels in the Tower of London. I will never cherish anything more, no matter how much it sparkles."

The two embraced, then Beatrice held her hand in the air, admiring her new ring and beginning to laugh. "You know, every young girl dreams of getting married. Many dream of marrying a Prince Charming. But I don't think too many of them dream of being proposed to by a stark-naked king betrothed with a keyring. Now that's hilarious."

CHAPTER 42
THE BLAZE

THE PAPERS WERE ABLAZE WITH NEWS OF THE SPECTACULAR FIRE. IT was a four-alarm fire that attracted brigades from districts as far as away as Bromley. Richard sat at his desk, enjoying his morning tea and reading the *London Times*, starting with a four-column, above-the-fold headline that declared: "Priceless Art from the Royal Collection lost in Fire."

Last evening in a secure storage facility located just south of London, fire broke out, destroying the entire complex. Included in the loss were an undisclosed number of priceless paintings that were part of the Royal Collection. The art collection belongs to the British Royal Family and is one of the most valuable and important assemblages of art in the world.

According to Palace spokesperson Percival Hammer-Smith, the art was being stored in the facility while major renovations of the Queen's Galleries at Buckingham Palace were being facilitated. The renovations started months ago, and reports are that they were nearing completion. Mr. Hammer-Smith is quoted as saying: "We are all heartbroken about this loss, one not just felt by the Royal Family, but by the entirety of British people and art lovers around the world."

The Royal Collection consists of more than 7,000 paintings, 40,000 watercolors and drawings, and about 150,000 old master prints, among other works of historical photos, tapestries, and the like. Fortunately, the art is dispersed amongst thirteen Royal residences across the UK. Those destroyed in last night's fire were among the most important and irreplaceable. No actual value can be placed on them since many of the pieces are considered priceless. Palace officials indicated there was no insurance available.

The collection is held in trust for the monarch, and as Sovereign he has sole control. Richard, Duke of Gloucester, serving as regent for King Charles, was unable to be reached for comment, but his office issued the following statement: "This is a tragic and irrevocable loss of the greatest magnitude. Some of the greatest art treasures known to man have been destroyed. His Majesty King Charles is devastated with the destruction of these national treasures."

Investigators are sifting through the rubble to see if there are any surviving pieces of art. However, the prognosis looks grim. At this time, there is no evidence of foul play, but the investigation continues. Although the palace has not released an official list of paintings, nor the actual number of pieces that were destroyed, it is well known that the collection included such masters as Giovanni Bellinim, Rembrandt, Gainsborough, and John Martin, the latter being one of the most famous British artists.

When questioned why these famous treasures of the realm were being stored off palace property, the palace spokesman replied: "The storage facility selected was the safest and most secure available. There was no such site on the palace grounds that would provide similar security and technology."

Palace critic Rupert Nettleson questioned the veracity of that statement. "Why couldn't the palace provide adequate security for the art on site since they guard the king and his family round the clock, which is far more important?" Sir Richard, the King's Regent, has announced that he has hand-chosen a team of investigators to examine the cause of the tragic fire. A report is due within a fortnight.

Richard smiled to himself. Of course, the coverage on TV was also constant, with images of the artwork plastered on every screen in Great Britain. Things were coming together—and it was time for another meeting with Sir Melvyn. The two met in the palace garden, where Richard triumphantly shoved his copy of the *Times* under Melvyn's nose. The other man looked ill.

"Melvyn, I want to congratulate you on the job you did," Richard crowed. "It looks like we were able to pull off the biggest art heist in history. I can't wait to get those paintings to Switzerland. I have some Middle Eastern blokes who are drooling at the thought of peddling them on the black market. They'll fetch millions, maybe even billions, and they all want a piece of the action."

"You told people about this scheme? Won't they go to authorities and turn you in?"

"Melvyn, you are really dim. Of course they won't go to the authorities. They are crooks, the lot of them. They deal in a dark world and the last thing they would do is get anywhere near the law."

Sir Melvyn could hardly bear to make eye contact with Richard. "I suppose that's good news."

"Good news!" Richard gloated. "Melvyn, it's money in the bank! Where are the paintings now?"

"They are all in containers just a few miles from the airport."

"Brilliant! I'll let you know as soon as the villa is prepared."

"Yes, sir," Melvyn answered.

"Cheer up," Sir Richard said. "At last, I believe you've found something you're actually good at. Lord knows, you haven't been good at much else."

Melvyn actually winced, and Richard laughed uproariously at the man's discomfort.

CHAPTER 43
HOME RUN!

HENRY AND HIS GROUP ARRIVED BACK IN DC BEFORE SUNSET AND were whisked back to the British Embassy. Julian and Sam were both tired from the long day's travel, but Henry was energized and pushed onward. Time was running out, and he was totally focused on getting to Cooperstown as soon as possible. He knew the judge could render his decision any moment now.

Samantha touched his arm to get his attention as they walked back into the embassy building. "Henry," she said, "let's go somewhere where we can plan our next step. We need to have a strategy in Cooperstown."

"Good idea. Where do you want to go?"

"Let's go sit in the Blue Parlor, where we had drinks. It's out of the way and private."

The threesome made their way to the second-floor parlor and sat around a small round table, their heads together.

"Henry," Samantha said, "I think that if we just walk in unannounced like some Joe Public and ask to see the journals, they probably would not allow it. We have no claim to them. So how about this? I will call the New York State Historical Society and tell them that the Duke of York, Prince Henry, is going to be in New York State tomorrow. I'll refresh their memories that you were Ambassador Carnegie's grandson and grew up in his house and would like to see some of the mementos they have in their archives. You know, for nostalgic reasons. I'll remind them that you spent childhood years in Cooperstown at your grandfather's camp. We'll play it up as a big deal that a prince would like to visit their museum and that the British Embassy is setting it up as an official visit. When you arrive with an entourage, they will be smitten with all the formality and give you access."

"I don't know, Samantha. I hate trading on my title. It's so not me."

"I know. But just this once it can come in handy."

"Fine," Henry agreed. "If we can even get pictures of the journals, we can ask Judge Lowenstein to subpoena them. I think it's our only shot."

"Agreed," Samantha said.

<hr />

The Lear 35 took off for Cooperstown right on time, with Henry, Samantha, and Julian aboard. It was a short flight, less than 90 minutes to a small airport just outside of Albany. After speaking with Samantha—and repeatedly stressing how excited he was to have a "royal visitor," especially one who was a Carnegie and relative of the historical society's biggest benefactor—the society's director had arranged for cars to pick them up at the airport and take them directly to the museum. Finding the right transportation in a sleepy village like Cooperstown wasn't easy, but finally Auggie Bush, one of the town's wealthiest inhabitants, volunteered his Bentley and a couple of local businessmen provided an assortment of Rovers for the motorcade.

Henry was ready to play his role to perfection. He had given up on his favorite jeans and was decked out in his finest English custom-made suit, looking every bit the young, dashing prince. Even Samantha had offered him a low whistle of approval when she saw him.

When the motorcade arrived at the museum's impressive col-umned *porte cochére*, the director was there to greet them, with a small group of local press, donors, and onlookers anxious to catch a glimpse of a real prince.

"Your Royal Highness, it is our pleasure to welcome you to Cooperstown and the New York Historical Society's museum."

Two young children bearing flowers appeared from behind the director and presented them to Henry.

Henry knelt to receive the children and accept the flowers. He was so taken with how adorable and innocent they looked that he leaned over and gave them each a kiss on the cheek. Cameras clicked and hearts melted at the sight of the handsome prince kissing the children. Henry rose, handed off the flowers to Samantha, and spoke: "Thank you so much, and thank you for your warm welcome on such short notice. I have been very anxious to see some of the Ambassador's mementos, and I'm grateful for your help."

Samantha leaned over and whispered in Julian's ear; "He's good, really good at this. With those looks and his charm he could get what-ever he wants for anybody."

Henry signaled for Sam and Julian to come forward and introduced them, using the titles they'd cooked up on the plane. "Director, I'd like you to meet my staff. This is Miss Samantha Smythe, chief protocol officer, and this is the head of my personal security detail, Julian Cox."

"Pleased to meet you, Miss Smythe," the director answered. "We spoke on the phone, I believe, when you arranged this very special visit. Thank you. And Mr. Cox. Welcome to Cooperstown and our humble museum."

As the gathering turned to enter the building through a pair of impressive glass doors, Henry paused and looked at the lake abutting the museum property. "Is that Otsego Lake?"

"Indeed, sir. You know it?"

"Yes. As a boy, my grandfather Carnegie had a camp along that lake. It was acres and acres. He called it Camp Bliss. I guess because he loved it so much. I remember sailing in the little boats he had made for us. We would sail over to some grand hotel and have lunch with my mother and father."

"That would be the Otesaga Hotel."

"Is it still there?"

"Yes, of course. And I was sorry to hear about the impending sale of your grandfather's camp. You should know, the museum is trying to raise funds to buy it before the sale goes through, but it's unlikely we could raise that kind of money in time to save it from some New York City real estate developer. Once acquired, there are plans to build luxury condominiums, something the town folks are adamantly against, but powerless to prevent."

"Such a pity. Why didn't the trust just donate the camp to the museum?"

"I only wish they had. We did approach the board chairman, a Mr. Whitman, on several occasions, but he turned us down, flat. He said the trust needs the funds to support other endeavors and was not in the business of doing Carnegie monuments."

Henry shrugged his disapproval.

The small group was escorted into the great hall, where a formal tea was set. After the appropriate receiving line introductions and a cup of tea, which Henry reluctantly sipped despite loathing the stuff, Samantha set the agenda into motion.

"Director, the prince would like to see the Carnegie artifacts now. Can you arrange that?"

"Of course, Miss Smythe, immediately. After which I'd love to show the prince our most important exhibit. It's the Otesaga Indian tableaus. It's one of the most complete collections of the tribes of the area. Very informative and interesting."

"Yes, I'm sure, but after the Carnegie viewing."

"Very well. Shall we proceed?"

He showed them to the Ambassador Harding Carnegie room, which looked more like an elegant library than a museum. The walls were lined with books and framed pictures of dignitaries and world leaders. Comfortable sofas and wing chairs were distributed throughout. A huge oil painting of Ambassador Carnegie dominated the room. It was the very one that once hung in his home in Westchester when Henry was a boy. Henry, tearing up a bit, couldn't help but feel nostalgic and a twinge of sorrow as he looked at the picture. He remembered how much his grandfather had loved Charles and him. He always knew that he was the favorite, feeling a certain closeness, an unspoken connection. He also thought how horrified the Ambassador would be if he knew that his family was being deprived of the Carnegie legacy.

"This is impressive, director," he said. "I recognize many of the artifacts from when I was growing up. Miss Smythe, you see that oil painting of the yacht, next to the French doors? It was one of his most prized possessions."

"Indeed, she was a beauty. I see by the plaque she was called *Summerset*. She must have been something in her time."

They fanned out and looked through the bookshelves for anything that looked like a journal. A worry grew in his mind: what if they weren't here? He had convinced himself they would be successful, but it occurred to him that they might strike out.

As he turned away from a rare English antique breakfront that housed a number of the Ambassador's trophies, he spotted a tall mahogany bookcase with glass doors. Within the shelves were what appeared to be leatherbound journals, each with the year stamped in gold on the binder. Henry caught Samantha and Julian's attention and nodded to the bookcase.

"Director, would you mind if I looked at some of those journals? I'd like to read what the Ambassador had to say about certain events in my life."

The director paused to consider this unusual request. It was irregular to allow anyone to touch museum artifacts. "Normally we don't allow people to handle the artifacts, but...seeing as how you were his family, I see no reason not to allow it."

Turning to his assistant, the director ordered protective gloves, a standard procedure when handling museum artifacts.

"Thank you," Henry said.

"You are most welcome. Take your time, sir. If you like, we can have photostatic copies made for you and send them to your office. We did that once before at the Ambassador's request."

"Copies, you say? You have copies of the journals?"

"Well, not here, but a full set were made years ago and delivered by courier to the Ambassador's executor. I believe he was writing a biography."

Henry's heart started to beat harder. "Do you happen to remember his name?"

"No. He was an influential lawyer in New York. A Whitaker, maybe? Whiteman—"

"Was it Paul Whitman?" Henry said quickly.

"Why yes, that's it! Paul Whitman. Now that I think of it, I believe it was the very same Paul Whitman who is trying to sell your grandfather's camp! I remember we had to work the reproduction room overtime to get all the copies made, bound, and sent down to him. We sent the material by our own courier truck to ensure their safe arrival. Once there, our men had to unload the journals into a private vault. I remember them complaining about it. We aren't a moving service."

"Do you think they have those copies in New York?"

"I wouldn't know, but I can't see why not."

"I see," Henry said. "That's interesting. Now if you don't mind, can we have a few minutes to look at the journals? I'd love to see what my grandfather wrote about."

The room emptied except for Julian and Henry. As soon as they were alone, Henry bolted to the bookcase and opened it. "I don't know how much time we have," he said. "We're going to subpoena these for sure, but…let's at least take a look now. I'd say we start in 1970, when I was born, and skim."

"Got it, mate," Julian said, already starting to remove leatherbound books. "What are we looking for exactly?"

"Don't know," Henry said. "Anything about me. About family."

They each took a stack of journals to one of the tables and started reading.

<hr />

Henry was quickly and completely absorbed in his grandfather's writing. The Ambassador exhaustively detailed almost every day, with his schedule, his thoughts, stories about people he met and saw, and analysis of the big news stories of the day. Henry figured it made sense to concentrate on the entries that might mention him and Charles, so he began skimming around his birthday and the holidays and went forward from there. He gave Julian a different year, and both of them sat with their heads bowed, skimming as quickly as they could, the sounds of pages flipping the only sound in the room.

Henry didn't have to look far to find entries about himself and his brother. His grandfather wrote about them often, mentioning their major milestones, recalling visits to their home and games they played, and fondly looking forward to their future. As far as Henry could see, there was more than enough material here to satisfy the second part of the will, that his grandfather was intimately involved in raising him and Charles "as Carnegies." He easily located half a dozen entries in that first year where his grandfather called them "Carnegies" and talked about how tight the family was. Coupled with Whitman's deception in hiding the journals, Henry's hope began to rise.

But still, there was the problem of the first part of the will: having Carnegie blood flowing through his veins. He knew the trust's defense relied almost solely on this clause. Hopefully, he thought, this would be enough at least to convince Judge Lowenstein to find in their favor partially. Perhaps he would split the baby, vis-à-vis the biblical King Solomon's approach at getting to the truth.

Just then, Julian whistled. Henry glanced up and saw that Julian was reading from a journal dated 1975. "What?" Henry said. "What'd you find?"

"Henry, do you remember having an accident when you were a child? At your brother's birthday party?"

Henry thought back and the memory came to him almost immediately, but in pieces. It was Tyler's party. The whole family was there.

His parents had hired magicians and musicians, as well as ponies. He remembered being on a pony when a car engine had roared—he clearly remembered the bright orange car with the Confederate flag on the roof, the one from the TV show—and then his next memory was faces hovering over him, his father and grandfather. He remembered the pain. Later, his mother had told him she had never been so scared for his life, that he had almost died. It was one of his earliest memories, but it was incomplete, only a jumble of images and impressions, the ghost of fear and pain.

"You need to read this," Julian said, and he handed over the journal. Henry balanced it on his knee and started reading out loud.

Saturday, August 2, 1975

It's 4 a.m. and dear God, what a day. It all started yesterday at the birthday party for Tyler. I arrived just before lunch and had some fun with the kids. Liz had put a fabulous party together for Tyler's 6th. The place looked amazing and a herd of cute kids ran through the old house and garden. Then the nightmare began. Dear sweet Henry fell off a rented pony and landed onto a pitchfork. It was serious. We rushed the dear boy off to the ER at Westchester Medical Center. I demanded that the Chief of Staff be notified and personally direct Henry's care. A team of doctors operated on the child and had to remove part of his spleen. My heart was breaking for the boy, and seeing the horror on William and Liz's face was devastating. The doctors told us that Henry's spleen had multiple catastrophic puncture wounds and that the boy had lost a vast amount of blood. They made two recommendations: immediate blood transfusions and an experimental surgery where they would graft sections of a donor spleen onto Henry's. In time, the donor graft would adhere to Henry's spleen, allowing it to function properly. William, Liz, and I all were tested for blood type and it was decided that I was the best match. Two pints of blood were transfused from me into Henry within hours. When I was told that more blood would be needed, probably four or five more transfusions, in the next few weeks, I told the doctors that I would make myself available at any time. Dr. Morgan, the surgeon, also asked for volunteers to donate part of their spleen. I immediately accepted the challenge, was tested and found compatible, so surgery was scheduled. As I end this entry, I can only say what is in my heart. Please dear God, don't take this boy. He is so special to all of us. If you must have a life, take mine, for it is far more important that this innocent child gets to live his life than an old man gets to finish his.

Henry looked up, a confusing welter of emotions running through him. Chief among them was gratitude and love for the old man. He had always felt a special bond to his grandfather, and reading his concern for Henry was moving beyond words. But there was also a dawning shock at what he'd just read. Julian was staring at him.

"You don't think…" Henry said. "I had no idea. I mean, I know my mom said I almost died, but no one ever told me about this business with the spleen or that I had blood transfusions and all that. But if that's true…" His words trailed off. "Professor Greenway needs to see this immediately. Like, now. Before Judge Lowenstein issues his ruling!" He stood up quickly and held his hand up for a high five. "Holy crap, Julian. This might change everything!"

⎯⎯•◆•⎯⎯

Henry, Julian, and Samantha arrived back at the British Embassy in time for dinner, which was hosted by Samantha's Uncle Arthur.

Before he went down to the small and informal dining room, Henry placed a call to Professor Greenway and left an urgent message at his office. He called twice more, then again after dinner. Finally, during coffee, a staff member came and informed Henry that the professor was on the phone. Henry excused himself and ran into a private office. As he did, he grabbed the journal. He knew he shouldn't have taken it, but it was too important to leave behind, so he had stuffed it in the back of his pants and promised himself he'd return the original as soon as this was over.

"Henry, my boy," Greenway said. "Glad to hear from you! Now, what's so important you're burning up the line to reach me?"

Henry quickly related the story of the journals, Whitman's role in receiving copies of them, and finally his grandfather's entry about the surgery. Greenway listened and asked a few questions. When Henry was done, Greenway uttered a low whistle.

"My goodness," he said. "I thought you might find the journal, but...this is really a bombshell. Incredible! Can you get to New York tomorrow? We need to get this journal to Lowenstein as quickly as possible. And I'll need to make some calls tonight. We need some medical expertise on board, quickly."

"I'll be there first thing," Henry said. "Whatever it takes."

"Perfect."

Henry hung up and went to look for the others. He found Samantha in the Blue Parlor, where she sat reading from another journal they "borrowed." She looked up as he came in.

"This is amazing reading, Henry," she said. "The Ambassador was really something. There is no doubt he loved you very much, as well as your entire family. He also was a brilliant worker. What an empire he built. He knew and met so many important people."

"Yeah, he was amazing," Henry agreed. "I miss him. My dad loved him too. I'm told he personally negotiated my father's candidacy for vice president. Great connections and master deal maker." Henry paused. "I just spoke to Professor Greenway and he wants me to bring the journal to New York City tomorrow. Can you come with me? I'd like that. We can take Amtrak first thing."

"That would be lovely. Count me in. Henry, come sit next to me."

Henry sat down next to Samantha on the long, blue and white sofa.

"Henry, may I ask you a question?" she said, leaning toward him and tucking a strand of hair behind her ear.

"Sure. What?"

"You have had some extraordinary things happen in your life. The stuff with your dad and then his death, and your elevation to such an important spot in the royal family, and yet you are such a regular person. You accept your lot and never complain or acknowledge your station in life, much less take advantage of it. You take your looks for granted as if you were some average bloke. Why is that?"

"I don't know. Probably because I think of myself, as you said, like a regular guy. My brother does too. For reasons I can't explain, stuff just happens to me and my family. Some have called it destiny. I never wanted or asked for anything special. In fact, all I ever wanted was to be just like all my friends. I wanted to succeed in life, but by hard work and sacrifice, not by birthright. Does that sound weird to you?"

"Weird? No. It sounds wonderful to me. I think it might be the best part of you."

Henry smiled as he recalled what Star called the best part of him. In a way, it was refreshing that Sam liked him for something else. "Thank you. It's really nice to know you feel that way." Henry hesitated. "Sam, I know this might sound, I dunno, forward or something, but I'm really glad you decided to come with me today and are coming to New York. I know I've only known you for like a day, but I feel like it would be strange to be apart from you, like it's so natural to be with you that I can't picture you leaving."

Samantha laid a hand on his arm. "I know what you mean." Then she frowned slightly. "But...don't you have a girlfriend? Julian told me about some girl you have at school. Star something?"

Henry was at first puzzled, then remembered. Oh yeah. Star. "Well, yes and no on the girlfriend front. It's complicated," he said. "We've been together a long time. But lately, it's been kind of failing. I think it's a habit by now, for both of us. Don't get me wrong. Star's great, and I've been loyal to her. But the relationship is skin deep, if you know what I mean."

"So...what does that mean? You're split up?"

"I guess, yeah."

Samantha put her other hand in Henry's and gripped him with a sudden intensity. He felt his blood rush into his head and the world seemed to drop away, leaving only the two of them on a pinpoint.

"Samantha," he said, only because he liked the way the sound of her name felt in his mouth.

"You're driving me a little crazy," she said.

Henry didn't trust himself to respond and could only watch in amazement as this beautiful, smart girl leaned forward, her face growing in his vision until she eclipsed everything else, and then her lips were on his and they were kissing. Her kiss was so unlike Star's provocative ones. It was a gentle and loving kiss that evoked a stirring deep within him, an emotion he had never felt before.

The couple held each other, each not knowing what would come next. Henry whispered in Samantha's ear, "I'm frightened. I don't want to ruin anything, but I want to make love to you. Is that out of line?"

"It's not out of line, but I've never quite had anyone ask me like that before, not that many would have had the opportunity, mind you. But yes. I want to make love with you too."

Samantha led Henry down the corridor toward her room. As they entered, Henry actually felt nervous. How odd, he thought, since he certainly had more bedroom experience with Star than most guys his age could ever imagine. He could tell that Samantha was also a bit ill at ease and chalked it up to the probability that she was treading in unfamiliar waters. Clearly, she was not the type to have casual encounters with just anybody.

Henry took Samantha in his arms and looked deeply in her eyes. "Are you sure you are okay with this?"

Kissing him deeply, she answered by her actions, not her words.

They undressed each other carefully and slowly. Samantha's beautiful body was undeniable. Her flawless skin and perfectly formed breasts took his breath away. More deeply, the sense of connection he felt to her, the total ease with which their bodies seemed to recognize each other, was gratifying. His nerves vanished, and he allowed Samantha to remove his shirt and then his jeans. Henry stepped out of them and then his briefs. Clearly, Samantha was equally as smitten as he was.

He slowly and gently caressed Samantha, who encouraged him by saying how much she wanted to be his. Henry gently ran his fingers though Samantha's long blonde hair and then touched her face. Looking directly into her deep blue eyes, he could see that this beautiful woman was there for him.

In time, the foreplay turned to climax and the passion within them exploded. Afterward, they lay breathless, naked, and exposed.

"That was amazing, Henry. You make me feel so complete. I am falling in love with you. So you best mind."

"I hope you are, because it will be the best thing that ever happened to me. And by the way, I'm already in love with you and have been from the first."

CHAPTER 44
THE TRUTH BE TOLD

HENRY WOKE UP THE NEXT MORNING EXCITED AND HAPPIER THAN he'd felt in years. He rolled over and, instead of seeing an empty bed or Star, he saw Samantha, and a surge of joy and, yes, even love went through him. She was so beautiful as she slept. It all seemed like it was happening so fast, but it also felt like the most natural thing in the world. What he had said the night before was true: he couldn't imagine being separate from her already, and he had only just met her.

She woke up and smiled at him. "Hey."

"Good morning," he said.

"You ready for today?" she asked sleepily, a hand stroking his face.

"Oh yeah. I'm ready."

"Good."

They got ready and met Julian in a small dining room. The long-time security guard raised his eyebrows when they came in together, smirking knowingly at Henry, who ignored him and sat down to eat. When they were done, they caught a cab to the Amtrak station and then a train to New York, where they hurried to the offices of a law firm that was allowing Professors Greenway and Haverman to use some spare space. Both were already waiting when Henry came in bearing the journals, and both looked like they'd already been up for hours working. The table before them was covered with books and papers.

"Henry!" Professor Greenway greeted him, then shook hands with the others. "Sorry to be in a rush, but I want to go over our findings first, and then we need to get over to Judge Lowenstein's courthouse and file an emergency brief. So, let's see what you've got."

Henry handed over the journal, opened to the page where his grandfather described the surgery, and Greenway and Haverman both read it quickly. When they were done, they leaned back and exchanged a meaningful glance. Then Greenway pushed a book toward Henry so he could read the title. It was called *Human Organs and How They Work*.

"Henry, do you know what the spleen does?" Greenway said, opening the book to a marked page.

"Sort of. Well, not really."

"Here. Listen." Greenway read aloud: "In the human adult, the bone marrow produces all of the red blood cells, 60–70 percent of the white cells (i.e., the granulocytes), and all of the platelets. The lymphatic tissues, particularly the thymus, the spleen, and the lymph nodes, produce the lymphocytes (comprising 20–30 percent of the white cells)."

Henry nodded but looked a little puzzled. "Okay, but...I thought the blood transfusions would be important. How does this fit in?"

"Henry, dear boy, you had a partial spleenectomy and donor transplant. The blood transfusions are one thing, but from what I just read, your grandfather's partial spleen actually makes blood cells."

The shocking realization dawned on Henry. This was even better than he had hoped.

Greenway continued, "The defense has rested almost all of its case on that one narrow point. That you must have Carnegie blood running through your veins. Assuming this is true, and we've checked with mul-tiple doctors to confirm, Henry, our whole position changes." Henry started to speak, but Greenway cut him off. "But it won't be easy. They will fight this tooth and nail. Boris here believes they will try to make the defense even more narrow, that you might have had Carnegie blood in your veins, but you don't any longer. You still with me?"

"Yes," Henry said.

Greenway chuckled and rubbed his hands together, and Henry could see why he was considered such a great legal mind. He obviously relished the fight. "We're really in the weeds now. It could be debated whether or not past transfusions leave a measurable DNA trace that would show Carnegie genetic material in your blood. We believe the defense will proffer that argument and could win it, depending on the results of testing. I'm assuming you'd be open to a DNA test?"

"Of course."

"But now they are the ones on thin ice. That's a very weak sauce on which to hang a billion-dollar decision, if you catch my drift. It is beyond dispute that fragments of Ambassador Carnegie's spleen were enjoined to yours, and over time they have melded into one. It's not a far stretch to argue that your hybrid spleen, part yours and part your grandfather's, is this very day producing white blood cells and voila! You have Carnegie blood in your veins."

Henry caught his breath.

"Wow. This is even better than I thought," he finally said.

"Indeed it is! Indeed it is!" Greenway said triumphantly.

Haverman leaned forward. "Henry, there's never been a case like this. We've searched every bit of case law we could find. Not only did you suddenly fill out an inside straight with this journal, you are likely to participate in a precedent-setting case! This could wind up in law books around the world."

"Holy shit," Henry said, then immediately, "Sorry."

Haverman laughed. "Holy shit indeed," he said. "By interpreting things as literally as they possibly could, I believe the trust might have created just enough rope to hang themselves!"

"I'm just...that's amazing," Henry said. "But will it hold up?"

"That's what we're going to find out," Greenway said. "But Henry, there's no denying the power of your story, or I might add, your personality and character. I think we're on very solid footing here."

<hr/>

They filed the brief that morning and requested an emergency hearing. To their total amazement, the judge himself called Professor Greenway within the hour, and Henry listened intently as Greenway nodded along on the phone, then said, "Of course, Your Honor. We'll be delighted to."

Two days later, Henry found himself back in Judge Lowenstein's chambers, sitting around a conference table with his two professors, the judge, and Paul Whitman and Leon Peck, representing the trust. Whitman and Peck were unsmiling and, aside from a perfunctory hello, ignored Henry. That was fine with him.

They all sat in silence as Lowenstein read from some papers in front of him, then cleared his throat, looked at Greenway, and said, "Well? I will say this is some of the most interesting reading I've had in my tenure as a judge. Is there anything you'd like to add?"

"Yes, Your Honor," Greenway said. "And thank you. We wanted to specifically address the claim that Henry does not have

Carnegie blood running through his veins. Over the last several days, we have continued to research the incident Ambassador Carnegie wrote about in his journal and have located the relevant medical records. We've forwarded copies to you and to the trust. These records confirm that the plaintiff was seriously wounded in a freak accident on August 1, 1975, and rushed to the ER. The record substantiates that the plaintiff underwent emergency surgery and had a newly developed procedure performed. This procedure actually transplanted segments of a donor's spleen, which were grafted to that of the plaintiff. That donor was Ambassador Carnegie. After years of residency in the plaintiff's body, the two spleens became one and function normally.

"I have also presented medical evidence as to the function of the spleen for the court's consideration. In summary, one of the major functions of a healthy spleen is to produce white corpuscles, a major component of blood. Hence, it is our contention that the hybrid spleen resident in the plaintiff is technically making blood cells that are in part producing Carnegie blood."

Greenway paused dramatically, then continued.

"Your Honor, we have also provided evidence to the effect that for several weeks after the emergency surgery, the plaintiff continued to receive blood transfusions directly from Ambassador Carnegie, which indisputably allowed Carnegie blood to 'flow through his veins.' Clearly, this event alone meets the will's first qualification. As to the will's second qualification, we believe the Ambassador's journals show amply his involvement in the plaintiff's upbringing and the sense of family that the Ambassador felt."

Judge Lowenstein paused in thought and began slowly. "Thank you, counselor. That was very concise and enlightening." He looked over at Peck and Whitman, who were sitting with absolutely no expression. "Gentlemen, are you ready to proceed?"

"Yes, Your Honor," Peck said. "We are. Your Honor, pursuant to our proffered brief, we are in serious disagreement with the plaintiff's supposition. It is the defense's contention that the most important of the criteria set forth in Fillmore Blair Carnegie's will has not been met. That criteria being the requirement that Carnegie blood is running through a beneficiary's veins. Again, Your Honor, I stress the words 'is running.' There is no serious evidence that this is the fact. As a matter of medical fact, the plaintiff does not currently have Carnegie blood. Despite the claim that the plaintiff's spleen, part of which was donated by Ambassador Carnegie, is producing blood cells, this is not supported by scientific evidence. The mere fact that at one time, the Ambassador's blood was used in a medical procedure does not constitute a genetic connection of the type the will clearly means. By that standard, anyone to whom a Carnegie gave blood would be entitled to a part of the estate."

Judge Lowenstein made a few notes, then turned back to Greenway. "Gentlemen, what say you?"

"Your Honor, I respectfully submit that the will's language in question, as written in Fillmore Blair Carnegie's own hand, states: 'Must have Carnegie blood running through their veins.' The defense seems to want it both ways, Your Honor. They choose the most narrow interpretation when it suits them, and the broadest in other cases. Taken literally, there is no question that the plaintiff has had, and still does have, 'Carnegie blood' flowing through his veins. He has further stated that he is willing to take a DNA test, but the court should be aware there are mitigating considerations in play. While DNA is clearly a widely acceptable tool for measuring whether people are related and share the same genetic material, this type of testing is in its infancy and we are prepared to produce experts who will state that the white corpuscles, which are being produced by a spleen that is partially Ambassador Carnegie's, are not totally detectable by current DNA testing.

"And second, Your Honor, although the DNA testing is said to be as high as 99.9 percent accurate, the scientific community agrees that the acceptable accuracy rate is more like 97 percent. This is documented by The Council for International Organizations of Medical Sciences (CIOMS). Thus, one can easily calculate that there is up to a 3 percent chance of error. Therefore, we suggest that there is a reasonable doubt that DNA testing would by itself produce any satisfactory conclusions."

The judge finally looked at Henry when Greenway was done speaking. "You would agree to a DNA test?" he asked.

"Absolutely," Henry said.

"Okay, that's noted." The judge looked down again, read some more, then looked back up. "I'd like to thank both parties for coming in today on such short notice. I've received the new briefs and evidence, and I will take them into consideration as I issue my ruling. Thank you, and as they say, I'll see you in court."

The parties stood up, shook hands stiffly, and left separately. Once again, Henry was amazed how quickly these actual meetings happened.

CHAPTER 45
You Play with Dogs, You Get Fleas

Every day was more oppressive than the previous one. Deprived of sleep and racked with stomach upset, Sir Melvyn was filled with pain, guilt, and depression. He longed for the days when he was a free and an uncontrolled man…but those days were gone forever.

He had no good options. If Richard was successful in his plan to raid the treasury, confiscate the art, and kill Charles and Henry, Sir Melvyn was sure his days would also be numbered. Richard would never leave a loose end like him around. It was equally hopeless to go to the authorities. For all intents and purposes, Richard controlled the security apparatus. He had MI5 in his pocket, and from there, they could pressure anybody. Even his former colleagues in Parliament wouldn't help. They all knew of his association with Richard and most of them would only be too happy to see him go down. He thought of his nanny's old adage, "If you play with dogs, you get fleas." It was true. Melvyn was a marked man and he knew it.

He even ruled out suicide. There was no way he could bring himself to actually do it. Without any other options, Melvyn sat down to write a full confession. He wasn't sure who would ever read it, but at least it felt good to get it all out. Fueled with false courage from half a bottle of twelve-year-old scotch, Melvyn began documenting the whole grotesque saga one night. After hours of writing, he wrote his final words:

In the end, I can blame no one but myself. I sold my soul to the devil and he will have nothing less. I am weak and dishonorable. My greed, pride, and self-preservation have allowed me to commit the most grievous of crimes and treasonous acts. I have closed my eyes to what is right and just. I have betrayed my family, my country, my King, and worst of all myself. I am too much of a coward to do the right thing and end my life, one that is no longer worth living. I now regret and humbly ask for forgiveness from my wife and family, my country and my God. For those who read this, I beg understanding.

Melvyn held the three-page epistle in his shaking hand and then placed it on the desk. Reaching for his pen, he affixed his name at the bottom. A tear rolled down his cheek. Opening the top drawer, he removed a large white envelope with the official seal of the Office of the Private Secretary. As he placed the pages into the envelope, the phone rang. Glancing at the desk clock, he noted it was 7:16 a.m.

"Sir Melvyn here."

"Melvyn, get your ass over here now." It was Richard's odious voice. "I have some work for you to do. Don't dick around, just get here."

"Yes, sir, I'll be along directly." Richard rang off with no further words.

Before he left, Melvyn sealed the envelope and placed it into his briefcase. It was now up to him as to what would come next.

He walked through the foyer of his town house and encountered his loyal manservant of some thirty years.

"Good morning, sir, I hope you had a good sleep."

"Indeed, I wish I had, Boynton, I wish I had."

"So sorry to hear that, sir. I wish you a good day."

"Thank you, Boynton." Melvyn paused in thought, contemplating Boynton. He had relied on the man for more than thirty years. Boynton had helped raise his family and maintain his many homes. Sir Melvyn knew that Boynton could always be trusted.

He made a decision. Reaching into his briefcase, he removed the large white envelope. "Boynton, I have a very important and special favor to ask of you."

"Of course, sir. Anything. Anything at all."

"Please take this envelope. Put it in the safest place you know. Mind it well! Never open it under any circumstances. If anything should ever happen to me, please give it to the editor of the *London Times*. He will know what to do with it. This is very important. Can I rely on you to do this?"

"Certainly. It would be my pleasure. But, sir, are you in some kind of trouble? Is there something I can do to help?"

"Trouble? Not exactly. But this is an insurance policy and you are the only one who I can trust to safeguard it. Do I have your word?"

"You can count on me, sir. I'm here to serve."

"That will be all, Boynton." As he walked away, Sir Melvyn turned. He extended his hand to Boynton. "You do know you're the only person in the world that I can fully rely upon. You are a true friend."

Boynton simply bowed his head and whispered: "Thank you, sir. That means a lot to me."

CHAPTER 46
STONEWALLING

"**W**E'D LIKE TO MEET WITH YOU."

These words came from Paul Whitman, in a terse message to Professor Greenway, only hours after they left Judge Lowenstein's courtroom. The group, including Julian and Samantha, was just sitting down to lunch when Whitman called, and there was a general sense of excitement and surprise they would call so fast.

"They must be scared," Greenway said after he hung up. "So what do you say, Henry? You up to making a trip into the lion's den?"

"Any day, any time," Henry answered.

The meeting was set for the day before their next hearing with Judge Lowenstein. They met at Cavanaugh, Wolf, Whitman and Smith, in one of the opulent conference rooms with a stunning view of New York City. After they exchanged pleasantries and got coffee, Greenway took control, even though Whitman had called the meeting. This was all according to the plan Henry and his lawyers had cooked up ahead of time.

"Gentlemen," he said, standing up, "thanks for hosting us here, and I'm sure you have agenda items to discuss. However, before you begin, there is something else I believe you should know, something that we have not yet submitted to the judge but believe will have a material bearing on his case."

Whitman and Peck both looked suspiciously at Greenway. It was highly irregular to hijack a meeting like this. "Go on," Peck said.

"We were most gratified to find Henry's grandfather's journals, as you can imagine. They were located at the historical society in Cooperstown. These are, in fact, the same journals that Judge Lowenstein had issued a subpoena for and urged you to, what was the word, strenuously search for."

"Yes, we're aware," Peck said.

Greenway turned to address Paul Whitman directly. "I was very disappointed to learn that you were ignoring the subpoena," he said. "And before we alerted the judge, we thought it would be valuable to talk this over with you first."

"Ignore the subpoena!" Peck said. "That's preposterous! There's no way——"

"Mr. Whitman," Henry said, cutting off Leon Peck in mid-sentence. "You lied to me and the court. You have the journals here, in a big vault."

There was a dead silence in the conference room. Paul Whitman's face was a mask.

"I know this because I saw the documentation in Cooperstown, showing that the museum delivered photocopies of the journals by express courier to your office. The workers even remember unloading the journals into a vault. In your office. We haven't confirmed it yet, but I'd bet that the signature on the courier form accepting the delivery matches yours perfectly."

Whitman still didn't respond, so Greenway leaned forward. "In your sworn deposition, you said you had no knowledge where the journals were. If we were to ask Judge Lowenstein for an order to search the premises, one never knows what might turn up in direct conflict to your sworn statement. I'm sure you understand the implications if that were the case."

Leon started to talk, but Whitman laid a hand on the table. Without breaking eye contact with Greenway, he finally spoke. "This is outrageous. What I said in my deposition was the absolute truth. I said I did not have the journals, which I do not. I stand by that statement. I never said anything about the copies. I have no further information for you."

"I see, Mr. Whitman," Greenway said softly. "It looks like we'll have to ask the judge to settle this. Along the way, however, you should know there are some other questions we'll ask him to consider. Questions relevant to the management of the trust."

"What questions?" Whitman said in a voice dripping with venom.

"It seems that through our research and investigation, we found that the sitting Carnegie trustees all have proprietary interests in a vast majority of relationships between themselves and the trust. Also, the trustees are all, in one way or another, related to you either in a business arrangement or family ties. Apparently you are intimately involved in at least two of the trustees' businesses, either as an investor or as a board member or both. The trust also holds vast stock positions in addition to extending very favorable loans to enterprises owned or operated by some of the trustees. Notably, each of the trustees seems to have unfettered access to expense accounts as well as unusually high honorariums, all approved by the chairman of the trust, which of course is you. Lastly, your firm receives an inordinate amount of their legal fees from the Carnegie Trust and/or related activities. The appearance of a conflict of interests on so many levels is inescapable. Very cozy indeed."

Whitman glared at them, then suddenly stood up. "Gentlemen. What you have said is patently ridiculous and without standing. I will not waste another second on such drivel. This meeting is over."

Henry and the professors collected their papers, stood and exited silently. On the way out, Henry realized that Whitman and Peck never even got around to telling them why they wanted to meet in the first place. Oh well, he thought, they'd all be together in court again the next morning.

CHAPTER 47
BRASS ONES

"ALL RISE! COURT IS IN SESSION, JUDGE AARON LOWENSTEIN presiding."

Henry and the professors stood at the plaintiff's table. Not far away, the legal team from Cavanaugh, Wolf, Whitman and Smith stood at the defense table. Henry was impressed that Whitman was able to keep his expression so neutral. There was a reason Whitman was one of the most expensive lawyers in the country—that kind of self-control wasn't cheap. Still, all it did was fortify Henry in his plans. The night before, after making love, he had told Samantha how he expected this hearing to go.

"Are you sure?" she had asked. "That's awfully risky."

"It's only risky if I have something to lose," he answered. "Truth is, I have everything to gain. They can't touch me."

Remembering that, and remembering Samantha, gave him even more strength.

Sitting behind the bench, Judge Lowenstein peered down his nose through his old-fashioned bifocals. "Gentlemen," he said. "I have reviewed all of the findings and am now ready to make my ruling."

Before the judge could speak another word, Leon Peck rose. "Excuse me, Your Honor, may I approach the bench?"

"Yes, but make it quick," Lowenstein grumbled.

"I would like to ask for a recess so that the plaintiff and the defendant can perhaps work out a settlement."

Greenway, Haverman, and Henry all looked at each other and shrugged. This was not entirely unexpected.

"Professor Greenway," Lowenstein asked, "is your client willing to meet with the defense to discuss a settlement?"

"Your Honor, may I confer with my client?"

"Please do, but be brief."

Professor Greenway leaned toward Henry and Professor Haverman. "What say you?"

"Look, Henry, we have nothing to lose by hearing what they have to say," Haverman said. "We can always reject an offer if they make one. But remember, there is no guarantee that the judge will find for us. There is always a risk."

"What do you think, Professor Greenway?" Henry asked.

"I agree. We have nothing to lose by listening."

"OK. I'm good with that."

"Your Honor?"

"Yes, Professor Greenway?"

"The plaintiff has agreed to meet with the defense and with counsel present."

"Very well. Bailiffs, please escort them into a deliberation room. I will grant a forty-five-minute recess. If after that time the parties cannot reach a settlement, we will reconvene. If no settlement is reached, I will render my decision. Understood?"

In unison the men replied, "Yes, sir."

The deliberation room was grim at best. Old and battered chairs surrounded an ancient and scratched Formica conference table, scarred from years of fear and desperation. The windows were covered with dirty and broken blinds. Henry could almost believe that the austere surroundings were intentional, giving the occupants incentive to get out of the room as soon as possible.

Henry and the professors sat on one side of the table, with Paul Whitman, Leon Peck, and their team of associates at the other side.

"Gentlemen," announced Professor Greenway. "The ball is in your court. It's your meeting."

"Thank you, Professor Greenway," Peck said. "We have discussed ad nauseam the merits of your action and have concluded that a positive outcome for you is not likely. We are convinced of this because of the overwhelming evidence we have presented, and in particular, the indisputable evidence showing there is no blood relationship between the plaintiff and the deceased Fillmore Carnegie, the trust's originator, and his son Ambassador Carnegie. However, in the interest of soothing old wounds from years past, and in keeping certain unsubstantiated allegations designed to discredit the Carnegie Trust and its hardworking and dedicated board members from being recklessly smeared, we are in a position to offer a more than fair and equitable settlement to the plaintiff."

Henry and the professors glanced at each other and sat silently.

Whitman pulled out a single sheet of paper from his Gucci briefcase and read aloud: "This generous and simple offer is as follows. The plaintiff will agree to drop all litigation against the Carnegie Trust, its subsidiaries, its board chairman and members, and the law firm of Cavanaugh, Wolf, Whitman and Smith. The plaintiff will agree to and sign a nondisclosure order whereas no information regarding any element of this case, its settlement, or allegations against any Carnegie Trust board member or chairman or the law firm of Cavanaugh, Wolf, Whitman and Smith for improper actions, conflict of interests, and the like will be made public under any circumstances. In consideration of this agreement, the Carnegie Trust will agree to render the plaintiff a onetime cash settlement payment in the amount of fifty million dollars."

Whitman passed the single page over to Professor Greenway. Greenway read it again, looked up, and passed it to Henry and Professor Haverman. There was dead silence in the room as the men read.

"Are there any questions?" Whitman asked when they were done.

"I have one," Henry said. "Could you clarify what you mean when you said, 'In the interests of perhaps smoothing old wounds from years past'?"

"Of course. What is meant is there is, by some, a feeling that when the trust declined entertaining any consideration to William Carnegie, it might have been a bit less than altruistic."

"Thank you for that clarification, Mr. Whitman."

"You're welcome, young man. On a personal note, I hope you will accept our offer and, with it, we can bury the hatchet, so to speak."

Henry stared down at the single sheet of paper, slowly reading it again. Fifty million dollars was a lot of money. He stood up, seeming to fill the room with his athletic and handsome frame.

"Mr. Whitman, is this your best offer?" he asked.

"Yes, sir, it is."

"Well then, here's my answer." Henry took the sheet of paper containing the offer and ripped it into shreds. "You can take this offer and shove it up your collective asses!"

Mouths fell open around the table, including those of the professors, but before anyone could say anything, Henry spoke. "You see, gentlemen, and I use the term loosely, since gentlemen are usually men of honor who do not steal, misrepresent, or manipulate charitable endeavors to enrich themselves, their families, and friends. This is a matter of principle, not money. No money could ever repair the devastation that the Carnegie Trust thrust upon my father and our family. He was turned out penniless, stripped of his possessions, and rendered persona non grata. Our cars, homes, and prized possessions were confiscated and sold. Mr. Whitman, as chairman of the trust, you even directed that my mother's own engagement ring be sold and the proceeds given back to the trust, since it was purchased with money given to my father from the trust. To see my mother's heart broken and the sea of tears she shed when she was stripped of the very symbol of her betrothal was an unconscionable act of greed on the part of the trust, so directed by Mr. Whitman! You are all shameful low-lives and deserve to pay for your indiscretions. Gentlemen, and again I use the term loosely, you have far more to worry about than paying me a settlement. It is my intention to contact the attorney general of the State of New York, who will unquestionably initiate an investigation into the Carnegie Trust and the misdeeds of the board and its chairman. With respect to the missing copies of the journals and the whereabouts of the originals, I'm sure your testimony relative to that constituted obstruction of justice and perjury, both very serious crimes, especially for members of the bar. The blatant and incestuous nature of the trust's board and the cronyism shown among its members also provide ample fodder for investigation and possible criminal action, not to mention a public relations nightmare. Therefore, I make a final and non-negotiable counter offer to you. If you choose not to accept it, we will proceed as promised.

"My offer is as follows. Please write it down so you don't miss anything."

The defense team reached for their pads and pens.

"First, the trust will issue certified checks in the amount of $100 million each to my brother Charles and me in restitution for the suffering we incurred due to your lack of consideration and concern for my father and his family's personal well-being.

"Next, the trust will give a gift of $10 million to the Harvard University Law School in the name Professors Greenway and Haverman in lieu of legal fees they declined.

"Additionally, the trust will direct that a certain parcel of land and associated buildings known as the Carnegie Camp Bliss located in Cooperstown, New York, will not be sold by the trust but will instead be donated immediately to the New York Historical Society's Museum at Cooperstown. Further, an endowment of $500,000 annually will be gifted to the Society for the sole purpose of maintaining Carnegie Camp Bliss and related endeavors, in the broadest way.

"Next, the entire Carnegie board of trustees and the chairman, Mr. Paul Whitman, will resign. Prior to their resignations, they will: 1. Terminate all ongoing business relationships that present conflict of interests, up to and including legal representation of the trust by the law firm Cavanaugh, Wolf, Whitman and Smith. And 2, vote in two new trustees: Professor Greenway and Professor Haverman, who in turn will select the balance of the board.

"Lastly, Mr. Paul Whitman will write a personal letter of apology to my mother, Elizabeth, for his atrocious betrayal of a friendship and his total disregard for her well-being. That's it. Take it or leave it."

Paul Whitman, aghast at this proposal and seething with rage, stood and addressed Henry. "If you think that your proposal, which amounts to nothing more than extortion, has the vaguest chance of being accepted, you better pick up your crayons, young man, and go back to school. You're playing with the big boys here. Don't even think of trying to bully us. You're out of your league."

Henry, still standing with fire in his eyes and the will of Hercules, said, "Back to school? Crayons? Perhaps I will. When I get there, I will be sending you and your partners in crime some pretty colored pictures to your prison address. That is, of course, after you are publicly dragged through the mud, humiliated, and disbarred for your illegal and egregious actions."

Greenway and Haverman sat at the table in complete shock, staring at Henry with open mouths. Before the hearing, they had all discussed the likelihood that Whitman and the trust would offer a settlement. Haverman had estimated they would offer $10 million, instead of the $50 million they actually did offer. Henry had not told them of his plan or his counteroffer. He knew they wouldn't have approved—but he also knew that, as much as he respected and looked up to Professor Greenway as a father figure—this had never been about the money. It had always been personal.

Whitman and his team sat silently, looking at each other for several minutes. Leon Peck finally said, "My colleagues would like to step out of the room for a few minutes, if you don't mind."

"Of course," Professor Greenway said. "We wouldn't mind the opportunity to confer among ourselves."

Whitman and the other lawyers cleared out, and Henry turned to face Greenway and Haverman.

To his surprise, Haverman was grinning, but Greenway looked serious. "Henry, I wish you'd told us this was your plan. Paul Whitman is not wrong, you know. You are playing hardball with some very serious guys. They are seasoned professionals who won't scare easily. I'm sure it felt good to say that, but your allegations of malpractice could be very difficult to prove, and we aren't even sure Judge Lowenstein will rule in your favor."

"I know," Henry said.

"Henry, my boy, are you certain about this? We can get them back into the room and maybe negotiate the amount up a bit, but you know a bird in the hand is worth two in the bush. To turn down $50 million, you have to have pretty big brass ones. We could lose everything."

Henry smiled before he answered. "You know I'm not about money or anything like that. My father was wronged, and my mother was humiliated. Giving back that engagement ring broke her heart. She acted bravely, but we all saw what happened. No, I have no intention of recanting my position, and that is that. As for whether I have big ones or not…I guess we'll find out in a few minutes."

Now Haverman burst into laughter. Greenway glanced at his colleague, then back at Henry and his expression softened. "Henry, you know you're like a son to me. And I know it's not about the money for you. Of course. You should know that I have never been prouder of you and more impressed. You epitomize everything good in man. You are honorable, kind, generous, and stand for what you believe, righting wrongs and adhering to your values no matter the cost. Even if we don't win this case, you have won something far more valuable. You have won the respect and admiration of all us. That has no price tag. I applaud you and I am honored to know you."

"Ditto on that, my boy," Haverman said. "I have to say, I believe I enjoyed your counteroffer as much as I've enjoyed anything in my career. That was something to see!"

Henry smiled. "Thanks. It means a lot to me to hear you saying that."

"Of course," Greenway said. "I mean every word. Now, since the die is cast, all that's left is to see what will happen."

It was another ten minutes before Whitman and his associates walked back in, walking in single file like ducks in a row. As always, their faces were completely blank as they sat down.

"Gentlemen, we have discussed your counterproposal and we are amenable with one exception," Peck said. "Mr. Whitman will not write a letter of apology to the plaintiff's mother. It is totally out of the question."

Greenway started to speak, but Henry cut him off. "With all due respect, Professor, I'd like to speak first."

"Of course, Henry."

"Mr. Whitman, you don't know me very well, because if you did, you would know that all the money in the world, and all the kingdoms on earth, have little value to me. What is of value is integrity and humility and a sense of fair play. You have not played fair with my family and probably hundreds of others. You owe us all an apology, especially my mother. Without it there is no deal. Do you understand?"

"Are you saying you are not going to allow this counter-offer to go forward merely because of a foolish letter?" Peck answered.

"Yes, that is exactly what I am saying. And for the record, I don't consider an apology to a very ill woman who has suffered to be at all foolish. I consider it mandatory."

There was a knock at the door. They all turned to see the bailiff at the door. "Time is up," he said, "the judge wants you all back in the courtroom."

The men stood. Leon Peck whispered something into Paul Whitman's ear, prompting Whitman to shake his head in disagreement.

Greenway leaned over to Henry and covered his mouth as he whispered, "Are you sure you don't want to change your mind? You've got everything, control of the board, your inheritance, everything. Do you want to throw all that away?"

"My family is more important to me than all their money," Henry answered. "And besides, they need to be made accountable for their outrageous mishandling of the trust and lying about the whereabouts of the journal copies in their safe."

"Okay," Greenway said. "I understand, and we'll support you. This should be interesting."

They filed back into the courtroom as Judge Lowenstein took his seat on the dais. At the nearby defense table, the defense team was crouched in an intense huddle, whispering urgently among themselves. Lowenstein frowned.

"Gentlemen, are we ready to proceed?" he asked.

Greenway stood and answered affirmatively to the judge.

"And for the defense, are you ready?"

Reluctantly, Peck nodded to the judge.

"Very well, gentlemen," Lowenstein said, removing his glasses and gazing out at the courtroom, his face as blank as an unwritten check.

"I don't like the look on his face, Henry," Greenway whispered. "He's not looking at us, which is never a good indication."

"What do you mean, Professor?"

"This isn't my first rodeo. Judges are human, as hard as that might be to believe, and they often wear their thoughts on their face. Sometimes it's just a wry smile, or a glint in the eye towards the party that is favored. We played the sympathy card, your unjust treatment, and I don't see a shred of sympathy or empathy on that man's face."

Henry, looking concerned, whispered more to himself than Greenway: "We're screwed."

Lowenstein said, "This indeed has been an unusual case. One filled with little surprises and some groundbreaking legal issues. A fine line exists here between what is so and what is not. It is a judge's job to look at every aspect and weigh the legitimacy of each party's argument. Sometimes that is more difficult than not. In this case we are looking for the right answer, and after due diligence and considerable thought I have arrived at my decision, one that seems—"

Lowenstein was interrupted by a heated but hushed argument between Leon Peck and Paul Whitman.

Picking up his gavel, Lowenstein tapped the sound block in front of him. "Gentlemen, I ask for your attention and respect for the court."

"Your Honor," Peck said, "may I approach the bench?"

"Now? I'm about to render my decision. And besides, I'm getting tired of your little jaunts up to the bench."

"Your Honor, this is important, I assure you," Peck almost pleaded. "May I approach?"

"Very well. This better be important. Come forward, but make it brief."

Peck walked briskly up to the dais and began conferring with Lowenstein.

"Professor," whispered Henry, "what is he doing?"

"I have no idea, Henry, it's most unusual for just one party to approach the bench."

Peck finished his conversation and returned to the defense table.

Judge Lowenstein wrote something on his pad and looked up to address the court. "It seems the defendant has agreed to the plaintiff's proposed settlement," he said. "I will read the highlights into the record, followed by a formal and binding written agreement to be signed by all parties." He picked up a piece of paper that Peck had left on his bench and, adjusting his bifocals, began to read out loud:

"The court now orders that a cash payment of $100 million be made to the plaintiff and his brother Tyler, aka Charles. In addition, the defendants have agreed to a contribution in the amount of $10 million to Harvard University, School of Law; another donation of a property known as Camp Bliss in Cooperstown, New York, and an annual annuity of $500,000 to the New York Historical Society; the dissolution of the existing board at the Carnegie Trust with the election of two new directors, Professors Preston Greenway and Boris Haverman; the termination of certain contracts and agreements held by the trust as shall be delineated in the full settlement document; and a formal letter of apology from Mr. Paul Whitman to the plaintiff's mother. Lastly, the court grants the defendant's request that any and all details of this settlement be kept confidential.

"Please see the bailiff after we adjourn to sign this preliminary settlement agreement. Court adjourned."

Henry thought he could have heard a pin drop in the courtroom. The heavy pause was interrupted when the bailiff barked, "All rise!"

Greenway and Haverman slowly stood, stunned. Henry jumped to his feet and pumped his fist in the air, declaring victory, then turned to the defense table and flipped them the bird. Whitman refused to look in his direction, but Henry didn't care. He had won a complete victory.

"Well, Henry," Greenway said, "I have to say, this was an incredible victory. You are to be congratulated. You've done very well for yourself, but..."

"But what?" Henry asked.

"But we will never know how the judge was going to rule! He was just about to say. Not knowing will haunt me for years. C'est la vie!"

Haverman clapped Henry on the back. "Son, you really do have brass balls. This is a case for the record books. Now, I think I saw your pretty friend waiting for us outside the chamber. What do you say we go celebrate? You're buying!"

Henry laughed. "With pleasure!"

———•———

In the few days after winning his settlement, Henry still had trouble believing it was real. He had restored his family's fortune and, more importantly, secured an apology for his mother. He called her and Charles as soon as they left the courtroom to deliver the good news. It was all too good to be true, and Henry was only too happy to share the victory with Samantha, who gushed about how brilliant he was and how proud she was. Still, life didn't stop just for the victory, and it wasn't long before the moment Henry was dreading actually happened: he returned to Boston while Samantha went back to Washington. It was so hard to say good-bye to her, and they agreed to meet again in DC as soon as possible. The only thing that helped Henry was the knowledge that his time at Harvard was almost over and he would be reunited with Samantha soon.

Henry returned to Boston, determined to take care of a few last things, but the biggest of these was his relationship with Star. She had been a central feature of his life since his days at Hotchkiss. And yet... he had known for some time that the relationship was coasting on pure inertia and physical attraction. They hardly talked about anything serious, and he had to admit that he really had no idea how Star spent her time away from him, and she really had no idea what he was thinking or dreaming about. In just a few days, he already felt closer to Samantha than he had felt to Star in years.

Once he made up his mind, he felt a great sense of relief. He had no doubt Star would be fine. She was a strong and independent woman who surely would do well under most any circumstances, with or without him. In the end, she would pick up, move on, and find another Mr. Niner.

Star arrived at River House around 6:00 p.m. the day after Henry got back.

"Hi, Hank, did you miss me?" she asked, using a seductive tone of voice that meant she was looking for some bedroom action.

"Yeah, sure, I missed you. You okay?"

"Blimey, I'm good. Where's Julian?"

"Oh, he's out, should be back around eight."

"Brilliant! What you say you and me haul out Mr. Niner and have some fun?"

"Not now. But sit down. We need to talk."

A furtive look crossed her face. "Uh oh. We need to talk, eh? About something in particular?"

"Yes. About us."

"You and me us?"

"Yes, that us. I think we need to start thinking about what comes after Harvard. My stint here is done and it's time to move on."

"Where to? Where are we going?"

"It's not so much about where, but more about how. We've been together for a long time and it's been great, really great. You are an amazing lover, but you know as well as I do that physical attraction isn't the only thing people need. They need an emotional connection, a sense of togetherness, and most of all an elusive thing called love. These important elements do not have a place in our relationship."

Star had sat down on the far end of the sofa at first, but now she slid over and put a hand on his thigh. "Hank, baby, do we need to talk about this now? It's been an age since we've seen each other. Can't we have some fun first, and then have this old boring talk?"

Henry gently pushed her hand away and slid further away. "No. I'm serious, Star."

She pouted. "Serious? So what? You're serious about all that tosh about emotional connections and whatnot?"

"Yes. We've been together a long time, since I was basically a kid. But things have changed. We've grown up."

Star leaned back. "Are you seriously breaking up with me? Is that what this is about?"

Henry took a deep breath. "Yes. It's been great, you know that, and you're just gorgeous, but I just don't think—"

"Spare me the humiliation," she said suddenly, viciously. "Do you really think you're allowed to sit there and condescend to me like that? You think I'm some kind of puppy you can just take back to the pound?"

"What? No. I don't think that at all. I just think we've grown up in different directions. Fact is, Star, I really have no idea what your dreams are, what you want out of life. I just don't see us as compatible."

"I thought we were plenty compatible!" she said. "As for what I want out of life, I want you. How is that unclear?"

"I'm sorry, Star."

"You're...sorry? What does that even mean? Do you have someone else? Is that it?"

"Star, it has nothing to do with anyone else."

"So what then?" she demanded. "You at least owe me an explanation! Is it because of all that money you just got? You think I'm after your money like some gold-digging slut?"

"Star! You know me better than that. I don't care about that."

"Then what? Why are you doing this?" She was starting to cry now.

"I told you," he said. "This is about each of us finding people who will grow with us as we become the people we need to become. And I don't think we are those people for each other. That's all there is to it. I have no hard will and…I hope we can stay on good terms."

He watched her face as it went through a remarkable series of emotions. Her eyes glittered with tears, then she almost sneered with anger, and finally she took several deep, calming breaths as if she had reached some conclusion.

"Okay, if you're set on it, then I understand." She uttered a short, bitter laugh. "I have no choice really. But you're right. It doesn't have to end poorly. We can each walk out with our heads held high."

Henry realized he'd been holding his breath and let it out in a big whoosh. "I'm so glad to hear you say that! And you should know that I'll always support you, any time. All you have to do is let me know what I can do."

She nodded, but he thought she looked skeptical. "Right, thanks. So…what's the next move? What's the plan?"

"Well, I need to be out of this flat in a couple of days. I'm going to Washington, DC to see the British ambassador and work on some business matters. Then who knows? I'll probably go to see my mother and brother."

"And what about Julian? Will he be going with you to Washington?"

"Probably. It's his job. At some point that too will have to be sorted out."

"You know, Henry, you are one lucky bloke. The looks of a Greek god, a royal heritage, and now the bankroll of a billionaire. All you need is love, and you'll have it all. I'll miss you."

"Thank you, Star. If you like, you can stay here until I must leave."

"Will I have a chance to say good-bye to Mr. Niner?"

"I'm afraid not. I'll sleep in the spare room, and you can have the other one."

Later that evening, Henry sat alone on the terrace at River House, looking out at the familiar city and thinking about his future. He was perched on the only open area of terrace—everywhere else was cluttered with scaffolding and other construction material from a renovation job that had been going on forever. The clutter was distracting, but in a way it fit Henry's mood. Everything was changing, and he still had some important decisions to make.

Harvard's law school commencement was coming up. He was contemplating whether he should skip it or not, risking the wrath of his mother. He had deprived her of seeing him graduate from Hotchkiss years ago, and pre-law undergraduate school, so he knew she'd be beside herself if he skipped Harvard Law graduation too. Henry hated pomp and circumstance, which literally would be playing as he marched down the aisle. As a prince, he also knew he would attract massive attention from the press that would only get worse if word got out that the Queen Mother and King of England were in attendance. What a nightmare.

Henry also considered how disappointed Professors Greenway and Haverman would be if they were robbed of the chance to witness "their boy" take papers. He sighed, then decided to put the question aside for now.

As darkness crept up, the lights across the river began to twinkle. Boston had an impressive skyline. After years at River House, he could point out the various important buildings and sites that glowed in the evening darkness like diamonds spread across a black velvet cloth. As he had so often before, he perched on the low parapet, dangling his feet into thin air and sipping an ice cold Budweiser. Clad only in boxer shorts, he had the feeling of unrestrained freedom and flight. In an odd way it was almost cathartic, liberating him from the oppressive past and formidable challenges of the future. The early evening breeze ran through his thick chestnut hair, giving him the sensation of soaring. It was liberating. He had so much to face, so many dragons to slay and a future to unfold. His hard-fought legal victory and vindication for his family was the first of many.

The responsibilities of his title and newfound unimaginable wealth were more burden than gift. As he sat contemplating, he turned abruptly. In the shadows, he saw someone walking toward him. The figure was coming along the wall abutting the next-door apartment, and his first thought was of his neighbor, the slightly odd South African poet who seemed to be lurking around his windows at all hours. The darkness hid everything but a silhouette.

"Julian, is that you?"

"No, it's not Julian, it's Badger."

CHAPTER 48
OPERATION WAR HERO

IT WAS CALLED OPERATION WAR HERO, AND WHEN WORD CAME DOWN to Sergeant Thompson that it was time to put the plan into action, he felt his heart grow heavy. He was about to kill a man he admired, a man who had saved his life in a grubby safe house in Belfast; Charles had shot the IRA terrorist who was lying in wait for him.

But still...Thompson had no illusions about what would happen to him if word of his history got out. He would be sent to prison as a serial pedophile. His life expectancy in prison would be short, and before they killed him, Thompson had no doubt he would be treated savagely by both guards and inmates. In order to protect himself, he had no choice but to help assassinate his king.

Sitting alone in his room after getting the order, Thompson sobbed and allowed himself to wallow in self-pity. He had no idea why he was this way, riddled with bizarre and perverse urges. The first time he did it, he was only sixteen years old, growing up in a rough neighborhood. During that first act, the feelings had been so intense, so overwhelming, he couldn't have stopped himself if he had wanted to. It wasn't until later that the self-loathing overtook him and he holed up in his room alone, a monster hiding in his cave. But soon he rejoined life and the old compulsions came back as strong as ever. They grew in him until he couldn't resist and he did it again, and once again he was overtaken with a self-loathing so intense it crippled him. This had been his pattern for years, always terrified about being caught but help-less against the sense of god-like power he felt over his tiny victims. Sometimes he wondered if he was possessed. Finally, one day he acted out and was caught. He was hauled into juvenile court, where at 17, he was fortunately charged as a minor, forced to go to a rehabilitation program, and released into the custody of his parish priest. As part of the lenient deal, when the rehab program ended, Thompson was "strongly" encouraged to enlist in the Royal Army.

It didn't take long before he received a call from Richard, who was looking for a mole to place into Charles's unit and had discovered Thompson's dark secret, which he ruthlessly used as leverage. From that moment on, Thompson would never be his own man again.

Now, Thompson felt like he was fast approaching a moment of reckoning.

"Sir," he said to Colonel McIntosh, "it looks like tomorrow night will be a good time. We're making a raid on a safe house and the lieu-tenant will be leading Delta Company. I will arrange to be with him. I'll get rid of his driver, so it will be just him and bloody me. When we get out of sight of the squad I'll find a nice dark corner and the lieuten-ant will meet his maker. I stole a gun from one of the Micks and will use it to inflict the wound. Then I'll shoot myself in the arm, just a graze, but convincing. I'll put his body in the jeep and drive back to command headquarters hospital. That will be that."

"Well planned, Sergeant. Now you say this will be tomorrow, right? About what time?" McIntosh asked.

"I don't know, but probably after 2300 hours. That's when most of the action happens around here."

"Brilliant. Then you have my permission to proceed."

"Yes, Colonel. What about my money and discharge?"

"No problem. Since you will be wounded, they probably will put you in the hospital. I will have orders drawn up to transfer you to London and then process you for an early honorable discharge, with full privileges. I'll even give you a bloody medal for bravery. As far as the money goes, you tell me where it should go and how much."

"Ninety thousand pounds, deposited into a London bank in my name."

"Just as you say. Ninety thousand pounds in your name. Will the Barclays Bank do? Or do you have another choice?"

"Barclays is fine. And don't double-cross me. A man with nothing left to lose isn't afraid of anything."

"Don't be daft," McIntosh said. "Just take care of your end and I'll take care of mine."

As Thompson hung up the phone, he began to breathe heavily. He had pains in his chest and was sweating like a work mule. Panic had set in. He had just sold the life of one of the most decent blokes he had ever known.

On the long walk back to his billet, Thompson resigned himself to his lot and prepared to commit the atrocious act to save his own hide. He rationalized it all as self-survival. He could only hope that he would be able to live with himself thereafter.

CHAPTER 49
A FALLING STAR

H ENRY WAS CONFUSED.
"Badger? Who the hell is Badger?" he said, recognizing the person behind the silhouette. "Stop kidding around, Star. Grab a beer and join me."

Star rushed toward Henry, her arms held out in front of her.

"Star, what the hell? Are you nuts?"

As Star came closer, Henry saw that her eyes were wild and filled with tears.

Now in a full sprint, Star reached Henry's perch on the parapet. Realizing that Star was about to push him to his death, Henry moved to the left and crouched, while holding on to the wall with all his might.

She was moving too fast to react and tripped over a piece of scaffolding. She tumbled over Henry with a shout, flipping over the wall and falling four stories to the street.

Henry couldn't believe his eyes. As he rose, he saw Julian, who had arrived just in time to witness what had happened. Julian ran to Henry's side, grabbed his arm, and pulled him away from the wall. "Are you okay? Wasn't that Star? Did she just try to kill you?"

Barely able to speak, Henry replied, "Yeah, it was Star. What could she be thinking to do such a stupid thing?"

Looking over the wall, the two men saw Star's lifeless body impaled on a decorative post on the high wrought-iron gate. Her blood was quickly filling the cracks and crevices of the century-old cobblestones that lay beneath her suspended body. A small group of students began to form around the scene, some covering their mouths in disbelief and horror. Moments later the wailing of a siren could be heard approaching River House.

"Get away from that wall! Don't let anyone see you," yelled Julian.

"Why? I didn't do anything. I was just sitting there having a beer. I had nothing to do with this."

"I know, I know, but it could look bad, just do what I say, Henry, and don't ask questions. This is dodgy business here. I'm going to ring the police."

Julian picked up the phone and dialed 911. When he got off, he told Henry to put some clothes on and sit back from the wall as they waited.

Campus security arrived first, followed by the Cambridge police. Henry sat in a chair with Julian standing squarely behind him. He gave the police a full account, but it was clear they were skeptical, even with Julian's eyewitness statement.

"Now let me see, young man, you said you were sitting on the ledge and she came running at you with the intention of pushing you off?" asked a burly Cambridge cop.

"Exactly. That is exactly what happened, officer, exactly!"

"Now why would this girl want to do that? Were you a couple?"

"Yes, sir. We were sort of a couple, but we were just in the process of breaking up."

Julian frowned, and Henry realized he had said too much.

The cop raised an eyebrow. "Ah, a jilted lover perhaps. Maybe an argument, a little pushing and shoving?"

"Officer, I saw the entire thing," Julian interrupted. "Star was going to push him off the wall. She came running at him. I heard her call herself Badger, which makes no sense at all. She must have flipped out."

Noting the clearly educated English accent, the officer quipped: "And who exactly are you? Manners the butler?"

"I'm Julian Cox, an officer in His Majesty's Special Forces." Julian produced his papers.

"British Special Forces? What are you doing here?"

"I'm on assignment as a special security detail for Prince Henry. The gentleman you're talking to is Prince Henry, Duke of York."

"This guy's a prince?" A wary note crept into the cop's voice as he inspected Julian's very authentic-looking badge and papers. They heard a sound and looked up to see another cop walking through the terrace door. The cop, still holding Julian's badge, said, "Captain."

The new cop was older, with silvering hair. "Officer Riley," he said. "What's going on here?"

"Sir, it seems that young woman hanging off the gate tried to kill the prince here. His security guard tells me it was an attempted assassination."

"Prince?" the captain said. "Prince of what?"

"This is Prince Henry, Duke of York and brother of the King of England," Julian answered. "He is a Harvard student. The young lady who attempted to kill him was Star Patterson, a British subject here studying theater."

"Really, and you are?"

"As I told the officer, I am Julian Cox, the prince's security detail and an officer in His Majesty's Special Forces. Assigned to the prince."

The captain nodded. "Well, now I've heard it all. Let's see some IDs."

Henry reached into his jeans and produced a wallet containing his international driver's license and a Harvard student ID, which he handed to the police captain. The first cop handed over Julian's military ID and other papers.

"So where does it say you are a prince?" the captain asked.

Henry smiled. "Well, sir, they don't issue IDs when you are a prince. But you can check the records, you'll see my name is the same."

"If you are an English prince, why don't you sound like the other guy?"

"I was mainly raised in the United States and never really developed a British accent."

"And what about this Star woman? Does she have some ID? They didn't find anything on her body."

Julian spotted Star's oversized purse sitting by the terrace door. He grabbed it and handed it to the captain. "Maybe something in here."

The captain unzipped the purse and noted, "This is one of those expensive French Louis Vuitton bags. My wife has been after one of these for a long time, but they are pretty pricey, especially for a student actress." He rummaged through the bag. "Let's see what we got here. Four lipsticks, a bottle of nail polish, two combs, a brush, Boston T pass, a bright red thong, a set of keys...What are these?"

The younger sergeant chimed in: "Those are birth control pills."

The captain dumped the purse upside down. "Candy, gum, more makeup, another set of keys, and a wallet. Not much in the way of ID here, just some money...quite a bit of money at that! Like $2,500, and maybe another four hundred British pounds. Too much for a struggling actress, wouldn't you say? Was this Star babe a hooker by any chance?"

Henry looked at Julian in disbelief. "No way, officer."

As the captain put Star's purse down, he suddenly froze and inspected it closely. "Lookie here! A secret compartment. Let's see what we got." He unzipped the compartment, removed the first of two items, and held it up. "Looks like a passport. British, to be exact." Opening it, he turned to the photo. "Good-looking chick." He showed the picture to Henry. "Is this your girlfriend, Star?"

"Yes, captain. That's her."

The captain flipped a page. "You say her name was Star, huh? And you're sure that's her?"

"Yes, sir. We were dating for several years."

"Star Patterson?"

"Yes, sir."

"Not according to this. Says here that her name was Marcella Hunt."

"What?" Henry said, shooting Julian a confused glance.

"I said this passport belongs to someone named Marcella Hunt, which you identified as someone you call Star, Star Patterson. Got any idea how that happened?"

A stunned Henry grabbed the passport, looked it over, and passed it to Julian. "What the hell, Julian?"

Julian closely inspected it, then looked up, confused. "I'm bloody cocked by this. I assumed she was vetted before I even got here. It never dawned on me to do a background check. Why would it? She was already part of your life."

"I don't understand why she would spend more than five years telling me her name was Star. I don't get it."

Julian just shrugged.

"Okay, boys. We're going to need to get to the bottom of this," the captain said. "O'Reilly," he said to the cop, who was still standing there. "Make sure the scene is secured. Collect and log this evidence and have someone call the medical examiner. And as for these two," he pointed to Henry and Julian, "have these two Brits come down to the station for a little more conversation."

"Right away, sir."

As the two police officers turned to leave, a third cop approached and whispered in their ears.

"I see. Are you certain?"

"Absolutely, Captain. I personally checked."

"Very well." The captain looked back at Henry and shook his head in amazement. "So it really is Prince Henry?"

"I prefer just plain Henry."

"Okay, just plain Henry. It seems you are a lucky prince. The corporal here talked to the administration, then checked downstairs and found a videotape camera that surveils the roof. And by Jesus, it supports your story 100 percent."

"That's great, I guess." The shock was starting to wear off, and Henry was only too aware that Star's body was still hanging from the fence below and medical personnel were draping the area off as they prepared to lift her off the cruel spear-like iron.

"Captain," Julian said, "I'm assuming we're free to go? No trip downtown?"

The captain shrugged. "For now, yeah. No reason to hold you. But don't go too far. I'm sure we'll have some questions."

"Of course," Julian said. "Thank you."

Then the cops were gone and Henry wandered back into his apartment, still trying to process what had just happened. Star had tried to kill him. And who the hell was Badger?

CHAPTER 50
OPERATION WAR HERO II

IT HAD TAKEN SOME SEARCHING, BUT SIR MELVYN HAD FINALLY FOUND Shaun McCabe. He was living in a rat-infested boarding house in Peckham, one of the most dangerous areas of London. The whole neighborhood was a den of drug dealers, gangs, prostitutes, and fugitives. It wasn't a place where Sir Melvyn even felt comfortable walking down the street in broad daylight, but now he found himself standing outside a greasy pub called The Chaulk and Ghost Tavern.

Melvyn had been practicing what he would say for hours. He had to act tough and decisive, even though this act of murder was so repugnant to him that he could no longer sleep. And yet he had no alternative but to follow Richard's orders. When Melvyn walked into the pub, Shaun was already there.

"Ah, I remember you," Shaun said. "You're the bloke who came to see me in prison. The one who got me to testify and allowed me to escape the holding cell at the courthouse. That was a good move; I got to lob a grenade and take out the bloody king. Long live Ireland!"

"Shhh, are you daft? You can't say anything about that, especially here in public."

"Are you kidding me? This place has no ears. And if someone did, they'd get cut off if they repeated anything."

"Let's get out of here," Melvyn said, terrified someone would overhear. "I've got a car outside. We can go for a little ride."

"No blinking way. If you want to talk to me, it's gonna be right here in public. I have no desire to go for a one-way drive with anybody. So what do you want?"

"Well, as you know, you have friends in high places. I understand they have been taking care of some of your needs. You know, like a few pounds here and there and, more importantly, not being hunted by the law."

"Yeah, what about it? I'm sure you didn't come here to tell me how good care the bloody Limeys have been taking of me. Get to the point."

"Very well. You see, someone wants you to do a repeat performance for them. This time in Belfast. There's this particular lieutenant that needs to be, shall we say, made a war hero. All you have to do is go to Belfast, which I will arrange, and follow this chap. Bring a sniper rifle with you. This lieutenant is going to be taken out by another bloke, so what we want to do is eliminate that chap, which at the same time will eliminate any witness. And you better damn sure hit your mark."

"Yeah, right. How do I know I'm not going to get deep-sixed the minute I've pulled the trigger?"

"You don't. But you've been living at the pleasure of some pretty important people who could have made you disappear a long time ago. Let's say it's payback time. You do this, and you will be able to live under the radar. No harassment, no running and hiding."

"Is there some dosh for me?"

"It could be arranged. What do you think of five thousand pounds?"

"I think it bloody stinks. I like ten thousand better. You know there is a lot of risk here for me."

Hesitating, Sir Melvyn reluctantly agreed. "Very well, ten and not a pound more. After you get the job done I will make sure you get paid."

"Are you bonkers? After? Listen, Sir Big Shot. I ain't stupid. I didn't come down in last night's cabbage lorry. Up front or no deal."

"Hmm. The best I can do is five thousand now and the rest after you do your job. Do we have a deal?"

"Okay, Shylock. But you better not screw me over, or I'll be on your doorstep. I swear on my blessed mother's grave. I will! And you know I will!"

Sir Melvyn had come prepared for this. He fished out five thousand pounds from his breast pocket and handed it to Shaun. He had another five thousand in his other pocket just in case.

Then he filled Shaun in on the details.

"By the way, Shaun, if the other bloke chickens out and doesn't do in the lieutenant, you put both of them away. Make it look like an IRA sniper attack. After it is over, you disappear immediately. Do you understand?"

"Two? You want me to do two? That will cost you more."

"Don't be greedy. But if you have to do both of them, there will be a bonus in it for you."

"There better bloody be, Sir Big Shot!"

CHAPTER 51
SHATTERED TRUST

HENRY SAT ALONE FOR SEVERAL HOURS, TRYING TO MAKE SENSE OF everything. It still seemed surreal: Star had tried to kill him. And, maybe even worse, he felt like someone had yanked hard on his reality and sent it spinning. Was she Star? Or Badger? Or someone named Marcella Hunt? None of it made any sense, and he felt like he was looking at a puzzle that didn't have a solution. Why had she tried to kill him? Why did she change her name? It made sense she'd want a more glamorous name than Marcella, considering she was in show biz, but now he found himself wondering if Star had something to hide.

Before long, evening fell and he found himself wandering around his apartment, seeing it as if through strange eyes. He needed someone to talk to, someone who knew him well and understood him. He thought of calling Samantha, but it would be too hard to explain all this over the phone. So he knocked gently at Julian's door.

"Hey, Julian, you in there?"

Julian opened the door and Henry saw that his friend looked pale and drawn. "Come in, mate," Julian said, letting Henry follow him into his tiny room while he dropped back down on the bed and held his head in his hands. "Henry, I just wanted to say how sorry I am that I was not at your side when you most needed me. I'll never forgive myself for that. You could have been killed, and it would have been entirely my fault. You don't know how horribly I feel. It's…"

"Cut it out, Julian. I'm fine, and you will be too. Nothing that happened was your fault."

"No, Henry, that's not true. If I were properly on duty, Star never would have tried anything so stupid. She would…"

"Julian, I told you to cut that self-recrimination. You did come to my aid just at the right time."

"Come on, Henry. We both know it never should have happened. I was a day late and a pound short. If Star hadn't tripped over that stuff on the terrace, it would have been you impaled on that bloody gate post bleeding all over Harvard Yard, not her." He took a deep breath. "The honorable thing for me to do now is to self-report myself to my commanding officer for negligence of duty. For a long time now, things have been far too casual around here. My first duty is to protect you and know where you are at all times. But things got too comfortable and protocol was sloppy."

"It wasn't sloppy. What are you talking about?"

"It was, Henry, and you know that too. Half the time, more than half the time, you went to classes and meetings without me. And I allowed it…just plain dereliction of duty and laziness on my part. Another thing that bothers me is how no one figured out who Star really was. When I arrived on the scene and replaced Ollie, I just assumed that Star had been properly vetted. I can't understand how this could happen."

"Julian, I met Star on an airplane years ago on my way to Hotchkiss. Simple as that. Ollie was with me, and neither of us thought much about it. Then she turned up at Hotchkiss and we became an item.

Later she followed me to Harvard, just more of the same…she simply fell between the cracks when it came to vetting."

Julian shook his head. "No. I should have known she was a problem. I let Star capture my trust and deceive me into thinking she was OK, someone not to worry about."

"Star had everyone convinced of that, Julian, especially me."

"But I should have seen that. Anyone who would two-time you should not have been trusted."

"Two-time me?" Henry uttered a short, bitter laugh. "Don't worry about that. I always sort of figured she had others, with her erratic comings and goings and long periods of absence. With her ferocious sexual appetite, it's not surprising. Did you know for sure that she was fooling around behind my back?"

Now Julian looked positively green with guilt. "Yes, I knew from the first day I came here."

"From the first day? How could you know that quickly? Why didn't you tell me?"

Julian stood and turned his back to Henry, unable to face him. "I knew because from the first day I met Star, she seduced me, and our liaison continued for years, right here and behind your very back. I'm so ashamed! So embarrassed that I betrayed my duties, but most of all that I'm unworthy to be your friend."

Henry stared at Julian's back in disbelief, betrayal, and anger. Then, without another word, he wheeled around and left the room.

He spent the rest of the night locked in his room. His last thought that night was that he wished Samantha was there to comfort him.

When the sun came up in Cambridge the next morning, both Julian and Henry rose from an almost sleepless night. Julian reached for the phone and placed the call he had planned all night.

A clipped English accent answered on the second ring: "British Embassy, how may I direct your call?"

"May I speak with Samantha Smythe?"

"Who's calling, please?"

"This is Special Agent Julian Cox, His Majesty's Royal Army."

"Please hold, sir."

Seconds later, Samantha was on the line.

"Hello, this is Samantha."

"Samantha, this is Julian, Julian Cox."

"Of course, Julian, right. You sound awful, is everything all right? Is Henry all right?"

"Yes, he is. He's safe and sound, but we have a big problem up here."

Julian filled Samantha in on the previous twelve hours, leaving out no details.

Samantha held her breath as Julian talked. When he was done, she exhaled and said, "Oh God, Julian, this is too unbelievable. Had Henry told Star that he was leaving her for me?"

"I don't know, but I don't think so. Henry is far too decent and a gentleman to do that flat out. According to Henry, she was alright with the break-up. Still wanted to remain friends. Why do you ask?"

"Maybe she tried to kill him in a jealous rage. Maybe she wanted him so much she couldn't stand him being with someone else. Henry did say she was a bit out there."

"I suppose that's a possibility." Julian hesitated, then plowed on with his story. "Well, you didn't know Star, or should I say Marcella. Her real name was Marcella Hunt. Anyway, I don't know how to put this delicately, but Star was not by any means monogamous. If you knew her you would realize she was not the type to get too emotionally attached."

"She had other men…while she was with Henry?"

"Yes, no question about it, she was two-timing him for years."

"How can you be so sure of that?"

Julian took a deep breath before answering. "Because I was one of them."

Samantha exhaled a deep sigh of astonishment. "You? Right there in the very apartment where he lived?"

"I'm afraid so. I'm so sorry, Samantha, but I am beyond ashamed and mortified. I have nothing to say to defend myself. I acted unconscionably and let lust blind my duty and judgment. I don't think Henry will ever forgive me, and I know for sure I will never forgive myself."

There was a stony silence. "Look, right now we have something really important to do," Julian said. "We need to figure out how to handle Star's death. The media will go wild once they figure out who Henry is."

"Are the police going to arrest him?"

"No, no! Thank God! They found a video surveillance tape that backs up Henry's account 100 percent. I also witnessed the whole thing and will back up Henry's story. He is totally innocent. But the press is going to have a field day with this nonetheless. The reason I called you was I wanted to get in touch with the ambassador. I didn't think he would take my call directly, so I called you, hoping you could connect us up. I need to have some direction from him."

"Of course. Hold on, I'll find him. He's probably in the pool or working out in the gym. I'll transfer you back to the switchboard and they will hold the call until I sort this out. OK?"

"Right. And Samantha, I'm so bloody sorry and ashamed."

There was a click and the switchboard operator picked up.

"Sir, please hold for the ambassador."

Julian held his breath until the aristocratic voice of the British ambassador came over the line.

"This is Ambassador Sturbridge. Is this Julian Cox?"

"Yes, sir, I felt I needed to call you and fill you in on the situation here."

"My niece Samantha gave me a ten-second synopsis, but you better start from the beginning."

Twenty minutes later, the ambassador was up to snuff. "Sticky wicket, man, really sticky. Grotesque, one might even say. I think the best thing is to get both of you here at the embassy and then develop a strategy. I'll send the Lear for you immediately. Can you be at the airport by, say, 3 p.m.?"

"That may not be possible, sir. The Cambridge police told us to remain in the area for future questioning if they need us."

"I see, Julian, but they did not charge either one of you. Right?"

"No charges, and the tape I mentioned definitely clears us completely."

"I'll check with our legal counsel, but I'm bloody certain that Henry has diplomatic immunity. For that matter, serving in your capacity, so might you too. "

"Well, like I said, the video pretty much clears us. Immunity may not even be relevant."

"We better make sure we get a copy of that video...God forbid anything happens to it."

"I'm not sure how I could get a copy of it. I don't think they will just hand one over to me."

"I'll have our legal counsel contact the Cambridge police and see what they can do. I'll also have them look into the immunity bit, it could be good to have that in one's waistcoat pocket. Let me make a few calls and see what can be arranged. I'll have Samantha coordinate this. Stay put and near the phone. She'll call you soon. And don't let Henry out of your sight. Do you understand?"

"Yes, sir, I'll stand by and await her call."

The phone clicked off.

It was a few hours later when Samantha called. She explained that the ambassador had reached the U.S. State Department, which in turn called the governor of Massachusetts, who contacted the chief of the state police. The chief ultimately called the Cambridge police and arranged for unrestricted travel for both Henry and Julian. The Cambridge police also agreed to allow a copy of the surveillance tape to be delivered to the State Department for forwarding to the British embassy. Finally, Samantha confirmed that the Learjet would be arriving at Logan International at 3 p.m. to take them back to DC.

"So that's the plan. You got that down, Julian?"

"That's pretty amazing. It must've taken a lot to pull that off, the coppers and all. Don't worry, we'll be at the airport."

"And Julian, tell Henry…Well, just tell him I'm waiting for him." Samantha rang off.

CHAPTER 52
GOD SAVE THE KING, PART II

S HAWN ARRIVED IN BELFAST THE MORNING AFTER HIS MEETING WITH
Sir Melvyn. He easily found the billets where Charles and his
men lived, and then staked out the building dressed as a repairman.
He couldn't get too close to the actual building since it was protected
by military police, but it didn't take long for him to spot Sergeant
Thompson. He didn't get a glimpse of Charles himself, but he wasn't
worried about that. Thompson would lead him to Charles.

Shawn stayed in position as night fell and the activity level in the
billet picked up. Around 2230 hours, the British troops began to assem-
ble outside the company headquarters, obviously geared up for a night
raid. After changing into a British military uniform, Shawn intended
to follow the mission in a beat-up milk truck commandeered from one
of his old IRA mates. The old truck would blend into the city.

He slouched behind the wheel as two lorries filled with troops
passed through the compound gates, followed by a military jeep. As
they passed his position, he raised a pair of tiny binoculars and studied the lorries, then grinned. Both Thompson and Lieutenant Charles

were with the convoy following in the jeep. He let them get several blocks away, then pulled out and began to follow.

The convoy rolled down the deserted streets and followed Crumlin Road into one of Belfast's most troubled neighborhoods. This was a high-conflict area, where some of the worst fighting of the Troubles had occurred. The whole neighborhood was crawling with IRA safe houses. Shawn was careful to hang back, knowing that the troops would be on high alert.

The convoy turned off the main road and entered a maze of twisting narrow lanes. Shawn was sure they were headed for a safe house for yet another raid, and watched as the convoy coasted to a stop on a narrow road with tattered old houses leaning over the broken street. They didn't even bother trying to hide their presence—they would have known there were eyes on them from every window—as British soldiers poured from the lorry and hit the ground, heading for their target building. Thompson and Charles stayed in their vehicle.

Shawn stopped the milk truck and jumped out, then hid behind a stoop, close enough to hear and see the action.

The British busted into one of the houses and shots immediately rang out, shattering the quiet night. There was shouting from inside. Charles and Thompson stayed in the jeep as British soldiers began exiting the building, some running, some pushing IRA soldiers ahead of them at gunpoint. The scene made Shawn's blood boil—he was going to enjoy killing one of these Limey pricks.

The jeep suddenly lurched into gear and headed for an alley between houses. Shawn followed on foot, dodging from house to house and staying close without being seen. Thompson and Charles didn't even bother to look around, they were so focused on the fighting in the building and alley.

"Sergeant, what are you doing?" Charles yelled as the jeep vanished into the dark alley with Shawn now sprinting behind it. "We need to be near the men! Why are you here?"

The sergeant skidded to a stop, causing Shawn to duck behind a group of trash cans. Charles half rose in his seat as Thompson got out of the jeep, turned back, and raised a pistol, one he'd confiscated from an IRA captive, and pointed it at Charles. The king's face was slack with shock, and tears were streaming down Thompson's face. Shawn found himself enjoying the scene immensely. There was nothing better than Brits killing Brits.

He was close enough to hear Thompson as he spoke. "I am so sorry, sir. You have no idea how much I wish I didn't have to do this, but I have no choice. It's a matter of survival. You saved my life and now I must take yours. It is something I will regret the rest of my life."

The sergeant fired a single round that struck Charles just below the heart. Charles looked down at the wound as the first rivers of blood poured down his uniform, then back up in confusion. Then, without a word, he pitched forward and his body rolled from the jeep and onto the cobblestone alley.

It was time. Shawn swung his rifle around and brought the sights up to focus on Thompson's skull. He exhaled smoothly and pulled the trigger. The bullet struck Sergeant Thompson squarely in the center of his forehead, rupturing his skull and spraying his brains over Charles and the jeep. Then, just for the hell of it, Shawn fired a second shot, this time at Charles. He was grinning as he thought, "I just shot the bloody King of England!"

He savored the thought for a heartbeat, then slung his rifle back over his shoulder and fled into the night.

The phone rang in Richard's apartments at 7 a.m. It was Sir Melvyn.

"Sir, I think we should meet. I have word from our Irish friend."

"Right. Be at the palace in an hour. We'll take a walk in the garden."

When Melvyn arrived, he was escorted to the walled garden behind the south wing. The meticulous grounds were filled with the beautiful plantings from around the world. A light rain fell, making the greenery glisten. To Melvyn, it felt like tears.

Richard waited for his henchman under a beech tree at the far end of the garden. He sat on a classic bench designed by nineteenth-century British architect Sir Edwin Lutyens.

Melvyn slowly walked down the garden path toward Richard. His head was down and his shoulders slumped in profound defeat. The news was still so fresh that the sound of the palace was still normal. Nobody in London knew that soon they would be mourning a king.

"So, Melvyn, what say you?" Richard said as Melvyn approached.

Melvyn cleared his throat and croaked out the news. "I heard from Shawn. Things went just as planned. Sergeant Thompson followed orders and shot Charles in the heart. After that, Shawn shot Thompson in the head and reported that he actually saw gray matter splatter over the jeep and Charles's body. And then…the bastard said he shot Charles again just for the pleasure of putting a bullet in the king."

"You say he shot both of them? Bravo, that's my kind of bloke. Putting on the belt even though you have suspenders. Did you speak personally to Shawn or was it a message from Colonel McIntosh?"

"No, it was a live conversation, over the phone from a call box outside of Belfast. He wants his money now. More because he shot both of them."

"More? You tell that greedy mick cocksucker that he is in no position to negotiate with me or anyone else. There's no extra pay. His bonus is that we let him live for another day. Got that?"

"I suppose I do, sir."

Richard sat and savored the news for a minute, while Melvyn felt like he would vomit, like he deserved to be surrounded by the awful funk of Richard's body odor for the rest of his life.

"I'm guessing this news will go public within the hour," Richard said. "Once they confirm who got shot, it will go viral in the press and the world will learn that they are minus one more king." Richard chuckled. "You better get your black suit out, Melvyn, you'll be in need of it."

CHAPTER 53
UNTHINKABLE

T HE SILVER LEAR ARRIVED IN BOSTON AT PRECISELY 3 P.M. EASTERN
time. It glided down the main runway and onto a secondary tarmac that terminated at the private aircraft terminal. The lobby was all
but deserted when Henry and Julian arrived by taxi from River House.

"Gentlemen, British aircraft 1243 is arriving at this time," the
attractive attendant said as they came in. "Please proceed to the door
marked Gate A. Once the aircraft reaches the terminal, a land crew
member will escort you aboard."

Flight 1243 was the official British Embassy Learjet 35 aircraft. It
was the very one that Henry and Julian had "borrowed" twice before.
When the jet came to a full stop, the air stairs gracefully unfolded from
the sleek fuselage. Henry glanced up to see the Union Jack boldly displayed on the tail and once again wondered, "How the heck did I ever
get wound up in all of this?"

As soon as the stairs hit the tarmac, Samantha bounded down the
steps to greet Henry. She threw her arms around him and whispered
into his ear. "Henry, I'm so sorry this has happened. Don't worry, my
uncle will help you. He's promised to sort this all out."

Henry embraced Samantha so tightly she could hardly breathe. "Sam, I had no idea you'd be on the plane. I'm so happy to see you. I love you and need you so much right now. Thank God you're here."

"I love you too. We'll talk later, now let's get this plane in the air."

As the threesome walked up the stairs, Samantha turned and gave Julian an ice-cold glare. She didn't speak to him at all on the seventy-eight-minute flight to DC, where the party was whisked into an official Range Rover and sped through the streets to the British Embassy, where Henry was immediately shown into Ambassador Sturbridge's office. The ambassador was waiting as Henry came in.

"Your Royal Highness, please come in and sit down."

"Thank you, Mr. Ambassador, but as I've said before, please call me Henry, and I shall call you Arthur."

"As you wish, sir, er, Henry. Right! Now, shall we make a start of it? While you were in transit I had our people look into the details of this incident. Pretty grim business, if I must say so myself. But the good news is that you and Julian are clearly innocent of any misdoings. I am assured by the State Department that the matter will be dropped. They have also assured me that we will have a copy of the videotape clearly showing your complete innocence in this matter. It will be here by tomorrow morning, or sooner. However, they have little or no influence with the press. I'm afraid it will be a media circus once the details of this become public. And that is just a matter of hours at best."

Henry slumped into his chair and sighed. "That's horrible."

"Henry, I think you should consider returning to England. It would save you from being hounded by the press and having to face endless questions and prying paparazzi."

"But won't that make Henry look guilty?" asked Samantha.

"We can have the Cambridge police handle the press. They are very satisfied with the investigation and will put the matter to rest as best as anyone could."

"I guess that means I'm going to miss my law school graduation," Henry said. "Boy, is my mother going to be put out. This is the third time I've stiffed her."

"Well, we don't have to make that decision at this moment, and you could always come back. But you should seriously consider leaving as soon as—"

The door to the office burst open and the charge de affairs rushed in. The ambassador looked surprised at the sudden interruption and half rose, but before he could say anything, the man said, "Excuse me, sir, so sorry to interrupt, but..." Then the charge de affairs looked at Henry and realized who was in the office. He pulled himself up short, gave a short bow, and the blood drained from his face as he gulped nervously.

"Yes? What is it?" the ambassador demanded.

"I need to speak with you, sir. It's urgent."

"Well, go on."

"Um, sir, perhaps we should go into the hall. Please."

The ambassador's brow creased, and he looked like he was on the verge of ordering the charge de affairs to speak up, but then he reconsidered and said, "Very well. Let's go."

The two men disappeared in the hall as Henry, Julian, and Samantha exchanged puzzled glances. This was a bizarre turn of events.

A phone on the ambassador's desk began to ring insistently. Sam jumped and gasped.

"What?" Henry said. "What is it?"

"That's the crisis phone," she said, starting at the red phone on the desk like it was a snake. "That phone is connected directly to the Prime Minister's office. It's a secure line, used only for the most extreme emergencies."

"Extreme emergencies? Like…what? What does that mean?"

She shook her head. "I don't know. An attack on the homeland. War. Something very bad."

"Well, should we answer it?" Henry said.

"I don't think so, but maybe we should go get my uncle."

As Henry rose, the office door opened and the ambassador returned, looking grave. He crossed the room to Henry and sat in an empty chair next to him. "Your Highness," he said, forgetting that he was supposed to use Henry's Christian name, "I'm afraid I have some troubling news. It's—"

"Is it my mother?" Henry blurted out. "Is she okay?"

"Yes, she's fine," the ambassador said. "But it seems that your brother, King Charles, has been shot in the line of duty while in Ireland. He is critically wounded and has been flown to London. Your mother and Prince Cyril are at his side."

Henry gasped as he was seized with shock. "What? You…you can't be serious? Charles? Shot? No! No! Not Charles. Not him too! God, don't do this to me. I can't bear anymore."

Samantha reached out to comfort Henry.

"I'm afraid so," the ambassador said. "I'm so sorry to be the bearer of this news."

"How bad is it?" Henry said. "Is he dying?"

"The seriousness of the injuries was not detailed beyond critically wounded," the ambassador said. "The Prime Minister and your mother have been trying to contact you at Harvard with no success. They contacted the embassy and asked us to help locate you and help expedite your return immediately. I explained you were already here."

Henry stood up abruptly. "I need to go back. Now."

"Yes, sir, of course." The ambassador cleared his throat. "You'll need protection, Henry. We'll arrange for everything. I'm sorry to bring this up, but…should your brother succumb to his injuries, you are the next in line for the throne."

Henry turned to the ambassador with a cold glare. "I don't want to hear that. Not another word. You got that? Charles will be fine, I know it, he has to be!" But in his heart, he was hardly convinced.

The ambassador looked down and let Henry spill his anger and confusion out. After a moment, as Henry visibly struggled with his emotions, the ambassador continued, "The royal aircraft is on its way, sir. You will be home by tomorrow mid-day."

"Uncle, couldn't we send Henry home in the Lear?" said Samantha.

"The Lear's flying range is too short to reach the UK. However, if it could refuel along the way with a brief stop, we could have Henry on his way later tonight and in London by first thing tomorrow morning."

"Then let's do that," Henry said. "I'm not waiting around here all night while my brother is in a hospital. He needs me, and I must go."

"Of course, sir."

Henry turned to Sam, and she saw how closely he was holding himself together. "Sam, will you come with me? Please?"

"Of course I will," she said. "I love you, Henry. Nothing would keep me from being with you, especially now."

"Thank you."

Julian suddenly spoke up. "I'll go as well, Henry. I'm your security detail. Then when we get to London, I'll self-report for my failure."

"Fine," Henry said. "But let's not worry about that now. We'll deal with it later. And now," he announced to the room, "I need a phone. I need to call my mother."

"Yes, sir, of course," the ambassador said. "You can have my office as long as you need it. Use the red phone, it's a direct line to Downing Street. They will connect you directly. And, Your Highness, the bar over there is fully stocked."

CHAPTER 54
BOTCHED!

THE HEADLINE FLASHED ACROSS BBC CHANNEL 4 AND THEN AROUND the world: "King Charles Near Death After Shooting By IRA Sniper!"

Richard was closely watching the television in his office. He frowned. Near death? That bastard was supposed to be dead. He turned the volume up and leaned forward to listen as the well-groomed announcer came on.

In the early morning hours in Belfast, Ireland, King Charles VII was critically wounded by sniper fire. His driver, Sergeant Percival Thompson, from Liverpool, also a victim of the sniper, was killed instantly when a bullet struck his head.

King Charles was doing his military service and was soon to return to London and take his throne. After the shooting, the king was taken to the local Belfast military facility and then flown to an undisclosed London hospital.

No details about the attack have been made public at this time and a full investigation is underway. In a press conference, General Sir Archibald

Coventry, supreme commander of the armed forces, announced the tragic incident and pledged a full and complete investigation would be conducted.

The screen cut to a shot of General Coventry saying, "The country is once again devastated over the targeting of yet another young king at the hands of the IRA. Our hearts and prayers go out to the Queen Mother, and the king's younger brother, Henry Duke of York, currently studying abroad."

A rapid montage of clips followed, showing the boys growing up, attending school, Charles's graduation from Eton, and Charles in his uniform. Then the anchor came back on:

Doctors have not given any official prognosis as to the survivability of King Charles and have said nothing more than that his wounds were serious and life-threatening.

Richard, Duke of Gloucester, now serving as the King's regent, was unable to give an interview. The Palace Private Secretary Sir Melvyn Batton told the press that the duke was so distraught by this senseless act of barbarism he could not appear in public. In his stead, Sir Melvyn released the following statement from the regent: "This insane act against King Charles, his family, the throne and the people of our great country is reprehensible."

It is reported that the Queen Mother was shattered by the news that her oldest son had been so savagely attacked. She remains wheelchair bound after a similar attack on her late husband, King William IV. The current whereabouts of the Duke of York, next in line to the throne, are unknown.

Seething with rage, Richard clicked off the TV and reached for the phone. It rang three times before it was picked up: "Sir Melvyn residence."

"Yes. I want to talk to Sir Melvyn right now."

"And may I ask who's calling?"

"Tell him it's his boss. He'll know who that is."

"As you wish, sir."

Melvyn was having his breakfast when his manservant entered and told him that he was wanted on the phone. "Who's calling, Boynton?"

"He wouldn't say, sir. He just said to tell you it's your boss. Quite peculiar, if I must say so myself, sir."

Melvyn paled and dropped his fork. "I'll take it in the library, Boynton. And please do not disturb me."

"Of course, sir. I'll set a fire for you."

Melvyn hastened to the library. It was a room of considerable size and housed many of the first editions he had collected over the years. The morning chill was still in the air and the fire that Boynton had set was just now coming into its own.

"Sir Melvyn here. Good morning, sir. How are you?"

"How am I? You stupid sod. I'm not well at all. Have you seen the news?"

"Not yet. I was just having breakfast and papers have not come yet."

"As usual, you are a day late and a pound short. Turn on your TV. It looks like the good sergeant buggered up his job. Now we have a wounded king who might very well survive. Get your arse over here now. Meet me at the palace in forty-five minutes."

CHAPTER 55
A Nation in Prayer

WHEN THE MILITARY MEDEVAC HELICOPTER TOOK OFF FROM Belfast, Charles was in a deep coma and barely clinging to life. The doctors and nurses worked feverishly to stabilize the young king and transfused liter after liter of blood into his system.

The flight time from Belfast to London was one hour, twenty-five minutes. Every second counted. In order to save critical time, the police cleared the car park at Victoria Hospital, London's most prestigious trauma center, so the helicopter could land directly at the ER entrance.

By the time the copter arrived at the hospital, the world had learned of the shooting. Within hours, every news outlet and TV station was covering the story. Churches opened their doors to those who sought prayer and solace. Charles, who had been relatively hidden from the public eye, suddenly burst onto every TV screen and every newspaper. The public response was overwhelming as sympathy turned toward the young king who had been gunned down, just like his father.

Despite the news flashing around the world, one person remained unaware: Beatrice. She had left Charles in Belfast, promising to return as soon as she could. Her mood was giddy at the thought of rejoining

Charles, the kidnapping already fading in her memory. She was excited to tell her family about meeting the love of her life.

Beatrice arrived at her London flat very late in the afternoon and decided not to go into the office. Instead she made herself an early dinner with a tin of salmon laid over some greens and a couple of slices of toast. Around 10:30 that evening, Beatrice decided to call it a night, closed the novel she was reading, and went to bed. As she lay waiting for sleep to come, she thought about Charles and smiled to herself, already counting minutes until they could be reunited. Around eleven o'clock, Beatrice fell into a deep sleep.

The phone broke the silence, causing Beatrice to wake suddenly. The clock on the nightstand read 2:30 a.m. Worried, she picked up the receiver. "Hello, who's there?"

"Beatrice, it's Josh. I see you're back. I tried at the Fitzwilliam in Belfast, but they said you had checked out this morning."

"Josh? What on earth! It's 2:30 in the bloody morning, couldn't you wait till I got in? A girl needs her beauty sleep, you know."

"Beatrice, I'm sorry, but something just came across the wire. I thought you should know right away."

"Something in Belfast, about my story?"

"No, nothing like that. It's about Charles. The reports are still very sketchy, but apparently he's been shot, maybe even killed. Everything is going bonkers here and the newsroom is hyperventilating."

"What did you say? Are you kidding?"

"No, goddamn it, no. I wish I were. All we know now is that he was shot by an IRA sniper and they flew him to a hospital here in London. He's probably just getting there now."

Beatrice was now wide awake, her heart pounding. "Tell me what happened."

"No one has all the details, but the night guy saw the report on the wire and called me into the office."

"Do we know what hospital?"

"No, but it has to be one of two. Either Victoria or King's College. They are the best and both have trauma centers. We sent teams to both, just to make sure."

"I'm coming down right now. You keep your ears open. I need to know which hospital."

"Right. I'll be here." Josh rang off.

Beatrice pulled her hair back in a ponytail, put on a pair of jeans and a T-shirt, grabbed her purse, and flew out of her flat. The streets were deserted, so she ran four blocks to the Strand and finally was able to hail a black cab. Trying to control her hysteria, she gave the driver the studio's address.

The cabbie was an older chap and rather chatty. "Mum, did you hear on the wireless the bloody Micks killed that young king, just like they did his father? Bastards!"

Not wanting to hear this, Beatrice probed, "Are you certain he is dead? Did they say that on the wireless?"

"Well, not exactly, dead that is, but it didn't sound like he was going to make it."

"Oh, please, dear God...Just get me to the studio."

———————

The newsroom was in chaos. Teams of people rushed around, trying to connect bits and pieces of information. By the time Beatrice arrived, Josh had been able to find out which hospital had Charles. "Calm down, it's going to be all right," he said. "He's at Victoria Hospital."

"I'm going there."

"Are you mad? They aren't going to let a reporter anywhere near the bed of a dying king."

"Dying? Who said he's dying?! What do you know?"

"You know all I know. It was just an expression, a bad choice. But seriously, you won't be able to get near him."

Beatrice agreed that Josh was right, but she wasn't interested in Charles for a story. She was the girl Charles was planning to marry, but now she realized fully how they had made a mistake. She and Charles had kept their relationship so secret that no one, not even her family or friends—or his family—knew of it.

Glancing at her finger, she saw the makeshift ring Charles had given her at the Fitzwilliam. She smiled, thinking of him naked, the man she loved, the King of England, on his knees, when he proposed. He had promised her a proper engagement ring once they were back home. Beatrice racked her brain. Who would know about them, their relationship, that they were betrothed? Who could confirm it? Certainly not a hotel clerk or a chamber maid—the media would have a field day with that.

There was Captain Morgan, but all he could really confirm was that they knew each other and had met in a bar. Otherwise, there were no letters, notes, or anything that connected her to Charles.

"Josh, I need your help," she said in a rush. "I don't care about Charles for a story. We...we weren't just friends. It wasn't just professional. Josh, I'm in love with him and he with me. We..." she stopped and took a shuddering breath. "We're engaged. I know it's not much, but here's the ring he gave me." She showed him her finger.

Josh looked at it and laughed. "Big spender, huh, that Charles? Must have raided the Tower of London for that beauty."

"It's just temporary," Beatrice said, stung.

"Right. I've heard that before." He smirked. "Bea, if you want to get the story, I say go for it, but you don't need to feed me this load of tosh. Save it for the official blokes at the hospital."

"But it's true!" she wailed. "Please, Josh. Please believe me."

He shook his head. "I don't know. You're asking me to believe that the King of England proposed to you and gave you a bit of wire as a ring, but no one knows at all about your relationship, and now you, who just also happens to be a reporter, fancies to see him at his bedside?"

She grimaced and a tear spilled down her face. "I know. It sounds… preposterous."

"I'll say. And to be honest, I'm having a bit of a tug at it myself, even though I know you well and that you are a sincere and honest person."

"But—"

"Bea, look, it doesn't matter if I believe you. All I know is that if you walk into the hospital with that story, you'll either get laughed out of the building and probably this business, or you'll get locked up."

"Oh, God. You're probably right." Beatrice collapsed into a nearby chair, held her head in her hands, and wept. She worried she would never see Charles again. If he were to die, she would never have said good-bye and told him how much she loved him. Just a day or so ago the two of them floated on cloud nine, planning their future and making love at that shabby Fitzwilliam in war-torn Belfast.

Josh walked away from her, over to the wire printer. He picked up a sheet of paper, read something from it, then looked up at Beatrice, his face a mask of shock and confusion.

She looked up. "What? What is it?"

"This just came through," he said. "The AP is reporting that the army issued a brief statement."

Beatrice grabbed the paper from Josh's hand and read it out loud. "The young king is in a deep coma and is being administered blood transfusions. We have no further updates at this time and can only ask the people of the British Empire as well as the entire world to pray for His Majesty's recovery."

"Oh God," she moaned again. "What shall I do?"

CHAPTER 56
MYSTERY WOMAN

IT WAS A GRIM SCENE. CHARLES LAY UNCONSCIOUS IN THE VERY ROOM where his father had laid after being attacked. Although it did not look like a typical hospital room, with its posh accoutrements it offered all the necessary state-of-the-art medical monitoring equipment needed for intensive care.

Liz sat at her son's bedside, as she had years before for her husband William. Physicians and nurses paraded in and out every few minutes, checking Charles's vitals and adjusting the equipment that was keeping him alive. The Archbishop of Canterbury joined Liz later in the day and suggested they take tea in an adjoining parlor. Liz refused and sat stoically in her wheelchair next to her critically injured son, hoping that each breath was not his last.

Around 4:00 a.m., Charles opened his eyes and saw Liz. He tried to smile, then murmured something. Liz sat up with a jolt and pulled her chair as close as she could to the bed, then put her ear directly to Charles's lips. He spoke again.

"I'm okay, Mom."

Charles closed his eyes and looked like he was sinking back into sleep again. Just before he nodded off, he opened his eyes again and turned his head toward Liz. His face was filled with urgency and Liz feared the worst. Using every bit of strength he had, Charles whispered several sentences to her: "There's a girl…her name is Beatrice Randton. I love her. We are betrothed. Can you bring her here? I want to see her. I want to say good-bye."

"What?" Liz said. "A girl? But where?"

There was no reply. Charles had slipped back into a deep abyss.

Liz rolled her chair to the door and called her faithful aide. "Myrtle, are you there?"

"Yes, Ma'am, I'm right here. What can I do?"

"Please call Prince Cyril. I need his help. Right away. Have him come here. Tell him I desperately need him."

"Of course, Ma'am, immediately."

Prince Cyril arrived in the door quickly. His face was a mask of concern as he came in and gave Charles a stricken glance before taking Liz's hands. "What is it, Liz? How can I help?"

Liz lost all her control at the sight of Cyril's concerned expression. She burst into heavy sobs and Cyril bent to hold her. "I can't believe this!" she wailed. "Not again!"

"I know," he soothed her. "It's so unfair, such a good, good man. I'm so sorry."

He held her until the worst of the tears had passed, then said, "What do the doctors say?"

"Nothing, just the same thing, over and over. That he is in a coma, that he has lost over 10 percent of his blood and his condition is grave. They don't know if he will survive. He was shot twice, the one bullet barely missed his heart but caused severe damage to his chest and lower abdomen.

The second to his head wasn't as serious, but it's too soon to know the extent of any damage to his brain. Potentially, it could be worse than the other wound. They performed surgery a couple of hours ago and did what they could. That's all they will say, and probably all that they know."

There really was nothing that Cyril could say to give Liz any encouragement. "You said you desperately needed my help, what I can do?" he asked.

"Charles gained consciousness for just a few seconds. I could barely hear or understand him, he could only whisper. He told me that everything was going to be okay and not to worry."

Cyril waited while Liz wiped away fresh tears.

"Then he seemed to be drifting off again, but just before he went under, he said he wanted to see a woman named Beatrice Randton. He said he loved her and begged me to bring her here. He told me that they were betrothed and wanted her here, beside him to say..." she heaved a heavy sob before finishing her sentence, "good-bye."

"Beatrice Randton?" Cyril said, sounding genuinely surprised. "Who on Earth is that? I don't believe I've heard that name, have you?"

"Never! And I certainly didn't know that he was in love with anyone, or for that matter that he ever had a girlfriend, much less betrothed! He kept it a secret. Do you suppose she is someone he met in Ireland? Maybe she's Irish and that's why he hasn't mentioned her?"

"I have no clue, Liz. But if this is his wish, we will grant it. I think you must be right about her being in Ireland. If she were seeing him here in London, we surely would have known about that. Probably everyone would...there are no secrets here. I will see if they can track this woman down."

"Thank you, Cyril. I always can count on you. But please hurry. We must find her as soon as possible, for Charles's sake."

Cyril stepped out of the room and reached for the nearest telephone. By the time he arrived back at his office, his staff was working at lightning speed to find the missing paramour. He had warned them to use the utmost discretion, since there was no way of telling who this young woman was. He feared the worst. Perhaps this Beatrice was a woman of ill repute, the kind lonely soldiers often fancied while serving far from home. Worse, she might be an Irish IRA sympathizer and, God forbid, a Catholic! That could be catastrophic to the monarchy.

Hours went by. Call after call did not turn up any leads. All of the British IRA infiltrators were contacted to no avail. Everything was coming up a dead end. Time was of the essence, since there was no guarantee that Charles would survive long enough for them to find Beatrice Grandton and grant what might be Charles's dying wish.

At half past six, Cyril sat at his desk, feeling useless and spent. Even with his multitude of resources, no one could find this elusive girlfriend.

One of the household staff popped her head into Cyril's office, expecting it to be empty so she could clean and empty the bins. "Excuse me, sir, I thought you had left. I'll come back later and do my bit."

"No, it's okay. I'm just sitting here racking my brain. You won't disturb me."

Noticing the real distress in Prince Cyril's face, the housemaid could not help but step out of her station and offer some comfort. "Sir, you look so tired and so worried. I hope everything is okay. We're all praying for our young king."

Looking up from his desk, Cyril gave her a wan smile. "It's Evelyn, right?"

"Yes, sir, Evelyn Brown. Thank you for remembering. If there is anything I can do, please allow me. Cup of tea perhaps?"

"Thank you, my dear, but I'm afraid not. I'm looking for a ghost. A person that no one seems to know. It's like this woman named Beatrice Randton never existed."

"Beatrice Randton? I don't know her, but I do know someone named Beatrice Grandton. Not personally, you see, but I know who she is."

"Really? Grandton, you say?" Cyril thought back to his conversation with Liz. She had said she could barely understand Charles's muffled whispers. Was it possible Liz heard wrong? Were they looking for a person with the wrong name?

"You know of her? How is that possible, she's in Ireland?"

"Well, maybe that is where Beatrice Randton is, but Beatrice Grandton, the one I know, is on BBC 4. She does the news and special reports. Quite the looker, if I must say so myself. Now that you mention it, I think I saw a BBC special that she filmed in Ireland."

"Filmed in Ireland, you say?"

"Yes, sir, she covers the Troubles over there, and she's quite good at it."

Cyril jumped up from his chair and rushed toward Evelyn. "I say, woman, are you certain?"

"I think so. No, I'm pretty positive. She's so young and good-looking, I always watch her shows, mostly because I fancy to see what she is wearing. Silly, isn't it, sir?"

"Not silly at all! If you have the right woman, there is a big bonus in it for you. And a new frock, just like Beatrice would wear."

Cyril was immediately on the phone with his staff. Within minutes, he was supplied with a complete biography and contact phone number for one Beatrice Grandton.

CHAPTER 57
HEAR MY PRAYERS

BEATRICE ARRIVED BACK AT HER FLAT AROUND TEA TIME. SHE HAD NO appetite for anything but a cup of chamomile tea, hoping to calm her shaking body. The small career girl's flat was just a place to sleep and hang her clothing. Nothing fancy, but it was very convenient to get to the TV studio and the Tube.

As she looked around the room, she realized that if Charles were to die there would be absolutely no trace of his existence in her life. Not a single snap or little handwritten note. It was surreal that Charles could be taken away without her ever seeing him again. She had wanted to race to the hospital and demand to see him, but she knew Josh was right. They would think she was just a journalist after a story, and not his fiancé. The more she thought about her dilemma, the more depressed and upset she became.

Around seven, the phone rang. She gave it a gloomy look. There was no one she wanted to talk to, but then she wondered if maybe it was Josh with news. Reluctantly, she picked up the receiver.

"Hello, this is Beatrice."

"Beatrice Grandton?"

"Yes, may I ask who is calling?"

"Well, you don't know me, and I certainly don't know you. I am Prince Cyril, Charles's step-grandfather."

"Prince Cyril?" she echoed. "Is this some sort of joke? If so, tell Josh it isn't remotely funny."

"No, dear, I can assure you this is not a prank but a matter of the utmost seriousness. I can only assume you've heard that Charles is in the hospital here in London. He woke up briefly and asked for you by name. I want you to come to the hospital and see Charles."

"He woke up? He asked for me?" Her heart did a happy flutter.

"Yes." The prince hesitated. "I'll tell you it was a shock, but he told the Queen Mother that you and he were betrothed, that he loved you and wanted to see you."

"Oh!" She couldn't keep the joy from her voice. "So he's awake?"

"No, dear. I'm afraid he slipped back into unconsciousness just after. I won't be disingenuous and tell you he's fine. He's in grave condition. His mother is sitting vigil by his bed, and we think you should be there too."

Beginning to sob and sinking in a confusing welter of emotions, she said, "Of course. I'm on my way."

"Right. I'll have the security people escort you up to his rooms. And Beatrice, please hurry." Cyril rang off.

Beatrice rushed out the door.

———◆———

Victoria Hospital was located on the far side of London. The early evening traffic was heavy and the ride seemed endless. When the cab arrived at the hospital entrance, Beatrice jumped out of it even before it came to a complete halt.

At least six police cars and two military vehicles were stationed in the car park. A makeshift command post had been arranged at the main entrance, and visitors were being screened as they entered the lobby. Beatrice walked up to the uniformed guard and identified herself.

"I'm Beatrice Grandton. They are expecting me."

"Yes, ma'am. Someone will escort you. Please wait for a moment."

"Right, but hurry, please."

A young female officer led Beatrice through the crowded lobby. She recognized a couple of the cameramen and reporters from other stations and hid her face. She desperately didn't want to become part of the story. Just beyond the lobby, they made a left into what appeared to be a small rotunda that housed several lifts. The officer placed a small key into the lock next to the lift. The doors opened to reveal one of the most opulent lifts Beatrice had ever seen. The rich, dark paneled walls were pinstriped with gold leaf and the floor was covered in an intricately laid marble sunburst pattern. A crystal chandelier lit the cab. There was just one button on the panel next to the door which was labeled: "Private."

The double doors opened as the lift arrived on the ninth floor. The reception area was also paneled. Two royal military guards stood at attention next to a pair of floor-to-ceiling oak doors bearing the royal crest. At a desk, another armed military guard asked Beatrice for her identification and searched her purse. After the routine security check, the officer opened the doors and asked Beatrice to follow her. Beatrice's eyes opened wide as she walked into what could have been one of the public rooms at Buckingham Palace. High ceilings, chandeliers, and Oriental carpets covered the herringbone wood floors.

She was amazed to see this kind of decor in a hospital. The room was set up like a parlor with comfortable seating scattered about. A marble fireplace with a heavily carved mantel was the focal point of the room. A woman sat in a wheelchair next to the hearth, looking at the low flames. Standing behind her was a tall man dressed in a distinguished gray double-breasted suit. He was handsome but elderly. The escort motioned to Beatrice to come forward.

"Ma'am, this is Beatrice Grandton. Beatrice, this is the Dowager Queen Mother. And Prince Cyril, may I present Miss Beatrice Grandton."

Beatrice curtseyed. "Your Highnesses, I am pleased to meet you." Then she said, "Where is Charles?"

"He is here, dear, just down the corridor," Prince Cyril interjected. He then turned to Liz and said, "Shall we go through?"

Liz broke away from her close study of Beatrice's face, her expression softened by the obvious distress in the young woman's look. She shook her head slightly. "And he never told me," she said. "Yes. Let's go see him."

They walked down the corridor and into a room that looked more like a royal bedroom than an intensive care unit. Life-support equipment whooshed and clanked along the back wall. An ornate placard bearing the royal coat of arms had been hung over the headboard.

Charles lay propped up in a hospital bed. His still and pale body was covered to the neck, with his motionless arms lying at his side. A two-day growth covered his young, handsome face. Beatrice was surprised. Since she had known him, Charles always was clean-shaven and meticulously groomed. She put her hand to her mouth and made no effort to stop the tears streaming down her face. "Can I hold his hand?" she asked Cyril. "Can he...hear me?"

"Of course you may hold his hand. As for his hearing you...we don't know. It's doubtful."

Beatrice sat next to the bed and slowly reached for Charles's hand, afraid it would be cold. When she felt the reassuring warmth, more tears spilled from her eyes. She talked to him softly, then prayed to her God asking for a miracle…one that would save the man she loved.

In the wee hours of the morning, Cyril approached Beatrice. "Dear, I think you should go home now. Charles is stable and the doctors won't be back until tomorrow morning, so there is nothing more to know until then. Please, I'm certain Charles would want you to get some rest."

Reluctantly, Beatrice agreed, adding, "I'll be back the first thing in the morning." She was escorted down the corridor, into the lift, and then out to an awaiting palace vehicle to go home.

CHAPTER 58
A Brother's Remorse

THE LEARJET CARRYING HENRY AND HIS ENTOURAGE ARRIVED IN London on an early, misty morning. There had been a 35-minute layover in Newfoundland, where the plane was refueled and reprovisioned. Since only four of the eight seats were filled and there was virtually no luggage or cargo, the plane was a bit lighter.

As soon as the plane touched down, Henry, Samantha, and Julian were whisked into a waiting car with a military escort to take them directly to the hospital. A rather significant security presence surrounded Henry, given that he was a heartbeat away from being the next King of England, a very weak heartbeat at that.

As they drove, Henry turned to Samantha. "Sam, I think it would be best if you don't go to the hospital. It will be a bad scene, reporters everywhere. We don't want them to start speculating as to who you are and why you are here with me. And besides, my mother is probably not up to meeting you. She has so much on her plate. It would be—"

"Of course, Henry, whatever you think best, I totally understand," she said. "I'll go to my parents. They have a place on Lexington Mews. You can call anytime, day or night, and I will be there."

"That's a deal. Driver, drop me off at Victoria hospital and take Miss Smythe wherever. Julian, you come with me, it would be expected."

With the aid of the military escort, the driver scooted through morning traffic and arrived at the hospital. Henry and Julian jumped out as the car sped away. They slipped into the hospital through a back door without attracting undue attention. When they arrived on the royal floor, Liz was sitting in the parlor room by the fire.

"Mom, Mom, it's Henry, I'm here."

Liz looked up, and Henry was struck by how much she had aged.

"Oh Henry, thank God you have come," she said. "This is just too much for me to bear."

Henry fell to his knees and comforted his sobbing mother, even as his own grief overwhelmed him and he shook with sobs. Charles was his big brother, the one he looked up to and loved as only brothers can. Charles had protected him and allowed him to escape Eton. Charles had taken on the responsibilities that were thrust upon them and let Henry have his own life. And it was Charles now suffering the same fate as his beloved father at the hands of Irish rebels. It took a little while before both Henry and his mother could regain their composure.

"Mom, what are they saying? Is he going to be alright?"

"They just don't know, Henry. The doctors have done all they can. They seem optimistic, but I'm not sure if they are just putting on a charade for me."

Cyril walked into the room. "Hello, Henry. Good to see you, but I'm sorry it's under such dreadful circumstances."

"Thank you," Henry said. "And thank you for being with my mother. She needs as much support as she can get."

"It's my pleasure and duty. Your mother is a wonderful woman who has had more than enough suffering in her life."

"May I see Charles?"

Pulling Henry to the side, Cyril whispered, "Of course. But I must warn you it's a grim sight. He's been through a lot, and the jury is still out on his recovery."

"I see. After I visit him, I'd like to sit down with you. There are some things I'd like to discuss."

"Right then, come through, and we'll talk later."

Walking into the hospital room where his brother lay near death was one of the hardest things Henry had ever experienced. Tears welled up in his eyes as he was overwhelmed with anger, fear, and despair. It all seemed so senseless, so cruel and unfair. Henry leaned over Charles's shattered body and spoke softly: "Charlie, it's me, Henry. I'm here." He picked up Charles's hand. "I love you, bro, we all do. You can't leave us now. Please, please come back to us."

Henry leaned over and kissed his brother's forehead, physically shaking, and said again, "I love you, bro. I'm so sorry that I left you in this nightmare of a country to fend for yourself. I will never forgive myself for being so selfish and pigheaded. Can you ever forgive me?"

Suddenly Henry looked up and saw a very attractive woman in the shadows. Wiping his tears away, he was startled he hadn't seen her before and astonished at the breach of privacy. "Who are you?" he angrily demanded.

"My name is Beatrice Grandton, and you must be Henry."

"So? What are you doing here?"

"I heard what you said to Charles. That was amazing."

Henry scowled. "You have some nerve eavesdropping on a private conversation. You never answered my question. Who are you, and what are you doing in my brother's room?"

"I'm Beatrice. Charles and I are engaged to be married."

"Married! I never heard any of this. Are you some kind of—"

"Please, Henry, hear me out. You heard nothing because we have kept our relationship and wedding plans a secret. We met while Charles was in Belfast and fell in love. We decided to wait until Charles finished his military service and returned to London to make the announcement."

"What? Did you tell my mother this? Is that how you ended up in here?"

"Yes."

Abruptly, he reached out and grabbed Beatrice's hand. "You don't even have a ring! How do we know that anything you say is the truth? Did you just show up here and tell this tall tale?"

"I didn't just show up. I am telling you God's honest truth. I didn't just tell your mother. Charles woke up and asked for me. He told her that he was in love with me and was going to marry me. He begged her to find me so I could be by his side. Prince Cyril called me at home and summoned me here. Trust me, it was as much a surprise to your mother as it is to you."

Henry shook his head. "And if I ask my mother, this is the same thing she'll say?"

"Absolutely. It's the truth."

Henry stared at her for several long seconds, then nodded. "I see. So you met him in Ireland? Then maybe you know why he was allowed to be in harm's way like this. How could a king be exposed to sniper fire?"

Beatrice looked anguished. "I wish I knew. Charles rarely spoke of his royalty or his service. He is such an unassuming, humble, and loving person. He told me that he was doing his duty and being with the men who were defending their country. I do know that he applied for an early discharge, but it was denied, so he dutifully accepted that and willingly waited until his proper term was completed."

"Denied? Who would dare deny a request from Charles?"

"He said the command officer. He could have overruled it, of course, and I told him that. But Charles wanted to earn his stripes. He viewed his service as fundamentally the right thing to do. He felt he needed to earn the respect of the people, all the people. That's what I love most about Charles, his humility and deep sense of duty."

Henry sighed and turned back to his brother. "Damn you, Charles," he whispered in agony. "You should have just left."

Beatrice came to stand next to Henry and together they gazed down on the king they both loved. The king who may soon be taken from them.

CHAPTER 59
CONNECTING THE DOTS

FOR THE NEXT TWO DAYS, BEATRICE, HENRY, CYRIL, AND LIZ TOOK turns sitting vigil at Charles's bedside, day and night. Henry still had many questions, but he knew those would wait until his brother was out of the woods. The doctors were sounding more cautiously optimistic every day and told the family that Charles might wake up at any time.

It finally happened in the early morning hours on the third day. He opened his eyes briefly, looked at Beatrice and smiled, then fell back asleep. The others rushed into the room and they waited throughout the morning and early afternoon, almost afraid to hope. Then, in the late afternoon, Charles opened his eyes again, this time meeting his mother's eyes.

"Charles, can you hear me?" Liz said softly.

"Yes, I hear you. I'm going to be alright, don't worry."

She thought that it was just like Charles to worry about everyone else but himself.

"I know you will, sweetheart, I know." Liz laid a careful hand on Charles's forehead. "Sweetheart, I met Beatrice. She is lovely and I see in her eyes how much she loves you."

Charles smiled weakly.

"When you are up to it, I want to hear all about her and how you met, all the details."

"Is she here? I must see her. Please."

"I'm here," Beatrice said, a sob of joy catching in her throat. "I'm here."

"Great! And Henry too? I want to see Henry."

"I'm here, bro. Standing next to you, as I should have for all these years. I was so selfish and I'm so sorry."

"Don't be, you are here now and that's what counts."

Days Later

As Charles began to heal, Henry started his informal investigation, beginning with Prince Cyril. He demanded to know exactly how his brother ended up in a dark alley, guarded only by a single soldier, during a high-risk raid of an IRA safe house. He vowed that he would stop at nothing and was willing to spend millions to find out what happened.

Late on a cloudy afternoon, Cyril called Henry and asked him to join him in his office. Henry showed up at the appointed time.

"Please, Henry, sit over there, near the fire."

"Thank you, sir." Henry came in and sat down, waiting.

Cyril took a deep breath. "Well, I've made some inquiries. Fortunately, I still have a lot of friends in the army who are loyal and trustworthy people. I've got some interesting information, maybe more than interesting."

"Okay," Henry said in a hard voice. "Go on."

"Right then. Well, you see, Charles was a bit naive about things. Can't blame the lad, he didn't have a father or elder to guide him.

Seems he took advice from his regent, Richard. And there lies the rub. I spoke with a major-general who was willing to put me in touch with a lower level officer who manages a records division deep within the bureaucracy. This chap was kind enough to research Charles's file and found a specific directive that had come down from a Colonel McIntosh directing Charles to be assigned to Belfast. Not only to Belfast, but in the thick of it, in one of the most dangerous of military assignments. The unit that actively seeks out IRA rebels. It is considered very risky duty, the very riskiest indeed."

"So Charles was purposely assigned to the most dangerous of posts?"

"It appears that way, Henry, exactly."

Henry paused. "Why would an obscure colonel want to assign Charles to such hazardous duty? What did he have to gain? How did he even know Charles? Was he a mole for the IRA?"

"Excellent questions! I did some deeper digging and I found out that this Colonel McIntosh once was Brigadier General McIntosh, a high-ranking officer in MI5. He got himself involved with some nasty business and was demoted, transferred to Ireland, and put back into the Royal Army. He never faced any formal charges. A deal was struck with his superiors."

"Okay, seems odd that a guy like that would have any command over my brother, but I'm not sure I see how it's related."

"Guess who ran MI5 and called all the shots back then?"

Henry shrugged. "Who?"

"None other than Richard, the regent. Henry, this is a man with plenty to gain if something happened to Charles or you. He would be next in line to the throne, assuming Edward isn't interested. Now we don't have any smoking gun here, just circumstantial evidence and hearsay for now. We need to do a lot more homework before we can prove anything. I'll do my best."

But Henry barely even heard the last part. What he did hear was that Richard had the most to gain if something were to happen to both he and Charles. Already, pieces were falling into place in his head, like a puzzle clicking together.

"Oh my God," he said softly.

"Yes? What is it?"

"While I was flying to the States years ago, I met a girl on the plane. We became…rather close. She was a British girl who went by the name of Star Patterson. She followed me to Hotchkiss and then Harvard. Four days ago, that girl tried to kill me by pushing me off a terrace. She tripped in the process and went head over heels, falling to her death."

Cyril leaned back and gave a low whistle. "Blimey. Does your mother know about this? She said nothing to me!"

"It was hushed up by the State Department and I was completely cleared of any suspicion."

"What do you know about her? Did she have a motive?"

"No, not that I know of, and it only got stranger. At first it didn't make any sense. Star was a party girl, but not the jealous type. After she died, though, we found out Star was an alias. She had a passport in the name of Marcella Hunt. I couldn't figure it out. All the years I'd known her, she'd never told me anything about her real name. And then, right when she attacked me, she called herself Badger. Like I said, it just didn't make sense."

"Henry, Badger is a code name often used in MI5 for a mole or assassin. It's after the animal which is known for being relentless, never backing down."

"Wow."

"So do you think that her attempt to kill you is related to Charles's circumstances, his being put in harm's way and the like?"

"Maybe? Star was no saint and apparently liked to play the field, right in my own backyard, right under my nose. But now that you connect the dots, it is most peculiar."

The two men sat and stared at each other in stunned silence. Finally, it was Henry who said, "I think we have to assume these are related."

"Yes," Cyril agreed. "Henry, if this is true, I don't think you and your brother are out of danger yet."

CHAPTER 60
TRUTH AT LAST

SIR MELVYN ARRIVED AT BUCKINGHAM PALACE LATE AND WAS USH-ered into Sir Richard's office. Richard was sitting at his desk staring out the large French windows at the lovely private garden.

"Sir?" Sir Melvyn said carefully as he edged into the office. "I'm at your pleasure."

Richard turned and fixed Melvyn with a look of pure loathing. If anything, his odor was worse today, and Melvyn thought that Richard looked like the personification of evil.

"You're late," Richard snarled. "I detest being kept waiting, especially by morons."

"I'm sorry, sir, but the phone never stopped ringing once the news—"

"Just shut up. I'm sick of you and all your excuses. You can't get anything right, can you? The good Sergeant Thompson botched up his job. Now I am told Charles might recover. And this is to say nothing of the other one, that brat Henry. He also lived, despite Badger's efforts... the stupid bitch wound up dead herself. Probably deserved it!"

Sir Melvyn didn't respond.

"I'll take your silence as an admission of incompetence. At least tell me the art is ready to go. If we don't move now, the whole thing could fall apart."

"Yes, sir. The art is in storage at the hangar. All you need to do is give the order and the plane will be loaded and depart."

"Then I'm giving the order. Tonight. Arrange it immediately. Call and let me know once the plane leaves. See to it personally. Now get your pathetic arse out of my sight. Make sure all that art makes it to Switzerland. I've got people chomping at the bit for it."

"As you wish, sir."

Melvyn was preparing to rise when the two massive oak doors were flung open and Henry burst in, followed by two security guards who were attempting to stop the intrusion. Sir Melvyn jumped to his feet and grabbed his attaché case. He glanced at Richard, then Henry. But Henry only had eyes for Richard, so Melvyn took the opportunity to hasten out of the room as Henry advanced on Richard's desk.

The regent heaved himself up from his chair. "I say, what is this all about! Get out of my office!"

"You can't order me to do anything, you disgusting stink pot," Henry snarled, shaking off a guard's hand. "I'm a prince."

Both guards backed away instantly.

Richard didn't move, but his eyes narrowed dangerously as Henry stood directly in front of his desk.

"I know you had something to do with my brother's shooting. He never should have been there in the first place. You set him up, didn't you?"

"How dare you come into my office and accuse me of something so vile!" Richard said. "I told you once to get out. Now get out!"

"Screw you," Henry said.

"Guards, I order you to remove this man from my office!"

The guards hesitated for a moment, obviously not sure what they should do. Then Richard roared, "GET HIM OUT or you'll be in the brig tomorrow!" That spurred both guards forward and they grabbed Henry by his arms.

Henry looked like he might fight back for a minute, then allowed the guards to escort him from the office. As he left, he said, "You're going down, fat man. I promise you."

"Shut the door on your way out," Richard said, sitting back down and breathing hard.

Moments later, Henry exited the palace, heading for Julian's waiting car. He didn't know where he was going exactly, but he had no doubt of Richard's guilt and was determined to make him pay. Before he could reach Julian's car, however, a black Jaguar pulled up and the window rolled down.

"Excuse me?" said the trim man behind the wheel. "Prince Henry? May I have a word with you?"

Henry stopped. Nearby, Julian jumped out of his own car and raced over, his hand already reaching for his service revolver.

The driver glanced over and saw Julian. "You needn't worry," he said quickly. "My name is Sir Melvyn Batton. I work for Sir Richard." He looked like the words might make him physically ill.

"Yeah, I just saw you in Richard's office. What do you want?"

Julian reached them and Henry motioned for him to wait.

"I need to speak with you," Melvyn said. "It's urgent. Please."

"Go ahead. Say what you want to say."

"Not here," Melvyn said. "Can you come for a ride?"

"No way," Julian said. "No chance you're getting in that car."

"You have my word," Melvyn continued. "I don't mean any harm. But for God's sake, please let's go now. Before he sees us talking."

"He? He who?"

"Richard."

Henry's heart thudded faintly. So this was about Richard. "Okay, I'm getting in. But Julian is coming."

Henry climbed into the front seat and Julian in the back, while Sir Melvyn slowly drove down the winding drive and joined the busy London traffic. "Just circle," Henry said. "What is it you want to tell me?" He was amazed to see Melvyn's eyes fill with tears.

"First of all, I want you to know that I am riddled with guilt," Melvyn began. "I have been coerced into acting in the most egregious of ways. I have been manipulated by Richard into doing things that are nothing short of treason, murder, and corruption of the most serious nature."

"What are you talking about?"

"I don't know where to begin." Hesitating, then taking a deep breath, Melvyn continued, "I'll start at the beginning. Richard is a power-hungry maniac. From the moment he gained the regency, he has been hell-bent on looting the Treasury and eliminating both Charles and you so he could take the throne."

"So he was involved with Charles's shooting?"

"Indeed, he orchestrated the whole thing," Melvyn said. "You see, Charles was a naive young man who was disposed to please. Richard, a master exploiter, opportunist, and scoundrel, had convinced Charles and your mother that it would best serve the country if he went into the military after graduation from university. All that sounded fairly reasonable. But it was Richard who engineered Charles's transfer to Belfast into a military operation of the most dangerous sort. He convinced Charles it was the most patriotic thing he could do and would impress his subjects. Charles fell for it hook, line, and sinker. Once there, Richard used an old MI5 colonel to help recruit a sergeant to shoot Charles and make it look like a sniper. Richard dubbed the operation War Hero."

"Wait, wait. One of Charles's own men shot him? A traitor!"

"Yes, sir, of the worst sort."

"Where is this sergeant? Will he talk to me?"

"No, he's dead."

"Dead? How?"

"Once the sergeant shot Charles, Richard paid another killer, an IRA fugitive named Shaun McCabe, to kill the sergeant. This McCabe is the same fellow who tossed the hand grenade at your father years ago."

"What? You must be kidding."

"No, Henry, I'm not. It's the God's truth. Richard had arranged for Shaun's escape years ago. Since that time, Richard owned Shaun and kept him as a sleeper for future dirty deeds."

"Is Shaun dead too?"

"No, but you'll never find him. He lives in the shadows. Richard is the only one who can contact him. I really don't know how."

"So Richard tried to have my brother assassinated?

"Yes. But it didn't quite work. Through the grace of God, the sergeant mucked up the shot and just severely wounded him. God willing, he will survive."

A black well of hatred bubbled up in Henry. "And what about me? You said Richard wanted to eliminate both of us." Even as he said it, Henry already knew the answer. He could feel it in his bones, but he wanted to hear it out loud.

"Yes. Richard blackmailed a woman to seduce you. You've been under total surveillance for years. She was supposed to kill you as well. I don't know her name. Only that she was code-named Badger."

"I know her name," Henry growled. "So from the beginning, she was spying on me?"

"Yes. And from what Richard said, she owned you sexually. She was playing you in order to keep you close so she could report your every move."

A sick feeling overcame Henry. He had been played for a fool for all these years. And the sex was nothing more than part of the trap, the hook that kept him performing like a circus animal. He was repulsed.

"Alright," Henry said. "I've heard enough. Stop the car and let us out."

"But…there's more," Melvyn said a little miserably. "Please, hear me out."

"Go ahead then. But you should know as soon as I get out, I'm heading straight for the police."

"Yes. I know. But Richard isn't done yet. From the very beginning, once Richard was appointed regent, he launched a scheme to siphon off millions of pounds from the Royal Treasury. He brought me in as the secretary and Keeper of the Purse…blackmailed me, really. I had no choice." Melvyn produced a ledger from a compartment in the driver's side door and pushed it toward Henry. "This is a ledger that meticulously itemized each and every transaction, called them charitable donations…Millions of pounds now reside in numbered private accounts in the Cayman Islands. It's all here."

"Oh my God, what a monster. Not only is he a murderer, he's a crook of extraordinary proportions. It couldn't be any worse."

"It does get worse. Richard arranged to have hundreds of priceless paintings, some by the world's most treasured artists, removed from the palace under the guise that the galleries needed to be restored. He then staged their destruction in a warehouse fire."

"I read all about that fire. It was all over the Boston news."

"Yes, a world tragedy. But the truth be told, he switched the paintings and now plans on stealing and reselling them on the black market."

"Incredible! This is outrageous!" Henry paused. "Why are you telling me this? You're an accomplice!"

Now the tears spilled from Melvyn's eyes.

"I am telling you because I can no longer bear the guilt and remorse. From the beginning I knew these schemes were lunacy, but I was forced to go along with it, blackmailed into submission, just like all the rest of them—Badger, the sergeant and his colonel, even the Irish rebel. At first he stole just money, then the art, but when it turned to treasonous murder I no longer could justify being part of it. But the harder I tried to move away from it, the more pressure Richard applied. The more control he took. He not only threatened me and my reputation, but he implied he would kill me and hurt my family. Richard has no boundaries. He is capable of anything, and I had to take his threats seriously. But now I can no longer stand silent. At some point, every man has enough and can no longer live in fear and despair."

"It's a bit late, isn't it?" Henry said, his voice pulsing with rage. "My brother lies dying, millions have been looted, and priceless artwork is missing. Your remorse isn't worth a damn at this point."

"Henry, please, take these ledgers. They will help convict Richard. And as far as the art goes, we still have time."

"Time? How so?"

"Tonight a private plane has been arranged to transport the stolen art to Richard's villa in Switzerland. It departs at 9:00 p.m. from Leicester Airport, just outside of London. I'll be escorting the cargo. If you act fast, you can stop it." A short silence drew out, then Melvyn continued. "For God's sakes, Henry, you can stop the madness. Once they leave this country, those paintings will be sold on the black market and never be seen again."

Henry nodded. "Okay. That's good to know. But...what about you? What do you want out of all this?"

"Only a clear conscience at the end of my life. Redemption, Henry. At least some small measure for being a coward. I'm willing to face whatever consequences there are for my actions."

"Too bad you didn't grow a spine years ago."

Melvyn shook his head. "I know. You'll never know how sorry I am. But Richard is dangerous. Very dangerous."

"So am I," Henry said.

Melvyn glanced over at the young prince, then put his hand into his pocket and withdrew a small revolver. In the backseat, Julian lunged forward and grabbed Melvyn's wrist.

"Take the gun," Melvyn said. "You should know Richard carries one as well. Take this...and go stop him."

CHAPTER 61
COWARDLY HEROISM

"HOLY GOD, HENRY, THIS IS SCANDALOUS," PRINCE CYRIL SAID. They were meeting in a small room at Victoria Hospital, where Henry had just filled Cyril in on Sir Melvyn's story. The elderly prince shook his head. "This could rock the monarchy to its core. The Republicans in the House of Commons will seize on this as the last straw and move for the complete dismantling of the monarchy."

"Can you do anything?"

"Let's start by trying to save that art from leaving the country. I'll make some calls. There isn't much time. I'll start with Sir Lloyd Mertens, the commander of the Royal Armed Forces. I have access to him. I think he's the only man who could do something on such short notice."

"And what about the ledger? What should I do with it?" Henry said.

"We need to hold on to it. It is the best evidence we have. Let's have it put under key here at the hospital. I'll have the chief of staff put it in their vault."

Despite his order, Richard decided that he could not rely on Melvyn to get the art packed up and transported to Switzerland, so he showed up at the airport to personally supervise the transfer. In all, some 219 pieces of priceless art were painstakingly packed into crates and loaded onto the Gulfstream.

As the last crate was being loaded into the cargo compartment, the ground crew secured the hatch. The plane was now fully packed, including most of the passenger cabin. There was just one seat left. It was reserved for Sir Melvyn, who was already aboard standing at the top of the flight steps. He waved at Richard and gave the all-clear sign.

The twin Rolls-Royce engines revved up with a whine as the ground crew moved to stow the flight stairs and remove the stop blocks from the wheels. The plane would be aloft in minutes, carrying billions of pounds in stolen art.

There was a disturbance on the tarmac. As Melvyn turned to enter the plane, a convoy of military trucks sped onto the cement. Two M35 cargo trucks screeched to a stop in front of the Gulfstream and three others surrounded the aircraft. A Royal Army captain jumped from the lead truck and barked a command to his men: "Dismount and take position!" Troops poured from the trucks, their rifles at ready.

Henry was the next to emerge from the truck and sprinted to where Richard was watching, his face slack with shock at the sight of the troops suddenly surrounding his precious cargo.

"You!" Henry yelled. "You're a thief and a traitor!"

Richard's head swung around and his face filled with malice at the sight of the young prince. "This is none of your business," he bellowed. Then turning to the troops, he yelled, "Arrest that man!" He pointed at Henry.

The troops seemed bewildered and held their positions.

"You have no power here," Henry said. "It's over. You lose."

"I said ARREST HIM!" Richard yelled again, his face purpling.

Henry approached. "Did you hear me, you murdering traitor? You lose. We know what's on the plane. We know you tried to kill my brother, tried to kill me. We have your ledger."

That seemed to snap Richard back into reality. The big man whirled around and looked up to where Sir Melvyn was standing on the top of the stairs, then suddenly lunged with surprising speed for someone so large and grabbed Henry by the shirt. A revolver seemed to materialize in his hand, and he held it to Henry's head.

A dozen rifles were instantly trained on Richard, but he was blocking the shot with Henry's body. Henry's nose was assaulted with the stench and real fear set in. He could tell that Richard was totally irrational.

Suddenly, a voice rang out from behind them, on the steps. It was Sir Melvyn. "Richard, put that gun down! Let him go! You've done enough!"

Richard looked up at his abused puppet. "Shut up, you sniveling worm. Bugger off. I'm going to fix this little twerp's wagon once and for all. He's been a pain in my arse as long as I've known him. Go get the car. And we're taking him with us."

"No," Melvyn said. "I'm not doing it. It's over."

"Then you're killing him," Richard said.

Melvyn's hand shot into his pocket and emerged with another gun. Things were moving fast, but Richard hesitated in shock. It was his last mistake. Three shots rang out: one hit Richard in the head and the other two near his heart.

A sudden volley of gunfire shattered the night air as the troops, reacting on pure instinct and not knowing if the gunman was going to shoot Henry next, trained their rifles on Melvyn. They were led by the young captain, who dropped to one knee and squeezed off three perfect shots. Melvyn tumbled down the stairs and slumped to the ground, dead.

Henry was rooted to the ground in shock, surrounded by the bodies of Richard and Melvyn. The young captain rose and approached.

"Sir? Are you okay?"

It took a moment for Henry to focus on the captain, and when he did it seemed like a dream.

"Ollie…"

CHAPTER 62
SIX MONTHS LATER

THE CONVOY OF RANGE ROVERS PULLED UP IN FRONT OF KENTWOOD Manor, a royal baronial estate situated in tranquility just outside of London proper.

A footman approached the head vehicle and opened the door for Henry and Samantha. "Good afternoon, sir, good afternoon, mum. Welcome to Kentwood."

"Thank you."

"I hope your journey was pleasant. Please follow me, sir."

Flanked by armed military guards, the couple walked slowly through the grand entrance. As they entered the great room, they were met by Beatrice. She looked thin and tired, but put on a broad smile.

"Welcome to Kentwood. I'm so glad you're here."

The manor house was stately and traditional, but it had obviously been fitted out as a convalescent home. Henry leaned over and kissed Beatrice on first one cheek, then the other. "How is Charles?"

Beatrice lowered her voice. "To be frank, Henry, he's coming back, little by little. He looks wonderful, but the injuries were massive and his brain has been affected by the coma. He is aware of everything, but at times he has trouble doing certain things, like writing and critical thinking. His speech is good, for the most part, although occasionally he stumbles and cannot get the words out fast enough. He requires daily physical therapy. The doctors have not been able to give a definitive prognosis on his further recovery. So we take each day one at a time." She put a tissue to her eyes to wipe away tears. "He refuses to marry me because he doesn't want to be a burden. He's quite stubborn, and once he has made his mind up there's no changing it. It pains me to see him like this."

"Where is he? I'd like to see him."

"In the solarium with his mother and Prince Cyril. Come, I will take you."

As they walked the wide halls, Henry's mind raced. The last six months had moved with the velocity of a bullet. After the shooting at the airport and the death of Sir Richard, Parliament had met and appointed Henry as Charles's regent until the king fully recovered. At the same time, thanks to Sir Melvyn's ledger, most of the stolen money had been reclaimed and returned to the Treasury. The priceless artwork was likewise restored to its rightful place in the newly renovated galleries of Buckingham Palace. Finally, Charles had remained king and been moved to Kentwood Manor to recuperate.

"Here we are," Beatrice said, as she arrived at the solarium and escorted them in. "Charles, honey, Henry has arrived with Samantha."

Charles walked over slowly, extended his hand, and gave them hugs. "Henry, Samantha...thanks for coming."

Henry looked Charles over from head to foot. He was still very handsome and looked quite normal, with the exception of a slight scar on his temple. But Henry knew that appearances were deceiving, and he could hear a slight thickness in Charles's speech that had never been there before.

"Of course," Henry said, "we came as soon as we got the call."

"Come, sit, and join Mum and Grandpa Cyril."

Henry and Samantha joined the group as Charles began, "Henry, I've asked you here to do me a favor. And I hope you will."

"Of course, anything," Henry said. For months, he had been struggling with his own survivor's guilt, and his guilt over the fact that he had left Charles years ago to carry the weight and responsibilities thrust upon them both by his father's death. For years he played and schooled in the United States while his brother bore the burden of duty. On some level, Henry felt that if he had not abandoned his brother, Charles's lot might have been different. As a team of brothers, they might have been more vigilant and seen the troubled waters created by Richard, perhaps diverting his treachery. It seemed so unfair that he was healthy and in love, free to do whatever he wanted, while his big brother had paid such a dear price to do the right thing. He would gladly do anything to repay Charles for his selflessness.

"This is a big favor that involves both of you," Charles said. "Samantha too."

Henry and Samantha exchanged glances. "Go on, bro."

Reaching over to the side table, Charles grabbed a file folder with shaky fingers. It was gilded with the royal crest. He opened the file and, removing the top page, handed it over to Henry. It was on royal letterhead. Henry read the title of the document: "Letters of Abdication." A heavy stone of fear sunk in his belly. He looked up at his brother.

"Henry, I've been in consultation with the Prime Minister and other members of the government, plus endless doctors. We all came to the same conclusion: I am not fit to fulfill the duties of the king. I realize that I have made great progress, but by all medical accounts, I will have lapses, perhaps mental confusion, and even more serious physical problems to come. There is even a possibility that I could go blind due to some lingering effects from the bullet. The doctors say that the weight of the office will most assuredly affect my health and jeopardize my recovery." He took a deep breath, then continued, "Henry, will you take this crushing burden off my shoulders? Will you be our king?"

Henry's life flashed before his eyes. Beads of perspiration broke out on his forehead. Ever since he had been thrust into this royal mess, he had rejected every aspect of it. As a teen, he had run away and hid from the reality of his situation. He even hated British tea. The only thing he ever wanted to be was an American, a lawyer, and to settle down with Samantha and raise normal kids with normal lives. He was looking forward to enjoying and sharing the Carnegie fortune he had fought so hard to recover, far away from England and the horrid memories it lavishly ladled upon him for all these years.

But then he looked into his brother's pleading eyes. He knew Charles was right: he would never be fit enough to serve. His every instinct told him to resist, decline, run. But his sense of love and loyalty to his brother, who he had admired for so long and to whom he owed so much, forbade him to do anything except honor the favor.

Westminster Abbey

It was coronation day, and the Abbey was splendid. Today, Henry would be the third member of his family to assume the throne as the head of the British monarchy.

From a strategic location far above the Nave, BBC 4 had set up a mobile studio to televise the historic event. TV anchormen, technicians, and even lip readers with binoculars were jammed into the tight space.

Matt Kensington, who had been recently promoted to BBC's lead anchorman, was the talking head. He had covered the coronations of both Henry's father and Charles.

"Ladies and gentlemen, they are playing the Grand Processional march, which has played at every coronation since King Henry V ascended to the throne. And now there's Henry, walking down the aisle. He has grown into a strikingly handsome man, but there are already signs he will be an unconventional king. He has chosen to keep his Christian name and will be known as King Henry IX."

"Indeed, he has grown into a handsome chap," chimed in Prudence Purnell, another BBC anchor. "You know, Matt, King Henry is a media sensation. His face has been splashed all over every newspaper and magazine cover worldwide. But, alas, this king is spoken for. He's engaged to a beautiful young British debutante named Samantha Smythe."

"Yes, a pity for those lasses," Matt added. "But Henry's story has been marked by tragedy and pity from his earliest days, from the loss of his family's fortune to his father's death in a terrorist attack, the attempt on his own life, and of course, the plot against his brother. Yes, this is truly an unpredicted reign."

"So true," Prudence agreed. "This is a royal family unlike any other in modern times, but then we all know that being royalty is a dangerous job. Wait! Isn't that them seated at the front of the Abbey?"

The camera focused on the five figures seated in front of the Abbey.

"Indeed," Matt said. "That is the royal family. They are seated in the Chairs of Estate in front of the Royal Box. The woman in the wheelchair is the Dowager Queen Mother, Elizabeth, mother to two kings, Charles and now Henry, and widow to another. Next to Elizabeth is the abdicated King Charles, who despite looking hale and hearty, continues to struggle with his grave injuries. The woman to the right of the Queen Mother is Henry's betrothed, Samantha Smythe, the third daughter of a rather successful British banker. She was a debutante in her teens, but she is definitely a commoner. Needless to say, our unconventional king doesn't care in the slightest. The final woman is Beatrice Grandton. She is one of our own, a former reporter for the BBC. It is rumored that the two are to be married, but a wedding date has not been announced."

"I can't wait, Matt," Prudence said. "The only thing I like better than a royal wedding is two royal weddings. It's been announced that King Henry will be marrying Samantha next May. I wonder what she will be wearing."

"Ah," Matt said, "Henry is now approaching the steps leading to the dais. He has stopped directly in front of his brother and seems to be saying something. Let's get a close-up, shall we?"

The camera zoomed in to record Henry talking to his brother Charles.

"Can you tell us what they said?" Matt asked one of the lip readers.

"Indeed," the lip reader answered. "He said, 'Charlie, I love you, and I know you love me. I'm sorry, so sorry.'"

"Wow! Did Charles reply?"

"Uh, hold on. Yes! He said, 'God save the king.'"

"Amazing moment," Matt said. "Now, let's watch. I believe we are just seconds away from crowning our new king."

Henry proceeded up the steps of the dais. Sitting on the raised platform was the Coronation Chair, known as the King Edward's Chair.

"The King Edward's Chair is an ancient wooden throne dating back to 1296," Matt said in a quiet tone. "Back then, King Edward I had it built to contain the coronation stone of Scotland, often referred to as the Stone of Scone. The stone is an oblong block of red sandstone used for centuries in the coronation of the monarchs of Scotland, and later the monarchs of England and the Kingdom of Great Britain. There are so many legends associated with this relic that it is hard to know which are accurate and which are not. Nonetheless, the stone, considered to have deep religious significance, has played an important part in every coronation for centuries. It is actually taken from safekeeping at Edinburgh Castle in Scotland and installed beneath the wooden throne only for coronations."

"Matt," Prudence said, "I see the Archbishop of Canterbury walking around the Abbey. What's that all about?"

"It's part of the Coronation ritual. The Archbishop goes to the east, south, west, and north corners, asking if those present are willing to pay homage to their new ruler. After the assemblage responds affirmatively, the archbishop is free to administer the Coronation Oath. Of course, Henry is technically already the king—that happened the moment his brother signed the Letters of Abdication. This coronation is strictly ceremonial in nature."

Silence fell over the booth while they watched the proceedings below.

"It looks like the archbishop is beginning," Matt said, his voice heavy with excitement. "This oath is sacred, since the king is also the head of the Church of England, as well as political. The constitutionally elected Parliament directly governs, and the king must pledge his allegiance. There is always a fine line here. Most Brits think the king has the ultimate power, but that is not the case. Parliament is the actual government of Great Britain."

The camera moved in for a close shot of the king. "You can see the archbishop handing the king a Bible, which symbolizes the connection between the king and the church."

"Matt, can you tell us about the robes the king is wearing?"

"Surely. The robe that His Majesty is wearing was hand-tailored for him by a firm called Ede & Ravenscroft. They have been the robe maker to sovereigns since 1689. More than twenty-seven tailors and artisans worked on it. As you may remember, there was some controversy as King Henry strongly objected to the expenditure for the robe, not to mention other coronation-related expenses. Some even said he contemplated wearing his famous jeans. However, at the insistence of the Queen Mother, Henry agreed to heed his mother's wishes. She prevailed upon him that the people of England needed to have their traditions, and it would disappoint them and be an unsettling start to break centuries of protocol.

"With respect to the robe itself, it features a potpourri of materials. Everything from the finest silk, mantua, satin, damask, sarsnet, and gold. You see the train? It is over six yards long and made of extraordinarily fine purple silk velvet trimmed with Canadian ermine. The Royal School of Needlework did the intricate embroidery in painstaking detail. His Majesty's robe was designed in the strict design guidelines of previous coronations.

"Ah, the king is now seated upon the King Edward's Chair. Do you see the canopy being carried by the four senior clergy members? That canopy will be placed over the new ruler's head while the archbishop anoints the king with holy oils. He makes the sign of the cross on the king's hands, head, and breast while conferring a blessing. It is the most religious part of the ceremony and dates back to the very first Christian kings. It signifies the connection between the monarch and God."

They waited while the archbishop anointed Henry, then Matt picked up the narration again.

"There now. The king is being presented with a pair of spurs and the sword of state. The sword symbolizes the power of a monarch and his duty to fight enemies in order to preserve peace."

"It looks like the Archbishop is handing the king some kind of golden ball?"

"Yes, that is the Sovereign's Orb, made for Charles II in 1661. It is encrusted with more than 100 precious and semiprecious stones and topped with a cross symbolizing the Christian faith. It's a priceless artifact."

The massive Abbey's organ began to play, accompanied by a regiment of trumpeters sounding the royal anthem.

"This is it, ladies and gentlemen, the crowning!"

The Abbey was filled with the joyous sound of the Westminster Choir boys, some two hundred strong, singing Handel's "Zadok The Priest," dating back to King George II's coronation.

ZADOK THE PRIEST, AND NATHAN THE PROPHET ANOINTED
SOLOMON KING.
AND ALL THE PEOPLE REJOICED, AND SAID:
GOD SAVE THE KING! LONG LIVE THE KING!
MAY THE KING LIVE FOREVER,
AMEN, ALLELUIA.

All across the realm, millions of people held their collective breath.

Henry, now holding the Sceptre with the Dove and the Sceptre with Cross, slightly bowed as the Archbishop of Canterbury placed the St. Edward's Crown on his young head. At five pounds, the crown was heavy, but nowhere near as heavy as the burden of the awesome responsibility now formally placed on young Henry's reluctant shoulders. Gone were the days of flouting social rules. Gone were his tight jeans and privacy. He was a king, a servant of the people and God.

He silently mouthed three little words.

Turning to the lip readers, Matt said, "What did he say?"

"He said, 'God help me!'"

The organ began the Grand Recessional March. Henry turned and bowed toward the main altar, paying homage to his God and church, and then began the long, lonely walk down the aisle. His robe trailed behind as hundreds, even thousands of photographers snapped the majestic scene. Dictated by tradition, the archbishop, his mother, and brother led the procession as the congregation joined the choir and erupted, singing the praises: "Long live the king! God save the king!"

As Henry proceeded down what felt like an endless aisle, his world seemed to be crashing in upon him. He looked around and saw hundreds of strangers standing and bowing as he passed. What now? For the first time, Henry really prayed to a God who he had held a grudge against ever since his father's life had been snatched away by an IRA terrorist. He didn't exactly know why he prayed...just now and in that moment...but he looked to a higher power for help. After all, who else could help? He was the king and they don't get any higher than that, at least not in this world.

Henry looked down the aisle again as he moved closer to the narthex. It was then that he saw the brightest of lights streaming through the enormous stained glass window at the back of the Abbey. The streams of light radiated like a sunburst and then narrowed down to what looked like a single ray of light marking the path ahead. His thoughts turned to his father and how he had always given him the soundest of advice and shown him the right path to follow. He suddenly felt an enormous power come over him. His heart was filled with courage and his mind clear with determination. He saw the sign, he felt the call, perhaps a divine intervention, perhaps his father reaching out from eternity. Who knew?

But what he did know was that, at last, he was ready, willing, and able to embrace the hand that was dealt him. He would make it work for him, Samantha, his family, and of course the country he was destined to serve. Even the heavy Crown of St. Edward now seemed feather-weight. His eyes shone and his shoulders straightened as this newfound spirit filled him. The epiphany gripped him as strongly as any force he had ever known. Thousands of bells tolled announcing the new reign. He felt that he had made peace with his destiny and that God would truly save the king. He knew he would fear not greatness.

The End